Caging Curiosity

A Song of Cages and Liberties

Volume I

Tayo Olajide

Caging Curiosity

A Song of Cages and Liberties

Volume I

"These imagined orders are subjective, so in order to change them we must simultaneously change the consciousness of billions of people which is not easy. A change of such magnitude can be accompanied only with the help of a complex organization such as a political party, an ideological movement or a religious cult"

--Anonymous

In loving memory of my father
Stanley Olajide

Contents

x

The Epidemic

Adeolu ran as fast as his legs could carry him as the news of the illness of his twin sons reached him. Fero, Adeolu's half-sister from a different father, had run to give him the message in his cave hideout, a two-mile distance from Adeolu's abode in the western part of the city. He ran past Muniru and Albert, Islam, and Christian converts, respectively, who had volunteered to help dispose of the dead, pushing wheelbarrows made from felled trees in which were littered dead bodies old, young, female, male, and naked. Their clothes were made from dead animal hides. The majority of the folks wore hides from dead rabbits, while the men and women of means wore hides from lions, leopards, wolves, sheep, horses, and other exotic animals. An industry existed for clothes made from animal hides, and Muniru and Albert own the two shops at opposite ends of the market where people purchase their clothing.

Adeolu ran quickly across the rows of mud houses on the outskirts of the city until he got to the rocky plains where houses were built with wood on trees and land in neat rows of shacks surrounding the marketplace. In the center is one of the king's many palaces where he holds and carries out judgments. The highly placed in the societies build their houses on land with an extension on trees and nearby topography.

Adeolu owned such a place west of the city's many mud and treehouse shacks. He sprinted across the rows of shacks through the middle of the market, which was scantily populated as a result of the Igbonna disease that had plagued the town. His house was close to the freshwater spring where all the city dwellers came to get their daily water needs. His wife owned the tie and dye factory where the elites came to make colorful clothes from cotton materials for their celebrations and festival parties.

This part of town was filled with fishermen and merchants who came from other lands through the seas and made their landings with smaller boats. The eastern side of town was less populated; water was brought to them through an aqueduct that Adeolu helped design and build. It was where the real elites lived and was less populated. It was where the king's second palace was situated.

He ran quickly inside, with Fero in close pursuit. He saw his wife, Enitan, sitting on the floor wailing and in her hands were their twin boys' lifeless bodies. He fell down beside her, held the boys in his arms and shouted at the top of his voice, "Why?" The pain and misery reverberated in his words as they penetrated the stillness of the moonless night.

The noise attracted many of their neighbors, who consoled the family. Adeolu was a very handsome young man, nearly twenty-eight years old, standing six feet tall, with a square and even jaw. He was one of the few folks in town who was cleanly shaven. He found a mixture from squeezing the juice out of ginger and mixing it with ground pawpaw, one of the many ideas he planned to commercialize.

He looked up with tears in his eyes, standing his full six feet and dwarfing everyone in the room. He turned to Enitan and asked, "What happened? They were healthy when I left two nights ago."

She replied with more wailing, "I don't know! The gods gave them to me and now they have taken them with the plague they have visited upon us."

Adeolu, clearly angry and agitated, shouted, "You must have fed them, clothed them, taken them somewhere!? That was the question I asked. Woman, you must answer me. What did you do?"

He was sobbing and falling into her arms. Enitan stood up, leaving Adeolu lying on the floor and said, "We got them new clothes from Muniru. Fero had told us he was giving some incredible discounts; it was too good to let go."

Adeolu continued to lay on the ground, sobbing, when Muniru and Albert came around and entered the compound where the people created a pathway for them. They took the children's dead bodies outside, took off their clothes, dumped the bodies in the wheelbarrow, and were neatly folding the clothes and putting them into a hidden compartment on the side of the wheelbarrow when Adeolu appeared and said, "Where are you taking the bodies of my kids? Give them back to me. I will bury them myself."

Muniru replied, "Were you not present when the king declared that the bodies and clothing of those that succumb to this plague be incinerated?"

"It is dangerous to keep such bodies in cemeteries and to keep the old clothes; one might even contract the disease if the clothes are kept around in the house," Albert added.

An alarm went off in Adeolu's head; this clothing angle was an angle he had not thought about previously, *What if more people are dying because they wore dead people's clothes? What if there is a conspiracy between these two merchants and religious zealots to not burn these clothes and instead resell them back to the citizens of Idumagbo?* With those thoughts he kept quiet, looked at Muniru and then at Albert, and then let out another throbbing wail, thereby obfuscating the details his thoughts might have put on his facial expression.

Muniru, a diminutive, fifty-five-year-old Islamic cleric, had very long tribal marks on both sides of his face. His folks also had similar marks. He was afraid at first when he heard Adeolu's remarks but relaxed when he saw Adeolu burst into another rant of wailing.

Albert, a bearded, twenty-nine-year-old Christian, was six feet tall, and an orphan was raised by Portuguese missionaries who had died of the disease.

"He said "my parents died of this disease too"".

Adeolu nodded and continued wailing.

He stood up, then went outside to meet Muniru who gave him a grim look.

He said "he is suspicious"

Muniru responded with a sneer as they wheeled their carts outside of the western part of the city onto tracks in front of the rows of shacks, where other people came in and dumped their dead into the wheel cart.

After they exited the city walls, Muniru and Albert laughed uproariously and were discussing what their share was going to be. Adeolu followed them soon afterwards surreptitiously and caught up with them a few hours later. He watched them from afar, pitied them when he saw what they were going through, carting all the bodies, and wheeling them along. None of the elites would volunteer any of their horses to pull the carts for them.

They got to the woodlands outside of the city walls, where they had been dumping and burning the bodies. They dumped all the bodies into the pit. Then they went and looked for tree branches, shrubs, and dry grasses to add as fuel to the ensuing fire. Muniru brought two flint stones out from his sack and simply rubbed them against one another. Promptly, the fire lit up.

Adeolu watched silently as the two continued performing their tasks in silence, never speaking a word to each other. It was as if they knew that someone might be eavesdropping.

Then suddenly, Muniru broke the silence. "You took more dead bodies than I did, which means you have more clothes than me."

"No, I did not! We took exactly the same number of bodies. I kept count in my head, and we alternated the places where we picked up the bodies."

A disgruntled and grumpy Muniru said, "You will have to count the pieces of clothing. I counted mine; there were fourteen. And I am sure you must have, like, twenty pieces with you."

A clearly unsatisfied Albert pulled out all the pieces of clothing from the hidden compartment in the cart and counted fifteen pieces of cloth items before saying, "It is fifteen. Should we throw one into the fire to make it even?"

"Ah, please stop! No, don't do that. I will take this fifteenth piece while you will take the next clothing item where our bounty is an uneven split."

Adeolu then stepped out of the shadows and said, "So this is how the dead people's clothes get recycled back into the economy."

Muniru and Albert were taken aback. They ran for the nearest trees to their sacks, drawing swords.

Adeolu calmly said, "Drop your swords, because if I should take out mine, I will have to kill or incapacitate both of you. You know I am a skilled swordsman and can defeat you with my eyes closed."

Muniru spoke first. "We do not get paid for doing these jobs; the king just assigned this dirty job to us by fiat. No one acknowledges or appreciates us."

"Is that why you are recycling the disease-ridden clothes back into the populace so that you can enrich yourself?" Adeolu said angrily.

"No, I cleanse my own by sprinkling holy water on it, a mixture that my parents left for me. It has always worked magically for me. No disease can exist after I sprinkle it with my holy water," said Albert.

"And I say the Shafa'ah multiple times on the clothes, interceding for the new owners of the clothes and inviting the Malaikahs to preserve the new owners of the clothing from contracting this same disease."

"Indeed; and that is why the number of deaths seems to have multiplied lately—and you have suddenly come into a lot of money?" Adeolu asked.

Muniru, speaking in his low, squeaking voice said, "You cannot link the deaths to these recycled clothes."

"I don't have to. All I need to show is that you profited from the deaths of their sons, fathers, daughters, and mothers," Adeolu replied.

"And then what?" Albert said in a roaring voice to an unperturbed Adeolu. "You will be burned alive!"

"The punishment given to those who practice ritual killings," Muniru said, looking at his partner in crime. "We did not kill anyone; we even helped to clean up the deaths!"

"You profited from their misery and you disobeyed the king. The people want to see a spectacle that will purge them of their miseries; don't be that burning spectacle," Adeolu said.

Adeolu brought out a bag and asked that they dump all the clothing items into it. He watched as they both obliged and dumped all the clothing into Adeolu's bag. Adeolu then said, "I will go and test these items, if they are free of disease, I will give them back to you and you can do as you wish. If they are not, and I can prove that they led to other deaths, I will have to let the king and the people know." He then calmly asked them to leave.

After they left, Adeolu hurled the sack onto his shoulder and took a different path back to his caves, a section of pristine caves uninhabited, hard to get to, where he did all his work.

At the first sound of the crow, just as the dawn began to break and the first vestiges of sunlight started to appear on the horizon, Adeolu crept out of the cave where he had been hibernating for the last few days. The concoction he had made and provided to the new set of rats had not worked as he envisaged, and all the rats had died off one by one. He would have to go and lay new traps for his new set of rats as another idea of the kind of leaves, herbs, and tree bark he could mix together to generate the right medicine to treat the Igbonna disease that had gripped the towns and surrounding cities in recent months.

It had been over four moons now that they had been searching for a cure to the Igbonna. He looked across at the bamboo shelves containing almost a thousand gourdlets of various concoctions he had mixed over time to try to rid the cities of the epidemic currently ravaging them. He looked at almost a hundred amulets he had gotten made with the help of Wura, the prominent and revered witch in the town. The amulets contained ground leaves, ground bones of exotic animals, feathers of different birds, and some metaphysical powers that were invoked by speaking esoteric commands, the language of the gods in which only Wura and a few of her witches understood. These amulets could ward off any bad spirit causing illnesses and other people's witchcraft.

At the thought of Wura, his mind drifted for a while as he reminisced on their intense and wild lovemaking some few weeks ago before he quickly snapped himself out of it and urged his spirit to concentrate by whispering a few spiritual commands, "Behold, it has been said that the tornado that blows against the palm tree can only succeed in making it bend, but it will not break nor move it; I command my heart not to waiver henceforth," before bursting into such uncontrollable laughter that he became teary-eyed.

After the fits of laughter subsided, his thoughts went back to the previous week when the king of Idumagbo, King Abiodun, had sent for all the leading herbalists, medicine men, babalawos, mediums, witches, and wizards in the land and outer lands to come and diagnose, analyze, and tell him what is going on in Idumagbo. Most of the lands around the coast of West Africa were inhabited by nomadic hunter-gatherers who moved around in bands of fifty to a hundred men, women, and children. In these same lands lie the city of Idumagbo, a hundred miles from the coast of present-day Lagos, inhabited by ten thousand people of all races; Europeans, Africans, Mongols, and Arabians, and several African hunter-gathering tribes engaging in fair trade and practicing religious tolerance.

In the last few weeks there had been an epidemic outbreak which had killed about fifteen percent of the city's and surrounding villages' population, leaving many more enervated and unable to work on their farms and other day-to-day tasks. This had taken a severe toll on the economy of the city, as the news of the disease had spread to many other surrounding villages and cities and some traders had started staying away or finding alternative markets for their goods and services.

He remembered the king's words spoken on the night of the meeting, "Which one of the gods and many orishas have we offended that we had to pay with the lives of many citizens?" and he called on the wise men and men of means in the city and environs to help proffer solutions. After many sacrifices and many spiritual sanitizations and cleansing of the towns, still, the Igbonna continued unabated, leaving scores of deaths day by day. Some people have started panicking, seeking shelter in distant cities, towns, and in the forest to seek alternative means of livelihood.

The thought of the king's words reverberated through his head—his own losses, the death of his twin sons—and he sighed whispering to himself, "If only they knew that this has nothing to do with any of the orishas." It was a thought he dared not say publicly lest he be disgraced, called a charlatan, and flogged publicly, probably hanged for heresy against the thousand gods of the land. He knew there must be a way to let the citizens and poor folks know the truth and enlighten them, but he knew that this was also not possible because for him to do that, he might be directly putting countless members of his cult out of their jobs and invariably signing his own death warrant.

Adeolu was the son of the late King Oyeade and his Arabian slave girl. His mother had died shortly after his birth and he was raised by his grandmother, Keniola Adun, who some people thought to be a witch because of her almost limitless wisdom and extra level of perception. She lived alone in a little compound on the outskirts of the city, far away from the city center; however, some people would often visit her seeking her wisdom and knowledge because of her reputation as a woman that had been to many lands of this world. Some said her wisdom was boundless.

During the reign of King Oyeade's father, King Adebayo, husband of Keniola Adun, King Adebayo was killed while on a trade mission in another town while Keniola, the queen, was captured and sold into slavery. She was sold to Arabian slave traders who took her to Timbuktu, a province of the Sahelian Empire which ran from the northern tip of the continent southwards on. There she worked in the gold mines, learned to speak the Arabic language, converted to a Muslim, and learned to read and write before becoming a medicine woman, a rare feat for a woman at that time. She learned to read and write, remarried to a wealthy landowner after many years of mistreatment by hordes of men that came across her world. She once shared with some folks how she traveled from the coast across the Sahara, sometimes on camel, and she endured frequent assaults along the journey; but the thought of her son kept her hopes alive. She really wanted to see her son Oyeade again, but she was not able to do so. By the time she got back home, after more than ten years of sojourn, Oyeade had died and Abiodun was king.

Her entrance back into the city was not pomp and pageantry, as she suddenly appeared in the city again out of nowhere during the reign of her second son, King Abiodun. King Oyeade's wife had no children, but he was able to have one during a tryst with a Nubian slave.

Adeolu went to live with his grandmother, Keniola, when she suddenly appeared in the city ten years ago. He went to help her with her daily activities and gained quite a lot of knowledge and wisdom from his grandmother.

He was apprenticed to a man called Babagun, the man that taught him more medicine and psychology initiating him into the cult of the wise ones, "the Oro". He went to live in Karounwi with Babagun and Ogunde, where he learned to be a skilled fighter and a medicine man. It was at Karounwi that Adeolu met Enitan, and it was from there they decided to get married. Enitan came from a very notable family with lots of land and industry in and around Idumagbo, and it is in one of these lands that Adeolu now resides.

Adeolu snapped out of his thoughts and peered through the little opening in the cave. He slipped his hand through the opening and reached for the gourds he had placed outside for fetching early morning dew. He saw that it was nearly full, and that gladdened his heart. He now had fresh water to mix his next set of concoctions.

He took one of the gourds, offered some prayers to his ancestors, and then mixed a few leaves with bark and the water from the gourd, gulping it down. He quickly moved his mouth left and right grimacing and then spat it out. He mixed some of the water with other concoctions and placed them in different gourds. He went over to the insects and animals he had sprinkled the water from the dead bodies on. He had collected a lot of water samples and blood from the bodies that the epidemic had claimed, hoping to see if he could replicate it. He had been, so far, very careful not to allow the sample to touch any part of his body.

Many famous herbalists in their lands had fallen to many diseases while trying to combat them because they failed to take proper precautions. Adeolu's grandmother had taught him that if he was going to be a medicine man, he had to be very careful and take extra precautions when handling potent medicine and herbs. Even the smell of these herbs and medicines could be very lethal. She had taught him that safety and security should be the highest priority. And the most important task was to protect himself because when he was alive and kicking was when he would be able to diagnose diseases and administer treatment on others.

He had gone around to the families with dead members observing that the infected kept passing out watery feces, constantly vomiting and had pains below their abdomen. In some households everyone would be infected and all would die of the debilitating disease, while in some other households while everyone was infected, a few would break loose from the fangs of the disease and survive. Still in other households, not everyone would be infected. He knew he was looking for a missing link, and he had to find it. He knew once he found the missing link, he would get to the root cause and defeat the disease.

The thought of not being able to put his finger on the missing link had been haunting him since he'd tested the clothes he collected from Muniru and Albert finding out that the clothes could not harbor this type of disease. How it was transmitted from one person to the other was still a mystery to him. In some households, he saw cases where some people were seriously afflicted and would die in a matter of hours, while some others were afflicted but could still carry on major daily activities, while others were simply not affected. It baffled him, in the enclosed spaces where they lived, they touched one another, their clothes touched. What was the medium through which these diseases agents transmitted themselves?

He had examined the ones that were infected and saw they barely ate their meals and they were passing watery stools. He made sure he did not use his hand to touch the stool. He covered his hands with banana leaves, as his grandmother had taught him. He later dipped each one of the infected rats and insects into the gourd with the concocted mildew water. He had performed similar experiments with the clothes he took from Muniru and Albert by covering a set of rats with the clothes for two days, and they seemed to be well and continued to feed well after two days, so he knew that the clothes could not have been transmitting the disease.

"Maybe Muniru and Albert successfully prayed away the disease agent," he thought before dismissing it. He remembered that his grandmother had taught him to rely on his instincts and all his senses. He should dismiss that which called for the invisibility of things.

He looked at his time stick and saw that the shadow of the sun made it approximately close to midday. He learned how to tell the time from an itinerant Arabian sojourner who was caught in one of the animal traps meant for larger animals, like the lions and antelopes in the forest. He felt pity on him, released him from the trap, gave him food and water and they became very good friends. On one of his many sojourns to other world cities and during their conversations, he had showed him how to use the stick and the sun to tell the time. He had shown other members of the Oro cult how to tell the time, as well as measure it using an hourglass. He held in his hands one of his most esteemed possessions, the hourglass given to him by the Arabian sojourner. He had not seen glass before this, and he quickly saw how useful it could be.

He hurried quickly and walked briskly out of the tunnel of caves and was on his way to the midday meeting that King Abiodun had called of the elites and the powerful in the city and environs. He took a swig from his special palm wine concoction and he saw that the sun was brighter than he had earlier anticipated. He had spent a lot of time wandering inside the caves and inspecting his rats and insects, lizards, and many scarce animals like chameleon, porcupines, and small, colored snakes. He often purchased these exotic animals from travelers and foreigners traveling through the city and surrounding villages. He also sometimes captured other animals by laying traps in the forest while he wandered in and outside of the city.

Apart from occasional meetings, celebrations, and festivals, Adeolu rarely ventured outside of his comfort zone and kept to himself most of the time. He understood the people of the city. Most were honest farmers who cared for the well-being of their families and were satisfied with whatever harvest they reaped. The wealthy elites owned almost all the lands. They leased it to the farmers at sometimes exorbitant prices, and when the harvest was small and the peasant farmers were unable to make the payments, the elites usually took a member of the family as an indentured servant, as custom demanded, until the debt was fully paid. The mainstay of the economy was cotton. Individual farmers planted on rented or leased lands. They made payments in cotton to the landowners, who collected the cotton and made many of their indentured servants wove it into clothing materials that were sold in the markets. It is this clothing market that attracted many people to Idumagbo.

Adeolu was neither wealthy nor a peasant and made a living by courting the wealthy elites providing knowledge and solutions to their everyday problems. He helped the peasants a lot, but the peasants didn't have ways to pay him except through produce. He would forgo payment when treating the peasants and as a result, a lot of people owed him plenty of favors. He had not been particularly wealthy but managed to gather knowledge by studying nature and becoming very wise. He was a conscientious man and strove for perfection in everything he did. He loved his wife, Enitan, because he knew that Enitan also loved him, supported him, and gave him freedom to do his work, even when she sometimes scolded him for being a lazy bone and not wanting to farm.

Adeolu's wife, Enitan, was a beautiful young woman of twenty-six years with silky, long hair, sweet, dancing grey eyes, and golden-brownish skin, an offspring of a wealthy landowner with mixed ancestors. She got clothes from the cotton makers and dyed them into blue, red, or black. Sometimes she made designs with those colors in a craft known as tie-dye.

She supplied the market women with these clothes making her a wealthy woman and a market leader.

As he reached the footpaths where he had his horse tied up, Adeolu untied the horse and was about to mount it when he heard the neighing of another right behind him. The rider dismounted and he saw it was Wura.

"You did not sound like you missed me when I left you the last time," Adeolu said.

Wura was a dark, pretty, middle-aged widow who everyone considered to be a witch because of her weird manner of dressing in red and dark-colored clothes and wearing a funny hat shaped like a triangle with feathers from all the known birds in the area. People often would get on her good side when they asked her to name the feathers on the hat; she was unusually charmed by this. She was a widow of one of the most powerful medicine men in Idumagbo and she learned a lot of her craft from him.

"I never knew I gave you the impression that you are the only one who knows how to give pleasure," she said, smiling.

They moved toward each other embracing. "I am on my way to the king's palace. I take it you are also on the way," Adeolu said.

"No, I came here to speak to you about the clothes you took from Muniru and Albert," said Wura.

"What about them?" he asked, straight-faced.

An equally game faced Wura replied, "The clothes are not responsible for the diseases."

"How did you come to that conclusion?"

"I received a sign from the goddess that the clothes are not responsible for the multiplication of deaths."

Adeolu wanted to respond by saying rubbish but he held himself back. There were three sides to Wura that he knew of. One was her ability to get information because of her network of witches, second was her ability to quickly understand herbs, plants, leaves, and their mixture, she gave the women of Idumagbo the capability to straighten and relax their hair from a mixture of ground coconuts and a mixture of oils from olive seeds, and third was her weirdness of seeing the future and things other people could not see or were not privy to. She did not argue or try to disprove the third one because disproving it was like striking at the heart. He had done it once and had to apologize for it in order for their friendship and all its benefits to continue.

"Surely, the disease did not multiply from recycling the clothes," Adeolu said.

"I am glad you believe me."

"Your visions and predictions have the highest rates of being correct so far," said Adeolu.

"You know I don't make mistakes. I tell it the way the goddess shows it to me."

"Did Muniru and Albert come to you to seek your help with this?" asked Adeolu. "I am going to stop by their houses and let them know they can come get the clothes. I have no further use for them. But I will be insisting that they start burning them."

"How will burning them solve any problem? Burning them is a waste of scarce resources," she said.

Adeolu seemed to be lost in thought for a few seconds and then said, "Then they don't get to keep the clothes and make a profit selling them."

"I will make a point of duty to ensure that the proceeds from the resale find a way to get back to the less privileged members of our society," Wura responded.

"Then I'd better get going before the meeting starts without me." He mounted his horse, made some noise, and galloped away into the distance while Wura took her horse and rode away in the opposite direction and shouted, "I will see you at the palace soon!"

To reach King Abiodun's palace in the eastern part of the city, Adeolu passed the previous palace belonging to his own father, King Oyeade. The palace walls had all crumbled and there were no slaves with torches standing outside of the compound (signifying a streetlight in modern days).

He saw a flicker of light inside and was curious to see who could be in there. He walked inside and shouted a greeting at a short distance to alert the person.

The person turned; he realized he had not seen the man before and as such, may not even be related to him. What was he doing there? Maybe he was one of the people that were defacing the house. The man was dressed up in a leopard skin wrapped around his waist, with raffia palm adorning his shoulders down to his knee. His face was painted with white chalk, giving him an eerie look. In his right hand, he held a machete. He must be a man of means, thought Adeolu, and as he walked closer, he suddenly recognized the raffia palm wearing man as Sango, a warrior, and a priest of one of the city's many deities from an adjoining village. He was about six feet tall and had unusually large hands. He was belligerent and liked people singing his praises. He also served as one of the commanders in the king's army. Rumor had it that he was gunning for Balogun (commander of all commanders) of the king's army in Idumagbo.

"How is your body, my elder?" Adeolu asked respectfully. The prevalent culture was to respect whoever was older than you.

Sango responded, "I am as strong as the bone that makes the carcass of large marine animals and the steel that has gone through fire and no fire can ever melt it again."

He grinned and then shook Adeolu's hands.

Adeolu then asked, "What can you be looking for in an old abandoned palace?"

Sango laughed before he replied, "I have come to pay homage to the spirit of the departed king."

Adeolu replied sarcastically, "That is so gracious of you to remember our father. You are a very loyal man."

Sango laughed, showing some very blackened teeth before responding, "I almost forgot that you were an illegitimate one, son of a slave," followed by more laughter, chuckling, coughing, and more coughing.

Adeolu cautiously ignored the remark and avoided moving too close to him and said, "I wish I had asked that I be brought into this world, perhaps I would have asked that my Maker spare the shame of birth from a slave."

Sango looked at him and then laughed again.

Adeolu then said, "I see you are carrying a bag; do you have the antidote for our maladies and the cure for this epidemic?"

"Yes, yes," Sango retorted. "Who else can diagnose and cure if not me? I have heard the news reports that you have accused two illustrious men in this town of spreading the disease on account of their volunteer efforts."

"Who are these illustrious men that have made such accusations?" Adeolu asked, feigning ignorance.

"You think I was born yesterday, asking me a rhetorical question like that?"

"No, I didn't mean it that way. I'm only trying to get the names of the people maligning my name."

"Well then, you should know that they did not cause the disease"

Adeolu stared, saying nothing, and Sango continued.

"You should not pursue that angle, because that angle is simply not true. And do not mention this when you get to the palace, and also do not speak against me. I have warned you. Now let us hurry so we can make it on time for the palace meeting."

Adeolu was worried more than anything else. He had no intention of bringing this up because it was not the cause of the disease replication and bringing it up would only raise more doubts than any solution.

***

Upon getting to the palace, they met King Abiodun, seated on the throne in his all elegance. Aremu, the king's brother and crowned prince, in his princely garment, was seated beside him. Chief Abioye the right hand chief (Otun), Chief Arese, the left hand chief (Osi), Wura, the leader of one of the witch covens in the realm, Adun, the king's second wife and the leader of the alternative witches coven, and Enitan, leader of the market women and the wife of Adeolu, were all seated on mats right in front of the king and his brother. Sango and Adeolu, on entering the king's court, prostrated flat on their bellies and chanted praises to the king

"Long live the king, may the crown stay on your head for a long time, may your feet always wear shoes of comfort, and may your houses be filled with gold."

The king's praise singers and drummers followed suit and started beating the talking drums and echoing the praises of Sango and Adeolu.

"The king is crowned with the crown of the greatest, the king with the power to decide the fate of mortals, the king that vanquishes his enemies, the king with the clothes of wealth and honor, we honor and give you glory!"

King Abiodun, stood six feet and two inches tall, his head unshaven and only hidden by the crown on his head, middle-aged, with grey hairs around the temple area, was a physically strong man but lacked good cognitive skills. What he lacked in cognition, he thoroughly compensated for in raw, brutal strength; he used to be the city's reigning wrestling champion.

He stood up and lifted his fist up, signifying silence. The drums and the singing came to an abrupt end.

The king spoke. "We have not summoned all of you here for a celebration. You have all been summoned here because the town is in pain. Its citizens are sick and are unable to tend to their farms. The market is no longer brimming with trade as it used to be. Who have we offended? Why are the gods against us at this time? We have not missed any sacrifices to any of the thousand deities that protect our kingdom. Why has this epidemic befallen us?"

He continued his lamentations in an almost teary voice. "My people have suffered, and the goats no longer cry as goats; neither do the birds squeak as they do, nor the fishes swim as they do."

The right-hand chief, Abioye, spoke next. "We consulted widely, and we believe that the gods of our favorite ancestor, Orisanla the Great, need appeasement."

Chief Abioye spoke further. "We should all remember that the Ifa oracle said seven years ago about the approaching seven rings of fire. Can we see that the seven rings represent seven years and the fire represents seven different types of deaths? Our Orisa is angry, and we should give what is due her. Our refusal to give what is due her will spell further doom for our beloved city and its inhabitants."

The king's right hand continued, "Lately, the goat does not bleat as it does, the cock does not crow when due, and our farms are filled with unharvested crops. These are some of the signs that Orisa said will occur if we do not provide her with the annual dues."

He ended his tirade by saying, "Have I spoken well or not?"

The people in the palace chorused, "You have spoken well!"

Muniru the Alfa stood up next, signified his intention to speak, and the king beckoned him on. He said, "The true worship of one true Allah is the surest way to get this disease cleansed from our city. We have called for prayers, and I am using this opportunity to invite all citizens to come to the mosque and pray for the health and safety of Idumagbo."

He continued, "In the last few weeks I have been very sad, because I have become a ubiquity in the homes of many people when they see me and my friend in their house. It is always sad news."

"We visit the bereaved and help them dispose of their dead and their belongings by burning them in the way and manner in which the king ruled."

Albert the Christian, leader of the Christians in the town, also stood up and said, "Jesus Christ is the only true way to everlasting happiness, and this epidemic is a symptom that shows us we have sinned and fallen short of the glory of God. We can only appease God not by bringing goat sacrifice but by bringing our broken and contrite heart to him and asking him to forgive our sins. Only then will our sins be forgiven, and this disease eradicated from our city. I enjoin everyone to join us in fasting and praying so that this disease and evil machinations can be defeated."

He then continued, "There have been some insinuations that some people have been profiting from this proliferation of this disease and that we can put a stop to it if we adopt some hygiene. I tell you this is not true because no one can make a profit from other people's miseries; the profit will also be a misery to him."

Sango then stood up and signified his intention to speak and the king beckoned him to do so. "I greet everyone in the court today. Those that are older than me I greet you with all humility, and those that are younger than me I greet you with pride and confidence. May today be a great day for all of us"

He asked a rhetorical question by staring directly at the citizens present in the king's court. "Which one of the sacrifices to our deities did we miss, or have we missed?"

He then turned to his left, where Chief Abioye and his retinue of Diviners sat and asked again, "Tell me which one of these sacrifices we missed?" Sango was known to be a very vindictive person who does not forgive and does not forget any slight and will not stop until he either kills his opponent or chases them out of the city. Sango and Abioye are both Ifa devotees, but the king awarded all the festival goats and sacrifices to Abioye year after year, even when it was clear that the sacrifices were not potent enough and the prayers and intercessions seemed not to be getting to the deities.

The Diviners looked at themselves and then nodded and spoke in unison. "None."

"Then why did the right hand say we missed the rituals for the Orisanla, the first among the thousand gods? Is the king's right hand trying to profit from our collective misery?"

Chief Abioye jumped up suddenly and used his body to hit Sango and said, "Are you calling me a liar?"

Sango replied, "No, I am not; your children said so" referring to his team of Diviners by pointing at them.

"Should you be referring to those that are still under training and compare their knowledge and wisdom to mine?" Abioye responded.

"They are as qualified as you, and they have earned their stripes to sit in this court and deliberate with the king. By assaulting me here, you have desecrated the head. You have shown yourself an enemy of the people and you are not worthy of a chief in this town," Sango added.

As soon as Chief Abioye heard that, he reached inside his robe and brought out a large knife, with which he tried stabbing Sango. This caused some commotion but Adeolu stood up and dragged him down, collecting the knife and tossing it to one of the king's palace guards, who had also drawn their swords, ready to protect the king.

Sango could not be bothered as he continued to ridicule the right hand. He said, "I don't think you can best me in a duel; you think your drawing your sword is going to shake me?"

The king looked unperturbed and said nothing. A majority of the court took sides with Sango by murmuring that Abioye had his turn to speak and should not have interfered with Sango's speech, even though the polemics were all directed at him. The king's right hand had no choice but to sit down with shame.

The king and Abioye had a long interesting relationship. The people were aware of Abioye's incompetence and had complained to the king several times, but the king refused to retire him and appoint a new right hand.

After tempers cooled down, Sango continued his tirade and this time chose his words much more carefully. "As many of you here know, I lost one of my wives and five of my children to this epidemic and I have nearly been rendered powerless by its unending rampage. It is as a result of this that I decided to seek help from my fellow Oro cult members across the Yobaland, and they have provided me with the antidote. I will start administering the medicine according to a plan that we will put in motion today."

He continued. "This disease has been defeated with help from the thousand gods and members of the Oro cult. We made sacrifices to all the thousand gods; we did not single out one of the gods and make sacrifices. All the thousand gods were duly taken care of and they have repaid us by giving us the antidote. I have administered this medicine on my sons, and they have recovered, and I await orders from the king reimbursing me for my expenses and providing me with the funds to make the medicine available to all men."

Everyone rose up and chorused "aye-aye" and they broke into a song. *"Sango has done it for use, he did it in the past and he has done it again and will do it again for Idumagbo!"*

Adeolu then rose and signaled to the king that he would like to speak. The king beckoned him to go on.

"I greet the king, King Abiodun; may the crown be long on the head and may the shoes fit the feet for a long time. I thank you for giving me the opportunity to stand before you here and speak to the people. I greet the king's right hand, Chief Abioye; your friendship with kings did not start today and will continue for many years to come."

Abioye smiled and was happy on hearing this, making a mental note to also help Adeolu out someday.

"I greet the king's left hand, Chief Arese; your time will continue to be a blessing to the people. I greet Sango and many others that are seated in court today for being part of a historical rejuvenation of this society. I thank my grandmother, not present here, who is an erudite scholar and a woman of wisdom for the knowledge of medicine that she has given to the Oro cult members. The practice of medicine is beyond just administering my medicine to sick patients; it also includes painstaking investigation into what causes diseases and epidemics. My elder, Sango has done very well and has produced some medicine from his work and through the guidance of the thousand gods.

"I am also a member of the Oro cult and I was privy to some of the discussions that were instrumental in bringing about this medicine, and I can say as a matter of fact that the medicine is not the cure."

Sango grimaced where he sat but kept his cool. Despite his veiled attack that morning, this boy still went against him.

"For instance, I know as a matter of fact that three out of Sango's children died, even after Sango administered the medicine."

There were slight murmurs from the crowd.

Adeolu responded by saying, "Yes, Sango claimed that he added some secret potions known only to him to the original medicine from the Oro, which made it more effective, and that was what led to the cure of the last child and his second wife. He has since refused to share whatever secret potion he mixed with the original potion, as is the tradition of the Oro. The Oro has not given blessings to this new medicine and he knows that, and he still came before the people to promote this medicine."

Adeolu concluded, "I thank Sango for his wisdom and knowledge, and for having the love of the city and its people, and courage to push this medicine through, and I pray for those that this medicine will be administered upon that their body will receive it well. I also pray for blessings from the thousand deities to be sent down upon him that he should continue to increase in wisdom, and may he not die young and many of his offspring outlive him."

Everyone chorused: "Ase!" meaning amen to all these prayers.

Sango was left with mixed feelings. Adeolu looked in the direction of Sango and asked, "How long does it take for the medicine to become effective after the sick individual takes the medicine?"

Sango, sensing a trap, replied, "It will take a few days for the full effects of the drug to be noticeable on the sick individual."

Adeolu, having anticipated this kind of answer, replied, "What about those that just recently contracted the disease? If the medicine is really effective, we should notice the improvements very quickly."

To which Sango replied, "Yes, it will be noticeable immediately."

Adeolu looked at him and then the king, and gave a common proverb that goes thus, "If work is taking time for us, no one should not take work's time for granted. We humbly ask that the king allow this medicine to be administered on his son Itiade. I know Itiade recently contracted the illness two days ago and has started developing the symptoms."

Sango's gaze toward Adeolu became very focused. Both tried to stare each other down, a thousand thoughts going through both of their minds. Who would be the victor in their mind game? What would happen in this battle of knowledge, divinity, and wisdom? And who would triumph in their morbid game of power and death?

Then Aremu, brother and heir to the throne of Idumagbo, a tall, very dark, man with dreadlocks and scars on his face and body, taller than his brother the king and one of the tallest in the kingdom, who could be forceful and fiercely loyal, spoke, never looking in his brother's direction and never asking for permission as others had done previously. He said, "We know of Sango's antecedents of peddling medicine that we later find out is not even potent. He has passed around placebos in the name of medicine several times. We should not allow him to hoodwink us."

Sango was visibly very disturbed and looked angry. The atmosphere was charging up.

Aremu, unperturbed by the change in the atmosphere, looked hard at Sango and continued. "Do not bring any of your medicine near my brother, you charlatan."

Sango stood up, wanting to defend his pride. The king signaled him to take his seat back.

Aremu continued, "A charlatan will always be a charlatan. Do you remember the time when myself, my wife, and our daughter had an accident and were mauled by a lion?"

The crowd responded: "True talk, we remember!"

"A lion that terrorized us in the city, I later fought and killed."

The crowd responded again: "True talk!"

"I lay on the bed for days, and I watched as you administered medicine upon medicine on my wife and daughter, which produced no results until they gave up the ghost. I had similar gangrenous tissues from the wounds I sustained from fighting with the lion. It was Adeolu that provided the means and medicine to heal my wounds. I recovered very well, and I am still as strong as ever."

Adeolu stood up, visibly pleased. A man that loved the theatre at the king's court, he bowed to the people, and the people clapped and cheered for him.

"We should also not forget that Sango did not ask for help from the Oro because he was not ready to share glory with any member," Aremu said.

Sango stood up, heckling him, saying, "You do not know that! I share my glory all the time with my cult members."

Aremu continued showering praise on Adeolu, ignoring the heckle from Sango. "If Adeolu were around when this incident happened, I am sure my family would still be with me today."

Adeolu had gone on one of his numerous discovery trips and only came back a few days after Aremu's wife and child had passed, to a dying

Aremu, and was able to make a potent medicine that reversed the gangrenous wounds all over his body.

"You should not forget my daughter, named Moremi, after King Adebayo's mother, Queen Warrior of Idumagbo, a very prominent woman who led many battles against the northern invaders after her husband the king was killed during a raid."

He concluded by saying, "Sango, be truthful. We know your antecedents. You are only trying to fool us while you make money out of our collective misery."

He spoke with such confidence and arrogance in front of the king that it left the people bewildered and murmuring. Unbeknownst to everyone else, Queen Adun had duly informed Aremu that the witches had claimed the throne for him, and he had nothing to fear from Itiade, whom they had put a curse on and would never be king. Queen Adun was the king's second wife and the leader of a witch coven. All the king's courtiers were aware of the tension between the king and the heir to the throne. King Abiodun had always shown favor toward Itiade, and it was an open secret that he wanted him to be king over Aremu, but he had named Aremu the heir shortly after he was installed as king because of his loyalty and his brotherhood, and now he was lording over him.

No one really knew why the animosity between the king and his brother came about. They never spoke about it openly to anyone. It was rumored that Aremu had a sexual relationship with a Nubian slave who was the king's palace lover. The king had noticed the unusual beauty in this Nubian when she did her daily chores in the king's compound. He privately asked that she be brought to him every evening for his relaxation. Aremu, the king's young, virile brother, also noticed the beauty at the same time and wooed her for himself, fell in love with her, and was thinking of marrying her and securing her freedom.

The king found out only after Itiade was born and could not believe that his own brother could do that to him. Aremu claimed that he did not know that his brother, the king, was sleeping with her as well. Itiade's mother kept her mouth shut and never revealed to Aremu that she was sleeping with his brother the king, despite professing her love for him. Even though the king bought her gifts sometimes and showed her favors, he never signified that he was going to take her out of slavery or make her one of his wives. Itiade's mother evaluated both and ended up playing both the king and his brother and had taken to the grave the knowledge of who was actually the father of Itiade. The people had always wondered. Some of the people thought maybe because Abiodun had not fathered a child from his two wives, he could not possible be the father of Itiade, while others thought, with the kind of love the King showed towards Itiade, he had to be the father.

The king stood up and raised the scepter then waited for silence to reign. He then spoke. "Sango has served us well in this community. He has commanded our armies and has won many battles. He has performed feats of medicine that put the worst of diseases and epidemics to shame. Let me remind you that there was a year in which pregnant women were dying at birth. It was Sango's medicine that saved Itiade and Itiade's mother's life. Then, our beloved Adeolu was not yet a man," said the king.

The older people chorused, "True, true."

He continued, "Sango and his medicine have my blessings today. I am thoroughly pleased with the work he has done so far. I am proud of his accomplishments."

The people chorused his name: "Sango-ooo!" and the king's band beat some drums and he broke into a grin, bowing slightly to the people.

The king continued. "Sango has put a lot into this medicine, and I have walked with him along the way and I believed him when he saved Itiade's life as an unborn baby, and I also believe him now that Itiade's life is on the line."

The people broke into a frenzy and Sango's name reigned in the air, much to the discomfort of Adeolu, who kept a straight face.

"As soon as Itiade is healed and has recovered fully, I will provide multiple workers for Sango to produce much medicine for the whole city, and we will make this medicine free for all sick individuals in the whole village".

"We will also make Sango a very rich man and install him as the new Balogun (commander of the king's army) of Idumagbo!"

King Abiodun gave his final ruling by saying, albeit prematurely, "Balogun Sango is the war chief of this city and oversees the defenses of the whole city and is head of the whole army and will supervise any war in which the city is involved."

Then the king raised his scepter again, signifying end of court, turned his back to the people and entered the inner chambers.

The king's panegyrists then echoed what the king said and pronounced that this was final asking the court whether the king had spoken well or not. All the members of the court replied that he had spoken well.

The Disease Agent

Several days had passed since Sango administered the medicine to Itiade. Sango had since been installed as the Balogun of Idumagbo land and there had not been any significant improvement in the health of Itiade. Sango had practically moved into the palace, as the king gave him a room allowing him to come and go as he pleased while he treated Itiade.

Adeolu, on the other hand, had returned to his caves where he received a message from Abeni that Barto came around, so he hopped on a boat in order to cut the almost day-long journey to around four hours.

He alighted from the boat onto the docks and walked a few meters to the center of town where the fish market was situated. A few folks on the street said hello to him and he walked the rest of the tiny road to Abeni's bar. Idiape, a fishing village thirty miles west of Idumagbo, was easiest to reach by boat from Idumagbo, a town where fishermen bring their fishes and traders buy fish, salt, and dried it before transporting it to other village markets for sale. Fishes were brought to Idumagbo for sale on market days.

Idiape was a far-flung trading and fish market with no army, and all the regional principalities and powers agreed to keep it as a trading zone with no oversight. A disruption to the city would disrupt the food supply and it could lead to unrest. As such, Idiape was a no-man's-land and could be very dangerous. Only a very dangerous man with magical or mystical power could provide the rules.

One such person was Ekunogun, who people rarely saw but respected, even when he was absent. Upon getting inside, he sat down and asked for *bruks* (a locally brewed wine from the palm tree). Abeni came around to serve him in a wooden cup and then sat down beside him. Adeolu had met Abeni, a middle-aged mulatto woman, a few years ago in the company of her younger brother, Araba, at a function in Karounwi. Adeolu was intrigued by her and decided to follow her to Idiape for a few days and had been a regular visitor ever since.

Abeni was considered the most beautiful woman in Idiape, Idumagbo, Karounwi, and its environs. She was a middle-aged woman of forty-two years old. She came with her father and mother to Idumagbo when she was around two years old. The father, Hubertino, a Caucasian, a carpenter by profession, brought the technical know-how of making clothes from cotton to Idumagbo. The mother, Eunice, a black African and a weaver by profession, came on a boat with Abeni. They never told anyone what made them come to the hidden coastal town. They exchanged their knowledge and technical know-how for lands and chieftaincy titles from the late King Adebayo.

They gave birth to a son, Araba, whom they sent to train as a soldier of Idumagbo under Babagun in Karounwi. Abeni currently owned the only bar at the end of town and was considered by many as a wealthy woman whose virtues could be bought for cash and kind because of the company she kept. She tried to stand up and defend women and children who had been abused, sexually and culturally. She did not have many elite friends and she was considered a pariah for the people she chose to associate with, and was seldom welcome anywhere. She was happy because she had protection from Ekunogun. No one dared disturb her business.

Things actually got worse for her and her brother after their parents died many years ago. Mulattos, Albinos, "sekembas (street name for an Albino)" were not uncommon; however, a lot of people think them weird due to their unusual hair and blue eyes. Araba was in the king's army at Karounwi before he disappeared. No one knew the reason why, but weird rumors were spread about his relationship preferences.

Abeni made a living by entertaining men and women in her little, out-of-the-way bar and sometimes she rented out rooms to men of means who came seeking hedonistic pleasures with their many concubines and sometimes captured slave girls. Abeni also had in her employ a few indentured slave girls of various origin; this often delights the many men that come pouring in night after night every day after a hard day's work on the farm to satisfy their hedonistic fantasies.

They also used the bar as an avenue to discuss and gossip about the latest news in the town, who was dead, who was celebrating, and who was sleeping with whom, whose child was a bastard that the husband was unaware of. And sometimes the bar happened to get long-distance travelers that brought news of happenings around the world while they also had good opportunities to satisfy the litany of debauchery whims available at Abeni's bar.

Last year, Adeolu had met a Portuguese traveler named Barto. They had drinks together and partook in a sexual orgy. During one of their sober moments, Barto told him an incredible story of how multiple cities in European lands were wiped out by a disease called the plague. He described the disease as a killer that was characterized by delirium, acute high body temperatures, and formation of big bumps all over the body. He was astounded when Barto later told him that they later discovered that the disease was caused by rats that were brought in by ships. Adeolu had asked that Abeni contact him anytime Barto showed up again. Barto showed up, and Abeni sent him a message and here he was.

"Where is he?" asked Adeolu.

"Who?"

"You know who I mean, don't get me started."

"Is that the way you greet a lover?" asked Abeni, who was dressed in goat leather trousers sewn together tightly with ropes extracted from yucca fiber and a blouse made from leopard skin reaching just above her navel.

"There is fire on the mountain. Your prettiness and beautiful body is not the only thing that has brought me here today," said Adeolu, eyeing her lecherously.

"I was hoping you were going to say you missed me and had come here to see me," she replied tauntingly.

"Where is he? People are dying, and many more people are going to die if I do not hurry and produce an antidote."

"Take it easy. How can you take this problem upon yourself like that? The king has even commissioned Sango to make the medicine," said Abeni.

"The king made a mistake, and I will make him see that when I find the solution and provide the medicine."

"Calm down. Barto is around and is currently attending to his business," Abeni said after a few seconds of both silently ogling and sizing each other up.

"I have always known you to be a reliable and gracious person; your beauty is unrivaled in all these principalities." he then went over and gave her a big hug, slightly placing his hands on her hips.

Abeni blushed. She had never married because she could not make a choice among the many suitors she had; old, young, powerful, and wealthy men from all walks of life sought her hand in courtship.

"You are the only man that tickles my fancy, and I know you tell your wife Enitan the same thing."

"I praise my wife with much better words than the ones I say to you," he said.

"What other words can beat 'your beauty is unrivalled in all principalities'?"

"Wait until you become my wife and you will get the most beautiful words out of my mouth; words that will make you moist, juicy, and mushy with me," he said, and winked playfully at her.

"Is this your way of asking me to marry you?" she queried seductively.

"My dear, you are a princess and you deserve to be treated as such. And once I make the kind of money that can provide for you, I will be here kneeling at your door begging for your hand," he responded.

"I will slide into your arms and we will take the boat and row back to Idumagbo."

"We will have a house near kings and chiefs in the eastern part of Idumagbo."

"No, I want to live in the west, so I can come back to Idiape and take care of my little bar," she added.

Adeolu looked confused and then said stutteringly, "Your wish is my command any day."

"How is the situation in Idumagbo?" Abeni asked changing the subject and taking a much more alert position.

"Bad, very bad."

"How bad can it be? You are not dead yet."

"If I die, Idumagbo will be no more in a few weeks."

"Really? You are so full of it."

"My dear, I don't think you get it. I am the only one with the kind of knowledge and power that can fix the epidemic, transform Idumagbo, and make it into a powerhouse."

Abeni looked at him, said nothing, and encouraged him to continue speaking.

"I have dreams of building boats that can sail across the seas and discover other lands. If I die, it will be a caging of minds for many generations to come."

"Your father came from a different land across the seas. I suppose he would have told you a few stories about the lands beyond the sea."

The truth was that Hubertino, an inveterate gambler, became a recluse after he perceived that others cheated him out of his earnings. He became even more bitter after his wife passed, his wife has been his sole confidante, she listened to him always and took care of him, pampered him. Abeni loves her father, he was ingenious during his time but now has tremendous manic episodes, she never shared it with anyone, keeping the memories of her father clean in the eyes of the public.

Barto stepped into the bar from one of the adjoining rooms and followed in tow was an Arabian Nubian lady with blue eyes. Barto, a short, wiry Caucasian with shifty eyes and very little hair on his head, often traveled the coastal towns of these lands. Few people knew what he did. He often went to speak with Ekunogun. Some people thought it was mere consultation. People like Adeolu and Ogunde thought the relationship might be more than that.

He looked at Adeolu but did not remember him, signaling to Abeni to bring him another drink. Abeni stood up from where she was, walked to the bar, snatched up a wooden jug, poured a large helping into a large wooden cup, and passed it to Barto.

He took a big swig, then said, "Abeni, can you please provide some music?"

"The musicians don't come until evening," she replied.

He took another swig from his bottle while Adeolu continued to study him, wondering how he would be able to approach him. He still could not believe he did not remember him after what they did together a few years ago.

Abeni then moved closer to him, wanting to refill his cup. He stopped her in her tracks and said, "I want to have a special good time tonight." He winked, and then laughed.

"I will find for you the prettiest girls here tonight," she said, and laughed as well.

Adeolu moved closer to them and asked Abeni to pour him a cup. She did, and he took a mouthful then said, "This wine has gotten better over time, would you agree with me?"

Barto said, "Indeed," and shrugged his wiry, little body.

Adeolu then said, "We were here together some years back and we had a great time with some very awesome people here."

Barto looked at him, shrugged and said, "I have an awesome time with many people whenever I come here."

"Don't mean it like that, I meant we were very good friends and we spoke at length on other matters. And you told me about the bubonic plague that killed many people in a land across the seas," said Adeolu.

Barto nodded his head. His mind seemed to have been suddenly engaged. His eyes shone through the darkly lit bar as he peered under the fish oil torch to look at Adeolu before saying, "Yes, that was a terrible time over there, and the people were lucky to discover the causative agent."

"We have a similar case in which multiple people have died, mostly women and children and few men," said Adeolu.

"Tell me about the symptoms." He was suddenly inquisitive as his eyes lit up.

"Constant vomiting and stooling, open sores on the body."

"you don't seem to have lots of flies around in Idumagbo, I see a lot of beeswax torches burning during the day to keep flies away and wild bergamot and horsemint flowers torches at night"

"Yes, we got that angle covered, ever since my ancestors understood that mosquitoes transmit another form of fever that kills in a few weeks."

He continued "We even have potent herbs we can use to cure the mosquito-transmitted disease. The causative agent could not have been flies"

"So, that leaves water and the air?"

"That symptom description fits a disease agent."

Adeolu nodded and repeated, "disease agent."

"That's why whenever I come around here, I drink only this," he said, pointing to his cup of bruks.

Adeolu said, "The reason why most men are not dying is that they drink bruks more than they drink water?"

Barto made a squeaky sound indicating affirmation, then spoke. "It's unfortunate and ironic that the men who don't drink bruks are the ones dying."

Abeni said, "Maybe that's why fewer people are dying in Idiape and Karounwi when compared to Idumagbo."

"Idumagbo is more heavily populated than Idiape and Karounwi with the Disease agent?" said Adeolu.

Adeolu continued, "you mean the medium carrying the agent that is causing the infection."

Barto nodded smugly.

"The disease could be transmitted through three mediums, touch, water, and the air we breathe," said Adeolu.

Barto and Adeolu started at each other for a while with Barto's expression nudging Adeolu to finish his comments."

"It isn't touch, because I just confirmed that wearing patients' clothes doesn't cause the infection."

"It has to be water, if it had been air, there'd probably be no one else in the villages."

"It must have been horrible," Barto continued. "I've often come around to Idumagbo on the western side and took walks around the areas where the river opens up into the seas. I have seen folks pass feces into the river."

"Water and feces; what about that? The river separates into two; the heavier part with the feces flows directly into the seas while the lighter and filtered part flows into the lake where the city gets its drinking water."

"Then some of the feces must have gone into the drinking water or someone violated the water code and passed feces directly into the lake," he replied, grinning.

Adeolu's eyes lit up, he said, "I have to test the water and if the water tests positive, then we have to enforce the water code and ensure that the lake water is cleaned up."

Barto said, "That's a good point. Afterward, you will have to come up with a good medicine to cure those that are already afflicted."

"Do you know of any such medicine?"

"I cannot remember vividly, but it seems that it had in it some brine mixture."

"Thank you, Barto!" A grateful Adeolu took Barto's hand and then pumped it before walking to Abeni. He gave her another hug and then quickly slipped out into the night. Abeni ran after him and said, "I wish you luck, we are all rooting for you to figure this out!"

Adeolu ran and got on the last boat going back to Idumagbo. It cost more because there were two extra hands on deck who would hold the beeswax oil torch to navigate properly. It was a big risk, and oftentimes people have gotten lost at sea, never to be seen again. Some appeared back onshore a few days later with grueling stories of how they survived and navigated their way back. He sat at the back of the canoe and allowed his thoughts to drift and not concentrate on the difficult trip he had undertaken.

***

"And I suppose this is going to bring back our twin sons as well?" said Enitan.

Adeolu, realizing he had been insensitive, said, "We will have many more sons together. The twins are gone. The Creator who gave them to us has taken them."

"I can't believe you said that! You barely come home at night. Am I supposed to make the babies all by myself?" she said before bursting into uncontrollable sobs.

Adeolu moved closer and hugged her close, with a lone tear dripping down his left eye.

Adeolu and Enitan's relationship and marriage could be termed at best, unconventional. Enitan made a lot of money from her business and financed her husband's endeavors whilst being aware of his many other women.

"Do you remember when we first met?"

Enitan nodded, drawing him closer into her embrace and then said, "At the Karounwi Army games."

The King's army usually held games like running, jumping, wrestling, archery, swordsmanship, and spear and axe throwing every year. The year he met Enitan, Adeolu had won a lot of medals and was the athlete of the year.

Adeolu said, "Do you remember how we had gone away for the whole night and everyone was looking for us the next day? How we could not leave each other alone for the next seven days, before we decided to get married?"

Enitan smiled and laughed softly then said, "we were the cynosure of all eyes, and everyone wanted us to be married including the King thereby forcing my Fathers hand."

"We are soulmates connected more on the sublime that the real and our coming together is definitely for a purpose which we both shared, and we know it is for the good and betterment of the society."

"To pursue a meritocracy-based society…"

"We will always be soulmates even after any of us depart this world, our actions today will create a better life for our children."

The laid beside each other and then fell asleep together.

"Enitan," Adeolu called out to Enitan waking her up, "this disease may have taken away our sons, but if we are not careful, it will eventually take away all of us. Together, we can defeat it." He then narrated the story about Barto to his wife.

Enitan knew that Adeolu's mind was troubled and would not rest until he found a cure.

"Please go forth and find a cure. We shall overcome this epidemic," she said.

Adeolu took some wooden bottles and ran out of the house to the stream to take the samples that he wanted.

***

Olori Jade, the first wife of the king, who had been childless, went to the king to commiserate with him and said, "My husband, my head and the paramount ruler of Idumagbo, I think it is high time we started to plan the installation of Aremu after Itiade passes. His health is deteriorating, and it does not look like Sango's medicine has helped him at all."

The king looked up from his morning nap and suppressed the anger boiling inside of him before replying calmly, "The time for my death has not come yet and I can still have more heirs. If not with you, then with Adun, and if not, I will take another wife."

Jade looked surprised at the king's calmness, as she was hoping to get him worked up, so she pressed him further. "We have been together for over thirty years now, no issue. You have been with Adun for more than twenty years, none yet, except for—Itiade—from an unknown slave girl and now you think more will come from another woman?"

Abiodun simply ignored the comments and went back to his nap. He knew they were intended to provoke him.

"You make everyone think I am the one with the problem, whereas you are the one that failed to make me into a mother. I am a fertile woman."

Abiodun could not resist not responding, "Indeed you are, and the fruits you have borne are there for all to see."

Jade, now more agitated, said, "Aremu will be king whether you give your blessings or not." The words were not taken lightly by the king and his temper rose, "get away from my sight, you barren, evil woman."

Jade stared at Abiodun with hands akimbo, rolled her eyes, and left. The king could not comprehend why Jade would want Aremu to be king after him, and he still could not understand why Adun was not standing up for Itiade, her adopted son, to be king. Itiade had been given to Adun at birth to take care of as her own, when his actual mother passed away a few days after childbirth. He suspected that both wives were in cahoots with each other against him, and their wish was to install Aremu as king after him. He had been unable to determine what drew them close. They used to be implacable foes before, and he was the one that used to preach tolerance and love. Now he wished for the days of the past when they were enemies.

He knew that Jade was the leader of the witches and he had ridden partially on her strength to the throne of Idumagbo. His suspicion was that Jade must have made a pact with Adun, but whatever Jade's reward would be in this pact eluded him and it drove him mad. He had sent some of his spies after both of them and they had not given him any useful information. He had started having thoughts whether he still had control of the security of the city. This was one of the many reasons why he decided to make Sango the war chief, hoping he would be loyal, and he could start getting some useful information about his subjects once again.

Ever since Ayesa (mother of Itiade) died, he rarely got sexually excited; it was like passion for sexual satisfaction from a woman suddenly vaporized, and only the thoughts of Ayesa aroused him. He always fought to drive such thoughts away from his mind and hoped no one could see inside and discover the lewd feelings and thoughts for a dead woman. He, once again, thought to himself that if he could seduce Adun, buy her some wonderful gifts, make love to her, he might just be able to extract important information from her. Some semblance of a plan started to form in his head.

***

Adeolu woke up from bed and was very pleased with the work he did yesterday in his cave. He had finally gotten a breakthrough in his experiments. Some of the rabbits and rats had recovered as a result of one of the solutions he had swabbed them with and also mixed into their meals and in some cases, force-fed the solution to them.

The solution contained a mixture of squeezed sugarcane and sea salt, but there existed a problem. The solution must be made according to specific proportions of salt and squeezed sugarcane, however, all the gourds contained mixed proportions of the solution, and the measurements were taken and kept by Fero. He had been unable to determine the proportion used for generating the current solution that cured these animals so he could commence large-scale production for the citizens of Idumagbo.

Adeolu loved his niece as a father loves his daughter. She called him Father, to his delight. Fero lost both her parents early in life and he had been her guardian ever since then and they had grown very close and even closer as she grew very interested in his line of work. She had mixed these solutions a few weeks ago and she usually kept records of such measurements, he believed, as he had instructed her to always do. He had learned that she stayed overnight at the king's palace to take care of Itiade, the king's sick son, whom she had grown fond of since they both converted to the Islamic religion a few years ago. He thought that there might be something between them, but he quickly dismissed it, and chose to believe that they were just favorite relatives. Even though the kingdom has not expressly forbidden such relationships, he had seen first evidence of the destruction it can do to family lineage. He also reminded himself to thwart this if he was in any way correct, as he remembered what his grandmother taught him about inbreeding, which produces feeble offspring. No one had told him anything yet and he was just presently cautiously observing.

Fero could be very passionate about what she believes in; he remembered when she first came to live with him and Enitan, she never wanted to go to the farm but took keen interest in Adeolu's work. He encouraged her, and he was not sure how that was going to play out. Eventually, if she learned the craft, she would not be an initiate into the Oro and subsequently would not have access to a lot of information that would make her successful in that profession. He sometimes worried, but nevertheless continued to teach her.

He had never been really concerned about her conversion to the Islamic faith. He felt the time had not come yet to explain to her the real truth about religion. Now he needed her to come and help him with the measurement recordings; she must have taken the measurements for the potions put in each gourd.

After waiting a few more hours, he felt that he should go down to the palace himself and ask her for the recordings. He had abandoned going to the palace since the king gave Sango the go-ahead to administer his medicine on Itiade and afterwards, on the rest of the citizenry. Fero mentioned to him a few weeks ago while they were working in the cave that Itiade seemed not to be responding to the treatment and might be getting worse. He had serious doubts on the efficacy of Sango's method, but since the king ruled before he could speak, he had to find some way to ensure that all ended well.

He entered the compound and saw the commotion and saw that a lot of the family members, the King's wives, Jade and Adun, with several of the household assistants huddled together, with Sango sitting beside Itiade, chanting and praying to the ancestors to come to the aid of Itiade—and spare him from the shame and ignominy that would follow if Itiade suddenly died. Adeolu saw Fero in one corner of the room. Their eyes met and he signaled to her to come and she met him, and he told him that he had found the cure. She responded by shouting, "Allah has shown us the way!"

Adeolu responded and told her cheekily, "No, it is Orunmila (one of the thousand deities) that has shown us the way, and we need someone to lead us through these roads and you are that person."

She looked at him bewildered.

"You will let me know which proportions you mixed inside this gourd," he said, tapping a gourd in a bag he had draped over his shoulders.

Fero took a step back from Adeolu, moving further from the room away from Adeolu before replying, "Father, there are more than a thousand gourds in there."

Adeolu then reached into the bag on his shoulders and brought out the gourd and handed it over to her. She took it, looked at the markings on it, they were part of an index number into the material proportions it contained.

She responded, "Yes, I remember the gourd, but I can't tell what proportions are in it unless you tell me where you took it from."

Adeolu stared at her with an expression that was begging for more answers.

She then continued, "The position of the gourd and the markings on it forms the index to their proportions. Do you happen to remember where you took it from?"

"Of course, I remember the position where I took it from," Adeolu responded, trying to picture the position where he took the gourd from in his head.

"Very well, let's get to it then."

The folks in the room grew curious about what was going on and started to file out of the room into the courtyard. They feasted their eyes on Fero and Adeolu, trying to decipher what they were talking about. Adeolu caught a snide comment from Jade, who said, "All these charlatans, they should let the poor boy go and rest."

Adeolu ignored the sneer and the snide remarks from the queens and said, "The king has given me permission to treat Itiade with my newly discovered serum, which I plan on administering to him in a few minutes"

Adun, Itiade's mother, said, "Anything is welcome at this time. We want him alive. He is just a boy and not interested in the throne of the king. All his enemies must surely die and let him live."

Adeolu said, "Can someone bring me a jug of water?"

Fero quickly signaled one of the house assistants (Iwofa) to get the water and it materialized. She placed the jug of water beside the almost lifeless body of Itiade and the defeated spirit of Sango, his face ashen, stood up as soon as Adeolu stepped closer. Sango said, "My work is almost done here. It is now in your hands."

Adeolu nodded in affirmation and avoided Sango's fiery red eyes, then blew his breath into the jug of water, then raised the jug to the sky and prayed in the name of Orunmila, saying, "The gods of infinite knowledge, divination, wisdom, and fortune-telling, who reveal the past, solution to problems in the present, we come to you with our humble word offerings. We have been to the east, to the west, to the south, and to the north in search of a solution and you have met us at the point of our needs. We call upon you today as our forefathers have called upon you and you heard them, to hear our cries today as we administer this medicine on your son. Let it be potent and let it revive Itiade."

He further thanked Orunmila for giving him the solution that he would be administering on one of his subjects and asked that the full potent power of the medicine manifest in the receiver.

Everyone chorused: "Ase! (Amen!)"

He then took the gourd and poured some of the contents in Itiade's mouth, poured some in a jar of water, took out a piece of white cloth from his waist bag and soaked it in the jar of water and used it to wipe Itiade's face, neck, and parts of his upper body, and then asked that everyone should leave the room and let him get some fresh air.

Everyone started filing out of the room except for Muniru the Alfa, who stayed perched in a corner and said, "I am not going to step outside because Itiade is a convert and is under my tutelage, as well as Fero, and as such I have a right to be here so as to give spiritual counsel."

Adeolu looked at him, stepped closer to him and whispered into his ear, "Don't even let me get started with you. If I should open my mouth here, you will surely meet your Maker."

Muniru scampered outside quickly.

For a brief moment, Queen Jade and Adeolu locked eyes together and when she, Adeolu, and Itiade were within earshot and no one could overhear them she whispered to Adeolu, "Adeolu, you are defying the gods and you shall suffer for it!"

It was as if she had a premonition that the time had come for Itiade to be cured and healed. He stared at Queen Jade and they both held each other's gaze for a while and his heart nearly missed a beat. His theories and assertions about fake witchcraft vaporized for a brief moment and he started to think that this woman might possess some unseen and supernatural powers after all and not just make-believe and tricks like some of the others. Then he quickly dismissed the thought and replaced it with a thought that she is just a very intelligent woman who has the uncanny capability to understand human emotions and motivations, channel and use this information for her own selfish ends.

He continued to look at her and told her, "Queen Jade, you are the one defiling the gods. You are refusing the healing of your stepson. Anyone that is on the side of evil can never triumph."

She responded furiously, saying, "The gods' wish is to have Aremu become king. If Itiade is alive it will make it more difficult. This epidemic is from the gods; you are the one defiling their wishes." She rolled her eyes, hissed, and then walked out.

Adeolu walked outside of the room where Itiade was kept and beckoned Fero to come back inside. He told her, "There are many enemies around; don't ever leave the room under any circumstance. If you need to do anything outside of here, detail an assistant that you can use for your errands."

She responded, "Certainly, Father."

He then walked out of the room, and one of the palace assistants told him that the king wanted his presence in the palace immediately. He walked across the courtyard and into the larger compound housing the king's palace. He saw Sango huddled in one corner and the king standing in the other corner leaning against the wall. The king looked to him and asked, "How is he?"

He replied and said, "It is too early to tell. The serum I administered is fast-acting, and we should notice improvements in a few hours—or at least before the sun comes up again."

Adeolu continued. "We should start making preparations to get the medicine into the hands of the sick people before we start losing them."

The king looked at him and pretended he did not hear the statement. He looked at Sango and asked, "What was the outcome of your spying into the whereabouts of Adun?"

Sango looked at the king and then at Adeolu, using his eyes to ask whether he should speak in front of Adeolu. The king beckoned with his hand to continue; he had brought Adeolu here so that he could hear as well. He had come to believe that he could be trusted, particularly seeing how Fero had stood beside Itiade during all these trying times.

Sango then said, "I received a report from one of the spies that has been trailing Adun for a few weeks now."

The king shifted impatiently. "Does the spy have any incriminating thing on her?"

"Apparently, yes. She has been at many meetings between Queen Jade's coven and Wura's coven."

"What can she be doing at a witch coven's meeting?" the king inquired offhandedly.

"My king, Adun is a witch. She belongs to Wura's witch coven, and it is an open secret in the city and its environs," said Sango. "There seems to be some conspiracy going on between the covens; they are planning something, and we have not yet discovered what it is. But it seems it has to do with your succession."

King Abiodun seemed to be lost in thought for a few minutes while Adeolu continued to listen to the conversation with rapt attention. He found it quite fascinating that the king did not know that his second wife was also a witch. Quite a number of people were privy to such knowledge. He then wondered how many things this isolated king does not know. In his own wisdom, a king that is not privy to some crucial information is probably not in charge of leading and ruling the citizens.

After a brief period of silence, King Abiodun thought 'she must have recently joined' then said, "Jade I know of her witchcraft practice but not of Adun, go on, tell me everything you found out."

Sango continued, "Yes, my king. She was present at a meeting hosted yesterday at Idiaba, and one of our spies was able to infiltrate this meeting."

"You had someone in their meeting?" the king asked.

"The person reported to us that an agreement was reached between Queen Jade and Adun that Aremu should be the next king and that Itiade should be named the next heir so as to maintain the current political equilibrium."

"What insolence! A political equilibrium where the gods' deputy, king of the land, is not on the scale?" a furious King Abiodun said.

Sango said, "May the body be strong, my king."

"Please don't do, as your might and power can reach," Adeolu said, speaking for the first time in this conversation, which he still did not know why he was included.

"What is Queen Jade's benefit in all of this?" the king asked.

"Whatever Queen Jade's gain is, currently remains elusive, it is a mystery that needs to be figured out," Sango replied.

The king demanded, "You had better get that reason quickly, because you can see that my wives and my brother seem to have taken up arms against me."

"My king, the goal is not to offend you but to try to shed more light on this. May I please talk?" Adeolu asked.

Adeolu then continued. "What about Sango's gain in all of this? Why don't we get the chiefs of the kingdom to also investigate?"

Sango was visibly very angry, and the king noticed this, then decided to ignore Adeolu's suggestions and said, "I have to quickly put down this plot and deal decisively with the masterminds."

Sango, visibly pleased now, said, "Yes, my king. We are working on getting this information on why Queen Adun can be against her own son and conspire with Queen Jade."

Then they noticed some quick movements outside the palace doors. Sango quickly dashed for the door and saw someone hurrying quickly toward the passageways with the intention of exiting through the palace's outer walls. He bellowed orders to the guards around to give chase to the phantom figure. When he returned, he saw that the king was even more alarmed than ever and had summoned the prefect of the palace guards to beef up the security around the palace and not allow anyone to exit or enter, and also shut down the city gates and no one should enter or exit and all strangers in their midst should be accounted for in the next few days.

Sango then bowed to the king and said, "My king, I have it under control. The man will be caught. He is still within the palace grounds and I have ordered our finest horseback riders to start looking for him with the help of our trained dogs. He will soon be caught."

The king sighed and said, "I want reports brought to me as soon as you have them. Send your trusted lieutenant to brief me if you are not around."

He then sent for the right hand and the left-hand chief, who would constitute a war council immediately. The king's butler came inside and said to him that there was a message from Fero. The king overheard this and asked that the messenger should be brought inside to give the message.

The messenger came in, a captured loyal Sahelian native and he said, "Itiade is awake."

The trio all stood up and were suddenly alert and quite elated. They moved quickly toward the door of the palace to get outside into the courtyards. It seemed the news must have reached the queens' quarters as well, as they had also stepped into the courtyard leading to the room that Itiade was sleeping in. The king signaled to the prefect not to let anyone into the room. The king stepped into the room, followed by Sango and lastly by Adeolu. Itiade stood up and gave the king a feeble hug. The king responded and asked him to rest so he could further regain his health.

There was some commotion outside in the courtyard with the announcement of the arrival of Aremu and his soldiers, who had gone on a trip to the coast on behalf of the kingdom. He heralded the king by kneeling before him, clasped his two hands together into a fist and laid it in the king's hands. The king was taken aback by the gesture but nevertheless took his hands, signifying acceptance and affection. Aremu then said, "My king, the son of great and prominent kings, the king with the beaded crown, I bring you good tidings. The chiefs of the coast send their greetings and loyalties with many great gifts, and they promised bigger and greater trading volumes between our communities in the coming years."

King Abiodun responded, suppressing whatever animosities existed between both of them, "You have done very well, my dear brother. Great things continue to await you in this great empire of mine."

As they were exchanging pleasantries, a soldier walked inside and whispered into Sango's ear. Then Sango said, "The intruder spying on us in the palace court has been caught."

Sango was not expecting any kind of jubilation, but he noticed the king's face was expectant, so he continued. "The spy said he spied on behalf of Queen Adun."

There was palpable silence in the room and a heightened tension as everyone glanced in the direction of the king. King Abiodun then said directly to Sango, "Place multiple guards around Itiade and ensure that strict protocols are maintained around meals served to him."

Sango responded, "Yes, my king. Such plans are already underway."

"Bring the spy into the palace court for judgement."

The soldier whispered into Sango's ear again. Sango then quickly said, "My king, I am afraid he might not be in a proper state; a lot of force was used in extracting the information from him."

"I said bring him! I want him to make that confession in my presence and I can send him directly to the gods," he said with a tone of finality.

King Abiodun, Aremu, Adeolu, and Sango all filed into the palace court where they met the right hand and the left hand of the king, as well as the prefect of the palace guards already in their seats. A few minutes later a disheveled and almost naked individual was brought in and placed on his knees in the center of the court, with only raffia palms covering his torso. He had lost some of his teeth, and it was obvious he was in a lot of pain.

Sango started the questioning by saying, "You have been brought here for judgment by the king, lord of Idumagbo and second only to the gods, to be sentenced for conspiracy, mutiny, and treason."

Arese, the king's left hand, stood up, cutting Sango off and said, "My able king and my very capable and loyal chiefs, I greet everyone in the name of justice and fair rules for which Idumagbo is known. It is customary for the charges against the accused be mentioned before going to questioning."

The people in the palace court, including Adeolu and Aremu, nodded their heads in agreement.

The king raised his fist for silence and the room grew silent, then said, "Sango, please continue," in apparent disregard for whatever Arese had said.

Sango continued. "You were caught eavesdropping on the king's conversation with his chiefs in his court and passing it to fellow conspirators in order to topple the king. Is this true or not?"

The very scared individual held his badly battered and bloody jaws in his hands, looked around then nodded his head. Sango said, "You need to speak so we can all hear you."

He murmured, "Yes."

Sango then continued. "Who specifically sent you to do this."

The individual, looking lost again, said, "it was the queen, Queen Adun; she sent me."

Aremu was taken aback as to what was happening and he responded before anyone could talk. "Why would she order you to do something like that? She is a member of the court and has the privilege to be part of anything that is being discussed in the king's court."

He responded, "I do not know. I was paid very well."

The king then spoke. "The truth is that there are certain items that are not usually discussed with women and females, certain traditions and ceremonies that the female cannot partake in. We are all aware of these traditions."

Aremu said, "So you believe this individual over your queen?"

The king ignored the slight from Aremu and looked in the direction of Sango and then at Adeolu and then at the palace guard prefect and then said, "Place Queens Adun and Jade under house arrest and send soldiers to arrest all of the witches of their respective covens. Seek more information on the extent of this conspiracy and we will have a trial."

Aremu protested, saying, "This is not going to be a fair trial; it looks you have your mind made up."

The king was now visibly and angry and he said to him, "Aremu, do not give me any inclination that you are part of this plot. Currently I do not have any evidence against you but what you say here can implicate you in a way you may not understand."

Aremu kept quiet from then onwards. Sango quickly bellowed out to his lieutenant and he was seen giving them orders to begin the arrest of all the witches in the city.

Adeolu was taken aback by the rapid happenings and he wanted to have a chance to warn his friend and concubine, Wura, so as to elude capture so he said to the king, "My king, there are still many more people sick in the city and we need to move fast to ensure that we do not lose any more citizens by quickly producing the antidotes and administering it to them."

The king was silent for some brief moments and he said, "Everything you need will be given to you. The medicine will be free to all those that are sick, and you will be well reimbursed for all your expenses."

Adeolu replied, "Thank you, my king."

Fero and Itiade were ushered into the king's court and then Adeolu said, "Itiade, look at you! You look like you were not even sick for one day."

Everyone around laughed and congratulated Adeolu for a job well done. Aremu beamed with all smiles as he hugged Itiade, his favorite "nephew," and Fero.

Adeolu then quickly used that opportunity to excuse himself from the meeting by saying, "I need to get to work and take care of the remaining sick people." Sango also came over to where Adeolu was, took his hand and said, "Very well done," then gave him a hug and then whispered, "Be careful of the insatiable hyena."

Adeolu smiled, then said to the king, "Fero will also be coming with me, as I will need her to help with the medicine. She deserves as much accolades I have as she was instrumental in getting us to this cure."

The king smiled, stood up, and then said, "We the people are forever in your debt, Fero, and someday we will make good on this debt."

The rest of the people then applauded her.

Aremu broke the applause when he said, "I have always believed Adeolu could do it; he is the best medicine man in this part of town. He might be young, but we know he understands his trade and craft better than everybody else. And we also recognize some charlatans who claim they can deliver; by the special grace of the gods, we shall soon dispense with them."

Sango's face glowed with anger.

It was generally known that Aremu and Adeolu were good friends, having grown up around each other, especially when Grandma Keniola arrived back from her forced sojourn. The king glanced around before saying, "I am very grateful to you, Adeolu, for your hard work and for not putting me to shame. A great reward awaits you; a reward greater than whatever you can ever dream for."

The people around chorused, "Say it! Make him the Lord Medicine of the city!"

The king ignored the chants of the people.

"Be careful of who you choose to be on your side because they might come back to haunt you; choose your friends carefully," he thought as he had never really liked Adeolu.

Adeolu bowed to the king, grabbed Fero's hand, and pulled her out of the court toward the exit. "Father," Fero said, "Matters are really getting crucial and I am afraid for Itiade's life. Itiade told me that it appears that some sort of sexual relationship may exist between Aremu and Queen Jade."

Adeolu replied, "That would be an abomination, sacrilege, and it is a death penalty on Aremu if such can be proven."

She said, "I thought the same myself, and that is why I wanted to be beside Itiade at all times and fight and get him to clinch the throne of his forefathers."

Adeolu replied, "Aremu seems to be fond of Itiade in a congenial way."

"Are you suggesting that he might be Itiade's father?"

"I don't think that ever came out of my mouth; or did it?" Adeolu said cheekily.

Fero continued in her line of reasoning unperturbed. "It will mean that Aremu is also having an affair with Queen Adun."

"Will that not be a weird or wild occurrence?" Adeolu added.

"When something weird and wild occurs, be on the lookout for a weirder and wilder occurrence; that is one of your quotes."

Adeolu thought that Fero may certainly be on to something and he changed the topic slightly by saying, "It is amazing how things change; despite me being a nephew of the king, no one ever gave me a chance to ascend to the throne of my forefathers. Rather, they see me as a bastard son of a whore slave who was not entitled to the throne."

Fero looked at him quizzically and said, "Would you like to be king someday?"

Adeolu replied, "It might be a weirder and wilder occurrence that is about to show up."

Fero laughed and Adeolu joined her and they both laughed heartily.

"We need to be careful not to be caught up in the family brawl that might develop from whatever has happened in the palace tonight. As a matter of fact, we should take no sides. This is a family that has never considered me as a legitimate son of a king worthy of the throne." They quickened their pace and walked out of the palace grounds and navigated to the footpath on the way to their cave.

Fero stepped into the cave where the gourds were kept and saw that some of them were on the ground. She looked up on the wall where she had arranged the gourds in an MxN matrix and asked her dad, "Which position did you find the particular gourd that contained the working solution?"

Her father pointed to a position. She looked at the position, memorized the number index, and led her father into an adjoining cave containing drawings and letters on a wall. She then said, "Father, the solution contains ten gourds of squeezed sugarcane and ten gourds of concentrated brine."

"Great," her father replied. "We need to get the supplies down here and get to production quickly." Adeolu had taught her how to write using the Roman and Arabic numerals; she preferred the Arabic numbers because they were less clumsy. Adeolu had learned the Arabic numerals from her grandmother, Keniola. Most trades in the city used the roman numerals.

They walked back toward the outer cave where the gourds were kept, and they saw the silhouette of two people. Adeolu quickly dragged his daughter into the shadow so that they were not discovered, and they peeped from the shadows. Adeolu then saw one of the two men was Sango; he must have followed them from the palace, he thought, as he could not remember bringing him to this location. Only himself, Enitan, and Fero actually knew this location.

Then Sango called out his name, "Adeolu, come out! I have not come to harm you but to make you an offering so that peace can reign between us."

Adeolu stepped out from the shadows and said, "Sango, how good to be honored by your presence. You are welcome to our laboratory, although I cannot remember inviting you."

Sango returned the pleasantries by saying, "I am very pleased to be here, and I apologize for not giving you a heads-up. It was not my wish to just barge in like this."

"Apologies accepted. Speak of what brings you to my humble abode."

He looked at Fero, signifying he was not comfortable with her around. Adeolu said to Fero, "Please go to the adjoining room."

Fero curtsied and left Sango and Adeolu.

"The kingdom is in disarray, and I have the keys to give to the prince that I like. I have the king on my whims and caprices and hanging onto my every word."

"How does that concern me and the medicine that I want to provide to all the people?"

"I am here to ask that you let me share in your glory so that the king can continue to trust my prowess as a powerful medicine man and when the time comes, I can hand over the keys of the kingdom to you."

Adeolu was surprised by the offer but kept a poker face and replied, "Planning with you might be considered a mutiny. I am satisfied with the crumbs from the king's table and the lives I am touching every day as a result of my work but there is no way I will share my glory with you."

"You did not contribute anything to the investigation and the final antidote, but you were putting detractions along my way and promoting a spurious one"

Sango laughed covering up his embarrassment and said, "You will do better than that if the kingdom is in your hands."

Adeolu ignored the comments and said, "The king trusts you already by naming you as the war chief."

"I do not think I can rely on that, especially all the riches that he promised me, none of which will be forthcoming because I failed to get a cure for the disease."

"We shall see. The king does not like changing his cabinet for some reasons not yet known, so there is a greater chance that you will be left alone," Adeolu said.

"Not having me in your corner will be a colossal mistake on your part."

"How do I even know you have the keys to the kingdom?"

"You were privy to the discussion earlier today; why do you think the king brought you in and included you in the discussion? I asked him to."

Now Adeolu knew that Sango was probably manipulating the king for his own ends and this would probably not end very well, so he said, "You are my elder and I respect you very well and I will give almost anything you

ask of me except my wife."

Sango laughed, extended his hand, and they both shook hands and

he exited the same way he came through.

The Witches Trials

It was a fortnight later, and Adeolu and Fero had produced medicine for the remaining sick people in the kingdom and the king invited everyone to a feast and he has asked Adeolu to give a speech. Adeolu began his victory speech by saying, "When you pass feces, you pass out demons as well. These demons, whether they get into your water or food, they will make you ill, so you should always pass your feces not in open waters that we fetch to drink and take our baths, but inside a special constructed hole of which I will lead a delegation to a special sample that has been constructed in my compound. May the owners of the realm of the invisible, the light, and the force of this earth that we walk upon not let us walk in dangerous ways that may lead to untimely and gruesome death. We may have the medicine to cure this but I assure you the demons don't stay the same; they change, they mutate, and they are dynamic, and they will bring a different mutated disease to afflict you and may you not be one of the people that will die before we find a cure for it. Let's keep our shit hole in a separate place around our house and let's keep the place clean and never bring anything we are eating or drinking near the place."

The people rose from their seats and gave him a resounding applause and they shouted long live Adeolu! A section of the people decided to add *Prince* to his name, and they chorused long live Prince Adeolu! Someone even shouted, "The next king of Idumagbo!" After the applause and adulations died down, the king rose and asked all the citizens at the feast to sit down.

The king spoke and said, "I thank you, all the people of Idumagbo, for your endurance and perseverance in the face of this daunting epidemic, and especially for believing in me, your king, to be able to search out this matter and not desert me."

Some of the people responded, "You are a good king." It was such a tepid chorus.

The king continued. "I use this opportunity to encourage those that have families and friends that have left the city as a result of the fear of this disease to reach out to them and ask them to come back home. We have the cure; we have surmounted this evil."

The crowd broke into shouts and chants of: "We are overcomers!"

He continued his speech by saying, "To those that have lost family members and loved ones, their deaths are not in vain. Their deaths have signified a new breakthrough on what we can and cannot do. It has opened new avenues for our economy to make new products and services, the house of shit (toilet), a new way to research, make new medicine and treat diseases and above all, it has exposed the fraud and impotency of our witches and their witchcraft."

There was a slight pause as the king looked around for a brief moment and Adeolu kind of understood where this was going to lead to.

"We used to believe that they possessed powers to make charms and heal our sick, but now we know that they are charlatans and conspirators utilizing their group network to further advance their cause of domination over the ordinary man in the community, to foment trouble and spread diseases, hate, and strife."

King Abiodun continued, "We have it on good authority that the witches of our city deliberately caused the disease to spread by trading in dead people's clothes, enriching themselves at our expense, wanting to use this to topple my authority and as a result of this, and by the powers conferred on me as the lord and king of Idumagbo land, I have issued an edict to arrest all the witches in the land; those that claim they have powers and those that just belong to the evil associations for the sole purpose of advancing their evil desires and those of their family and children."

A hushed silence fell over the crowd. A few people wanted to make a spirited escape, causing commotion, and they were promptly arrested by Sango's men.

"I have asked that Sango and his men go and pluck them from their houses and put them in prisons across the land. In seven days,' time we will have a public trial as our forefathers have done before us. We will give them an opportunity to explain why they should not be hanged or burned at the stakes for murder and misleading the populace with their chicanery."

Someone in the crowd shouted, "Burn them all!" Then the crowd broke into chants of: "Burn them all! Burn them all! Burn them all!"

King Abiodun paused to enjoy the chanting, smiled, then continued. "Olori Jade and Adun have been arrested. They are my wives. I love them so much; but I have to do what is right for our community and for the future and prosperity of our offspring. I will leave Providence to be the judge of all."

Another hushed silence descended over the assembly as the king quietly sat down. The king's voice-maker and town crier stood up and said, "Has the king spoken well or not spoken well?" of which a loud chorus of: "He has spoken well!" reverberated throughout the assembly and their loud chants energized and confirmed what the King thought, the people want a spectacle, a bloodletting to satisfy their souls. The king's entertainers rolled out their drums and played scintillating music to the ears of the citizens and they danced and sang the praises of Adeolu, King Abiodun, Sango, Fero, and Itiade.

Adeolu awoke suddenly from a deep, inebriated sleep with the words of the biblical Proverb that was once shared with him by a traveling and wandering Christian preacher who told him, it is the glory of their God to conceal a matter but to search out a matter is the glory of kings. The cure of this disease was a real glory onto himself after he had searched out the matter. He had dreams of a future in which he was clothed in fine silk Arabian robes, riding on fine stallion horses, and having his wildest fantasies with beauties from all walks of life fulfilled. His fame knowing no boundaries, and already his feat of curing this disease had traveled far to all other city environs and he had started getting more visitors than he normally and previously got.

Then he heard some rumbling noises outside of his courtyard, which made him stand up and walk across the courtyard compound. He heard someone whisper his name so he stepped back, grabbed a piece of cutlass to arm himself, and stepped outside of the compound and he followed the sound of his name: "Adeolu, Adeolu, here, here!"

Suddenly, Wura appeared from the shadows of the night dressed in a black, fitted *dansiki*, which allowed her to move stealthily through the darkness at incredible speeds. She pulled Adeolu into the surrounding shrubs and said, "I am here for your help. Sango and his soldiers have been to my house. They have arrested all members of my household. I only managed to escape because I went hunting for the last few weeks and some people warned me on my way back, so I took a detour down here."

"Wura, why here?" Adeolu replied.

"You are the only one I can trust, and this will be a test of our friendship," she said.

Adeolu still looked shocked with many different thoughts racing through his mind and also a nagging fear that if he were caught conspiring with Wura, it may put a dent in his ambitions. He quickly recovered his composure and said, "How are you? I hope you have not been hurt."

She replied, "No, not yet, but will soon be if you don't act fast and let me know how you can help me get out of this town fast and elude Sango and his goons."

"I have been very busy making and distributing the medicine to the sick and there was no way I could warn you; many of Sango and the king's servants were working alongside us too."

"You know that the disease did not spread as a result of the clothes—" Wura began before she was cut short by some noises behind her.

Suddenly appearing through the footpaths were several soldiers dressed in full battle regalia, wearing battle shirts made from dyed cotton and raffia palm and cowrie shells. They whispered some commands and a few of them scattered in attack formation and surrounded Adeolu's compound.

Wura and Adeolu quickly clambered up a nearby tree, within eyesight and earshot of each other.

Sango, their general commander, soon appeared, followed closely by a tiny, wiry man, Salim, Sango's personal lieutenant. It was renowned that he was more wicked than Sango and he ate his meat raw like a carnivore. Salim was another converted Muslim but a foremost Sango loyalist. "Will it not look good if we catch Wura here with Adeolu?" he said, grinning, showing his darkened teeth from too much kola nut eating.

"It will be killing two birds with one stone," Sango replied. "That will be good." Then with a sneer and a grunt of irritation said, "If you had done a very good job, Wura would not have escaped from your traps in the first place."

Sango continued. "With Adeolu, we shall see," and then his gaze fixated on the compound entrance. "Why have you not asked him to come out and see me?"

Salim then hurried from his presence into the compound with a few of his men in tow. Adeolu overheard everything that was said and was taken aback by this sudden subterfuge game that Sango was playing, and his mind started racing in different directions thinking what had he done to Sango to warrant such diabolical thoughts toward him? Then Adeolu whispered, "Wura, Wura."

She looked in his direction on the tree branch where she perched.

"Get down quickly and make a dash for it while the soldiers are searching for me in the compound."

She whispered back, "Where should I go?"

"Go to my caves where I have my laboratory and wait for me there."

Wura climbed down from the trees and made a dash for the bush in the direction toward the caves. Sango said, "I heard voices and rustling," and pointed in the direction of the tree that Wura climbed down from. He shouted, "Soldiers! Soldiers, come, she is here! Give chase and make sure you catch her."

The soldiers arrived to the shouts of Sango's voice and they gave chase in the direction where Sango was pointing and shouting, "Get them, get them."

Adeolu was about to climb down and show himself and prevent the soldiers from going after Wura, then changed his mind when he suddenly saw Fero and Enitan being led outside by Salim and some soldiers. Sango greeted them very well and asked, "Enitan, where is your husband, Adeolu?"

Enitan answered quickly, "Why is that suddenly your business, and is that why you decided to barge into our houses like common criminals? After all, is it not Adeolu that saved this city with his knowledge and medicine?"

She retorted and this continued, "Is this how you repay him or are you just jealous of his new status?"

Sango interjected, "Woman, that is not the way to address me."

"You cannot shut me up; you are incompetent, and everyone knows it. Neither can you silence Adeolu, my husband, the hero of Idumagbo."

"Enitan, you will regret this statement you just made."

It looked like Enitan was just reenergized and she said, "You are a jealous nitwit and a brute and you are envious of the renewed love between him and the people of the city."

Sango, seething with anger, and thinking this might escalate if he allowed this woman to continue her utterances, replied in a calm manner and said, "No, it is not like that. We were told that Wura entered into this compound and we wanted to search this place, but not without the knowledge of the master of the house."

"You lie; you are a liar," Enitan said.

"You already searched the compound and nearby surroundings without our consent, treating us like common criminals," Fero said.

Sango replied, "It was not our intention to barge into your house, but a fugitive from the king's law was seen coming around this location, and this fugitive is a long-known ally of your husband and that is why we are doing this."

Fero quickly catching on then said, "Father must be at the caves where he works. He mentioned to me that he was going to do so overnight yesterday evening."

"Then we had better find him there or he will have to explain his whereabouts to us," Salim said, wrinkling his nose and then added, "We searched every room in this compound and we cannot find him, nor Wura."

Salim's eyes glanced furtively from Enitan to Sango (he noticed Sango's expressionless face, which is a signal for him to continue) and then to Fero and further said, "If he is not there in his cave, then he will have a case to answer about his whereabouts as from yesterday night."

As soon as Adeolu heard this, he quickly climbed down from the tree he was hiding in and made a dash for the shortcut to the caves. He had to just get to the caves before the soldiers, otherwise Wura would be caught and he would be exposed as a fugitive protector. What does he even have to lose if Wura is caught? he thought. He does not owe her much except for some tidbits of information here and there, he thought while dashing through the bush. They have also done a lot together anyway, so she deserves some loyalty. He knew if he did not get to the caves as fast as possible, Wura would be caught and he would also be arrested, and his reputation would be tarnished as "one who disrespects the king." The king is second only to the gods, according to the tradition of the people of this land, and Adeolu knew that, although he rarely shared in any of these beliefs but yet still belonged to the highest secret cult in the land, the Oro cult.

Adeolu slipped through the back tunnel to enter into the caves, a path nobody knew apart from himself and Fero. He dashed through the interconnected tunnels to the cave room where he knew Wura would be waiting. He saw her glancing furtively at the gourds, charms, and amulets on the wall. He quickly said, "Hide, hide, the soldiers are coming!"

"There is barely anywhere to hide around here," she said.

He practically pushed and shoved her behind one of the rock boulders in the cave; she drew out a dagger. "I will not be caught, and I will have to go down fighting," she said.

Adeolu said, "Very well then, let's see if we can outsmart them first before starting a fight."

Salim and two soldiers arrived first through the main entrance of the cave and Salim shouted, "Adeolu, where have you been? We have been looking for you and we suspect that you are harboring a criminal and a fugitive!"

Adeolu shouted back, chiding him, "Is that how you relate with your superiors in the army? are you well trained at all or did you refuse the training of your parents?"

Salim laughed furtively and responded, "Move out of the way on the orders of King Abiodun and let us search this premises."

Adeolu brought out a leather under belt called an *ounde*, a belt laced with strains of fast-acting disease cultures sewn carefully into it such that when a gentle pressure of it is applied on a person's skin the disease cultures seep into the skin causing breathing difficulties, muscle thrashing, drooling, sweating, and high blood pressure, which can cause instant death if not treated within a few hours. Adeolu said, "If you attempt to move any closer here, you will be breathing your last."

Salim laughed and said to the two soldiers with him, "We are here on the orders of the king, he will not dare do anything. Go ahead and secure him if he does not move out of the way."

As soon as he finished saying the words, Adeolu, with one lash of the ounde, struck the two soldiers and they fell down suddenly and their bodies moving spasmodically, and some white foam started coming out of their mouths, nostrils, and ears. Salim stepped back quickly, drew a knife, and Adeolu whipped up the ounde again and was advancing toward Salim when Sango stepped in and said, "Halt whatever you are doing!" stopping Adeolu in his tracks.

He glanced furtively around, saw the two writhing soldiers, and drew out a long, two-edged sickle shaped blade from his belt, a blade that he stole from a traveling Arabian sojourner. The sojourner had come into the city and was looking to trade the two-edged sword that Sango now had in his hands, Sango had followed him outside of town and must have killed him and had not traded with him as he claimed when questioned because no one was there when the trade happened. The poor guy had no family, no friends, and no one to be an advocate and fight on his behalf. It seldom happens but when it does, it is usually perpetrated by someone who thinks he is above the law.

Then the drums of the Oro cult started sounding. The ordinary folks, also hearing the same sounds, thought that these sounds were made by the spirits inhabiting the forests; but the members of the Oro cult and initiates do understand and will usually give excuses to leave whatever meeting or endeavor they are currently in and if they cannot, they must let the cult know why they could not make it. If they do not plausibly provide an explanation, a severe physical punishment is meted out to the person. The person is treated as if he had gone rogue, so it could be instant death, and anyone that gets the killing done automatically wins more laurels and advances more in leadership of the cult.

It takes approximately a day's march to the meeting place from their present location. Several other members will be rising from nearby and far villages, also about a day's march, and for some a few hours' march.

Sango and Adeolu looked at each other. Sango then said, "You will have to let me pass through and search this place," and before Adeolu could respond, he reached into his bag, pulled out a gourd, and handed a gourd to Salim and asked him to administer it to the two soldiers. Salim took the gourd and sat down on the floor, untied the rope around it to open it and then poured some in the cup of his hand and asked the first soldier to open his mouth and poured it through his throat and asked him to gulp it down, which he did. He did the same with the second soldier and they watched them for a while before Sango said, "Did you do anything to the poison in your ounde?"

Adeolu laughed and responded, "Yes, I have an improved version of which I am the only one with the antidote and for me to help your soldiers you will have to vacate my premises and let everyone know that you violated my premises without a legitimate order from the king and that you have no significant reason to harass my family for hiding a fugitive."

Adeolu continued, "If you do have any significant reason, you will have to let me know who was the person that gave you such information so that I can cross-examine him."

Sango sighed, looked at the plight and suffering of the soldiers; they were part of the best and he did not wish that they would die soon so he said, "Give them the antidote and I will withdraw the soldiers to the perimeter and we will meet on the other side of town to discuss the upcoming meeting of the Oro."

Adeolu said, "Hmm, I will not fall for your usual ruse. Send for the staff of the king and ask that every one of your soldiers withdraw to a place where the caves are no longer visible. I will activate my traps and if they move into the perimeter, they will be killed."

The staff of the king signifies an order of the king, and whosoever flouts this order will be punished by instant death. Sango then nodded his head, signifying acceptance, and said to Salim, "Go and explain the situation to the king what has transpired here and ask him to give us his staff to broker the current truce."

Salim dashed out on a sprint and Sango ordered the rest of the soldiers to withdraw to a distance where the caves are no longer visible, but he said they must cover all entrances and exits from the caves so that no one can enter or exit from the cordon. Sango then led the soldiers outside of the surrounding caves and Adeolu slipped into one of the cave rooms took off his shirt and then looked upon the wall and grabbed his battle gear (aso igbale), put it on and then grabbed some hide skin bottles off the wall and hung the straps on his shoulder. He then glanced furtively at the wall and grabbed few more gourds and put them in his pocket and then picked a belt dagger and wore it on his armpit. He picked his bow and quiver of arrows and slung them across his shoulders. He then wore a flowing gown (agbada) on top of it to conceal his battle readiness. He went into a different room where Wura was. Wura ran into his arms and said, "Thank you so much."

"Wura, Wuraola, now that I see that this is beyond the ordinary and it looks more like victimization, I will protect you with all of my might," Adeolu declared.

After what seemed to be a long embrace, Wura pulled back and said, "I am not your wife; neither do I have any children for you. Furthermore, I am also your competitor, even though we sometimes collaborate on solving some issues. I do not understand why you are doing this for me."

"You mean, you don't know? You actually do complement me and, in some ways, and I cherish your knowledge, intelligence, and charisma— and of course, good sex. I would not want to relinquish all that on behalf of some flimsy king's household disagreements and conspiracy."

"Wait, wait; what do you mean by the king's household disagreement? I thought King Abiodun had caught on to our incredible acts of witchcraft and that was the reason he is hunting the two witch covens."

"He accused you of spreading disease by trading the dead people's clothes."

"A very false accusation; we did not even trade in those clothes."

"Yes, that is a complete fabrication on the king's part," Adeolu noted. "I was taken aback when Queen Jade and Adun were arrested, as well as all the members of both covens at various locations all over the city."

Both seemed to be lost in thought, then Wura spoke again. "Tell me about this king's household conspiracy."

Adeolu responded by saying, "The king distrusts his wives and he knows that in order to divorce them, he will have to discredit them because they are from very powerful families and are prominent witches as well, and he will have to kill them to show examples of what it looks like when you disrespect the king."

Wura continuously looked at him with a look saying go on, and then Adeolu dropped a bombshell. "The king's favorite son, Prince Itiade, is the son of Prince Aremu, the king's brother, and not King Abiodun. It is unlikely that the king can ever make any baby."

"What, you mean the king is impotent? I had thought so myself but never put any voice to it" she responded.

"We need to leave here very fast; there are certain details I have not figure out yet, but I am going on a hunch and whatever I have heard from conversations when I was around in the palace during the last few weeks before yesterday's event."

"I don't see how we can both get out of here together now that Sango's men have this place surrounded and have been instructed to not let anyone enter or exit."

"I have a very secret passage to a cul de sac room no one knows about, and this is where I have kept some food for days like this. You can hibernate there for as long as I am away. When I get back from *igbale* (meeting of the Oro cult), I will have a way to smuggle you out to a safe location."

He now led her along a narrow corridor and pulled down a secret ladder to climb into another narrow passage that opened to sunlight, with more than a thousand different plants lying side by side on the hallway. At a particular junction Adeolu said, "Wura, you will have to crawl under these plants and flowers, and please do not let the flowers and plants touch any parts of your body."

"I recognize the water hemlock," she said.

"All of these plants in this part of the corridor are poisonous and can kill you in a few minutes. It further serves to protect this hideout in case anyone mistakenly discovers it."

They both knelt on all fours and crawled underneath the plants, ensuring that the plants and flowers did not touch any parts of their body, until they alighted at a small cave where a bed made of straw with rows of shelves above where some dry edibles were laid. Wura decided to take a walk around the small cave inspecting each item. She took some of the dry edibles, took a taste, munched it, and then wolfed down the remaining. Adeolu watched her eating for a while, stood up and reached for a jar of water, poured some in a cup made from marble and handed it over to her; she collected it and then drank from it. Adeolu then said, "Conserve the food; you do not have too much food and I might be gone for a long time. I am going to lay further traps around the perimeter of the caves to be doubly sure they keep to their word, and I also have to go and administer the antidote to the two soldiers, then meet up with Sango before he starts wondering where I have gone to."

Adeolu came back to the entrant cave and saw that the king's staff was already placed on the premises, with Salim glancing around furtively and the soldiers still writhing on the ground. The poison had affected a lot of their glands; even if he gave the antidote at this time they would lose some of the functions of their internal organs but nevertheless, he brought out a leather skin bottle from under his gown and poured some liquid into a cup and then gave a mouthful to each of the soldiers. He was watching the antidote reaction and suddenly the writhing stopped, and the foaming of the mouth also ceased. They opened their eyes stood up and as soon as they regained their consciousness, they looked at the entrance that they came through and made a dash through it, colliding with Sango as he was coming back inside.

"I see that you have applied the antidote on my soldiers and now you have the king's staff. We will abide by the king's orders and keep a perimeter distance from your premises," Sango said.

Adeolu smiled and said, "What are you still doing here? You are already flouting the king's orders." Salim and Sango looked at each other, then retreated without saying any words.

Adeolu waited a few minutes, inspected the shelves around the cave, checking that nothing had been taken. He then walked down the path leading to where the soldiers had mounted their cordon. He saw five of them and Salim on top of a large rock. Sango was nowhere in sight, and he thought maybe he had started on the journey to igbale.

Without saying anything, he reached under his gown and brought out another bottle containing venoms from scorpions mixed with venoms from a poison tulip flower and a mixture of herbs that keeps the venom potent. He had cultivated a ring of receptacle flowers around the caves that can be receptacle for poisons and other fluids and can ooze it out when they are disturbed, or someone comes in contact with it. He then quickly retraced his footsteps, stepped into one of the surrounding bushes and searched for the perimeter of receptacle flowers and as soon as he found them, he applied some protection to his body and ate a few leaves and herbs from his pocket and then started spraying the venoms from the bottle using a kind of sprayer that he had built into the bottle cover.

While walking, his mind kept racing; first he needed to get information on the state of things. He knew the king must be expecting him to get his version of the story and he was not prepared to do that just yet; he needed to first figure out the current situation of events. Had judgement been passed on the other arrested witches? he would find out the execution date or whether they had been executed yet. The answers to these questions would determine his next move. Plus, he also had to figure out a way to get to igbale, which was currently a day's march; something told him that Sango was trying to deliberately delay him because he could make use of any of the king's horse chariots to get there in a few hours and complete the whole journey on foot in under half a day.

As soon as he rounded the perimeter, he saw a little bit of commotion between the soldiers and some visitors; Fero and an unexpected visitor, Babagun's son, Ogunde, a childhood friend who lives in Karounwi, a suburb of Idumagbo under the rulership of his father Babagun himself. Ogunde commanded a standing army of a thousand youths in their compound; he fed them and provided them with gainful employment on his farms and they trained every day in the art of warfare. They had sworn their allegiance to the current king of Idumagbo as their forefathers before them had done as well.

They embraced each other and since they were initiated into the Oro cult the same day, they often travel to igbale (meeting of the Oro cult members) together and must have come here to check on whether he needed a ride.

Sango was still nowhere to be found around the vicinity so he must have truly left for igbale.

Salim spoke up and addressed Ogunde with a slight bow of his head and said, "Ogunde, we have the king's orders not to let anybody enter these caves nor exit from them. We have reasonable intelligence and suspicion that Wura is hiding within these premises."

Ogunde responded by nodding his head, and Adeolu interjected by saying, "I will go and see King Abiodun and all of this will be resolved."

Fero, who had been looking on previously, now said, "King Abiodun has scheduled the trials of the arrested witches for three days' time, and the town crier has been going around making the announcement for all the citizens to attend."

"Oh, oh, then," Adeolu muttered and then responded, "I must be there to see for myself in three days; but now I need to speak with my friend and brother from a different mother."

Adeolu also continued and before saying anything, beckoned to Fero and Ogunde and when he determined they were out of earshot of the soldiers, he said, "Fero, go and bring some of our friends and supporters here quickly and let them stand guard with these soldiers here so as to ensure that they keep their end of the bargain."

"Yes, Father, I will get people from the mosque and some of mother's brothers."

"I have to go somewhere for an important meeting and will be back before the trials of the witches in three days. Also, when your brothers arrive here, you go and tell Grandma Keniola in Idiape about what is going on here and tell her that all things being equal, I will be with her in four days' time and after the trials and if I am not with her, she should know that something has gone wrong and should be on her way down to Idumagbo."

Ogunde and Adeolu walked back to the location where the soldiers were camped on a rock. They saw Salim and three other soldiers. Adeolu noticed that two were missing and proceeded to not say anything at first but Ogunde, also very self-aware of his environment, asked, "Where are the remaining soldiers?"

Salim responded, "They went to take a dump somewhere in the bush."

"I hope they respected the boundary of non-visibility to the caves."

A cry of anguish came from the bush and one of the soldiers appeared with huge boils on his face and body and his eyes were covered by huge boils so that he could hardly see.

Salim rushed to him while the remaining three soldiers retreated to a safe distance. Salim asked, "Where is Sekona?" (The name of the second soldier.)

The soldier responded, "I don't know whether he made it to the caves yet."

Adeolu asked, "What are you going to do at the caves?"

The soldier responded, "Salim asked us to do a reconnaissance and see if there were any movements in and around the caves; please help me! I don't know what I came in contact with."

Salim said, "We need to find Sekona."

Adeolu responded, "He is probably dead by now and any endeavor to find him will probably result in more deaths. I suggest that you abide by King Abiodun's staff not to desecrate my compound anymore."

Fero appeared with two men from the mosque, Aragangan and Omisola. They greeted Ogunde by prostrating and lying flat on the ground. Ogunde asked them to rise up and prayed for them. After the exchange of pleasantries, Adeolu addressed Fero, saying, "I have asked you and your friends here to ensure that no one goes against the king's orders by trying to gain access to these caves. I have fortified the perimeter to prevent unauthorized access, as you can see from the young dead soldier at my feet who tried to breach this access; the other soldier is probably dead in the bush."

Adeolu continued, "Do not fight these soldiers, just tell them that no one should try to breach the perimeters. Fero, make sure you let Prince Itiade and King Abiodun know about what has transpired here since yesterday and I will come back and fill him in on the rest."

"Yes, Baba," Fero responded.

Salim looked on in silence throughout the encounter and the exchanges and then said to the other soldiers, "Go and get some tools and bury this soldier." They dragged the body on the ground to a nearby spot to bury the dead.

Ogunde inspected the chariot and adjusted the harnesses on the two horses and both of them got on the wheeled chariot. Adeolu said, "This is an improvement over the last one that I saw."

"Yes, you know we have our soldiers continuously working as blacksmiths, bending iron, carpenters carving wood, and sometimes they improve on what we currently have. As you can see now, previously we used wood for the wheels and until recently we were unable to successfully bend iron into wheels."

Ogunde concluded and then asked, "Tell me more about the miracle medicine of Idumagbo. It has been the talk of the towns for the last few weeks and I cannot wait to hear from the horse's mouth directly."

Adeolu, with a smile on his face, said, "It is the work of the gods. They have shone light on what has been previously hidden, and I have a method now to unravel many diseases and also proffer solutions to problems."

Ogunde and Adeolu were very close. Ogunde is one of the few that Adeolu opened his thoughts to. Ogunde looked at him and said, "I know the gods have not shown you these methods, but you have been able to devise it from your curious mind and knowledge gathered over the years; I am really proud of you."

"King Abiodun has inadvertently begun a campaign of caging the curious minds of our people by instituting the arrest of the witches," Adeolu said, changing the topic.

"I mean apart from myself and few other men, the witches are the only set of people fond of experiments with the elements of the earth, its leaves, plants, trees and animals" he said before going into a long pause.

Ogunde, seeing that Adeolu was not interested in sharing more right now, continued on the topic of the security of the realm. "This introduction of iron and steel into our weapons and defense systems will make our weapons strong and durable; you should also look at our swords, cutlasses, and arrows.

We are moving away from stone and wooden arrow tips to use iron and steel, which can penetrate and cause more damage to our enemies. We are currently experimenting with a new device that a traveling Mongol traded with us. The Mongolian man told us he is a Dane, which means he is from a land called Denmark. We did not believe him, but we were interested in what he had to offer. This device can kill from a distance; it is called a gun." he continued.

"Really? That must be a device from the gods!" Adeolu exclaimed. "I have heard similar war stories of guns used in killing from long distances from other sojourners to our lands. They have not shown me what it looked like, they only described it."

"Yes, I know what it looks like," Ogunde said, and he stood up on the speeding chariot and pulled out a short hand cannon pistol from his belt, made of wood and an iron barrel, and handed it over to Adeolu, who took it and looked it over. He peered through the barrel with his eyes, put his finger on the trigger and was about to give it a squeeze before Ogunde asked him to stop and said, "If you do that, it will release the iron pellets inside the gun barrel; the Dane man called it bullets, and it moves at an incredible speed and tears through flesh and damages body organs in its path."

"Very creative craftsmanship," Adeolu muttered, thinking that he could have just killed himself if he had squeezed the trigger.

"I will show you how to use this properly as soon as we stop at a place to rest," Ogunde said.

The chariot continued to speed through the evening, as they had a target. Adeolu handed the gun back to Ogunde and Ogunde put it back in his holster pocket. Ogunde continued in an animated fashion, "We are making long-barreled guns which will enable us to kill our enemies at longer distances, even longer than the range of where the short-barreled one can reach."

Adeolu said, "You mean we will have means to kill our enemies at incredible distances before they even come near us?"

"Yes; no kingdom will dare go to war with us. Tributes will pour in from far and near. My army currently stands at twelve hundred strong, and Babagun has indicated that we need a secondary army, which my brother Isegun will lead, and will mostly be a cavalry with horses and chariots. We are currently building as many chariots as possible."

"Will we be forcefully conscripting young boys in order for us to get to these numbers."

"We pay them now, based on the craft that they are able to master and how much trade they can generate off the sale of their craft," Ogunde replied.

"Good. Our army should be a modern one. Forced recruits will run away in the heat of battle, as we saw in previous wars."

"True, and moreover, we have to be able to match the strength of the Sahelian kingdoms when they come down south to raid our resources, rape our women, and murder our children," Ogunde said. "Just recently, some of our agents brought news that the Sahelian army massacred many of our villages up north, capturing men and women for slavery in the Arabian regions."

"What about the 'general of generals' in Katunga and his soldiers?" Adeolu retorted.

"I was told he was up north engaging in a different battle with the Sahelian people when the raid from a different party of Sahelians came to some of our villages. After our meeting tonight, Babagun will be going to the defense council meeting at Katunga, where there will be a discussion on how we can defend the perimeters of our fatherland," Ogunde said. The chariot came to a stop at a river where the horses could drink. "We will have to walk the remaining distance by cutting a path through the bush."

As soon as the horses finished drinking water and had their fill of hay, Ogunde led them along a path and tied them to a tree. The men walked in silence as they cut their way through the thick bush to the igbale (the meeting of the wise ones).

At the igbale, each of the wise ones put on a white regalia signifying purity, and each was assigned a name of a spirit from the yonderland, given a white cloth and a hat signifying their hierarchy and tenure in the fold; Babagun was called the "Oluwo," (the wisest one), while the members of the "Egbe agba" (elders committee) wore a red hat and the rest of the wise ones wore a white hat to match their white regalia. There were about sixty members in attendance, Adeolu observed by doing a quick count. He walked toward Babagun and prostrated by lying flat on the ground; this was the father he knew, and he learned quite a lot from him but today he was paying obeisance not because he represented a father figure, but because he was the wisest one. He addressed him, "Wisest one, I hail. Your wisdom will continue to grow every day and we shall continue to benefit from the decisions of your wisdom."

Babagun responded, "My son, how are you and your family? I hope they are doing very well," without looking at him as he concentrated on the herbal concoction that his acolytes were mixing. Then he muttered a few words to the acolytes, which they heeded, and he then turned toward him and he could see that he was much aged but there was still the same fire and probe in his eyes with which people perceived he could see through the minds of humans. He put his right hand on his left shoulder and said, "I have heard some very good news about you, and also some disturbing news, and the disturbing news will be part of our discussion tonight. You had better come with convincing argument because this may lead to excommunication, and excommunication can lead to a severe punishment."

Adeolu bowed respectfully and moved on to greet order members of the *iwarefa* (a six-member council that advises the Oluwo). He greeted Chief Abioye, the king's right-hand man, who responded with an expressionless face and then he walked toward Sango and he noticed that Sango had a red hat on. He greeted and addressed him as an acolyte should address an elder. Sango blessed him, then turned to Adeolu and said with his teeth closed, "You may have an upper hand on the outside with your wittiness, but you are now within moments of your last breath."

Adeolu responded loudly to ensure that everyone within earshot could hear, "You came and asked that I share my medicine with you, and I did, as a loyal member of this cult. You promised that we could work together if I did not out you as a charlatan. I protected you from the wrath of the king then; now you are after my life by spreading untruths about my person!"

Sango looked at him and saw that other members were looking in their direction with keen interest in their discussion. Sango hissed, muttering something about he who is rude to the king deserves a punishment irrespective of whether he is a hero or a member of our cult. "Some kings have been members of this cult, but they have always been exempted from attending the meetings; however, King Abiodun is not a member but he is still respected as the second-in-command only to the gods."

Chief Abioye said " Adeolu is a responsible man of our community, a brave and assiduous one" speaking up in defense of Adeolu.

The big gong drum sounded only once to signify the commencement of the meeting. The meeting usually started with a procession, with Babagun leading and all others following into the hallowed grounds chanting the processional hymn: "Eeri wo ya, ayagbo, ayato." They chanted continuously until they formed a circle around a big fire on the hallowed ground. Babagun raised his fist and the drumming and chanting stopped, then he spoke. "I greet everyone! We are here today as our tradition demands to deliberate on the happenings within our realm and decide on how we will proffer solutions; we will also deliberate on the happenings amongst ourselves; celebrate our individual and collective successes. We will initiate new members into our sacred order; we will mete out punishments to our members that have erred against our sacred oath."

All members present responded, "Eeri wo ya."

Babagun continued, "First we will celebrate our successes." He called out Adeolu's name and said, "I am calling you out first because the gods blessed you with a solution that has eluded many erudite and senior members of this society and rid our cities, towns, and villages of the Igbonna that bedeviled us for many months."

He continued, "Adeolu performed a feat worthy of emulation; he painfully researched the disease, trying many different permutations of the solution. Adeolu has shown exemplary talent that we should all be proud of."

Everyone on the ground applauded, and some even walked up to him and expressed their thankfulness for saving one or more of their family members.

Babagun then called on his son, Ogunde. He said, "Ogunde has invented a new weapon that kills at a distance; this device is called a gun. He has led development of it together with the skilled blacksmith and craftsmen to produce many of these weapons for the armies that defend the realm."

Ogunde removed the pistol in his belt and fired once at the goat they'd brought for the demonstration. The goat bleated, fell on the ground, kicked his feet, and died. Everyone stepped back when they heard the thundering sound of the gunpowder and then stepped forward cautiously toward the dead goat to inspect it. They were bewildered and had not seen such magic of death performed from a distance before, although the majority of them did lay claim to killing their enemies from a distance through the use of some metaphysical powers of which there was no collective affirmation of success. Amongst themselves they laughed and called it just salesmanship.

The mere thought of non-members speaking ill against the members of the cult was scary for most people; there are different stories and myths about what harm came upon the people that had spoken against the supposed powers of the cult members.

Babagun continued. "The gun that Ogunde showed today has proved that this is possible."

They inspected the goat and they saw that it was dead, and they started clapping and Abioye, the king's right-hand man, an enemy of Sango, said, "I would like to possess such a weapon."

Sango added, "This kind of weapon will make my enemies fear me and I can be king of this jungle."

Ogunde replied, "A weapon will be provided for each member of the society at a specific amount, and this will be communicated in due time. Every member can come around to Karounwi to pick up their weapons and also practice the skills of shooting."

Babagun also called on Akara and Ogini from Idiape, a village far west of Idumagbo, and said, "Akara and Ogini showed tremendous amount of bravery on behalf of the people of the town and they singlehandedly fought off the Sahelian invaders who raided their village with the intent of capturing slaves. But unfortunately, in the battle to ward off these invaders, Ogini was killed."

Akara is one of the foremost runners in the Ogboni, meaning they can run a hundred miles in a day once they know where they were going. Navigation was terrible, but they asked other folks on the way; sometimes they were helpful, sometimes they were not.

Babagun continued. "Ogini was a great sculptor and craftsman, the maker of our gods."

They all removed their hats and said a few prayers to grant his soul passage to the lands beyond human comprehension.

Babagun then asked Akara to step forward and share a few words on his experience. Akara stepped forward then broke into an elegy song: "Mo ti rokun la fo so, eeeh moti rokun la pomi, ibi wo dele wun kor renikan oo, ooju mi so mi were," meaning, "I have gone to the river to wash my clothes and when I came back home, there was no one home and then my eyes dripped of hot tears."

Then Akara started weeping profusely while others resisted the tears from forming in their eyes for the tragedy of the passing away of a courageous brother; tears in their eyes could signify weakness. "Ogini stood for the good of our society and exchanged his life for its protection," Akara said.

Babagun, whose eyes also looked moist, then said, "We are warriors, custodians of our society's traditions and protector of our realm. Ogini has exhibited all of our attributes and we should not be weeping for him but celebrating him as he goes across into the spirit world."

Then they sang again, this time a celebratory song and danced to it: "Aiye a ma je ka gbagbe, aye lajo orun ni ile wa, ekun loni eerin lola, aiye lajo orun ni ile wa" meaning, "People don't let us forget, this world is a sojourn, the spirit world is our home, even though we laugh and cry day in day out, this world is temporary and the spirit world is our final home."

Babagun spoke again about the armies and the upcoming war with the Sahelian kingdoms and how the plan would be to amass a ten-thousand-man cavalry and another ten-thousand-man infantry army and invade the Sahelian kingdoms. "Once we get a foothold in their lands, we will never vacate the lands and it will be up to us to set the traditions and culture of our fathers on that land and set its people free from the alien culture of the Eastern people."

All the other members chorused, "Ase!" (amen).

Sango then spoke up. "We will make a humongous fortune from the lands in the region; I even heard that they have gold in plentiful supply."

Adeolu also spoke up and said, "We must codify our culture and bring the traditions of our people to these people in simple ways so that they can admire us. We have medicine, we have beautiful clothes, and our gods have not yet let us down."

"We will also need a way to build a garrison in their lands as soon as we capture their lands, so we will need to bring along some of our best masons and artisans to help us in achieving this aim," Ogunde interjected.

Babagun added, "Ogunde will be leading the infantry while Isegun, his brother, has been training with the newly formed cavalry division to counter the Sahelian cavalry men."

"Our plan will be to contribute a two-thousand-five-hundred-man army to the Yoba army to complement the ten-thousand-man army that the generalissimo will command."

Babagun continued, "We will be sending requests to all towns and villages to provide us with their able-bodied young men and we expect everyone to honor these requests for the security of the realm and the perpetuation of our culture and traditions."

Everyone on the hallowed grounds broke into groups of their respective towns and villages and each leader of these groups came forward and hollered, "Yes, we will honor this request! It is for the future of our kith and kin." Chief Abioye for Idumagbo, Ogunde for Karounwi, and Faleti for Idiape.

Then Babagun spoke again. "We have all spoken well, and now is the time to discuss what we are not so proud of, especially where our members have run afoul of our rules and edicts or disobeyed the king's or any of his appointees' laws. We will not tolerate insolence because if we do, our society will begin a slow descent into anarchy and we will become people of double standards, and soon we'll not be able to live up to what is expected of us and our society shall die slowly and shamefully."

Babagun further continued and called Jigijaga out for killing a traveling European man and his family and forcefully having carnal knowledge of his spouse, an act that was committed in front of many of our people and confirmed by Abioye, an elder of this society. "Jigijaga has not yet denied this and we have imprisoned him and brought him here for judgement." Babagun signaled, and two acolytes led a man whose hands and feet were tied to the center of the circle. Babagun asked, "Jigijaga, the people and this society have condemned you for the killing of a white foreigner and forcefully having carnal knowledge of his wife; how do you plead?"

Jigijaga responded, "I am guilty. Please be lenient with me. This was a foreigner and should have no consequence in our society."

Babagun then replied, "Foreigners are very important to the economy of our cities and villages. They come around and we trade. If we start killing them, word will spread, and no one will come around to our cities to trade. Also, this is expressly forbidden by the king and it is also very abhorrent because you are an honorable member of this society; for this reason, we shall not be lenient, and we shall apply the maximum penalty."

Babagun then concluded, "Did I speak well or not? If anyone has any reason not to support my ruling, he should say so now or forever hold his silence."

No one spoke up; not because they were afraid, but because they believed the penalty was just and right for the crime that had been committed.

Then, Jigijaga pointed with his tied hands in the direction of Sango and spoke for himself and said, "This society has already demonstrated double standards by allowing Sango to still be in our midst after killing a traveling Caucasian man and stealing his knife, which everyone saw. I saw Sango commit this act and he swore me to secrecy and told me that we as members of the Oro are exempt from such rules and we can kill foreigners and take their properties if we so desire, and that was what motivated me to do this."

Babagun waited a few minutes for some other responses and seeing that no one was responding, then said, "Jigijaga, we have no one to corroborate what you just said and if you had mentioned this earlier, before you were put on trial, it would have been believable."

Then Abioye spoke up. "I do not like Sango as a person, but I love this society, and we cannot make a ruling based on what a convicted murderer just told us, so we should, however, not take the words Jigijaga spoke lightly. We should get Sango to swear by the spirits of *ayelala* (one god out of the thousand gods who is always quick to act when someone lies before him) and the thousand deities of our ancestors; if he really did this and refuses to confess, he will die in twenty-one days."

Sango looked unperturbed and rose in his own defense and said, "I will definitely swear by Ayelala and all the thousand deities, and I will be vindicated."

Adeolu thought quickly, saw an opportunity, and believed that he may be able to nail Sango, his enemy, once and for all and said, "Before swearing to the spirits and deities, Sango should also drink the truth serum that will allow us to ask him any questions and the serum will make him tell us the truth."

Sango responded and said he had no problems with drinking the serum and answering all the questions truthfully. Little did he know that Adeolu had tested and improved on the previous version of the serum and it was now very efficacious, unlike what was previously used in which a lot of common criminals could beat; that was not very reliable. Adeolu had sprung a trap and Sango had entered.

Sango knew he could dare the spirits and the gods and tell falsehoods without any ramifications and so did Adeolu, and that was why Adeolu devised another trap.

Babagun then spoke. "In a week's time, the truth serum will be administered on Sango and we shall give that honor to Adeolu, who has an improved version of the serum."

Sango then knew that he had entered a trap; he knew Adeolu to be a very knowledgeable and wise person who had researched and devised many potent medicines. He would have to hurry, or else time would be against him; he had only one last card, and that was to ensure that Adeolu died tonight at the Igbale (meeting of the wise ones).

Babagun thanked everyone that contributed to the discussion and called for the executioner, who came forward brandishing a large cutlass and with a swift movement of the blade, the head of Jigijaga was severed from its neck and some acolytes came forward, grabbed it, and put it in a sack, and some dragged the body away to an already prepared grave. The head would be taken away by Babagun for some other potent medicine that they proclaimed; they will take then skin off the head, clean the skeleton, and hang it in a conspicuous place around their buildings using it to scare the uninitiated.

Babagun moved onto the next item on the agenda, which was Adeolu's case, and asked that Adeolu and his accusers come forward. Adeolu stepped forward, followed by Sango and then Faleti stepped out. Faleti, a middle-aged animal farmer who also doubled as an animal doctor, well-known for his potent medicine for treating all sorts of farm animals, short and stout in nature and with a heavy frame, cannot be easily missed in a crowd.

Adeolu could not understand why someone like Faleti would be spying for Sango. *What is he really looking for? Definitely not money,* he thought to himself. He had no recollection of any negative interaction with Faleti; they had always been cordial with each other. As a matter of fact, they'd met recently at Abeni's bar and they really had a great time discussing politics and happenings around the world. He was surprised that he was going to be one of his accusers today and he knew that this was going to be tricky. He did not have many friends that could stand up for him around this igbale except for Ogunde, but he doubted whether he would go against his father, Babagun.

Babagun spoke. "Adeolu, you have been accused of harboring a fugitive and disobeying the king's orders to arrest and try all witches in the realm for causing the recent epidemic and misleading the public on the actual cure and remedies. How do you plead?"

Adeolu said, "Not guilty."

To admit guilt would mean instant death with no appeal.

Babagun said, "I am not your prosecutor but will be a judge in this case, and I will ask that Sango begin his prosecution."

Sango started by saying, "Adeolu is on trial here today because he is one of us; if he was an ordinary man, I would have killed him and had his household decimated for failing to heed the words of the king, the second-in-command to the gods."

He continued, "As we all know, the king has declared that all the witches in the realm be arrested and be tried tomorrow night for misleading the people, spreading the epidemic, and giving false prophecies, so as part of our mandate to arrest the witches, we went to Wura's abode, only to be told that she was not there. We detailed some of our men to watch over until she came back while others followed her trail into a town where we learned that she was just at the town's prominent bar.

"We followed her trail from there and unknown to us, on her way home one of the members of her household had met her on the road and warned her that we were laying siege for her at home; that was how we missed arresting her.

"However, we also have spies in the town helping us with information and monitoring the situation, and one of the spies was Faleti, who saw the member of the household give that information to Wura. Faleti then followed Wura surreptitiously all the way to Adeolu's house. When he saw that she entered Adeolu's compound, Faleti quickly came to find and warn us but on getting to Adeolu's compound, Adeolu frustrated us and disallowed us from searching his compound and took us on a race to his cave hideout, where he also murdered some of our men, all for the sake of Wura."

There was a deafening silence in the igbale that lasted for close to forever before Babagun spoke and asked Faleti to corroborate the story or deny what Sango just said.

Faleti started by saying, "I like Adeolu and admire his ingenuity and prowess, and I will say we have always had a cordial relationship. But I am a patriotic citizen and loyal to the king until death, and when someone is rude to the king, he is rude to me and he is looking for my trouble.

"Also let it be known that I sometimes work for Sango and the king by getting information from the people by feeling their pulse and by asking rhetorical questions from citizens and reporting troublemakers, deviants, and rebels, and getting them arrested before their trouble conflagrates. On this day I was walking to the bar as usual to get a feel of what the people are saying about the king's recent proclamations when I saw Wura and the household member by the roadside. I quickly hid by the bush and I saw her get a message from the household member in which she suddenly changed direction of her travel."

Faleti continued. "I saw her turn back and follow a footpath that few people travel, and I followed her until she reached Adeolu's compound in Idumagbo. I also waited a while until I was sure Wura was going to stay a while, then I went to find Sango in Idiape, and I went to wait again but did not see Wura and Adeolu again.

"Sango and his men came later and then confronted Fero and Enitan, Adeolu's wife, who told them that Adeolu would be at the caves since he was not home. Nevertheless, Sango's lieutenant, Salim, and his men, searched Adeolu's compound but could not find him before they headed on to the caves for the continuing investigation, much to my surprise," said Faleti.

Sango then stepped in and said, "When we got to the caves, Adeolu refused the search and ended up killing two of the king's men." Sango concluded by asking Adeolu, "Where were you when we came to your house?"

Adeolu replied, "I was in my caves, working."

Sango responded, "Liar! Liar! You lie."

Babagun motioned for Sango to keep quiet and then said, "You dare not say that in these hallowed grounds."

Sango apologized and ask Adeolu, "Do you know where Wura is?" He quickly added, "Do you have sexual relations with her and is she your concubine?"

Adeolu responded, "I know you have always desired her, but she is way out of your class, and in any case, she was not with me in the night in question. Were you planning to watch us do the thing?" Adeolu concluded by laughing uproariously.

Babagun looked at Adeolu quizzically, not finding it funny, and then asked, "Do you know what we do to people that are rude to kings? We behead them and then feed their remains to Sopanna; the Sopanna daemon will devour all your family and all your properties."

Adeolu had no immediate response and later added, "I defended my properties not because I was hiding anyone but because I knew Sango was jealous of me and wanted to steal some of my research."

Babagun responded, "You should not have taken the law into your own hands. You know you could have reported him to the igbale to get justice, yet you acted irresponsibly and guiltily by even murdering the king's men."

He then ordered him to be arrested and be taken to a secret location for judgement at a later date. Ogunde, his best friend, came forward and asked that he put his two hands together and then tied them. Adeolu knew the procedure; from this place henceforth, he would be taken to the shrine of Sopanna and would be given a truth serum that would trouble his stomach and unbalance him mentally, which would make the unschooled confess to crimes if they are guilty and other feeble minds confess to crimes that they are innocent of. Adeolu thought he could probably handle the serum, but he may not be able to handle the politics and underhanded dealing that would go on in his absence amongst the members of the Oro cult, the king and his men, the kingmakers, and the title holders. He had to act fast and get a sympathizer who could help him on the outside during his incarceration; otherwise, he might be doomed to die soon.

Adeolu looked up, trying to catch Ogunde's eyes. Their eyes met briefly and Ogunde quickly shifted his eyes away. As he was being led away, Adeolu pleaded with Ogunde and shouted, "Ogunde! Help me on this and your songs will be sung for generations and generations to come!"

Ogunde shouted back, "You, this two-faced, double-dealing cheat! You who holds our traditions in contempt and has no regard for our king and title holders! You deserve what is coming to you."

Then they led him to the Shrine of Sopanna (another god out of the thousand gods worshipped by the inhabitants of Idumagbo) and they asked him to kneel down and Babagun gave him the serum to drink. He drank from it and he swore an oath that he knew nothing about the place where Wura was hiding. Then began the twenty-five-mile trek to Isanlu, north of Idumagbo, where the king's prisoners are kept. On getting there, he noticed how unkempt and ill-fed the prisoners were and all he could do was hope that things changed for him.

***

The next day at the trial of the witches, the king stood up and announced why the women were being tried. "They are being tried today because they are conspirators that have led our people astray; they have deceived us with their fake prophecies; they nearly ruined us with their fake medicine. It is unfortunate that my two wives are also part of these witches' covens and also conspired to make us paupers in our father's land."

Chief Abioye, who had returned from igbale early in the morning, also spoke up and said, "We will not tolerate conspiracy against the gods and the second-in-command to the gods. If you conspire against the king, you conspire against the gods, and then you deserve nothing but death."

Chief Arese also stood up and spoke. "We will not tolerate those that seek to profit from our collective miseries. Can you imagine reselling dead people's clothes, all in the name of making money?"

The crowd roared, "Kill them all!"

Sango also stood up and said, "We have all the witches but one, and she will soon be in our custody. We have arrested all her accomplices." (No one discloses what goes on at the igbale; that itself is a death sentence.) "They will soon lead us to wherever she is hiding.

Then Aremu came in with some warriors loyal to him, brandishing swords, and knives, and stabbed two of the king's men and attempted to free his lovers, Queen Adun, and Queen Jade. He was able to get to where they were being held and was cutting off the ropes that they were tied with before some of Sango's men descended on the other warriors and a free-for-all fight ensued. When it seemed that Aremu's men were getting the upper hand, Sango took out the gun he'd purchased from Ogunde the previous night and aimed it at Aremu and pulled the trigger. One of Aremu's lieutenants fell down. They quickly retreated to a safe distance, not knowing what happened, since they had not seen such weaponry before. Aremu had promised Jade and Adun separately and at different times that he was going to make them mothers of Kings as soon as he ascends the throne"

He had consulted Adeolu about preventing pregnancies and Adeolu had asked him to wear a cured sheep's intestine around his manhood and surprisingly it had worked and neither Jade nor Adun got pregnant. He told them as soon as he became King, he will no longer wear the Sheep's intestine.

The king, who was initially protected by his men, pushed them aside and also drew out a sword and he quickly retreated when he saw Sango reloading the gun he had. Once again Sango pulled the trigger and the gun bellowed and another of Aremu's men fell down on his back. This time Aremu and his men retreated, pulling the wounded lieutenant along with them, and fled the scene.

The scene quickly deteriorated, with the people fleeing in all directions together with the prisoners. Queen Jade was able to mix with the crowd and escaped. Sango's men apprehended Queen Adun and the rest of the witches and took them away to the king's dungeon.

King Abiodun then spoke to the remaining people present and pronounced death sentences on the witches and said they would be killed tomorrow at dawn.

Jade wandered far into the bush; she could not trust anyone and vowed that if she survived this, she would make sure that Abiodun and his son, Itiade, suffered hell on this earth. She later joined up with a roaming band of hunter-gatherers, the Kikuyu, where she met the leader of the band, a Caucasian, and his wives and big family. All his wives were his queens in his kingdom; he called himself "Ekun," while everyone referred to him as Ekunogun, "Lion of medicine." He moved around with his band of about fifty people, staying in a place for as short as two months and as long as a year. They were a band of about six families following him around with their own families, people bringing their children and families to follow him.

During his stay, news went around all the surrounding towns and villages, and even to very far-off kingdoms, and people brought their sick and their problems. Jade had never had any cause to visit him previously or hear about him so after traveling with them for a little while, Jade told him of her inability to have children and Ekunogun said, "We shall see what the gods have in store for you

The Dispersal

Fero woke up from where she slept in the cave after the incident at the king's palace. News had filtered back to her that Adeolu had been arrested and sent to the king's prison and she did not have any further details on that. She heard movements outside the cave and peeped through the opening in one of the caves and saw that it was drizzling slightly, and the guards had breached the first perimeter. She noticed the absence of the additional guards she'd brought; she had told them yesterday to run away when she shared the news of their father's captivity. They had either adhered to her instructions or were probably dead now, she thought to herself before realizing that the same fate could befall her here any second as well if she did not quickly find a place to hide before Sango's soldiers found a way to get inside the caves. She knew it was a matter of time before the rains washed away the infected perimeter fences that her father had set up.

She ran inside the caves and found the spot where she could climb into a hidden upper cave chamber. She still recollected the day Adeolu had first showed her, and she remembered what he said that day. "You have to keep this place a secret; it might mean the difference between life and death. No one should know about this."

She reached the tunnel of flowers and shrubs covering the entrance to the safe pod. She crouched under the shrubs, making sure none of the flowers and twigs touched her until she reached the entrance to the safe pod.

She opened it and she found Wura on one knee, ready to spring up and kill, and when she saw who she was she stopped herself and both were surprised. A million thoughts went through Fero's head and she felt slightly giddy because nothing was making sense; this was the king's enemy who was in her father's private cave and who the king's soldiers were looking for. If the soldiers found their way up, they would both be killed; even Prince Itiade would not be able to save her.

She looked at Wura and said, "Tell me everything from the beginning and how you got here."

***

Adeolu was writhing and grinding his stomach on the floor as his stomach and head continued to pound with the effects of the serum settling into his system, producing the effects that can make him likely confess and be summarily executed or keep him in perpetual delirium. His hands and legs were bound in chain, making him unable to feed from the dinner of watery yam pottage in a broken earthen clay pot in front of him.

One of the prisoners, named Bankudi, a man about seven feet tall with very menacing looks, had been watching him from afar and proceeded to help him by lifting up the clay pot and putting it to his lips, thus feeding him gently and as soon as he noticed that he was feeling better, he whispered into his ear, "Be prepared for dawn, the Albino is coming." Albino is the nickname for Araba.

Adeolu did not know what that meant, but he knew this might be his only chance to escape—or a trap where they would finish him off finally. One of the prison guards came up to them and said, "Whatever you two are discussing, it's time to break it off."

Bankudi moved away quickly to sit solitarily somewhere far but within eyesight of Adeolu. Adeolu slowly sat on his butt with his bound legs in front of him and contemplated the situation and started evaluating options; option one, he gives up and they kill him tomorrow evening. If he tried to escape at dawn with the Albino and it was a trap he would be killed and if it was not a trap, then he would have to make use of that opportunity.

Suddenly, two guards materialized in front of him, dragged him up and with them to a building where Ogunde was seated. He beckoned the guards to leave and he was left alone with Adeolu. Ogunde spoke. "How can you do this to yourself? I loved you like a brother. I cannot believe you can betray the king like that. What happened to our dreams of serving our fatherland and making it the best amongst all the lands far and near?"

Adeolu responded, "What do you mean? I labored many weeks to get the medicine to rid our villages of the epidemic, saving the king an embarrassment. What is my gain from betraying the Crown?"

He paused and then continued, "It is not so. The king is being misled and manipulated by a coterie of selfish advisors led by Sango. They are deliberately feeding him falsehood and cutting him off from all authentic sources of information."

Ogunde was silent and gave a nod, asking Adeolu to continue.

Adeolu continued. "The king is also carrying out a vendetta against his wives for deceiving him about the nature of the birth of Itiade. The king is not the father of Itiade and might be impotent or sterile and incapable of fathering a child and must be using this charade to cover up his shame."

"This is a very big accusation you make, Adeolu."

"I know, and you should know me that I seldom make statements if I do not have a way of proving it," said Adeolu.

"Even if you manage to prove this, it does not absolve you from the death sentence already passed by the Oro," said Ogunde.

"It does not; but it exposes the king's lies and the conspiracy and hold Sango probably has over him."

"What do you mean? I do not understand," Ogunde replied.

"It is a long story, and the short solution now is to get me out of here and give me medicine to help me clean my body from the serum they gave me," Adeolu said.

"The king executed Adun and the other witches tonight at Idumagbo. He is coming over to watch your execution tomorrow evening," Ogunde said.

"What about Queen Jade?"

"I was told she managed to escape when Aremu attempted to free her."

Adeolu grinned, a faint smile caressing his lips. "I will not give Abiodun the satisfaction; I will die before he gets here."

"No, you will not die, but face your execution as a man, like all men and titled chiefs before you have done. You'll face your execution like the gallant officer that you are!" he shouted, then came close to his ear and whispered, "Tomorrow morning at dawn, be prepared."

Adeolu could not believe his ears; he knew for sure that Ogunde always meant whatever he said, but he could not let him into the other plan with the Albino, a nickname that was given to Araba. As he was led back into the prison walls, he felt strength returning to his legs and hands. Tomorrow at dawn was surely pregnant with action.

Shortly before the break of dawn, four horses galloped toward the prisons with Araba riding on a very fast black stallion. Two of his trusted lieutenants were on two and the fourth one was rider-less. Araba was previously an inmate after he ran away from his military commission under Ogunde in Karounwi. Araba was a skilled swordsman, archer, and a brilliant military strategist. He found himself in prison suddenly without trial after he had a disagreement with Sango over a battle plan. He had never been considered a real member of the tribe because of the color of his skin; people tolerated him because of his mastery of the sword and warfare. Sango used that against him and had him dismissed and jailed.

Ogunde liked Araba for his mastery of the instruments of war and he saw himself as his mentor. When he was told that he had been sent to prison, he could not believe the crime which he was accused. Ogunde could not defend him because they were at different theatres of the war with the Maradians and before he could visit him in prison, he heard he'd escaped and gone on to a different land east of their city.

Araba had sent an emissary to Ogunde a few hours ago, immediately after he heard about Adeolu's imprisonment. He informed him that he had a plan to break Adeolu out of prison and take him with him so he could escape his execution. Ogunde had agreed to the plan with the emissary if Araba would lead the charge on the prison.

Now Araba was on the way and was going over the plans in his head. The guards on the inside would be asleep, but they would still have to storm and take the outer perimeter guards who would not be sleeping. There were three outer perimeter guards, and he and his lieutenants would each take one out.

As they neared the prison, they disembarked from their horses and hid them somewhere along the road. They then moved cautiously on foot toward the prison yard. They adopted a tactic in which one of the lieutenants moved ahead and would provide clues as to what was happening up front and could give signals to warn the others in case, he encountered any trouble.

The trio of them got safely to a corner leading to the cul de sac housing the prison yards. The forward lieutenant had gone around for a reconnaissance and he came back and said there were guards, two for each door, and they changed often and communicated using the drums; the next message would be soon. "We should go immediately after the guard beats the drum signifying a guard change." Then they laid out of eyesight of the prison guards, with each one sharpening their swords and knives.

They heard the bellows from the drum of the guard in the first guard post, followed by the second, then the third, and then it was all quiet.

Araba advanced zigzaggedly across to the first guard post and motioned his two lieutenants to go for the other two. On getting there, he saw that one of the guards was asleep and one was startled. He quickly, with one

swift slice of his sword, severed the head of the first guard. The second guard

he pierced in his stomach with the tip of the sword until it made an exit at the

back with the guard making a hissing sound as he passed on into the spirit

world.

He waited for a few minutes, then he heard his two lieutenants

coming back and the trio advanced toward the main prison yards where they

expected the remaining guards to be asleep.

Bankudi, one of the prisoners, saw the silhouette of the trio

advancing toward the prison yards and went to wake Adeolu and said, "It is

time to go; the Albino is here."

Adeolu rose quickly, the effects of the drugs they gave him seemed

to have worn off, but he still felt a little giddy. Then Araba entered and they

looked at each other and smiled. Adeolu then remembered him as a young

boy at Abeni's bar and then later as a young soldier at Karounwi with

Ogunde. He embraced him and said, "Thank you for coming to my rescue;

I don't know how I can ever repay you."

Araba embraced him too and said, "You are the one helping me;

there is a lot that we have to talk about. Let's get out of here."

Salim, Sango's commandant, materialized out of the darkness with

about twenty soldiers. Araba and his two lieutenants moved backwards and drew their swords. Araba passed his knife to Bankudi. They had no weapons to give to Adeolu, so he took a few steps back.

Unknown to them, Sango had sent Salim in the middle of the night with the soldiers to come and guard the prison yards before the king and his entourage's arrival in the morning.

Ogunde also materialized immediately after, surveyed the battlespace, and threw a sword in Adeolu's direction, deliberately throwing himself into the fray, and thus signified his intention to be in the rebel camp. Salim was surprised, because they had talked when he came, and he had not given him any inclination that he was going to be against the king. Salim said, "Ogunde, you too? You are being disloyal to the king?"

Ogunde then replied, "Honor comes before loyalty to the king. In this I would defend the honor of my friend against the king. He has not done anything wrong to deserve death. The king is wrong to execute the witches who have done nothing wrong but exercise their right to trade, and Adeolu has done nothing wrong to warrant this treatment."

He continued, "What kind of a king would reward a man and then turn around and accuse him of treason the very next day?" Ogunde, with the sword in his right hand and a gun in his left hand, declared the battlefield open by firing a shot at the detachment of soldiers running toward them. Two of them fell down immediately before it became a free-for-all.

Araba handled three of the soldiers together at the same time; Ogunde managed two while Adeolu fought with Salim.

Bankudi, with the knife, fought and killed the rest of the soldiers. In the few minutes that the battle lasted, Araba's two lieutenants were dead and all of Salim's soldiers.

They took Salim, bound him, and Adeolu gave him a message to the king. "If you do not rescind your decision to come after Adeolu, your kingdom will be torn away from you today and we will come and get you."

Then the four of them—Adeolu, Araba, Ogunde, and Bankudi—headed out of the prison walls and into the twilight. They quickly located the path where they hid the horses and they galloped far away at top speed from the prison yard.

They stopped at a stream near a farm for the horses to rest and drink water. Each of them was left to their thoughts and minding their business before Araba broke the silence and asked Ogunde, "Why did you join the fight? We could have gotten away without your help. You could have just stayed out of it; now you have complicated the whole process. Babagun will be infuriated and Sango might arrest him."

Ogunde interrupted Araba and said, "Sango would not dare arrest Father; if he does, I will raise a large army and bring the whole kingdom down."

Araba looked at him and smiled, patted Ogunde on the back and said, "You have always been a brilliant searcher of truth and a good soldier, but never a good politician."

"Indeed, you think your rebellion makes you an astute politician?"

"It is only a matter of time before you see what my policies will do to help and free the people of the corruption of the king and his elites. Moreover, before I left the Karounwi military camp, I had issues with Babagun on our relationship together. What do you think he will be thinking about us together now?" said Araba, looking glumly at Ogunde.

Ogunde looked on and said nothing. Then Araba continued, "Ogunde, that is why I am suspicious of your interference in this."

Adeolu looked at both of them, slowly catching on, knowing instinctively that a lot had not been said between Araba and Ogunde but refused to say what was on his mind and then supported Ogunde. "If Ogunde had not given me the sword, one of Salim's soldiers would probably have killed or wounded me. So, I believe he is justified in pitching his tent with us."

"What I don't understand is why he chose to leave everything he has ever worked for and follow us into a world of rebellion of which we do not yet have a plan to win?" insisted Araba.

Ogunde stood up and said, "Here were two of my greatest friends in the world; Adeolu, my oldest friend and age mate; Araba, my colleague, mentee and comrade in arms, accusing me of intervening to save their lives and putting my own career and that of my family on the line. I put it to you today that when greatness beckons, it is the man of valor that recognizes the time, takes the chance to sacrifice himself so as to etch his name on the sands of history. I mean, what would happen to my name, should it be missing when the grandmas were telling the stories by moonlight, when the legends die, the dreams end? I am going to be a legend when the stories of our adventures together are told."

Adeolu looked at him, rose up, and then hugged him. Araba then responded, "I am sorry for thinking you had an ulterior motive."

Bankudi, sleeping and seemingly oblivious to what was going on, saw the spate of hugs also and stood up and hugged Adeolu and Ogunde and then hugged Araba. The trio of Araba, Adeolu, and Ogunde then laughed. Adeolu said, "Since we are now official rebels, they will think that we are on the run and not dare to come back to Idumagbo; but we should surprise them. I would like to go back to my caves at Idumagbo; there were certain medicine potions that will be useful for our war efforts. I need to get them."

Araba said, "My camp is not far from here and I am sure some of my soldiers will soon join us here. I will go over to the camp and start preparation for the war effort."

"Adeolu, you go ahead with Bankudi and some of my soldiers," Araba said.

Ogunde then said, "I will come with you, Araba, and set the ball rolling for the war efforts. Bankudi and these soldiers will provide all the help Adeolu needs."

Araba smiled and beckoned for Ogunde to come along as a detachment of soldiers materialized from beneath the hills around them. Araba then asked two of them on horses to follow Bankudi and Adeolu and gave instructions that they should be back before nightfall tomorrow and if they were not back, they will consider them dead and will have to move the camp immediately.

The party of four travelled through the thick forest and the road less traveled to get into the city of Idumagbo. As the party of four neared the town of Idumagbo by nightfall, each climbed on different trees to have an unfettered view of the city's main road with human and equestrian traffic. Adeolu, from his vantage position on the tree, saw Salim and Sango riding back into town, galloping furiously, with a large battalion and a few hours later, Babagun and a detachment of soldiers riding out of town. Adeolu thought there must have been some kind of meeting and he would have loved to know what was happening.

Then he saw his wife, Enitan, and others, being taken in a horse-drawn cage with Salim and some soldiers. He wanted to come down and fight for her, but he quickly realized that this would be a futile effort. Instinctively, he knew that the guards he placed at his cave laboratory must have been arrested or killed as well. He hoped that Fero and Wura were still safe, so he signaled to his compatriots to come down and they took a detour back to the caves Adeolu used as his laboratory and workshops.

He led them through one of the private paths known only to him and Fero. The path led through a swamp of crocodiles, and he led them through the secret stone paths where the reptiles dared not tread.

On arriving at the caves, he noticed that there was still a detachment of about 10 soldiers guarding it from the front. He thought maybe they were yet to discover Wura's whereabouts. He told Bankudi and one of the soldiers to finish them off and asked that the other soldiers follow him to climb on top of the caves through one of the iroko trees. A typical Idumagbo woman or man would not climb an iroko tree, but Adeolu was different; an iconoclast extraordinaire who questioned everything and experimented with his life on the line.

Through one of the iroko tree branches, they lowered themselves down into one of the caves. Adeolu could see that they had laid waste to some of his artifacts, his important experiments, and many of his medicines all littered on the floor. He crept silently through the caves, hoping none of the soldiers would be inside. Then he led the other soldier through a crevice that led into an inner cave that led to the secret roof entrance to where he'd hid Wura.

He detailed the soldier in the adjoining caves to wait, still not wanting to give away this secret, and told him to make lots of noise if anyone tried to breach this place. The soldier nodded and he went inside the adjoining cave where the secret roof entrance was. He climbed through and came into the hall of poisoned flowers. He knelt down and started crawling underneath until he came to the entrance.

He opened the door and saw Wura and Fero lying on the ground, staring at nothing; the light of the moon providing illumination through a slit on the roof allowing the moonshine to seep through. They were startled at first and tried to reach for their weapons, then they recognized him and relaxed. Fero rushed into Adeolu's embrace, leaving Wura staring and wondering for a while before also embracing Adeolu and crying, saying, "I brought all of this calamity on you and the whole town."

Fero sneered, "The lust of a man for a woman can surely bring woes and perdition to a wealthy and prosperous city."

Adeolu sighed and said, "Fero, Enitan, was arrested this evening. Where were the friends you placed as guards?"

"I have not set my eyes on them. I figured they must have been killed or taken prisoner," Fero responded.

Adeolu, looking forlorn, said, "They are probably dead by now. Sango would not take them prisoner; I know the kind of person he is. He would think of them as the heads of snakes that should be permanently cut off, extinguished."

"I wish I could turn back the hands of time and never came to your house that night. Look at the calamity I brought upon the whole of the village," Wura said.

Adeolu looked on and then said, "The city is no longer safe for any one of us. We need to leave the city and join a military camp. We will have to fight for our lives and the lives of our remaining loved ones. If we die in the process, may posterity be our judge; may the lives of those unborn and those that were yet to join us in this world be our judge, and may they see my actions and your actions henceforth in the right light."

Wura and Fero sobbed gently and shed very hot tears.

Adeolu continued, seeing the tears in their eyes, "Now the fight is the fight for our future, the future of our offspring, their emancipation and their education. If we continue to let Abiodun lead us, he will lead us to doom and darkness and our generation shall perish and will have nothing to show for our lives on this earth while other generations in other places are making strides to better their communities. We will continue to wallow in fear, myths, untruths, and perpetual darkness."

He led them out into the hall of gardens, and they crawled and climbed down into the lower caves. They saw the Bankudi and the soldier detailed to guard the entrance. Bankudi said, "We killed them all; the other solder did not make it."

Adeolu nodded his head, grabbed a bag, and then silently started filling it with artifacts and medicine from the shelves around them. He instructed Fero to do the same and after they were done filling the bags, he led them silently to one of the cave's exits leading to a route less traveled into the darkness, where they journeyed silently through the forest until they got to a fork in the road leading in the direction of Araba's military camp.

Adeolu then stopped and told Bankudi to continue with Wura and Fero to the camp and that he would meet them in a few hours, as he had to go get his grandmother. Fero said, "I will come with you."

Adeolu said, "No, it could be very dangerous. They know I have escaped, and they will come for my grandmother."

Adeolu opened one of the sacks, took out his military uniform, put it on, and also took out two medicine belts (oundes) and some gourds and then a sword and a cutlass. He closed the sack and handed what was remaining in the sack to Fero and said, "Do not let anybody handle this; it can be very dangerous."

He turned back and then disappeared into the darkness.

He crept into the forest, sidestepping all major and minor roads, and used his cutlass to clear a path for himself through the forest. Then he heard the sound of thunder and he knew it was going to pour down heavily soon; he had to move fast so that he could get to his grandma's place before the rain started. The good thing was that the moon was also very bright, but the gathering of the clouds had been dimming its brightness. Then he decided to get back on the path to Keniola's compound and he broke into a jog so he could escape the rains, so he thought to himself.

Then the rains started heavily, and he had to maneuver back into the forest to find a shelter from the pouring rain. As he continued to cut through looking for a suitable shelter, he was thoroughly drenched. Then he started hearing voices in the distance and suddenly he saw a fire go up. His instincts kicked and he started crawling on his belly so as to get within earshot but out of eyesight. He got close and he could see that this was a detachment of King Abiodun and Sango's army.

Then he saw Salim and he heard him say, "Let us rest; we will start again as soon as the rain abates a little. One thing we know is that the old woman has nowhere to go in this rain and we will be surprising her as soon as the rain stops," before he broke into a dry laughter.

One of the guards asked, "Is she not the mother of the king? Why are we even after her?"

After Salim's laughter stopped, he said, "The king does not want to kill his mother but would like to use her as a hostage to trap Adeolu; Keniola and Adeolu are very close, and it makes sense to use her to draw Adeolu out in the open. Moreover, there is no love lost between the king and his mother; the mother still thinks Abiodun is a usurper and a murderer and that the throne of Idumagbo is being desecrated by Abiodun's rule."

The guards were taken aback by these revelations and Salim continued. "We are the spears keeping Abiodun in power, and a time will come when we will all be rewarded greatly for the parts we played."

Salim's last statements brought smiles to their already drenched and sad-looking faces.

As soon as Adeolu heard this, he knew he could no longer find shelter again and he had to brace the weather elements and get Grandma Keniola out. He traced his steps back to the main road. Now that he was sure no one was going to be on the road he broke into another jog and started whistling and singing under his breath while the rains spluttering on the ground provided the rhythms.

As he neared the barrier to the hut where his grandma resided, he took a detour as he had agreed with his grandma. He was also aware that there was no thoroughfare and that very poisonous flowers and plants that can cause instant death were along the narrow footpath to the house. Only those that were regular family members and friends were aware of this.

The detour took him to the back of the house, where he climbed a tree and took a horn placed there for the purpose and he whistled the password melody: "Eledumare soro fun omo re o."

He waited and then heard the response: "Ola a da," then he climbed down from the tree, saw a light come on in the hut and he walked toward it.

On seeing his grandma, he saw that she was still full of energy and it did not look like she was aging in any way. He laid down flat to greet her and she praised and prayed for him, saying, "Welcome, Adeolu, the brave and courageous one. Please stand up and greet me."

Adeolu rose up and gave his grandma a hug.

She brought out some water and kola nuts for him and asked him, "Do you want me to make you some warm dinner?"

Adeolu responded, "No, I have come to take you away from here because King Abiodun and his army are on their way here to either kill or imprison you."

Grandma looked at him and said, "He would not dare do that; I have not done anything against him, or his family and I have been a benevolent supporter of him. What does he have against me to do that?" Then she paused and asked, "Or have you done something that he now wishes to seek revenge on me?"

Adeolu suddenly broke down weeping; only his grandmother could elicit such an emotional response from him. Amidst the sobs he said, "I have been condemned to death and have just barely escaped. My wife has been arrested and is probably on her way to the gulag. I saw her been led to the king's prisons this evening. My home and properties have been confiscated."

Keniola continued to look at him with a facial expression that said, "How does all this involve me coming with you?"

Adeolu continued, "I am now a fugitive."

Keniola responded, "There is something I am not getting; you were just celebrated as a hero by ridding the town of the epidemic that has plagued the cities for many months now and suddenly you are on the run, imprisoned and condemned to death, your wife arrested, and here to warn your grandma to take off with you; what really happened?"

He said, "The king wanted to kill all the witches for no just cause and I hid one of them when she came to me in the middle of the night and I had no choice than to further protect her when she was about to be discovered."

"Oh-oh, you let your loins dictate your future."

"At the igbale I was accused of this and I was arrested and taken to prison to be executed the next day before some other loyal people came and rescued me, killing many of the king's soldiers. There is a rebellion camp with many youths ready to overthrow the king and install a new one, and that is where we can get protection and security from the king."

Keniola was thoughtful for a while and then responded, "What if I choose not to go and prefer to talk and negotiate with the king and his men? Remember the King is still my son."

The thunder cracked once again, and the rains began to simmer down and the rain clouds began receding. Adeolu then responded, "I do not think the king and his men are going to like that. I ran into them on my way here. I hid from them so they did not see me, but I could see that they were battle-ready, with garments of brutality and destruction adorning their bodies. I counted about ten men, including their leader, Salim, Sango's right-hand man; he is a sadist. Grandma, we have to go, we do not have much time!" Adeolu pleaded.

Keniola rose up, looked at Adeolu and said, "We do have some time; the moon is going to be reborn tonight." (Referring to an eclipse of the moon.)

"Grandma, what do you mean by a moon rebirth?" Adeolu recognized that there were some things he still did not know, and that was one of the reasons why he cherished this woman, who continuously surprised him with new education, new information, new knowledge. He would fight to elongate her life.

He asked, "Are we going to see the moon fall off and then a new one replaces it?"

Keniola rose up and said, "No, the moon will undergo a darkening for a few hours tonight and there will be no moonlight for several hours, and then it will come out and shine brighter than it had done previously. We will use the moonlessness to escape from our detractors."

She then went into an adjoining room, grabbed a sack, and started putting some of her personal belongings into it. Adeolu was happy, and quickly rose to start helping her and told her to pick only the things that were of immediate need. She responded, "I have been on such journeys a quarter of my life—unannounced, sudden, forced—you name it."

She took a piece of yam and put it in the sack and handed it to Adeolu. They then slipped outside of the hut and they could see that the rains had actually subsided. Then they heard approaching footsteps in the distance. Adeolu held his grandma's hand, looked up, and saw that the moon already had a dark shadow on it and they quickly slipped into the forest through a back path hidden in some trees.

Then they heard the commotion. "The old witch has taken out the moon!" There were shouts of these statements reverberating through the night followed by pandemonium as all the soldiers went running in different directions in the forest as the moon finally slipped under a whiff of dark clouds.

They traveled through the forest in silence for a while, sometimes in quick jogs, sometimes walking, and sometimes hidden in trees, when they heard footsteps approaching. It was usually Keniola who heard the footsteps first and alerted him that they should hide in the trees. Adeolu was surprised about her agility and her acute senses. Adeolu broke the silence by asking, "Grandma, would you like us to rest a while before continuing?"

Keniola responded, "Yes, let's take some minutes' rest." She did not want to show how anxious she was about trying to find a way to escape Idumagbo and look for new ways to convince others of an impending attack on Idumagbo. She thought that the Maradians would be on the attack by now and would probably take the city before daybreak. A few days ago, she was visited by the leader of the Maradians, a man she remembered vaguely, but the man told her that he was asked to seek her out by the king of Maradi, Bashir. She had not yet shared the information with Adeolu.

Adeolu spoke again, "Grandma, how were you able to hear people coming from afar?"

Keniola looked at him, then thought briefly to herself, maybe it was time to reveal a little bit of herself to Adeolu. She then said, "A long time ago, I ran and hid in the trees many times. Particularly I remember a time when I was chased after escaping from captors in Maradi. They chased me with dogs, and I learned how to cover my tracks and elude capture. It was there my senses got trained and in sync with the environment."

Then she asked with an endearing tone, "Adeolu, my grandson, where are we going?"

Adeolu looked at her, felt a bit ashamed and said, "Grandma, I do not have a personal place of mine to take you to, but I have a friend, a rebel leader, Araba, who will try to wrestle the throne from King Abiodun. We can hide with him for a while."

Keniola thought she guessed right about their destination and seemed to be lost in thought for a while before she said, "We should persuade Araba to move quickly or give us a detachment of soldiers and incapacitate Abiodun and snatch the throne from him."

Adeolu could not believe what he was hearing. "King Abiodun is your son and you want to seize the throne from him?"

"He ordered my arrest and was probably going to kill me. I have left the city for him and now he calls for my head." She ended her statement by saying, "It is my head or his head, and if I do not act fast, then I may end up being sorry. I have not come this far to have a lowly son behead me."

She continued, "If you do not know, Abiodun was not my only son; my first son, your father, was the rightful owner of the throne. I suspect that Abiodun murdered him while I was in captivity in Timbuktu."

"That is really interesting; we can really try him for that and get him to confess to that."

"How do you put a king on trial?" she asked.

"There must be a way."

"Adeolu, the only way will be to depose him, and we are on the right path."

They fell silent for a while before Keniola continued.

"I bore other sons for a king in another land."

Adeolu appeared not to be shocked with the piece of information he received just now, and he repeated it for emphasis. "Grandma, you have other children from another man that no one has heard of?"

She continued, "I am going to Idumagbo to settle this once and for all. If not, I will go to Babagun and try to see if I can sway him to give me command of the army."

Adeolu paid attention to what was said and particularly what was not said. "I will persuade Araba to give us some soldiers to overthrow Abiodun and make me king; I am also entitled to the kingship."

Keniola broke into a smile and said, "Well then, let's go to Iddo, the camp of Araba."

Adeolu looked at her, surprised, wondering whether he had told her about Araba's military camp at Iddo or not. And he knew he did not.

Iddo – Araba's Military Camp

Fero, Bankudi, and Oromodi, Araba's female lieutenant soldier, tall, slender, and one of the tallest women in Idumagbo and environs, together with Wura, arrived at Iddo camp just before dusk and the beginning of the rains. Araba and Ogunde welcomed them with smiles and praises until they saw Wura in their midst. They were alarmed, as she was not expected. Araba stood up and asked, "Where did you find this woman and why is she coming here with you?"

Fero responded and said, "Only my father, Adeolu, can tell you that," sensing the hostility and knowing that she had to be strong or things would deteriorate.

Araba, visibly uneasy, asked Ogunde, "It looks like Adeolu has kept a lot from us; did you actually know that he had Wura hidden?"

Before Ogunde could respond, Oromodi interjected and said, "Some very important visitors are around and are seeking your audience immediately."

Araba asked, "Who are these visitors?" And with a wave of hand he asked Oromodi to take Fero and Wura out of his presence.

"Bring them into the courtyard and announce them."

One of the soldiers then announced "Prince Aremu of Idumagbo is here seeking your audience."

He then signaled to Oromodi to come near and he whispered something into her ear. Aremu then stepped inside with some of his fellow soldiers and after they exchanged pleasantries, he said, "I have come in peace to seek your help in overthrowing my brother so I can set the people of Idumagbo free and rid the kingdom of corruption and the perverted practices of Abiodun."

Araba looked thoughtful for a while before responding and said, "Yes, I would like to overthrow your brother. As you can see, we have a lot of soldiers willing to do that here; lay down their lives for the survival of the kingdom of Idumagbo, which Abiodun has so desecrated." He continued. "We need a new system or process that will make our people prosper and not cause division by sowing discord among its different peoples."

Oromodi came inside the courtyard once again, interrupting the conversation and said, "There is no moon again; it just dropped out of sight. It has been taken out and I suspect that witch Wura. Immediately when we bound her in chains and threw her in our prison, we started noticing the darkening of the moon. We should kill her immediately before she kills us all."

Aremu was taken aback. "You mean you have one of the witches here? I thought Abiodun executed them all."

Araba, not wanting to give anything away at this time to Aremu, said, "No, we rescued one of them before the execution."

Aremu asked inquisitively, "Which one of them did you rescue?"

Araba looked into Aremu's eyes and now did not know what he knew said to Oromodi, "Go and bring the prisoner here into the courtyard."

Oromodi encountered Fero on her way back, who saw that Wura was in chains and started protesting and came into the courtyard with them and saw Aremu. Fero had never liked Aremu. Aremu had been indifferent to her anyway and when she saw Aremu, she was surprised and mumbled a greeting.

Aremu, knowing that this might be a spectacle, put on his political and Machiavellian hat and pulled Fero to himself in an embrace, saying, "My dearest relative, how have you been? How is your father?"

Fero, not surprised and not knowing what to say, responded in kind. "We are doing very well, and it is such a surprise seeing you here. I hope you are not on the run like us."

Ogunde and Araba kept on a bewildered look, knowing that they were not the best of acquaintances, while Wura looked on forlornly. Araba broke the awkward silence and said to Aremu, pointing to Wura, "This is the one we have," and then said to Wura, "Did you darken the moon?" Wura gave no response, not knowing what to say, and thought it best to play dumb.

Aremu then said, "Gentlemen, this is Wura, the witch Adeolu was accused of harboring, and this is the witch that would have cost Adeolu his life."

"Adeolu is not dead?" Fero responded.

Araba confirmed it by saying "Adeolu is not dead; we rescued him from his executioners yesterday before the dawn and he will soon be here with us to plan and depose Abiodun."

Ogunde nodded affirmatively in silence before speaking. "It is not possible for anyone to darken the moon. This witch did not do this and let us not provide her with powers or an aura which she does not possess."

Araba looked on and said, "Oromodi, did you hear that? No one is capable of darkening the moon and until we know how the moon dropped out of the sky, we will continue to keep her in prison."

Oromodi responded, "The soldiers are afraid that the world is about to come to an end and that executing Wura will bring the moon back and keep the world from ending."

Ogunde and Araba burst into laughter and Araba said, "I will come and speak with them later."

Fero stopped Oromodi and said, "My father is not going to like it; she has not done anything wrong. You cannot prove that she darkened the moon."

"It is easy for you to say; who knows? you may belong to the same coven," Oromodi replied.

Fero, not wanting to back down, directed her response to Araba. "You are no different from Abiodun, who decided to execute many people based solely on suspicion of witchcraft and sorcery, which he had no proof of."

Araba looked hard and was angry AT his orders BEING countermanded by an outsider—a female, for that matter—but decided against using his powers in an extrajudicial manner and asked Oromodi and Bankudi, "What is it that you have accused this woman of?"

Bankudi said, "She has not done anything against me; she seems to be a very nice woman and we got along very well on our journey to the camp."

Oromodi said, "I have nothing against her either, except what I heard from fellow soldiers about her being a witch."

Suddenly, the eclipse of the moon started receding as soon as it started and within a few minutes, the full glare of the moon was upon them once again and they all started rejoicing and to everyone's bewilderment,

Wura broke into a song: "Eemi la ni yo si bi ati fe ori bee naa lo ri," and started dancing. Fero joined her in the song and dance. After the excitement of the dance died down, Araba welcomed Aremu and Wura by saying, "The enemy of my enemy is a friend. Aremu and Wura are enemies of Abiodun and as such, they have become my friends today and together we shall vanquish Abiodun from the throne of Idumagbo."

Everyone around shouted: "Aye! Aye!" Aremu then proceeded and said that he had it on good authority that Idumagbo was going to be attacked by the Maradi people of the north in the next few days and as a matter of fact, they had sacked Idiape and the town was currently in ruins. Those that escaped said Abeni put up a good fight, but she was raped several times before she died, and her body was dragged throughout the whole town before they set fire to it.

The Maradi people inhabit the northern lands with their capital in Timbuktu and they attack the southern lands for slaves and livestock. They take the slaves and sell them to Arabs who take them on to distant lands across the Nile River and the Red Sea into the land of the Arabs. Most people, after they were sold into slavery, were never heard from again.

"My good, older sister. The cruel hands of the Maradians have torn her away from this world; but I will surely get my revenge, certainly in this world and not in the next," responded Araba.

News of the attack on Idiape had confirmed the demise of his sister Abeni.

Araba continued. "However, this will also be a good time to attack Idumagbo and overthrow the king."

Ogunde said, "The army will be severely weakened, and it will take some time to rebuild a formidable army that can repel the attacks from these north men."

Aremu said, "Ever since I received this news, I have come up with a plan."

Ogunde answered for himself and Araba, "What plans?"

Aremu continued. "We should go on the offensive, attack the Maradi people in their camp and then use that to sway the people to depose Abiodun and then make me king."

Araba was incensed by Aremu's statement and he immediately responded, "Why should we make you king? It is our army, the people's army. Why can't people use their free will and choose who they want as their king?"

Aremu laughed and said, "Would you like to be king too? Your ancestors have never been kings and you cannot be a king. Only those whose family the thousand gods have anointed can be king in this realm."

"So, it is you that was not even a legitimate child of the king that wants to be the king? We cannot even prove your parentage."

"By the virtue that Keniola the queen mother accepted me to live in the palace after my mother passed, proves that I am a legitimate prince of the land," Aremu responded, fuming.

Ogunde said, "Beware of where you are; you are not in the palace anymore and here you have no authority."

"I may have no authority here; the thousand gods have destined me to be the next king after Abiodun, and I will speak up and fight for what is rightfully mine."

"Who are the thousand gods, by the way; has anyone ever seen them? Oh, we know their maker Ogini was recently sent to the world beyond, what have they ever done for anyone?" Araba responded in unfeigned anger.

Aremu was very upset with the statement coming out of Araba's mouth but suppressed his anger at this blasphemy by biting his tongue and then offered a conciliatory tone by saying, "It is well."

Deep inside, Aremu seethed with anger but appeared on the outside to be unperturbed by Araba's outburst. He recognized that he did not have the army nor the authority to order Araba's arrest for blasphemy and he needed to keep his cool, so he switched the discussion. "We will surely find an alternate method to select our new king; maybe we can organize a wrestling competition for all contenders and whosoever wins will be the new king."

Everyone present laughed except for Araba and Ogunde. Ogunde then added his voice. "No, we should do better than a wrestling match to select someone that will rule over us. At the minimum he should be a man of knowledge, wisdom, and should be widely travelled, and we should let the people make that choice." He then continued, "I once met a European traveler who claimed to have come from a faraway place that he described as very cold, with only a few days in the year that the sun comes out. He told me that the people elect their kings; that each head of household represents a single vote and the candidate with the greater number of vote tallies will be the king."

He then pulled out the same pistol in his belt and showed it to them. Some of them had not seen a gun before. Aremu responded, "Yes, one of those was used by Sango to kill some of my supporters during the trial of the witches."

Ogunde responded, "I sold him that gun and made many more for Babagun's army."

Fero then chipped in, "Why don't we plan to overthrow this king first, and then discuss how we will proceed to elect a new king. Arguing and disagreement is not helpful to our quest. The long and short of it is how to ensure that we do not end up having tyrants as rulers; that should be our main focus and not who is entitled to rule."

Everyone nodded in agreement. Araba then asked, "Aremu, how did you come about the information on the Maradi people?"

Aremu responded, "I have a spy in their midst who informed me of the impending raid on Idumagbo."

"Who is this spy? Can he be trusted? When is this raid planned for?" Araba inquired further.

"It should be anytime between today and the next seven days," Aremu responded, evading the other questions on trust.

The evasion was not lost on Araba, who just nodded and said, "Then we need to prepare our own plans as quickly as possible."

"Do we know how many men were in the camp of the Maradi people?" Ogunde asked.

Aremu responded, "The spy said he counted six hundred men and that there were reinforcements on the way."

"The city of Idumagbo currently has about four hundred soldiers under Sango's command and it will take about a day's march to move the army from Karounwi to the defense of Idumagbo, as they are not even aware of this information yet," Ogunde said.

Arabas added, "The Maradi people attack on horses and are very swift and fast, and most of their raids end in a few hours, leaving destruction, sorrow, and tears behind them."

Ogunde said, "Then they will easily overwhelm the four hundred Idumagbo soldiers under Sango's command, who are mostly infantry. The archers battalion is in Karounwi and would have inflicted heavy casualties on the Maradians if they were part of the battle. Our best plan will be to send spies along their escape route and lay traps to kill them all," concluded Ogunde.

Araba thought for a little while before adding, "However, our overall goal is to seize power, and by killing the Maradians we have not seized power because news of the attack will get to Babagun, who will mobilize the soldiers down to Idumagbo as quickly as he can and that will make our plans useless from that point onwards."

"Can we get Babagun involved in this?" Araba inquired, looking at Ogunde.

Aremu said, "I sent emissaries to him first before coming here; he refused to see me."

Then there was some commotion outside as some of the soldiers started hooting the appearance of Adeolu and serenading him with songs. They also sang to the great Keniola, who was known to be the wisest woman of all times in the history of Idumagbo.

Adeolu and Keniola were announced and entered into Araba's court and they were given a rousing welcome followed by resounding applause. Araba spoke first, clearly taken by the highest high priestess and former Queen of Idumagbo in his presence. He said, "To what do I owe this honor, Keniola? Your stories of courage and resistance have preceded you and we welcome you into our midst with gladness. During the time you are with us, we shall know it for good and it shall be for a greater cause."

Keniola, looking very expressionless and taking in everything all around her, nodded and said nothing.

Aremu spoke next and said, "To a worthy mother, I am always proud to be associated with you, Keniola, and I count it as a great honor to be pressed into service for you. Keniola, you are welcome into our midst; a great woman that has known adversity and has known wealth. She has known suffering and she has known what sacrifice is all about. Welcome to our midst and with your wisdom, we shall prevail."

Ogunde went next and before anything, he prostrated flat on his stomach. Keniola smiled and asked him to stand up and he said, "Let me remain because I am not worthy of standing in your presence and I can only say that whatever wishes you have, I am at your command. Ever since I was young, I have heard stories about you, and I am very pleased to be in your very presence today and would be highly honored to wield sword with you side by side."

Araba called for Oromodi, who was standing nearby, and asked that she prepare a place for Keniola to sleep tonight. Keniola stood up and asked Araba whether she could speak. Araba asked her to proceed. Keniola said, "I have not come here to seek pleasure and sleep and wait until the Owner of days calls me home. I rose from my bed and from my home by my grandson Adeolu warning me that my own son, King Abiodun, is after my head and wanted to prosecute me for the crimes committed by his own nephew, Adeolu here. How absurd is that? Is that a proper and right decision for a king to make?" she asked. She looked at the faces of people she was speaking to and they responded by shaking their heads. She continued. "A king should make decision that suit his people the most, and the loathing of King Abiodun is the reason why all of us are gathered here in this camp. We hate him, and we would make him to abdicate the throne, peacefully or by force."

And they all responded, "Yes, that is what want."

Then they began the chanting, "Kill him! Kill him!"

Keniola looked at the passion displayed before her and smiled before continuing. "Does anyone here know the reason why I refused to live in the palace or in the city of Idumagbo?"

They responded, "No."

"Now I will tell you: it is because of Abiodun. He gave me and his father away for selfish purposes so that he could become the king." There was a gasp of aah-hah followed by deep silence from the audience. Keniola looked at Aremu and she saw that his head was down a bit. She thought to herself, now is not the time to talk about your complicity in this crime.

The rebels suddenly became energized and there was an instant connection between the soldier officers present and the old queen standing in front of them. The revelation of what King Abiodun did was quite abhorrent and could have caused him to lose the throne ever since Keniola returned from captivity but Keniola had kept quiet, not because she was impotent but because she knew that the revelations could lead to instability.

"Abiodun had no reason to suspect that I even know anything about it. I had gotten to know this after the crown prince of Maradi took a liking to me and then married me, although forcefully; the crown prince loved me but hated my regality and proud look, as he often said."

She continued, "The Maradian crown prince told me that one of the slave raiders had told him that it was one of my sons that gave them the whereabouts of where to find me and my husband, King Adebayo, so we could be captured, and that paved the way for him to be king."

The people listened with rapt attention and there was silence all around and you could hear a pin drop. She then continued, "We have a duty to take up arms tonight and march on Idumagbo because Idumagbo may likely fall into the hands of the Maradians tonight and it might take us a while to take it from them. I say we march on Idumagbo for the peace and prosperity of Idumagbo!"

Araba looked around and saw many of the soldiers were mesmerized by the speech from Keniola and knew instantly that at this point he might lose command if he chose not to go as she wanted. Keniola then continued, giving Araba a slight bow, "We proceed and seize the throne from Abiodun tonight and make fight or make peace with the Maradians. Our decision should be collective, which will build us a better society."

Araba started the applause, and everyone soon joined, then Araba spoke and said, "We will make plans immediately and move on Idumagbo tonight. It is about a half-day's march from here for the army."

Keniola said, "I would like to inspect our army.

Araba signaled Oromodi and Oromodi started the drumming, which alerted all the forces. Keniola then stepped outside together with all of the others, then Aremu said, "This is a very large army; we stand a chance of getting the throne back from Abiodun."

Adeolu listened to his grandmother and could not understand why she had not shared the information with him for so long. He consoled himself by thinking, *maybe she thought I would have misused the information and get myself killed.*

Adeolu moved closer to his grandmother. "I am with you, and together we shall avert the wrong done unto us and tonight we move for the glory of Idumagbo."

Keniola replied rhetorically, "We need to move fast; time is not our side. The Maradians are planning their attack as we speak. We have to get to Idumagbo in due time and we will need about fifty men that can run very fast without stopping so that the journey takes a quarter of its original length."

Aremu said, "That is three hours," hoping to get others to join to join with him.

Araba said yes, we can get these men and I will lead them. He called on Bankudi and said, "Go and inform our elite and specially trained soldiers to prepare to move out soon."

Araba came into the hut that Fero was in and asked her to come with him. Lately they had run into each other so much and he had behaved not like a brute, but like the kind of man she always liked. She could not bear the thought that she had started thinking about another man after not seeing Itiade for just a few days.

She stood up and then followed him and then asked him why he was pushing her pride in her face. Araba looked into her eyes she looked back hard but all she could she was love radiating back to her, so she melted and asked why in a milder tone. Araba then spoke. "Over the last few days you have been here, I have grown fond of you. The advice, training, and caring for the soldiers and your overall composure really helped my thought process."

Fero replied, "Really? I seem to have grown fond of you too. We have to take things slowly, so we know we are doing the right thing." Then Araba took her in his arms and planted a kiss on her lips. She was first taken aback and then thought she liked the feelings and the vibes she got from her relationship with Araba. He took off her clothes and then made sweet, passionate love with her.

Araba spoke and said, "In ten minutes, I will be going to war and will be attacking Idumagbo at high velocity with a handful of men. The rest of the men will be with you, and I will put the army under your care."

Fero looked at him and said, "You trust me that much already?"

Araba replied, "Let's say I have come to trust your family; Adeolu, your great-grandmother, and yourself, and I am now willing to lay down my life for you all to live and be happy."

Fero hugged him again and said, "I will do as you wish and will make sure you are proud of me." Both of them then held hands and walked together toward the large courtyard where fifty of the fiercest warriors that Araba had in his camp were waiting.

Araba entered into the courtyard and the first thing he noticed was Keniola, who was also dressed in full battle regalia. He made a decision not to talk about it until she eventually proved a stumbling block on the lightning attack on Idumagbo. Aremu was also dressed, and he believed he could also try to make the lightning attack. Adeolu was also dressed up in battle gear and Araba thought that Adeolu could make it based on their recent experience.

He then walked around some soldiers and thought that maybe around half of them would reach Idumagbo in three hours. He inspected the swords, bows and arrows, and knives; he saw they were all intact. Bankudi then bellowed out as the commander of the forces, "The forces are ready to deploy to Idumagbo at the command of Araba!"

Araba then went to Oromodi, who was leading the rest of the army, and said that the rest of the army should follow behind them immediately and ensure that they reach Idumagbo in half a day. He then said that this army would be under the command of Fero.

Oromodi proceeded and said, "Aye," and said aye to Fero as well.

Araba then said, "Army; move!" He looked at Fero and kissed her again, then jumped on a horse and the rest of the soldiers jumped on their horse as well. The horses would be tired in about an hour and a half and would feed for about an hour before they were ready to go again; at that point, each of the soldiers shall disembark and begin the run down to Idumagbo. He then wondered, what would Keniola do? Does she want to wait with the horses? He understood that whoever was present at the discussions after the battle had a lot to gain by influencing the decision on his own or for the future.

Adeolu also mounted a horse and Keniola galloped at measured speed first and then started moving faster with the command from Araba. Araba started galloping ahead of everyone and he galloped with Bankudi and Ogunde and they raced ahead of everyone and disappeared from sight.

After a few hours of galloping, they all came to rest at a predetermined site where the horses would feed and drink water. Then Adeolu saw Araba and Ogunde in the midst of some of the soldiers discussing in low tones. Adeolu and Keniola approached slowly and they told him that their spies reported that the Maradians had attacked Idumagbo and that Babagun and his army had also arrived and were currently in a free-for-all battle in the palace.

"If we start running from here, we should be in Idumagbo Palace before daybreak."

They all chorused, "Yeah!" They began running and after about an hour, Araba saw that Keniola was still running and did not seem as if she was ready to stop. He thought to himself that he had had a total misconception, thinking she was an old lady; she was quite young at heart.

Adeolu kept wondering about the same thing, and thought, why would he ever think of her as an old lady? Perhaps she must have been practicing and surprisingly hid her status and agility by covering herself everywhere she went.

Soon they reached the city gates in time to see the Maradian soldiers fleeing and they gave chase as well, cutting them down as they went.

Itiade's Call to Service

Ever since Itiade got converted to Islam he had not missed any call to prayers apart from the time he was down with illness, and he is seen more in the company of Muniru the Alfa and many of the Muslim converts. One of the few notable Muslims in the town of Idumagbo is Ibraheem, an Arab man who specializes and trades in tea leaves and palm produce. He has since settled down in Idumagbo town and married two women from the town. Because of his wealth he was able to afford many luxuries, like a horse-drawn carriage, a large house, and a large store in the center of the market.

Itiade had grown fond of Ibraheem and his family and ever since Fero disappeared, he had spent a lot more time with Ibraheem's family and most notably his youngest daughter, Saadia, who impressed him with her knowledge and gracefulness. Ibraheem noticed Itiade's closeness to his daughter Saadia, and wanted to stop it because the elder sister, Almitra, had no one courting her currently and he would love if Itiade courted and married Almitra, but he did nothing to stop the relationship but kind of encouraged it inadvertently.

However, he was torn deep inside because he had been supporting Aremu for the throne of Idumagbo and had been instrumental in providing some useful information on the Maradi people. He had already struck a deal with the Maradians to spare his folks when they arrived in the town. He had prospered a lot in this town and would not want to leave everything behind. He had suffered a lot and had traveled over two thousand miles over a twenty-year period with his family and friends before he found Idumagbo town and came to like the openness and friendliness of the people that inhabit its walls. They were a unique people that welcome strangers into their midst, accommodate them, and give them a chance to eke out a living in their midst without disparaging them or putting them under the knife. He found this openness very enchanting and exhilarating, which was quite different from many other places he had been in the last twenty years.

In some places, if you are a stranger and you wander close to their city, they pretend to like you during the day, but in the night, they seize, kill, and eat you for supper. He had lost some very good friends to the belies of so many humans this way and that's why he appreciated the people of Idumagbo for their hospitality.

The people of Idumagbo believe that all humans come from the same source and as such, discrimination is heavily frowned upon by the gods, and the culture welcomes diversity. His sons and daughters were some of the most sought after in the whole city and its environs. Their skin tone and their foreign looks made them very desirable by every youth of marriageable age.

Now he was in a dilemma because if Itiade chose to marry Saadia, he would not be able to support Aremu anymore. He knew how much Aremu wanted to be king and he owed quite a lot to Aremu; they had been friends from the very first day he came into the city and they had not had any disagreements between them at all.

Aremu was now in exile, and the odds of him becoming king were getting lower as he continued to absent himself from the eyes of the people and from major decisions that affect the livelihoods of the populace.

A few weeks ago, he received some unusual visitors; some Maradian spies posing as traders. They had come over to his store during the market day and told him they wanted to attack the city and that he should help them so they could take slaves and also impose Islam on the people inhabiting the city. He listened to them, gave them water and food, and said he would be in touch. As soon as they left, he quickly reached out to his trusted servant, Tela, to follow the spies surreptitiously so as to discover their campsite.

Tela was a native of the city, an orphan who found a place in the household of Ibraheem. Tela had been feeling double-minded since he had a chance meeting with Salim, who had been trying to get information from him about Ibraheem. He was not a fan of Salim and he refused to do his bidding then until they decided to give him a hefty sum of money and a position in

Sango's army; then, he could no longer resist. So, he decided to be a double agent; any information he received, he passed it on to Salim and his agents.

He followed the Maradian spies together with some of his fellow trusted servants and they came back and gave information on their campsite. This information Ibraheem promptly passed to Aremu. It was this same information that Aremu passed on to Araba and his rebels at their campsite. He did this because he was convinced that imposing a single religion on the people of this town would spoil its fabric and may lead to a collapse of the trading economy. He did not mind them taking slaves, looting, and leaving, as long as they did not harm his own family, but imposing Islam, which means they plan to stay and form a government, would not be good for the egalitarian society that Idumagbo and its environs is noted for.

With that, he knew he had to frustrate the Maradian invasion by making sure their invasion plans did not succeed.

Tela also informed him that the Maradian spies also went to see Muniru the Alfa, and he was surprised that Muniru never mentioned anything of such to him and he had given him enough chances to tell him, but he refused to give any information on what he knows. Ibraheem had always thought that Muniru despised him because he participates in the town's festival of the thousand gods and some other traditional religious festivals; he always criticized him by saying that partaking in this festival was an unclean act, ungodly, went against the teaching of the holy prophets and that Allah is not happy with him. The thought of what Muniru said about him often made him laugh, and he often wondered why he perceived him like that; maybe because he did not show the holier than thou attitude that he displayed with his stoic attitude. Was he the one that collaborated with Albert, a Christian, to sell dead people's clothes, and he helped pin that on the witches to get a conviction? *He is such a hypocrite!* Moreover, he had been a Muslim before Muniru ever heard anything about Islam, so he simply disregarded his comments whenever he heard about it from third parties and never thought anything about it.

However, he was now sure that if the Maradi people took over this town, Muniru would throw him to the wolves and brand him as an apostate. He would be doomed, and his life would probably not be spared. So, he asked Tela to inform Salim of Muniru's treachery and collusion with the Maradians—information that Tela had already shared with Salim. Nevertheless, he nodded, signifying that he would do so immediately.

Itiade, on the day of the night of the lunar eclipse, started the day by visiting Enitan, Adeolu's wife, at the prison. The guards would not permit him to enter. He threatened fire and brimstone to all but to no avail until one of the guards gave info that she passed away this morning and her body had been taken away to be buried. Itiade asked the guard, "What was the cause of death? Does anyone know? Was she executed?"

The guard replied, "No one knows. The first guard that checked on her met her dead; apparently, she must have died during the night."

He broke into tears and wept. He did not know how to take the news, so he went to Ibraheem's house to meet his new love, Saadia. He cleaned his face as if nothing happened and did not mention anything to Saadia. Saadia was very happy to see him. She said, "Good of you to come early today, it's almost time to go for prayers."

"I would not miss prayers for anything, and you have been a source of joy to me after my recovery."

"You mean after Fero ditched you."

"Fero was never my lover; she is my cousin. Her father is my father's stepbrother."

"So? I can give you many examples where brothers marry sisters in this town."

"I am aware of this and it is because of ignorance; the king's council will soon outlaw such practice."

"Indeed, why would they outlaw it?"

"Fero once told me that Adeolu told her that when offspring from the same parents, or of very close parentage, come together and have children, their children are most often weaker or malformed, with missing limbs or with mental issues, and die early."

"Wow, now I see; that is certainly true because if I look at the examples that we have in Idumagbo, I see a correlation between what she said and the children of these siblings. Most were often weaker than children of parents which were not siblings."

"Allah is indeed marvelous; he works in very mysterious ways," said Itiade.

They then held hands and walked together to the prayer house, where they spent a major part of the night sheltered away from the rain in one of the market stalls. They heard the noise about the lunar eclipse and they also came out to see and were mesmerized as well, seeing the moon receding behind a whiff of cloud.

"The world is coming to an end!" said Saadia, trembling.

"If it's going to come to an end, would it be giving us an advance warning?" asked Itiade, trying to act brave.

"Have you ever seen the moon appear and then disappear while it is still night?"

"It probably fell ill and needed to relax," said Itiade, trying to make light of the matter.

"We need to go find Father and the Alfa quickly so we can make peace and ensure that our place is secured with the Malaikahs."

As they stepped outside of the prayer house, they saw Albert and a couple of Christian followers with a gong chanting: "Repent, for the Prince of Peace has come! Now it's time to come clean of all your sins. Where you are going, you need neither clothes nor money."

The Islamic adherents were not far away either and they were led by Muniru and he had a similar message, not wanting the Christian converts to outdo them. "Heaven is not a place for spending money nor wearing clothes, repent of your sins now and be guaranteed a place in heaven with the Malaikahs!"

Albert, seeing the Islamic converts, heightened the pitch of his voice. "The kingdom of heaven is at hand! Come and confess your sins, give away all your belongings, and make heaven your permanent abode!"

A few minutes later, Sango appeared with a band of soldiers and shouted: "Silence! Who gave you orders to make sales without the permission of the king?"

Muniru inched closer and said to Sango, "Saving the souls of the people should not need permission from a king; you should join us to have a chance at making heaven."

Albert chimed in as well and said, "Tonight your soul is required; join us and be a Christian and you shall be absolved of all your sins."

"While we are still breathing, the world has not come to an end and you are making money behind the king," Sango said in an irritated tone before he barked orders to his soldiers: "Seize them!"

Their followers ran and dispersed in all directions while Itiade and Saadia continued to watch with unbridled curiosity.

Sango said, "Now you see that I have powers to even end your lives and make your ascension to heaven quicker."

"Sango, the law giver of Idumagbo, you do," Muniru started singing his praises.

"Sango, lord of Idumagbo, lord of the powerful and champion of the people!" Albert added his own praise.

"Now listen to me. I want fifty percent of everything you have made tonight. You bring it to me before the break of dawn, otherwise, I will accelerate your ascension to heaven." He then laughed uproariously while Muniru and Albert nodded yes.

Itiade and Saadia heard everything from the empty market stall where they had been hibernating and were more confused than ever before. There was silence between them as they walked solemnly to the prayer house.

A few hours before dawn, after the storm subsided, Salim led a few soldiers into the courtyard of Muniru's house, which also includes the prayer quarters, and called out to him saying, "Muniru, come out now! I know what you have been up to and I have orders from the king to come and arrest you."

He came out and asked, "What do you want? I already settled with your boss, Sango. I will bring his payments to him tomorrow."

"No, that is not what I am here for this morning. I am here on the orders of the king to arrest you for treason and collusion with the enemy."

Muniru was suddenly afraid, as his facial expression changed from impudence to one of consternation and panic and he quickly retreated his footsteps and ran back into one of the bedchambers. Two of the soldiers with Salim gave chase. Salim shouted, "Don't let him get away! He might be harboring some foreign fighters; be careful!"

His voice was suddenly drowned out in the clinging and clanging of swords and knives inside the bedchamber and a loud, deathly noise from one of the soldiers.

Then came out an unknown man, a Maradian man, middle-aged and average height, very dark in complexion with deep, groovy tribal marks running from the center of his forehead over his cheeks down to his chin. He was dressed in black and looked very menacing.

This was the foreigner Salim was talking about. His spies had seen him yesterday and had tailed him to Muniru's house. The unknown man followed Muniru outside into the courtyards and they both drew their swords.

Muniru said, "Here is to us as we set to take the town of Idumagbo for Islam."

The unknown man said nothing and just nodded his head.

Salim drew his sword as well as the other six soldiers with him. Salim then said, "You are outnumbered; save your life and the king can have mercy on you."

The unknown man spoke for the first time. "I won't be taken alive. I accept death, if that is what it takes."

Muniru, taking a cue from the unknown Maradian, said, "No mercy shall be accepted from pagans and animists."

Three of the soldiers went quickly against the unknown Maradian. They fought and killed him with two casualties while Muniru gave up as soon as he saw that the Maradian had been killed. Salim had instructed the soldiers not to kill Muniru, as he knew that Sango would be very displeased if he did not get what Muniru promised him.

Muniru was arrested quickly, his hands and feet bound, and was about to be carried to the king's prisons when Itiade burst out of the bedchamber and, not understanding what was going on, saw a man killed and he demanded that Muniru be released.

Saadia, an ardent Muslim, also drew a sword together with some other members of the household, blocking the exit out of the courtyard asking that Muniru be let go.

Salim said, "On the orders of the king, I ask that you vacate the exit now. I will only give this order once."

Itiade left the exit and tried to pull Saadia away, but Saadia said, "I will not allow this intolerance and grave disrespect to a man of God while I am here."

"There is more to this than meets the eye. Let's find out what the king has against him before taking up arms."

She refused.

Then Salim gave the order. The remaining soldiers with him drew their bows and arrows and aimed at the people blocking the exit. Saadia fell as one of the arrows hit her in the chest and she died immediately. Itiade fell down on her corpse and wept profusely. The soldiers took the bound Muniru and pushed him toward the exit, clambering over the weeping Itiade, the dead Saadia, and other corpses.

On getting to the palace grounds, Muniru was tortured severely and he revealed that the Maradi people were planning an attack on the town and their goal was to turn everyone to Islam and ensure that Idumagbo pays tribute to the Maradian king. As soon as the king heard the news of Muniru's confession, he summoned Sango and sent for Babagun to bring reinforcements into Idumagbo.

The news of the arrest of Muniru and the impending invasion by the Maradian army quickly spread around the city. The people started preparing for the defense of the town. Soldiers were sent to fortify the city walls and where there were no walls, traps were laid by digging large tunnels and pouring water and sharp stones into them and then covering them with tree branches and leaves to disguise the holes.

Itiade picked up the body of Saadia and carried it on his shoulders and walked down to the house of Ibraheem. He found him outside the courtyard with one of his wives and when they saw him, they ran to him and took the body from him. Ibraheem wept when he saw that it was the body of Saadia; he could not control the flow of tears from his eyes. He later summoned up courage and asked Itiade, "What happened to my little girl, the fairest one?"

Itiade, no longer weeping, narrated, and said, "We were in Muniru's house learning from the religious texts when suddenly Salim and some of his fellow soldiers broke in and asked for Muniru."

He paused and then continued. "Muniru came outside and Salim accused him of treason. Instead of surrendering he tried to escape by entering into the bedchamber and some soldiers ran after him and were killed in the bedchamber, only for Muniru to appear with an unknown man and both of them fought the remaining soldiers. The unknown man lost his life in the fight and Muniru was finally arrested."

Ibraheem nodded his head. He was aware of everything that was going on because Tela had briefed him and there was no way he could have known that Saadia was going to insert herself into the fight. He wept profusely because of the guilt he felt.

Itiade tried to console him and then continued. "The scholars, including myself and Saadia that were watching from a corner previously decided to join in the melee by preventing the soldiers from exiting with Muniru. The soldiers did not take it lightly and they shot arrows into our midst, leading to the death of Saadia."

Ibraheem's two other wives also came into the compound from the palace and said, "Muniru has confessed that a Maradian invasion is imminent and the king has commanded that everyone should prepare for the defense of the city."

Itiade said, "An imminent raid by the Maradi people? We need to prepare for our defense!"

One of the wives added, "He has also summoned Babagun and his armies and all other *Baloguns* (war chiefs) to report to Sango immediately for deployment."

Ibraheem asked everyone to go inside and he joined them, only to return with some tools to dig a grave for Saadia. While they were digging the grave, Ibraheem suddenly thought about Tela and asked Itiade at what time did the raid on Muniru's house start? Itiade replied, "It was early before dawn and it lasted about an hour."

Ibraheem thought to himself that Tela must have told Salim long before he asked him to inform on him. He muttered the words, "Thank God."

Itiade asked, "Why thank God? Saadia is dead."

Ibraheem responded, "I was not the cause of her death; Tela caused her death, not me," shifting the blame of death of Saadia onto Tela.

Itiade, looking bewildered, asked, "How?"

Ibraheem then narrated the whole story about the visit of the Maradian spies to him and how he refused but sent Tela after them to discover their hideout only to discover that Muniru was also in touch with them and also to discover that Tela was already sharing information with Salim and Sango.

Ibraheem then said, changing the discussion, "Itiade, now is the perfect time for you to take the throne for yourself."

"How can I do that? I have no soldiers nor followers, and neither do I understand what it takes to rule these lands," Itiade responded.

Ibraheem and Itiade finished digging the grave and both of them carried the body of Saadia and laid her gently into the grave and started shoveling sand to cover the grave. Then they both sat down while Almitra and her mother joined them, and they all locked in an embrace and wept together.

Ibraheem noticed the way Almitra held onto Itiade and thought, *I don't have to do a lot of work on my daughter, just Itiade.* Ibraheem thought such thoughts were very dangerous considering that he'd just buried one of his daughters. Now he thought of himself a great schemer and manipulator but a very bad parent. He later asked his wife and daughter to leave them because he had some important things to discuss with Itiade.

After Almitra and her mother left, Ibraheem turned to Itiade and looked at him thoughtfully for some time before saying, "We are going to be strategic about this and our first move in our quest to take the throne is for you to embed and ingratiate yourself as a loyalist to the king again so that you can have access to all information and discussions taking place in the king's hall and you will pass this information to me and I will help you to make meaning out of it so as to make a good decision."

Ibraheem continued, "The siege of the Maradians will take a couple of days and hopefully our defenses can hold them down until Babagun and his army arrives. Once Babagun and his army arrive, you must find a way to kill King Abiodun and wrestle the throne from him."

"No, I will not do that; he is my father!" Itiade responded.

"No, he is not, Aremu is your father, and you will be doing him a service because he is a tyrant and he is no longer useful to the citizens of Idumagbo and its environs."

Itiade was shocked beyond words; the words hit him like a tornado as he nearly lost his balance.

Ibraheem, seeing his discomfort, pressed on. "Abiodun has had cause to send notable and gifted people into exile; people that have helped our community immensely. We have to bring these people back and sue for peace."

"I don't believe you. How can the king favor me to be king after him if he knows that I am not his son?" Itiade said, cutting Ibraheem short.

"The truth is, I do not think he knows. He seems to be living in denial and that has made Aremu very bold and disrespectful of him. From all indications, he is a sterile man and not capable of fathering a child."

Itiade was very silent, and this encouraged Ibraheem to continue. "Do you even know who your mother is?"

"Yes, everybody knows it is Adun, King Abiodun's second wife," said Itiade.

"I can't believe no one ever told you; you were born to Ayesa, a Nubian slave woman working in the palace. She was a lover of the king and Aremu. The relationship between your mother and Aremu was a secret, while the relationship between Ayesa and the king was known. You only have to be wise to see that the king's two wives have no children, and the only child that the king can lay claim to is the one born of a different woman sleeping with another man, his brother, Aremu."

Itiade became very silent. He knew this must have been hidden in plain sight for a very long time. Then he became visibly angry for the deceit that had gone around him for a very long time and he said to Ibraheem, "It seems I am alone in this world and I have to fight for my survival. What would you have me do to take the throne?" he asked.

"There is a lot you have to do, but you have to first realize that you are only a pawn here. If you let Abiodun die on the throne, you will have to fight for the throne because Aremu will not give in easily," Ibraheem said. "However, if you seize the throne during this melee, a lot of people will urge caution. Aremu will have no more cards to play and Araba might halt his rebellion and even join you to protect the realm."

He continued. "After King Abiodun dies, you can leave the rest to me. I will handle Babagun and the other war chiefs and I will convince them to rally to your side and will also convince all the other chiefs; they all owe me one thing or the other. It will be my chance to get my payback. And one more thing, you will have to kill Sango; he has too much to lose.

"Let me go and start preparing the grounds for your ascension to the throne of Idumagbo as I go and speak with Chief Abioye and Chief Arese. I urge you now to go to the palace, stay on the side of the king, make plans with the king's men, and arm yourself for the defense of your lands. And you should come and see me every morning at a rendezvous place, here at Saadia's burial place," he concluded.

Itiade then looked at him, embraced him and said, "We shall avenge the death of Saadia and the rest of these people; their deaths shall not be in vain."

He traced his steps backwards, turned around, and broke into a run toward the palace.

On getting to the palace, he saw the pace at which the town's defenses were been buffed up; the frantic pace at which the soldiers were working, digging trenches around the palace, the marketplace, and uncovering the trenches around the city walls, the parade of soldiers back and forth. He quickly ingratiated himself, making himself useful by joining the trench diggers and ensuring that there were enough tools to go around.

He got on his horse and went around the city walls, inspecting the soldiers and giving orders to the soldiers to move fast. He then galloped to the

market square where the military headquarters was currently located. There
he found Sango, Salim, and incidentally, Tela. Sango seem pleased to see him
and he thanked him for his service in ensuring that the trench digging was
going according to plan. However, Salim still suspected him and refused to
say anything.

Tela was also suspicious; not because he was the king's heir, but
because he was an Islamist and a close confidant of Ibraheem, his master.

Sango noticed the distrust that was going on between Salim, Tela,
and Itiade, and saw perhaps a way for Itiade to earn their trust. He said, "Tela
was just telling us that he has sighted an advance party consisting of about
two hundred men and fifty horses of the Maradians, a half-day's march from
here. He also mentioned that this advance party has sacked many of our
farming hamlets along the way, destroyed farmlands and seizing the farmers
as slaves. These slaves were being held in giant cages that were built for this
purpose. The Maradian army is about two thousand men strong, with two
hundred horses, and they are about a day's march behind their advance
party," Sango added. "I believe the objective of their advance party is to
disrupt our defense preparation and throw us into disarray."

Sango continued. "Since we know their plans and their
whereabouts, our intention is to launch a surprise attack on their advance
party's position tomorrow morning before dawn. As we go along the way, we

will also be poisoning the farmlands and the water wells along the path to ensure that they do not have access to anything good from our lands."

Sango then looked at Itiade and said, "All this being said, we have chosen you and Salim to lead this surprise attack. So, I ask you to go and prepare to march at dusk and finish off the enemy before they even wake up. You and Salim will lead a company of one hundred men each. Itiade, you will head into them directly from the east while Salim will take a circuitous route and attack them from the rear. Salim and his men will start marching out now. Tela will ride with you and will show you their present camp."

Itiade listened attentively to all of this and never uttered a word, several thoughts racing through his mind. Is this a setup? If it is not a setup, how can he even trust Tela? He also thought, I am an expert swordsman and I have been trained in the art of warfare and I am capable. After much thought, he responded, "I will do it, and I do not have to go back to the palace tonight. Show me the men that I will lead so I can get to know them well."

Sango led Itiade, Salim, and Tela into the outer yard where the soldiers were, some sharpening their swords, knives, and arrows and some practicing with each other. Salim shouted an order and they arranged themselves into two companies. Sango then bellowed another order and one of the battalions responded and he asked whether they were ready to behead some Maradians and all chorused, "Aye-aye!"

Then he broke into a song. "Ko ni ja lomo koni ja lomo ogun ote yi o, ko ni ja lomo," (This time they will not kill our children and we shall all be survivors.)

He then continued, "We will go, and we will come back and the only people we will not see on our return are those that do not wish us well. We will not meet them at home." They all broke into the song and danced.

Salim, taking cue from Sango, also broke into another song. "We will kill many Maradians, we will sleep with their women, kill their children and their unborn babies." They also joined and sang it with him. Salim then mounted a horse together with twenty other lieutenants, who also mounted their horses. They took a back road, not wanting to go in the middle of the city for the fear that there might be some other Maradian spies lurking around. They galloped fast and disappeared into the night.

Sango spoke again and told the rest of the soldiers that Itiade would be leading them into battle. There was a temporary murmur of disagreement before one of the soldiers by the name of Albert stepped out and said, "Itiade is not a worthy leader to lead us; a majority of us are Christians and Itiade is an Islamist."

Itiade recognized him as the leader of the Christian converts; it was a new religion brought by some European men from across the seas in the north and he never could understand why they followed a God that died on a cross. He remembered having a hot disagreement with some of the Christian youths, Albert inclusive, when they preached to him and tried to convert him to their faith. There had been no love lost between them after they discovered that he had become an Islamist.

In matters of religion, he respected Adeolu a lot; he had been able to talk sense into the people and that had averted a lot of unnecessary bloodletting and fights. He worked with the Christians, the Islamists, and those worshipping the traditional gods of their ancestors. He did not discriminate, so he prospered.

Albert then said, "How can we trust Itiade, an Islamist, to lead us against other Islamists?"

Sango stepped in, seeing that his plan might backfire before it even started; this was a variable he never considered previously. He said, "Itiade is a prince of Idumagbo and the heir to the throne of Idumagbo and he is eager to kill the Maradians as you were. He has a lot more to lose if the Maradian triumph in battle, so I urge you to take him as your leader."

Itiade then spoke, looking at Sango, and said, "Release unto us Muniru and we will take him into battle with us."

Albert seemed genuinely happy and said, "Yes, release Muniru to us; we will gladly fight alongside him."

The other soldiers in Albert's platoon chorused the ask, saying, "Release Muniru now and let him fight alongside us!"

"I do not think he will be in a good state to fight. He will be by morning; give him good food, bathe him, clothe him, and let him know it is time for him to redeem himself in the eyes of his king."

Sango and his lieutenants seemed quiet after he spoke, but it seemed to be an uneasy kind of calm descending upon them. Then Itiade, sensing the tense mood, spoke and said, "Truly I am an Islamist, but before I am an Islamist, I am a son of Idumagbo, and so are all of you. I will fight to protect my heritage as a son of Idumagbo before any religion.

"My father, King Abiodun, is not an Islamist and neither is he a Christian; our generalissimo, Sango, is a proud worshipper of the thousand gods, and I would not condemn or seek his destruction. The freedom of worship is what gives Idumagbo peace, and that is why we are the center of trade and that is why everyone wants our land."

He continued. "However, they do not understand that it is just not the land but the culture and the heritage of our people that has sustained the trading and economic prosperity of our towns and cities.

"I repeat, I am first Idumagbo before any religion and I would die to keep it that way and I say to you, let us join hands to make our city one and not let religion divide us. I will not be a party to a war of religion, and I give it to you that we shall only triumph if we are one."

With that being said, Albert came up and gave a slight bow to Itiade and then faced the rest of the soldiers and said to them, "We fight not because we are Christians but because of our fathers and mothers who came to this land before us and have given us these customs that have allowed us to live in peace ever since. It is for these reasons that we fight; we fight to protect our common heritage; we fight for the future of our sons and daughters and not because of the religions that we converted to."

The spoken words electrified the men and they all broke into frenzied war songs which they danced to and waved their swords in the air. While the dancing was going on, Itiade consulted with Sango, Albert, and some of their fellow soldiers, discussing the routes and the best way to mount an attack on the unsuspecting enemy. Sango said, "It is better if we assume that the army will not be sleeping and that they will be marching toward us as fast as they can. Salim and his army will flank them in a few hours, and you and your army will run into them head-on. Should they be sleeping, the better for you; you just kill them all in their sleep. If they are not sleeping it will be a hard battle, but the tide will change if Salim and his soldiers appear in the rear as we planned."

Itiade beckoned to Albert and whispered into his ear to select two of his trusted lieutenants to watch the city gates to see if anyone will be hurrying outside when they exit through the gates. The plan was to catch any spies within the city gates and use the spy's method of contact to gain an advantage on the enemy. It was not unusual to find spies during such perilous times.

These lieutenants, having heard from Albert, decided on a disguise, and removed their army uniforms and put on sack clothes to blend with the populace. Sango was very pleased with Itiade's plan and he said, "I am very impressed with your strategy; you should join us in the army full-time."

With that being said, Itiade mounted his horse and rolled out with the soldiers toward the city gates. Many of the city dwellers stopped and prayed for them and wished them success in their campaign, while Albert's men flanked out watching for hurried movements. Soon they saw a woman making hurried movements toward the gates. Two of them followed quickly, one after the other. Albert also followed at a safe distance; the first follower quickened his pace so he could overtake the woman and be ahead of her.

When he overtook her and murmured some greetings to get her to speak back, she did not respond, feigning absentmindedness, and as soon as she noticed that the individual pestering her was not going to stop, she quickly changed direction by dashing into the forest. Both soldiers and Albert gave chase. They ran through the forest, jumping over dead wood and ducking branches. She got to where she had tethered her horse, jumped on it, but there was no way she could ride a horse that fast in this kind of environment; her plans had gone awry. She then drew her sword and the sword, not very visible to the second follower, she used it and pierced his chest; he died instantly.

Albert, seeing what happened, drew his own sword, and told the woman that she would not be killed if she surrendered and that he needed her to take him close to the Maradian camp. She did not respond.

The first follower materialized from the flank, drew his bow and arrow, and hit her in the leg. She knelt down, broke the arrow, and another one hit her in the second leg before she threw down her sword and surrendered.

Albert raced to her side and said to her, "You are from the Maradi people and where is your camp?" He paused a bit and looked into her eyes as she avoided his eyes. Albert cupped her face in his palm and asked again, this time more firmly than the first, "How can we get to your camp from here? What is your secret signal?"

The woman looked up directly into Albert's eyes and said, "Promise me you will spare my life."

Albert could not guarantee that, but he replied, "Don't worry; you will die a glorious death."

She then described the place of rendezvous with the advance team about three hours' march from there and what the secret signals were before she took a knife from her bag and slit her own throat.

Itiade and the rest of the army soon joined them. Albert disclosed what had transpired. Itiade, who had been watching the interrogation from a safe distance, said to Albert, "How do we know she told us the truth?" to which Albert replied, "We do not know."

"That being the case, we should tread carefully and discard the information she gave us. Who knows? She might not be the only one," Itiade said, providing guidance.

They sent their reconnaissance soldiers to flank the advance of the army so that the army could be warned quickly if enemy forces were ahead. Then they rode at a high speed into the night until they got a signal from one of the recon teams ahead of them to halt. They came upon the massacre, the bodies of Salim and his soldiers, who had been ambushed and killed. Tela's body was nowhere to be found.

Incidentally, another spy had seen them, he thought, and had warned the Maradian army, who ambushed them. They looked for trails of where the army could have gone. They had done a neat job to disguise their trail. Their best option was perhaps to turn back and try to defend Idumagbo now that it seemed that this plan had not worked. Perhaps Tela was indeed a double agent and had permanently switched sides, Itiade thought once again.

Itiade barked new orders and asked the army to turn back. This time they rode furiously and those on foot ran all the way back to Idumagbo. On getting to Idumagbo, they could see signs of battle as bodies littered the streets and they could still hear battle noises near the king's palace, so they raced straight to the palace.

On getting there, Itiade disembarked from his horse; he saw Sango and King Abiodun and many of the chiefs in the distance slugging it out with the Maradians. He rushed to their aid and in that moment the leader of the Maradian army got the best of King Abiodun and dealt him a blow to his head with the blade of the sword. The king staggered backward, and he then used the blade of the sword to slice through his stomach. King Abiodun dropped his sword, held his intestines in his hands, then fell face forward.

Itiade then engaged the Maradian leader in a sword fight. He got the best of him cut him on his shoulders; he dropped his sword before he fled into the midst of his other soldiers. Itiade continued to fight, killing many of the Maradians.

Sango and the chiefs also did very well.

Just when they thought they were going to bring the battle to an end, another army of the Maradian arrived and this time they pushed forward and replaced the weary people in front with fresh hands.

Albert, observing what was going on, knew that they were severely outnumbered. He selected a handful of soldiers and positioned them on the roofs of the palace houses, then used that to launch barrage of arrows on the new invaders. That stalled their attacks and they retreated to a safe zone where the arrows could not get them, buying some rest time for Itiade, Sango, and the rest of the soldiers.

That did not last long, as the Maradian army quickly found their own sweet spot and they started shooting arrows into the palace grounds where Itiade, Sango, and the rest of the Idumagbo army were holed up.

After a while, Albert and his army ran out of arrows and the Maradian cavalry also ran out of arrows and the fight became a free-for-all once again, with Itiade engaging about four soldiers at the same time. Itiade was already feeling tired and he signaled that Sango should sound the retreat so they could abandon the city.

Then when all hope seemed lost and with the impending defeat and loss creeping on them, and as the twilight gave way to the early morning dawn, hope was rekindled when Babagun rode in with the cavalry of a thousand well-trained soldiers. His arrival created a lot of excitement and renewed vigor on the part of the people fighting for Idumagbo. Babagun and the people's army, though a small one but well-trained and well-disciplined when compared to what the Maradians have, surveilled the battleground first. The Maradians noticed them, then they rearranged the army and turned toward the newly arrived army.

Babagun asked his soldiers to load their guns and gave order to fire; the guns boomed and many of the Maradians fell down. The Maradian army was very shocked as they had yet to encounter any wars with guns before. Babagun ordered the guns to be loaded again and another order of fire saw many Maradian soldiers dropping dead once again. This time the Maradian leader, Khalil, who was incidentally the son of King Bashir of Maradi, asked that they attack, and they raced forward and Babagun's army kept loading and firing, leaving many of them dead. The few that got to Babagun's line were cut down by swords.

The Maradian army, seeing what transpired, sounded their retreat and they raced quickly out of the town. Itiade and Albert ordered the soldiers after them. They saw Tela also chasing after the Maradians and cutting them down with his sword as they tried to escape, they gave chase, killing off many of them and they returned to the palace. They'd won, but it was a victory that had come at a very steep cost, a pyrrhic one.

Khalil escaped with his life with a few other soldiers and went to the mother camp north of Idumagbo to raise another army. Khalil knew he could not fail; he had to win this battle for his father, King Bashir and his mother, Queen Keniola.

Babagun immediately ordered his soldiers to cordon off the palace and not allow anyone near except for himself and Itiade. Babagun thought, *we need to make a decision on who will be the next king, and if the decision is not made very fast, it could spell doom for the city while law and order can quickly deteriorate.*

Then Babagun saw Adeolu, Araba, Ogunde, and Keniola fighting their way into the palace as they were been denied entrance. They had arrived on the eastern front of the battle and had been fighting their way in since, and they had raced into town when the Maradians sounded their retreat. Babagun asked his soldiers to cease fighting.

Keniola asked, "Where is Abiodun?"

Babagun replied, "He is dead, we lost him to the battle."

"What about Sango?"

"He has been wounded and he has been taken to the medicine man of the palace."

"What about Itiade?" Keniola asked, trying to take stock and assess the whole situation.

"He is fine, but exhausted. He fought bravely and displayed tremendous fighting skills."

Babagun continued. "We have started preparing him to take the throne of his father."

"That will not be possible; he is not entitled to that position. Let us summon all the chiefs and let us prepare to militarize this town because the Maradians are coming back; they do not give in easily," said Keniola.

Araba and Ogunde, with their men, entered into the palace courts forcibly while Babagun looked on. He saw that he was quickly losing control of the situation. Keniola pulled him to the side and said, "Announce me as regent and I will put everything under control for you."

Babagun said, "You know I cannot do that; it is beyond my powers. The throne either belongs to Aremu or Itiade. Since Aremu is not here, it should go to Itiade. Besides, Itiade fought gallantly defending this city and the people think of him as a hero right now."

"Babagun, you will be making a mistake if you announce Itiade. We need to do something noteworthy that our children's children will forever be grateful to us. We need to ensure that those who lead us are not tyrants and entitled, spoiled little brats. We need to ensure the people that are being governed have a say in choosing who leads them," Keniola said.

Babagun was taken aback and said, "How can we do that?"

"Announce me as the regent and I will put in place a system of government that will create economic prosperity for all individuals and ensure security of lives and property and make our people happy."

They closed their discussion, and both also advanced to the king's court. Keniola saw Itiade on the stool next to the king's stool and beside him was an Arab-looking man she thought she had seen before. Her eyes left Itiade and she glanced and saw Chief Abioye with Ogunde and Adeolu with Chief Arese. Araba stood beside Fero with Bankudi by their side, and also plotting their next steps. They knew the next few hours would probably determine their future.

Keniola continued to smile at everyone, giving orders, especially to Babagun, who was now busy doing her bidding and in effect she had assumed the de facto position of the lord and ruler of Idumagbo. She thought to herself, *this is going to be an interesting political theatre and, in a few moments, winners will start emerging.* For her it was either she gets the highest office, or she dies.

Then, from the corner of her eyes, Tela appeared. She remembered him; he was the one that brought the Maradian messenger to his hut in the forest. She wondered why Tela was still alive; it seemed the people of Idumagbo were yet to discover his treachery.

Babagun looked around and cleared his throat to bring silence to the court. He started by thanking the gods that gave them victory today over their enemies. He praised the bravery of the soldiers of Idumagbo who went on the offensive and delayed the impending attack for a lot of hours until reinforcements arrived. He also praised his own men that raced all the way from Karounwi without any sleep and got here just in time to thwart the attack.

He thanked Araba for also coming and pitching in his men in order to save the city and its inhabitants. He then deliberately ignored Adeolu and Ogunde and then praised Sango for his loyalty. He thanked chiefs Arese and Abioye for their war efforts and their thriftiness in keeping the economy of the city going.

Babagun also thanked Keniola for her courage in rising to the occasion and also showing up to defend the city and its inhabitants. He said, "There are a couple of things we have to get done today so we can secure this city from these invaders from the north, and first is we need to choose a new leader. We have many contenders for this throne; Aremu, the king's brother, who is not here today, and Itiade, who is presently with us here. Should we give the throne to Itiade because he is present here now or wait until Aremu comes?"

Araba stood up and said he would not accept the authority of Aremu or Itiade and that a better process should be instituted for installing new kings.

Kings should be made accountable to their people and not the other way around.

Fero also spoke up and to everyone's astonishment, she sided with Araba. Everyone expected her to be on Itiade's side. She said, "We have come too far as a group of people to rely on some traditions that bequeath power to offspring of those who lord over us. Our people have roamed these regions for millennia and settled this city a few centuries ago but never appointed kings until the arrival of visitors and travelers across the Nile River and the northern seas, sojourners from the lands of the pharaoh."

She continued. "Appointing kings was alien to us; important community decisions were taken by consensus. Why do we let the traditions of aliens influence our practices and induce us to fight each other?"

Adeolu smiled after listening to her; he was very proud of her right now. All the stories and parables he had told her, she internalized it.

Adeolu spoke next and in support of his daughter, saying, "We have come to a point where our health and wellbeing matters, our security matters, and decisions of such cannot be left to a single man or woman whose capricious tendencies can bring ruin to our lives. We must learn to tolerate and respect one other, be our brother's keeper, and build the largest trading city known to mankind."

Everyone in attendance rose in a chorus of "Ase!" meaning amen.

Keniola saw quickly that her plans were not going as she originally planned, and it was most importantly being thwarted by her own kinsmen, the people she loved the most. She then knew who she needed in her camp: Adeolu. She had taught him everything and he now had a mind of his own and could not be swayed. The only way would be to bring him into a benevolent task and push him into a trap and send him to jail. To do that she needed Babagun in her camp and she knew what to do to get Babagun into her camp.

She said to the people who stood there, "It is true that building a consensus is a better way of making decisions for our community, but who should be in that consensus is a major thing. Do we bring the young ones who were still suckling from their mother's breast or those with head issues? those are the things we need to think about first before agreeing to a consensus-driven leadership. In the meantime, the festival of the gods is here. This war and the instability of this dead king are why there has not been any plans to date, so we should all put hands together and plan for a befitting festival while I will be the regent. Babagun, our war hero, will lead all security forces in the city and enforcement. Araba will not bring his army into the city; his army will continue to be outside of the city and he will be heading the intelligence gathering arm of this regency. Ogunde will manage our economy and our purse."

She had intentionally omitted all her family members from cabinet positions despite the fact they fought very hard. Itiade was a war hero too, Adeolu is a war hero too, Ibraheem noted, and he instantly knew that Keniola was a master strategist. If he opposed her, he was not going to win; being a foreigner would work against him, although people don't mention it, but it would come to play to his disadvantage later, so he thought. "These people, they call themselves the Yobas," he muttered under his breath, very accommodating and at the same time, very discriminating.

Adeolu respected his grandmother a lot and loved her very much and believed that she had good intentions for the people of Idumagbo and environs, so he was the first one to chorus the ayes and everyone else within that vicinity chorused ayes, so did everyone else within the vicinity of the palace. Keniola then dismissed everyone saying, we know our duties, let's get to them and defend our cultural heritage.

Keniola beckoned to Babagun to follow her. Ibraheem stood in a corner and decided to study the atmosphere to determine his next moves. Araba put his arms around Fero, who looked very confused, much to Itiade's surprise, who was walking toward where Fero was. As soon as Keniola and Babagun were out of earshot and in privacy, Babagun said, "You should not have done that; no one is going to have you as a regent, you were a deposed queen and an itinerant traveler whom the people fear as a witch."

Keniola responded, "Yes they will, because you will provide them with this assurance that I am not a witch but a wise woman and a well-traveled woman with immense goodwill with neighboring tribes. You will tell them that would provide great and exemplary leadership."

"I never knew you were interested in ruling this city," Babagun said.

She replied, "No, I am not interested in ruling the city, only interested in setting the right standards. After my travel and travails, I have seen what a good and exemplary way to govern a country is." She paused and then continued. "To do this I will need your help. You are the only one in my generation that can help this community with this transformation; you have the army. I will build schools for our children after they come back from the farms to learn and master the written word so that we can send communication over long distances. I will build cloth markets and expand the cloth dyeing industries and we will have traders coming from afar to buy clothes from us. I will build large barns to store our yams and grains to provide for us during famine and with your help, we will build a greater army that will defend this country and will conquer other lands which will bring us a lot of wealth and above all, you will have me as a close confidante anytime you want. I know you have always desired this since we were youngsters; we can get a chance to be soul mates once again."

Babagun looked on and said, "Yes, I will do as you have said, but Adeolu needs to be in jail for the crimes he committed against our last king. The Oro is not going to be happy if he continues to live on this earth."

"Yes, I know, but he is a hero of the town and this is a time of war and we need every man who can wield a sword in battle."

Then Tela knocked on the door and said there was a Maradian visitor waiting in the court for her. She stepped out and walked down the narrow corridor with Babagun in close tow and she saw the visitor and blood drained from her face as she looked onto her son Khalil, whom she left in a hurry when running away from Timbuktu some seventeen years ago.

Khalil bowed and greeted her and said, "I bring greetings from my father, King Bashir, the ruler and sultan of Timbuktu. He wants me to make a deal on his behalf so we can have a truce and suspend this fight once and for all, pledge allegiance to the throne, and give up your Queen Keniola."

Chief Arese spoke up and said, "Keniola is not our queen, she was a former queen and now she is a war hero," and everyone broke into laughter.

Khalil continued, "If you do not surrender your queen, my father the king is not far away from here and he is coming with twenty thousand men and two thousand horses and he told me he will not spare a single man if you decide otherwise."

On walking in, Keniola instinctively recognized her son; the son she had for the king's brother, and she quickly instructed Babagun to tell his soldiers to seize him before he says things that could hurt her current machinations. Some nearby soldiers seized him by the arm. He did not resist but said the word, "Um, Um," the Arabic word for mother. Keniola grimaced slightly, ignored the motherly instinct welling up inside of her and gave an eye signal to the guards, who then grabbed him by his arms and took him away.

From Captivity to Captivity

Twenty-five years prior to the epidemic at Idumagbo, peace reigned in Idumagbo. Trade was fair, and the citizens fared well under the kingship of King Adebayo and wife Keniola. Queen Keniola, tall, fair, and very beautiful, with silky hair falling down to her shoulders, was revered by many Idumagbo citizens. She was an offspring of a female Ebira hunter-gatherer named Olosa and an Arabian soldier, Malik, who deserted his battalion to emigrate down with his parents and families to the western coast of Africa in search of greener pastures.

Her grandmother was of the Nupe-speaking people in the hinterland and her grandfather was a skilled traveling medicine man from Nubia. Her grandmother was displaced during a raid on their land by the people from Fouta Djallon and she found succor in the Ebira people and that was where she had a chance meeting with the father of her child.

Her grandmother gave birth to her mother in the midst of the Ebira people and the family stayed with them and taught them medicine. Her mother learned the most, to become a gifted medicine woman. Keniola's mother grew up in the midst of the Ebira people and she was quite different, as she was unmistakably very beautiful and every man in the tribe wanted to lay with her and have her as a wife. People also came from faraway lands to seek her medicine and the leader of the tribe was jealous of her popularity and wanted to subjugate her and use her knowledge for himself. She refused defiantly and ran away and on the same day she encountered the Arabian man Malik took her to the coastal lands and there they gave birth to Keniola, who then married Adebayo, who then became the king of Idumagbo.

King Adebayo and Keniola Adun held hands and walked down the promenade leading to the palace and were greeted by their subjects, many children running after them with Keni handing out nuts to them as she strode gently in her usual regal manner. Their son, Abiodun, followed, and had a scowl on his face. The queen had just reprimanded him for forcing himself on Ebunoluwa. King Adebayo pleaded with the girl's family and they agreed to keep it hush-hush, saving the Crown from a disgrace. King Adebayo did not know how to treat this matter and as soon as they got inside the palace walls, he gave Abiodun a slap across the face. Abiodun held his left hand to his face and said, "Why? Ebunola lay on me; I did not force myself on her and she willingly gave herself to me."

The king responded, "You had better shut your mouth. I hope you know that I was not born yesterday. Your type should never be a king in this land. I will ensure that you are stripped of your prince hood as soon as I get back from my journey to the waterside. We should thank the gods that your brother Oyeade, though sickly, has been very well behaved and he deserves to rule after I pass on."

King Adebayo and Keniola had two sons together, Oyeade and Abiodun. Oyeade, the firstborn, less energetic and sickly, whom a majority of the populace did not think merited the throne because of his feeble nature and a second one, Abiodun, was an athletic champion. King Adebayo also had a third son, Aremu, a product of his tryst with a woman on one of his travels. The woman had brought the son to the palace and ever since then, Aremu had lived in the palace with them. He was not even considered for the throne.

The king naturally favored Abiodun to be king, and this he had demonstrated by showing favors and showering gifts and praises on him, leaving no one in doubt as to whom he wanted to succeed him. Keniola favored her first son, Oyeade, and he continued to let the king know that his sickness should not be used to rid him of his heritage.

Now that Abiodun had been accused of such a despicable and heinous act, the king was suddenly at a crossroads. He would not want to put a man of questionable behavior on the throne of Idumagbo; that would be the end of this great and masterful kingdom, he thought. He was also far gone in age and his citizens and chiefs would want a pronouncement soon because of the history of such where there was no declared successor; it usually puts the sons against one another with each vying for the throne. He was determined that this would not happen with him, but he had been avoiding such conversations in the last few years so as not to hurt Oyeade and his beloved Keniola.

He drew his wife Keniola closer and Keniola said, "I know what is on your mind; your thoughts on who succeeds you and I hope you are no longer in doubt anymore; your mind should be already made up."

Keniola's firm commitment to her son Oyeade was so enduring, leaving no one in doubt as to where her loyalty lay.

Abiodun felt very uneasy and ran inside his room and was very moody, thinking of how he was going to lose his throne to a crime he did not commit. He should have known that the girl was devilish, taunting him with her body. Now he had exchanged his future as a king to a few minutes of fun. He thought to himself, *this is very unfair. How can I lose my birthright over a misdeed I never committed? I did not rape that woman.*

Abiodun agonized over this until Aremu came to announce that his bosom friends Abioye and Arese were there. This woke him up from his agonizing slumber. Aremu had always been his sidekick in the palace, and he often treated him very well when he showed loyalty to him above their parents. Abioye said to him, "Tonight is the maiden dance night, a night where young men can openly ask the lady of their desires out."

Abiodun replied, "Leave me alone, I am not interested in this women charade. All I want to do now is kill myself to escape the ignominy that is about to come upon me."

Abioye and Arese made bewildered faces, and both responded, "Kill yourself?"

Abioye said, "You don't mean it; you're the king tomorrow. Where would that leave us? We were hoping that when you become king, we will become chiefs."

Arese nodded his head and said, "Yes, we will be chiefs in this land of Idumagbo."

Aremu, also watching from the corner of the room, said, "And I will be the Balogun and the king's chief swordsman."

"You'd better get away from here. Who would make you a leader in this land; you, this illegitimate child?" Abiodun said, leaving Aremu scurrying away in shame.

After a few seconds of silence with Abioye and Arese staring directly at their friend Abiodun, Abiodun then opened up and said, "My father is going to take the throne away from me." He said, "I am a disgrace to the throne for sleeping with Ebunoluwa; I mean, Ebunoluwa accused me of raping her after I told her I was not going to marry her and her parents conspired with her and told the king that I raped her."

Arese's look changed and said, "You slept with Ebunoluwa despite the fact that you know I was wooing her, and my intention was to marry her?"

"Now I have lost everything for a few minutes of pleasure," Abiodun responded, ignoring Arese's statements.

Abioye stepped in quickly, not wanting the conversation to degenerate into something else, and wanted the conversation to stay on focus on what mattered most, the ascension of Abiodun to the throne of Idumagbo. Abioye said, "We cannot let that happen to you. You have made us promises to install us as your right hand and left-hand chiefs, respectively."

"I know, my friends, but I don't think I can keep these promises now. My father said as soon as he is back from his waterside trip, he will start the process of removing me as the crowned prince."

"So, no one knows yet?" Arese stammered a response, forgetting his earlier anger. Obviously, being a chief was better than marriage to Ebunoluwa.

"So, what are we to do in the meantime, wait agonizingly for your parents to come back and disgrace you?" said Abioye.

All three sat down in silence before Abioye then said, "We should go to Elegbara and ask him to take your father and mother's life and we make you king as quickly as we can."

"No, I would not want their lives to be taken. I would not want to commit two wrongs at the same time," Abiodun responded almost immediately.

Abioye grinned and responded, "What was the first wrong? Did you have to rape Ebunoluwa? She would have given herself to you freely."

Abiodun did not respond, which gave Abioye more leeway to talk. "You were just a deviant, and just like to violate women for no reason at all."

Arese looking thoughtful and said, "You did no wrong when you allowed yourself to be seduced by your friend's girlfriend. It is still no accident when your seducer was able to pass your escapades off as rape to your parents, which indeed is a rape. It would not be an accident if they met an accident on the way to or from the waterside. The natural order of things is just at its tipping point; you just have to apply a force. Either you force Ebunoluwa to confess to her cunningness and treachery or you make your parents take your side."

"Both options will be against you because the court of public opinion will convict you and you will not be respected by the people you intend to lead and rule," Arese concluded.

"The only viable option is time bound. If you really want the throne, you have to act now. Otherwise, you can kiss it goodbye," said Abioye.

"So, what do I have to do? Because I really want the throne," said Abiodun.

Abioye responded, "You must make a choice from the options that Arese just provided to you, and I am in support of the first option."

After some brief thought, Abiodun said, "Fine, fine, we will go with the first option—but with a finer twist. We allow Oyeade to ascend the throne and we first rule by proxy until we find a way to eliminate him as well."

"I say we ask Elegbara to do this for us; he is the perfect assassin for this job. We need to go now if we intend to give Elegbara the details of where he will find the king," Arese said.

The trio took a less-walked road and took a shortcut through the forest until they got to Elegabra's part of the bush. They were suddenly accosted by five of Elegabra's soldiers and one of them said, "Where were you going?"

Arese quickly moved to the front and said, "We seek Elegabra to give him his due for work he will do for us and it will be of mutual benefit to us."

The leader of the guards recognized Arese and asked them to follow while signaling to the other guards to fall back into formation. The leader of the guard, a man named Sango, asked that the trio follow him, and they seemed to walk for a while before they took a sharp curve in the forest leading down into some hidden gaps in the hills. They entered into an underground living castle where they passed through a waterfall before they came into Elegabra's abode. He was being entertained by some dancing women and had company of two Caucasian men and two Arab men. Elegbara was a tall, muscular, scruffy-looking middle-aged man with a graying beard and receding hairline who was notorious for assassinations and armed robbery of travelers. People paid him protection so as not to be attacked; if you had his protection, you would be spared.

He beckoned them to move close and then with a wave of his hand asked that the show be stopped and dismissed the dancing women. The visitors stood up, bowed, and quickly took their leave.

He asked in a slurry voice, "What do you want here, boys?" while standing up quickly and grabbing Abiodun by the neck, peering into his eyes saying, "Son of the king, what do you want from me? Are you trying to trap me for your father? Your father has never liked me; even when I have done him favors, he treats me with disdain, as if I am not a human."

Abiodun said, trembling, "Please let go of my neck and we can discuss how I can make you a great man in Idumagbo."

Then Arese spoke up for him. "We have come to seek your help in getting rid of the king."

Elegbara then released Abiodun's neck and said, "Speak of your mission and let me know."

Abiodun said, "I want my father and mother missing from this world and I want my brother to be king, and in return I will give you plenty of riches from Idumagbo, its lands, and its environs. Here is a token of two hundred cowries to get you started."

Abiodun took a bag of cowrie shells from his waist belt and tossed it in the direction of Elegbara, who caught it tossed it up and then tossed it to Sango for safekeeping.

Elegbara asked, "Where can I find the king and the queen and their entourage? You know it will be quite deadly if I should go into the city to assassinate the king and queen. Where is the weak link? Where can I find the king and queen with their guards down?"

"They are going on a trip to the waterside south of Idumagbo and will be traveling with a small party of soldiers and chiefs. Their plan is to rise very early tomorrow morning and take the forest shortcut."

Elegbara then raised his hand and said abruptly, "Now you must go. When the deed is completed, make sure you come around and make good on your promises, because if you do not, it will not be a pretty story."

The trio of Abiodun, Abioye, and Arese scrambled away from Elegbara and exited the underground castle through an exit where Sango led them through. Elegbara stood thoughtfully for a while and thought rather than kill the queen, "I can get a lot more money for that beautiful woman when I sell her up the coast." The mission of the two Eastern men that just left was to ask Elegbara to procure for them a highly cultured and well-bred female they could enslave and use to give birth to multiple male offspring. *Interesting ways to make money,* he thought to himself. He had not betrayed any of his clients yet, but he might do so just this time; the rewards were just mouthwatering. Nevertheless, it would be the same results: the king dead, the queen not found.

There were frequent rich Eastern travelers looking for people with unique births to enslave; kings and chiefs usually did this as a pastime to breed in order to have desirable offspring. He called out his boys and asked them to prepare the horses for a long travel. Elegbara had decided that he was going to kill King Abiodun and steal his queen and sell Queen Keniola to the Arabians. They offered him a thousand cowrie shells and ten horses. If he did not kill her, no one was going to know, and he was going to do the job himself. He might even have a taste of her before delivering her to the Arabs; a creepy thought crept through his mind leaving a grinning smirk on his face.

He knew the surrounding villages very well, having grown up and worked as a laborer in the evening on farms and fought in the evenings for money at some of the multiple bars across the entire reach of the people of the lands. He was on the move constantly, staying a few weeks at a time in one city or village, securing some work as a farmhand for a few meals and shelter and a few cowries. He had moved on so many times and had come back to the same cities and places many times, sometimes over many years.

He once worked for a family of wealthy Nubian landowners whose families came from Makoria and Alodia north of the continent. The families owned several horses and cattle and vast amounts of land used in growing cotton. This cotton was sold to the kings and queens of the land on credit and they employed people to weave them into clothes, dye them, and sell them in the markets across the lands. Through this they had been able to control the economy of the cities and the lands.

In some parts, their families had interbred with the other settlers of the lands and one of that offspring was Queen Keniola. Elegbara had once worked for Keniola's distant uncle, Abdallab, son of Dongolia, and he was the one that gave him his first assassination job. These two visiting Arabs had purportedly come from Abdallab, where they asked for a royally beautiful woman. Abdallab had directed them to Elegbara, not knowing that Elegbara was going to kidnap his own niece.

King Adebayo and Queen Keniola rode their horses on a trot out into the adjoining forest followed by ten soldiers and two chiefs. The journey to the south waterside was going to take two days. The plan was to get there in the evening of the second, rise again on the third day to have their meetings, and start riding back the same day. What they did not anticipate was their son Oyeade riding with them; he had overhead their parents arguing with his younger brother, Abiodun, and because he did not want trouble, he decided to stow away on their parents' caravan to the south waterside where the ocean empties itself into the lagoon.

They reached the city of Eko and they settled down amongst the sailors and other nobility from around the metropolis by building a tent near them and when the day broke, they went in search of Abdallab. They found him on the dock where he was negotiating sales of cotton. Abdallab was happy to see his niece; they saw each other at least once every two years. King Adebayo told him that the city of Idumagbo was flourishing and many more people came and settled and had been given lands and more people were being trained as weavers and more people were buying clothes and as such, they would be increasing their orders for the coming year.

As soon as negotiations were completed, they strolled into the market and went on inspection of what was on sale, sometimes shopping. They came across different exotic animals on sale and it was here that Keniola bought a baby leopard for her son Oyeade.

Elegbara had also traced them to the market and here he was looking at them a few meters away, stalking them and looking for an opportunity where they would be apart, and he could strike at one and steal the other without any pandemonium.

Suddenly, he saw the opportunity he had been waiting for; the king and queen were suddenly distracted when they saw their son Oyeade also strolling casually around the marketplace. Keniola was shocked and then waved to him. He saw them and knew he had been discovered but then pretended it was not him they saw and wanted to use the opportunity to quickly slip away.

Keniola also wanted to follow him. Adebayo held her hand and told her not to break protocol. Adebayo asked one of the two guards following them around in the market to go get Oyeade. The guard also pointed out to the king that he was breaking protocol; the king frowned, and the guard took a detour with the hope of accosting Oyeade on the other side of the market before he slipped out of sight.

Out of nowhere, one of Elegbara's boys struck Oyeade a blow to his head that sent him careening into other shop stalls, spilling the grains and fruits on the floor. Oyeade stood up and looked lost, as he was unable to fathom what was happening. He had ridden alone, and no one really knew where he was. A thought quickly flashed through his head; *Will this be my last breath?* before he then collapsed back onto the floor.

He looked up as one of his assailants appeared in his sight. He saw that it was not a familiar face. He took the last blow that blacked him out with a smile.

Keniola had also observed what happened and at that time she broke the protocol, snatching her hand away from the king. She ran toward the direction where Oyeade fell.

The king, not knowing what to do, also walked briskly into the sea of people that he had been avoiding since he got to this land and it was here, he felt the tip of the sword pierce his underside. He also saw the guard following him falling down in a mask of blood oozing from his face. It was there and then that he knew that the end had come, and his enemies had triumphed over him; he closed his eyes and breathed his last.

As Keniola was struggling through the sea of people to the place where she last saw her son, Elegbara's soft blow to the back of her head made her fall forward into his hands and he carried her and made a gruff noise asking people to move away and he whisked her into the forest where a horse was waiting. There he tied her hands and feet and gagged her mouth with a piece of cloth, preventing her from alerting other road travelers if she woke up suddenly. They rode the horses in silence for a while until Keniola woke up and started struggling with the ropes and the gag and in the process making herself and her horse rider fall down from the horse that was carrying them. Elegbara, having been salivating ever since, he stopped and then decided to take her into his tent to carry out his deepest imaginations. He removed the gag from her mouth, and she spoke up immediately and said, "Who are you and why do you have me bound?"

Elegbara said, "I am the person in control of your destiny right now and will determine whether your life ends or becomes very miserable."

Keniola replied, "I am the queen of Idumagbo, the birther of kings and queens and the Alodia of the kingdoms of the West, the niece of Abdallab, the son of Dongolia." When Elegbara heard the last statement, he was shocked; he could not believe that Keniola was in any way related to Abdallab and he could no longer carry out his earlier plans of having carnal knowledge of her because of his fear of what Abdallab could do to him and his business.

He quickly put the gag back in her mouth and then bundled her onto the horse again and then galloped as fast as possible to the place where he would meet the Arabs for the exchange. At the exchange, the Easterner named Isa and his Nubian counterpart received him. It was a quick exchange and they took possession of Keniola and they gave him a thousand cowries, put Keniola on a horse, and rode northwards toward Timbuktu, the kingdoms that asked for a royally beautiful slave they could breed with. They looked at her and they were very impressed; they knew they would be commanding a lot of money for her when they got to Timbuktu.

A few hours after the body of King Adebayo was discovered, Abdallab was notified about the death of a royal and the kidnapping of his wife. He was shocked that a crime of this magnitude could occur in the waterside, a town where there were multiple security personnel from the many ships. He quickly assembled a search party and he gathered intelligence by asking people at the marketplace about what they had seen. They had informed him that they saw Elegbara somewhere around the market and he knew instinctively that someone had paid for their lives.

A few hours later, Oyeade, the king of Idumagbo's legal heir, arrived at his door and he knew instinctively that this was going to be bigger than what he anticipated. He did not know that the heir was on the trip with them. Only very powerful elites within the community knew that he was uncle to Keniola, and the news of this might undermine his power and social status in this city he had lived in all his life, he thought.

Oyeade looked up and said, "We have to find my mother fast; she has been kidnapped. We need to find the perpetrators very fast before she gets out of the kingdom."

Abdallab replied, "We are making plans to do that just now and we have to gather some intelligence very fast."

Then Abdallab and Oyeade, together with what remained of King Adebayo's army, rode to the priestess of Eko, who informed them that

Keniola was being taken to a new kingdom for a sacrifice to their gods. "Before her sacrifice she will be a slave in the temple of their gods."

Oyeade and Abdallab left the priestess feeling despair and then organized search parties. Some went to the ship and dockyards hoping to get news about a slave party that left with a very important personality, and some other parties running came back saying that many traders reported seeing a large caravan of slaves leaving on a horse and in a haste. Abdallab believed this knowing some of the side businesses that he does is not trading on water but on land and with separate business partners and decided that the right search should go on land. They rode northward in search of Keniola.

Abdallab asked that Oyeade return to Idumagbo so as to be crowned king. Oyeade returned to the city of Idumagbo with the body of the dead king and the news of how the king died in the hands of some marauders. He also explained to the populace that their beloved Queen Keniola had also been kidnapped and no one knew her current whereabouts. This news was already stale, as the news had already reached the city and its environs, and the people trooped out in solidarity with him and had formed search groups to search the forests.

Abiodun, Arese, and Abioye also came out to welcome him and they all genuflected and hailed him as the king of Idumagbo. He rode to the palace, and there he announced that the perpetrators of the murder and kidnap were in their midst and everyone should watch because some very bad people were in their midst willing to cause war and disaffection. "We are sons and daughters of Idumagbo; our fathers and mothers settled and ruled these lands for thousands of years and we have not heard that a queen was kidnapped, and a king assassinated."

As he spoke these words, the words of his father, King Adebayo, reverberated in his ears, saying that he would disinherit Abiodun based on the news of his crime. He could not remember what crime Abiodun committed but he knew instinctively he was going to be at the mercy of Abiodun and his clique to be able to rule effectively in this kingdom and if he started asking questions, he would not get their cooperation but their angst, which could deteriorate into a coup.

Isa and his company of kidnappers rode for about five hours without stopping with about ten high-net-worth slaves until they got to a place where they found water and were resting and Keniola in her bondage, hands and feet tied, mouth gagged and eyes blindfolded, could not see anything and was unable to see that she had some intricate parts of her body exposed. Isa saw this, capitalized on this, and asked that she be brought inside his tent and this was where he raped her mercilessly.

Keniola cried and cried, as she has not been given this kind of treatment before in her life. She took it in her stride, and she resolved never to feel sorry for herself. She understood that she was in a very terrible position; she was a slave and she would have to act and behave as one though she would keep her dignity no matter what; not even death would make her blink and compromise her dignity.

They rode for several hundreds of miles until they got to a lake on the northernmost part of the kingdoms and here, they stopped at the lands of the Berber for a while. Isa left and went in search of buyers. He sold most of the slaves at this market but kept Keniola and they rode off once again into the night desert and traveled in the desert for several days before they arrived at Timbuktu market, the famous market in the north and south of the Sahara.

Abdallab sat down under the tree in front of his compound with some of his servants. They brought to him a young man who said he saw Elegbara at the market. He dismissed the man as soon as the man finished his story and sent the rest of the servants away. He had to quickly dismiss him so as to dispel any form of rumors against Elegbara. A couple of them had seen him with Elegbara in the past. They did not know what he did, but they did know he looked menacing. He knew that he needed to find Elegbara quickly and find out if he knows anything about the kidnap of Keniola. If he did not find Elegbara quickly and dissuade him from whatever his plans were for Keniola, his political and social standing in the city and environs would surely suffer. So, he bellowed to his two trusted servants and asked that they prepare a detachment of guards to follow him on a journey north.

They got to the Idumagbo environs shortly before dawn, as the dews were falling. They chose a suitable rock hidden from roads and footpaths and here they made camp until morning, then Abdallab asked one of his servants to follow him. He informed the others that if they did not see him in one hour, they should attack the compound he was going to. Deep in his mind he was deeply troubled because of the Faustian bargain he'd struck with Elegbara in the past; he had used him to install kings and assassinate his opponents. Now the chicken had come home to roost. He had not seen him or dealt with him in recent years; his only hope was that he still feared him.

He stepped into the path leading to Elagbara's compound and one of the guards accosted him and he immediately cut him down with his sword and a second guard refused to fight when he saw the swift manner in which his colleague met his death. Abdallab said to him, tell Elegbara that I, Abdallab, the leader of all chiefs and kings, has come to see him.

The guard turned back and fled through the slopes and disappeared into a ledge beside the waterfall that led into the courtyard directly opposite Elegbara's inner sanctum. Abdallab and his servant followed the guard into the inner sanctum where Elegbara was sleeping. Before he could rise up,

Abdallab had his sword on his throat and asked him not to move. Abdallab then asked him, "Where is my niece?"

Elegbara, still in shock, thought he had imagined that this was going to happen, just not the way he wanted it to, saw from the corner of his eye that more and more of his guards were showing up so he said to them, "Leave now, this will be something I will handle personally."

He felt more pain as Abdallab continuously applied more pressure and blood started trickling out of his neck. After the guards left the inner sanctum, Elegbara said in his very gruffy voice, "If you wanted to kill me you would have done so by now, so let's be civil. You take away the sword and let's talk."

Abdallab looked confused at first, then quickly changed his composure again and then asked again, "What have you done with my niece?"

"If you could only take away your sword, we would already be on the lookout for her."

Abdallab withdrew the sword from Elegbara's throat and said to his own personal guard, "Don't take your eyes off him; any false move, kill him."

Elegbara settled down, cleaned his neck with the back of hands and tasted the blood with his tongue before licking it all before muttering, "Blood is sacred, better not to waste it."

Abdallab continued to look at him with an expression that said, "I am ready to kill you if you don't talk."

Elegbara then said, "We will make a deal. Your niece Keniola would be about two days from Timbuktu. If we ride now, we can catch them just before they get into Timbuktu."

"Why do you care so much about her?" Elegbara asked after a few seconds of silence in which Abdallab was weighing whether it was worth pursuing.

"You are just an oaf. You should have looked for me and I would have doubled anything they asked," Abdallab replied, and then slapped Elegbara very hard with the back of his right hand. Elegbara wiped away the spit that came from his mouth as a result of the slap, knowing that he was trapped. He said, "I did not know she was your niece; if I had known I would have brought her to you first, and it would have cost you two thousand cowries."

"If we get her back you will still get your two thousand cowries." Abdallab said.

"Then we should ride now," Elegbara said.

"Whom did you sell her to?"

"Some Easterners; they wanted royal women to breed with, can you believe that?"

Abdallab gave him another slap with the back of his right hand and said, "You just turned my favorite niece into a rabbit."

Elegbara said, "We need to ride now," taking the slap in his stride and called for two of his strongest men and their horses. He informed them that they were riding to Timbuktu right away and gave no further information.

Abdallab met up with his men and asked four of them to join him in riding to Timbuktu and he asked the rest to ride back home and wait for him. Elegbara and his men joined up with Abdallab and his men; a total of eight men began the journey to Timbuktu in search of the captured queen, Keniola.

In the meantime, the body of King Adebayo was brought home to Idumagbo and all the people trooped out to bid him farewell as he was buried amidst lots of weeping. His body was wrapped in white clothes and displayed for everyone to see. People came from all walks of life, in and around the city, the surrounding villages, and some very faraway places like the coastal cities of Eko.

After the viewing, the kingmakers and some special class members of the Oro cult came in and they took the body away to a location where they now unwrapped the clothes around his body and painted his body with ochre, a natural clay earth pigment that is a mixture of ferric oxide and varying amounts of clay and sand, which is golden yellow in color. After this they began to say and chant prayers to the thousand gods, invoking the name of each of the gods one by one and saying prayers and cutting a piece of the body. They did this until all the names of the thousand gods were invoked and the body of the king was in a thousand pieces. Then they waited until the middle of the night before beginning the procession around the city and surrounding villages, burying each piece. A curfew was declared before the procession began; absolutely no one must see the procession, and everyone had been forewarned. Anyone caught during this period breaching the curfew will also be killed and his body sent to accompany the king to the great beyond.

King Adebayo was a good king and his lovely wife would surely be missed. The trio of Abiodun, Abioye, and Arese wept bitterly when the news of the death of the king and the disappearance of the queen was announced. Abioye openly wept more than the bereaved, which left everyone surprised as they asked, "Why is he crying more than the bereaved?"

They consoled Oyeade continuously for days after the burial and prevailed upon him to set up a search party, which was led by Abiodun, and they set out immediately only to return after a few days with the news that she could not be located. Oyeade was installed king in a very small ceremony at the palace because he refused to make it a big ceremony because of the circumstances in which he came to be on the throne. His brother Abiodun tried to convince him otherwise but he stood his ground and he went on to rule for five years before Abiodun quietly deposed him. Abiodun and his coconspirators became the rulers of Idumagbo and its environs for many years after that. Abiodun went on to have a very mighty installation ceremony.

***

On getting to the Songhai market in central Timbuktu, Isa completed the necessary paperwork and handed Keniola over to the market leader. They had her bathed, clothed her in nice clothes and fine gold jewelry, and put her hands and feet in chains together with other slaves and led them out into the open market, preparing for the market to open and for trading to begin. Isa sat in a corner of the market and observed as the market opened. Several men came in and priced the slaves and there seemed to be a lot of focus on Keniola. He liked his business, dealing with the luxurious goods that attracted the wealthiest clientele.

Then appeared the princes of Maradi lands; Audu, a very rough one, followed by his very meek and humble brother, Prince Bashir. Prince Bashir, though gentle, was the leader of large swathes of loyal fighting men. Most were veterans of several jihads across the Mediterranean seas and had now settled down with lands and they understood how to wield power. They were both offspring of great masters of the art of Eastern divination who later became kings and rulers of Timbuktu.

Prince Audu rode past and his eyes caught the beauties available for sale. He stopped, then asked for the price of Keniola and paid ten thousand cowries for her and he immediately took custody of her, loaded her onto one of the camels, and his party rode off to the part of the desert where they had their lands, with Prince Bashir in close tow.

Keniola was taken to the harem of Prince Audu and there she slept until she woke up in deep heat and felt someone on top of her. She tried to resist but she got several slaps and after a lot of slaps she was weakened and gave up and allowed her fate to take her to the darkest places she had not yet dreamed about and tears rolled down her cheeks. Audu repeatedly raped her several times over the next few months such that the other ladies in the harem took pity on her. They had their duties; they bathed her and prepared her for the prince, and they urged and encouraged her to show love to Audu, but she refused and remained defiant.

Then she became pregnant with a set of twin boys and Audu was still beating her; she was rather unfortunate with her pregnancy as she continued to suffer violence from Audu. She lived with this violence for many months until her pregnancy term limit was reached. While other women in the harem consoled her, she resolved never to show love toward Audu. She knew that her indignation toward Audu infuriated him more and she was already very used to getting sudden slaps on her face.

In Audu's harem, she met a woman named Miriam, a Caucasian, one of Audu's many wives. She told her that her former name used to be Agathe and they kind of hit it off together and became soul confidantes. They spent moments together and they helped each other out with their day-to-day tasks. Then on a day when she was about to give birth, they went out to fetch water from a nearby well and Keniola suddenly heard Audu's voice, but she could not answer because she had water on her head and was gritting with the pains and pangs of a coming childbirth. Some of the women in the compound came for her and took the pot of water from her head and asked her to sit down on the floor as soon as she reached the compound while one of them fanned her. Agathe also came to her aid and was trying to soothe her when Audu appeared suddenly with a whip and pushed Agathe away and started whipping Keniola. Keniola resisted and wore a very proud and indignant look on her face even with her pregnancy, which further incensed Audu and he continued to whip her.

Abdallab and Elegbara lost all their guards; some due to diseases and illnesses and some due to random acts of violence on their journey, but they were able to make it to Timbuktu at the first light and they headed straight to the Songhai market and perched on some of the empty stalls. They saw

Keniola in the distance on one of the trading platforms and Abdallab started walking across to see if he could purchase Keniola and just then, the entourage of princes Audu and Bashir rode in with pomp and pageantry. They seemed to be going somewhere but they stopped, and he could see Audu pointing to Keniola and some words whispered, and bags of money exchanged hands.

Prince Audu, Prince Bashir, and other princes usually made stops like this in popular markets in the kingdom and sometimes made a big purchase of the most expensive item in the market, and some strangers and rich landowners also do so on popular market days.

Then they took her, put her on a camel, and rode off and disappeared as quickly as they came. Everything looked pre-planned to Abdallab and he did not have enough men to start a fight there; even if he did, he did not know how far they would have gone before reinforcements would catch up with him, so staying action was a wise decision, so he thought.

Abdallab and Elegbara spirited to where their horses were stationed, hoping to trace the direction where the princes and their entourage went. After asking around for a few hours without any headway, they decided to stay at a local bar and ended up staying at the inn for several months. Abdallab was very frustrated because of their inability to locate the whereabouts of the prince until one day they stopped at a local bar selling cheese, honey, and *brukus*, a locally fermented crushed corn. They greeted everyone sitting in the tiny bar and bought some honey, sugarcane, and hay for their horses. They asked the locals a few questions and there was a man named Ibn who told them that the princes they seek lived about a hundred kilometers into the desert and they have a large settlement with lots of soldiers and he said some other Nubian folks also came to ask for the same prince around this time yesterday. Abdallab pressed him and asked, "Where can I find these men?"

Suddenly Ibn's eyes glanced right and he could see that the two had also entered the shop, one clearly Caucasian and the other Nubian, the Caucasian trying to pass as an Arab by trying to copy their tongues when speaking. Elegbara also stiffened, as he suddenly became very paranoid when he feels that he had to commit a crime; he glanced furtively at the two men. The two entrants, Makuria, a tall, muscular Nubian and Phillip, a Caucasian, also sensed the sudden silence from the three men across from them with the furtive glances back and forth.

Abdallab walked across and asked to pay for their drinks and to his surprise they obliged him. Elegbara and Ibn also joined their table and sat across from them. After exchanging pleasantries about the places where they had been, their families and friends, Abdallab asked, "Why do you seek Prince Audu?"

Phillip was not surprised, as he was expecting the question seeing that Ibn was with them, so he replied curtly, "We are going to kill him if we can ever find him."

Phillip looked at Abdallab and Elegbara, searching their eyes to see whether they could be trusted or would like to start a fight. He did not want to be going around telling everyone what the prince had done to his family. Abdallab stared at him and peered into his eyes, begging, probing the question. Philip continued. "It is going to be a long story."

"Make it short and straight to the point," said Elegbara in a menacing tone.

Makuria took out his sword and made to cut Elegbara before Phillip dissuaded him and before Elegbara even saw it coming, the sword cut him on his left forearm as he chose to retreat from the sword strike. Elegbara quickly drew his own sword and Abdallab stepped in front of him and said, "No, we will need all the allies we can get if we intend to get Keniola back."

Phillip also commanded Makuria to stop as well. Immediately after Abdallab left his front, Elegbara struck Makuria a blow with the back of sword, a blow which devastated him so that he fell down flat on the floor. He then went to him and offered him a hand and said, "I like to give the last blow and win."

Makuria grunted and snatched his arm away. Abdallab then replied to Phillip, saying, "It is going to be many long nights and we had better start discussing how we can achieve our common goal and what would make our alliance stick."

Phillip said, "When I tell you mine, I want to hear yours as well. This will let me know whether we can go into battle together."

"A few years ago, I and my brothers were Crusaders fighting in Jerusalem to claim the city of God back to its rightful owners. We had gone on a long campaign and I'd just recently got married to the most beautiful woman in the world, Agathe. She was pregnant with my baby before I left and but when I got back to our beautiful island of Crete, I saw that it had been ravaged by another fighting force that massacred the women and children and plundered everything in their path.

"I was downcast; I had lost my brothers in the Crusade and I was very much alone in the world. The survivors told us that the soldiers were from an empire in the continent south across the ocean. I was flabbergasted and could not believe that an African empire this powerful exists south of the Sahara. I was told they just left back to their ships. I was told that most of the women had been taken as captives of the army while the older ones and those not pleasing to the eyes of a particular prince were either raped, promptly killed, or decapacitated. We could still see the burning fires and wreckages left by the savage army and as for me, all that I had it seemed I had lost.

"I sought my wife, hoping I could rescue her and bring her back home and exact my revenge on this terrible prince, so I followed them in a small boat across the Atlantic to the Nubian kingdom of Kush. We landed a day later, and we were able to pick up their trail as they joined up with more armies from where they'd left for Nobatia. Makuria here is from Nobatia, a city in the kingdom of Kush. We fought together side by side in the Crusade with many of his city people, which we sadly lost.

"We quickly followed the invading armies, knowing that we could not fight these armies with our current strength; I mean, there was just two of us. Nevertheless, we followed, but kept our distance. By the time we got to Nobatia, everywhere was in ruins, as the invading army did not spare anyone as they went on a looting and destruction spree. Makuria lost his family and his relatives as well. We found some of his murdered relatives and we stayed behind to give them proper burials, and this is where we lost sight of the army for a few days.

After asking around for a few days, we heard that the army regiment led by Prince Bashir was the one responsible for the wanton destruction of lives, property, and rape. We heard he was from Timbuktu and he had led the army southwards back home.

Makuria raised about ten fighting men to follow us so as to finish up this barbarian prince and exact our revenge. We waited several days, recruiting men, and the trail of the armies grew cold, so we asked around and we were told that the prince lives somewhere in Timbuktu.

"We arrived in Timbuktu after about ten days and we camped our men outside the city, well hidden from passersby, and me and Makuria decided to visit the city and we sighted him for the first time when he visited the market to purchase a slave woman. We were able to follow him to a compound where we think he resides. This compound is heavily fortified with several guards, and the only way we can get to him is to lure him into the open.

"So yes, we know where he lives. I have camped out there for the last three hundred days and I have seen my wife only once and she was pregnant, and I am very angry, but Makuria asked me to be patient and not make a fool of myself. I have also heard from Ibn here that Bashir has a lot of other beautiful women in his harem from many places all over the world, especially the places where he has gone to war. He keeps the women as his spoils of war, and he impregnates the women at will and they give birth to sons for him. After they have given birth to sons for him and he is tired, he usually kills them or gives them out to some of his other officers, depending on his mood.

"So here we were now waiting for the opportunity to strike and break out my wife. I hope she has delivered the bastard child she is carrying; if not, I will claim that child as mine." He laughed, thinking of what other people might think.

Abdallab responded, "What an interesting story! When do we go there? Tonight, is probably the best time out of many days to come."

Phillip replied, "What is your story?"

"My niece was captured by this man, Elegbara, who sold her into slavery. She was the queen of her kingdom," Abdallab said.

"Elegbara was my assassin for hire, and he does jobs for me and I allow him to pick up other jobs. But this time he did a job that impacted me, and this is why we are here together to rescue my niece and return her back to her kingdom where she rightfully belongs."

"Does this mean he is no longer in your employ?" chided Makuria.

Abdallab ignored the statement from Makuria and said, "So if you know where they are keeping her, this would be a wonderful time for us to get her. Tonight, is the end of the Islamic fast and so there will be some celebrations and their guards will be down."

"The man you seek is not Bashir but Audu, his brother; Bashir is a very fine man and of good manners," said Ibn.

Phillip and Makuria arrived at the tip of Audu's compound just when the fast was about to be broken and all the soldiers on guard duty had gone inside for the fast-breaking ceremony and they heard some bit of commotion. Phillip saw his former wife for the first time when Audu pushed her and she seemed to have hit her head on some rock and was not moving, and then he could no longer resist it, so he asked the soldiers to follow him and they ran into the compound and engaged some of the soldiers, killing many of the unsuspecting soldiers breaking their fast.

Makuria fought with the Audu's guards, giving Phillip room to engage Audu directly and in the ensuing melee, Phillip bested Audu and he was hurt really bad when Phillip reached and sliced his left hand off and was about to thrust his sword into his stomach when Bashir came to the aid of his brother, saying, "He is mine to kill for what he did to Miriam," before thrusting his sword through Phillip's back. Phillip rolled on his back, looked at Bashir and said, "That is my beloved wife of many years. Her name is Agathe and your brother, Audu, killed her, so he deserves to die from my hands as well."

Bashir was astonished, then spoke. "You mean you came all the way across the oceans for her?" Phillip nodded before managing to crawl alongside her, dusted some dirt away from her head and kissed her gently on the lips. He looked back at Audu and saw that he was also in pain and he knew he was not going to survive the wounds. He looked back at his wife again, smiled satisfyingly and then gently closed his eyes and gave up the ghost.

Bashir looked at Phillip and said, "Dear friend, you seem to be an honorable person. Miriam was beloved by all and we will miss her and will ensure she gets a befitting burial—I mean, Agathe," he said, correcting himself.

After speaking all those words, Bashir was surprised to see that Makuria was still fighting the rest of his men and he seemed to be the only one alive out of the attackers. Bashir soon joined the remainder of his men and they engaged Makuria until he was tired, and he threw down his sword and gave up. He then asked his men to seize him and tie him up.

After the battle, Bashir headed to where his beloved Miriam was and saw that she was dead, then heard some painful noises coming from Audu. He went to where Audu was and said, "I love my women and would never hurt them, and I do not know why you hurt them. I wish you had concentrated your hurt only on your own women and not on those I own." He then gave him a finishing blow from his sword.

Bashir had never had any sons. He had about ten daughters from four different women unlike his brother, who had many sons and daughters. Abdallab and Elegbara had moved closer and were contemplating whether to join the madness going on but chose to wait to see if there could be an opportunity to snatch Keniola, who was now in labor a few meters away from them; they just did not know what to do. They saw Keniola give birth to twin babies, and they were relieved when they heard the cry of the babies. What they saw next bewildered them; they saw Bashir embracing Keniola and saying something like, "Everything is going to be all right from now on."

They retreated further into the hills where they were previously to plan the next attack. "How can one snatch a mother without her children?" Abdallab said.

Elegbara replied, "Just take her now that they have weakened defenses. I can count like five of their soldiers remaining. We can finish them off right now and escape with Keniola."

"No, it would be a tortuous journey for Keniola, and it would be a harrowing ride back to Idumagbo. The babies would certainly not survive," Abdallab said.

"Why would you care about the children? they were not from her husband but from her kidnapper. Let them keep the children," Elegbara said.

Abdallab looked at him indignantly, a look Elegbara understood and he quickly shut his mouth.

Bashir said to the people there, "My brother, Audu, was not a good man. We all tolerated him, but his behavior continuously put us to shame, the way he treated slaves and people was unbecoming of a prince."

The people in attendance nodded and he continued, "Henceforth, no one shall treat slaves horribly. They are our captives, and sometimes we paid money for them because they provide us with a useful service of which we need to sometimes show gratitude.

"Sometimes we put our lives in their hands and sometimes they provide us with good and strong offspring that are capable of wielding the sword; we should take care of them.

"Now that my brother is no longer alive, I claim all his property as mine, including his harem." Keniola stood up, held her babies in her hands and gave them to Bashir, who acknowledged her with a slight bow and raised them up and named them Khalil and Khaleb. The guards and the women in hijab chorused a cacophony of sounds which represented assent.

Then Bashir went over to where Makuria was bound and asked him, "Where are the others?" Makuria looked at his hands and feet and grunted something, which indicated that he should be untied. Bashir beckoned to his lieutenants and they untied his feet and hands and removed the gag from his mouth, and he said, "I will lead you to where we were previously stationed."

Bashir commanded one of the lieutenants to go to the next town and raise reinforcements to come and join them, then he got on a horse and asked the five other soldiers to follow him. They tied Makuria to one of the horses and they led him along the paths that he pointed to, which they had come through.

Elegbara, who was on the lookout on the hill, pointed to the advancing horses and said, "The prince is coming to look for us and kill us; we need to go and fight them and use the opportunity to rescue Keniola, whom they left at the compound."

"No, we have to hide and fight another day." Abdallab started running down the hill with the hope of finding somewhere to hide.

Elegbara followed behind for a few minutes before determining that it was going to be a futile effort and then decided to quickly hide behind a rocky ledge and as the first horse approached, he reached for the rider and pulled him down and quickly thrust his sword into the tummy of the soldier, killing him instantly, while one of the other horse riders quickly stopped the horse and circled around and swinging the sword Elegbara ducked and rolled over across the grassy hills, then stood up again and on the second advancement of the horseman he flew and drove his sword into his heart and he crashed from the horse onto the hilly grasslands.

The three remaining horse riders, including Bashir, that were previously chasing after Abdallab, stopped in their tracks. Two of them got off their horses and approached Elegbara with their swords drawn and they engaged each other continuously, giving Abdallab some time to put distance between them.

The third horseman had Makuria tied to his horse and he waited and watched as the three soldiers, including Prince Bashir, engaged in a duel with Elegbara. Elegbara got one of them before Bashir pierced his left side and blood gushed out, Elegbara held his side with one hand and the other hand holding the sword and he used that to continuously fight the two soldiers but gave up and they ended his life by severing his head from his body. Then the remaining two soldiers put his head on a pike and chased after Abdallab and was able to pick up his trail, they later found him some hours later and he gave himself up without a fight by kneeling down putting his hands clasped together on his head and bowing it. The soldiers and the Prince Bashir tied him his hands to their horse and then led him to join the other soldier that had Makuria tried. As soon as they got back to the city, news went around that King Al Mustafa the king of Timbuktu is dead and his first son Prince Audu is also dead and that the prince's younger brother Prince Audu had killed him. King Al Mustafa had been ill for some time now that the sons had taken over the affairs of the kingdom, Audu became the de facto ruler over all economics and financial matters while Bashir was in charge of the army. The chiefs had gathered at the central palace in the center of Timbuktu a three-story clay and limestone edifice with marble floors and gold walls. As soon as he got back to the palace, the prisoners were taken off his hands before he had some good chance to question and interrogate Abdallab and Makuria on why they were here, he had kept them alive because he was intrigued by such men, men that could take up such missions. Their mission intrigued him a lot since it had no financial reward based on what he had heard from the dead Caucasian, Phillip. He hurried into the palace where the ten Kingmakers who doubled as Judges for the land were seated waiting for him. Once in two years they bring other noblemen and rich landowners into the fold. Bashir knew he was going to be asked questions on why he killed his brother, he knew he can count on the two guards not to say anything and to corroborate his version of events. One of the kingmakers stood up and informed him officially that his father has died and that his brother has also died and that he is being considered as the king. They just wanted him to let them know why was it that his brother died from his sword during a duel with some invaders.

He bowed his head very low before saying, "I love my brother Audu very much and we do a lot of things together but during the duel with the invaders, he was severely wounded and was writhing in serious pains with half of his stomach outside. I took pity on him and ended his life because there was no way he would have survived."

One of the kingmakers also stood up and asked for a vote. One against vote was a tie and the kingmaker must bring evidence forward to justify his non-assent. It was a unanimous decision, and everyone united to have him as the next king, and they fixed the crowning ceremony for the day after tomorrow.

Makuria and Abdallab found themselves inside a dark jail with rats as companions and competitors for warmth and space. Abdallab instinctively did not trust Makuria again and when Makuria tried to speak with him, he responded by dealing him a blow with his fist, which resulted in fighting. They fought until they were tired. Makuria then said, "I had no choice. I wanted to give you guys a chance to also fight so I may have a chance of escaping, I have seen these guys; they were very diabolical. I have seen what they have done to others and I deserve to get a chance to escape from it," he said before dealing a blow to Abdallab, who fell face down on the floor, tired.

Obviously, he could not fight this muscular giant with bare hands. He had been able to control Elegbara, who is equally tall, with wits and money. As long as they were in this prison, he would have to fear for his life from Makuria. He stood up and said to Makuria, "I have forgiven you. I would have done the same if I were in your shoes," not meaning any of the words.

Makuria smiled and said, "We need to find a way to get out of here." Few weeks later, one of the guards appeared and said they had a visitor. They had spent eight days in total in the jail without food. The guards provided water without any meals. They ate by setting traps for the rats, killing, and eating them raw. The guard said that a princess had come to see them.

Just then a woman appeared, covered from her head to her toes, with only slits for the eyes to see. Abdallab moved closer to the gates while Makuria did not stand up from where he was, since he was not expecting any visitors. Immediately the figure stepped closer. Abdallab said, "Keniola?"

She responded, "Here I am. I was told that some people attacked the palace compounds hoping to free me; not in my wildest imagination would I have thought it would be you that would risk your life to come and rescue me. Thank you for looking out for me."

She continued, "I wanted to confirm that you were the one before going to meet the king and ask that he pardon you. The new king is Bashir, and he has shown me favor and he has been very kind to me and my children." She then made to leave.

Abdallab grabbed her hand and said, "Is this going to be a new life for you now? Have you now accepted your fate, and have I risked my life for nothing?" He could see the confusion in her eyes. "In that case, can you ask that I be given at least some proper meals, water, and clothes?"

She said, "I will try," then turned her back and left.

A few months after Bashir was installed as the new king, he started receiving a lot of official visitors, holding court with his chiefs, and attending to the kingdom functions. One of those functions was to receive routine reports from his head of the army and head of prisons. They had informed him that Keniola frequently went to the prison to talk to Abdallab and give him food. He barely had time to find out more about the prisoner Abdallab and he wondered why Keniola went to see his prisoners; he thought they came for Agathe.

In the meantime, he sent for Keniola. He had shown her affection and wanted to let her know that he would take care of her and would not want any harm to come to her and her children. Keniola came around a few minutes later with her twin sons, one on her back and the other in her arms. He went and took one from her arms and looked at the boy, smiled and said, "They are going to be very strong men." He laughed and handed him over to the mother.

"You sent for me?"

"Yes, I did. You look very happy and it seems you are being well taken care of, and your children look well-fed too," Bashir replied and then continued. "Have you found anything to keep you busy while you are at home here?"

Keniola replied, "Yes, I have been well taken care of and my children have kept me very busy."

Bashir thought, *so she is not going to tell me she has been going to the prison to see a prisoner of mine despite all the love and accommodation I have shown toward her.* "Would you like to join the women's weaving group during the market days? They weave clothes and sell to wholesalers who take it to the market," Bashir asked.

Keniola was thoughtful for a few minutes, then said, "I have looked at the weaving quality here and it surpasses what I have learned at Idumagbo. I believe I can do very well if I join the women, however, I have been going to the Arabic school with some of the princes and I do love the teachings of the Holy Book, algebra, geometry, philosophy and literature, writing and transcribing, and I would like to be able to continue to do that full-time."

Bashir was surprised by her answer and was even more surprised that she left out some major details of her daily itinerary. He received reports that she went to the school and that she was one of the brightest students. He was less concerned about that and now he thought that there was no harm in having her continue learning, so he replied, "If that is what you like, I give you my full support."

She was genuinely very pleased to hear him say that and she said thank you and waited for him to say she can go. Bashir asked, "Who are you? Where are you from and why were you captured and sold as a slave?"

Keniola, fearing that revealing who she really was might endanger Abdallab and Idumagbo where she came from, said, "I am no one and a child of no one, captured from my farms and sold into slavery."

For some reason Bashir did not believe this but gave the nod and dismissed her with a smile, saying he had some other state matters to address.

Keniola continued her education and training at the city school in Timbuktu for seventeen years and became one of the leading experts in diagnosing and treating diseases. She even pioneered some of the early surgeries of those days and her husband, Bashir, was so proud of her because she became so prominent that people from far-flung villages sought her knowledge and expertise.

Several years later, the twins had grown up to be teenager, then Abdallab fell ill in prison and Keniola was sent for in the middle of the night. Abdallab was never tried, as King Bashir completely forgot about him and Makuria in the prisons. Unknown to Keniola, Makuria had conspired with Abdallab and feigned serious illness and the prison wardens had allowed Makuria to carry him down to the sick yard (a compound where sick prisoners were isolated); this is where they were planning to escape from.

Free of the prison bars, their plan was to overpower the healers and then escape from there onwards. Unknown to them, Keniola had asked one of the guards to let her know immediately if anything was going on with the two prisoners so Keniola hurried to the sick bay, to the surprise of the guards.

On getting to the sick bay, she saw two of the prison guard's dead and was about to raise the alarm when he saw Abdallab and Makuria with bloody hands; she knew instantly that this was an escape and there was no real illness. Abdallab said, "We have to go, I have suffered enough here. I see you now have a great life here and if you want to stay here you are free to, but I have to go."

Just then the guard that came to inform Keniola stood up from where he was hiding and was about to run pass Keniola. Keniola snatched a spear left by one of the dead guards and threw it, hitting the guard in the back and killing him instantly. Abdallab beckoned to an unresponsive Keniola, saying, "It's time to go."

Keniola, coming out of her reverie, said, "To where? I have no homes again. I just threw away this new one."

"You are going back to your real home, your real position, friends, and family," Abdallab said.

Keniola knew she would not be able to live with the guilt of killing the guard and that the fear that she might even be discovered made her say,

"Now it seems I have no choice, I have to leave everything behind, just when I started liking my life here. It is all an illusion."

With that said, Abdallab grabbed her hand and they ran toward the nearest exit from the compound where they made it into the surrounding bushes. As soon as they got into the surrounding bush, Abdallab said, we need to travel southwards.

Keniola stopped both of them in their tracks and said, "Don't we have to get horses? It will take forever to get to Idumagbo from here."

Makuria replied, "No. Once they notice that horses were stolen, they will track the horses and it would be easy to have their horsemen track us and send an army after us. I would rather we go on foot because they will not know in which direction we went, even though the guards know that we are from the south."

Keniola remembered something and spirited back into the darkened city while Abdallab followed in close pursuit, but before leaving said to Makuria, "If we do not come back within a reasonable time, run for your life; and don't worry, if I am caught I will not bring them here."

He laughed and grinned, then followed quickly in the direction that Keniola went.

First, they could not find their way as they spirited through the darkened city streets and back corridors. Except for the occasional homeless, everywhere seemed relatively quiet. Keniola stopped in front of the compound that housed the school buildings, Abdallab, catching up, asked, "What do you want here? We should be on our way."

Keniola replied in a hushed tone, "Wait here; I need to get some curiosity potions."

Abdallab, not understanding, ran after her as they raced to one of the buildings. She opened the door and then picked up a leather satchel on the wooden table and started stuffing scrolls and a copy of the diamond sutra, which she had just started studying. They ran outside into the dark corridors until they got to where Makuria was.

When Makuria saw them approaching, he started running as well and they ran until they were tired. Abdallab was tired first, and Keniola had to stop. Makuria walked down to where they were and he asked, "Why did you stop running? We need to go. They are going to be after us very soon."

"We have to move in the night, avoiding other travelers on the road who may carry news back to the kingdoms and avoid major cities. If we are not eaten by the beasts on the way, we might as well become immortals."

Abdallab said, "If we put distance between us and them, we can stop at cities to get some well-cooked food. There will be no way Bashir and his army will get to us again."

"That is not true; Bashir and his people keep pigeons and they use them to send messages to their chiefs in other lands and Bashir also receives messages from his chiefs through these pigeons. As you can see if anyone sights us in these parts, it would take one pigeon message to capture us. So, don't let us delude ourselves, at least not until we are safely out of these environs."

Abdallab replied, "Well then, let's go, but I am dying for a good meal. I have fed like a rat in the last few years."

The next shift guards arrived on the scene, found the bodies of their colleagues, and also noticed that the prisoners Makuria and Abdallab were nowhere to be found so they raised the alarm, which woke the king up. The king was also informed that Keniola might have left with the prisoners, but her children were still inside the compound.

The king was very furious and as such, commanded the head of the army to bring out the cavalry and search the entire countryside for traces of the fugitives and bring them back to him. He also commanded that the pigeons be sent out with a message to all the chiefs that they should send a message back to him once they sighted the prisoners, and they provided a description of two men and a woman traveling together.

***

King Abiodun deposed his elder brother, King Oyeade, a year after their father, King Adebayo, died on a trading trip. He took over the reins of government and had his brother under house arrest and told everyone that his brother was ill and that his illness had incapacitated him.

Adeolu was a few years old around this time and did not understand what was going on. Adeolu was a product of King Oyeade and a Nubian slave girl who took care of him. The Nubian slave girl bore the child after Oyeade died and told everyone that the child belonged to a different man, and that was why Abiodun and his accomplices allowed him to live. The truth would later come out.

King Abiodun, who was the head of the security forces in Idumagbo, together with the chiefs, took over the rulership of Idumagbo and imprisoned the de jure king. The de jure king, unaware of what was going on since he was not feeling very well most of the time, was kept under house arrest until one day. Oyeade called for his nurse who kept him company and told her he would like to take a walk in the courtyard. The nurse agreed and led him down the stairs into the courtyard where the king's garden lies and a soldier on guard stopped her and told her that Oyeade was not allowed into the king's garden. Oyeade was shocked and asked, "Who gave you that kind of order when I am the king and the law giver of this city?"

The guard replied, "No you are not, and you have not been king for five years now. Your brother Abiodun has been crowned king and he has been ruling in your place."

Oyeade was shocked inside but appeared unfazed on the outside. "Do the people know that I am still alive?"

"Well, I did not know you were alive until I saw you now, so I am very well shocked. This is some news; it is as if you just came back from the dead," the guard replied subtly.

Then a young Salim appeared and asked that the guard take Oyeade back to his quarters, the king's quarters. Abiodun had lived in a different palace in the same palace compound and had some people worried; only a handful of people knew about Oyeade's existence. Everyone thought he died until he took a walk in the garden as reported by the guard who saw him. Abiodun seldom went into Oyeade's palace to speak with him. Abiodun gave orders that he should not be allowed to come outside, and Salim was his personal guard, who was also complicit. Oyeade had come out when Salim was running a different errand for Abiodun and had met an unsuspecting guard.

Salim pushed Oyeade inside the palace walls and asked the palace guard to come inside with him and stay on guard inside. Oyeade asked, "Soldier, what is going on here and why were you handling me roughly?"

Salim replied rudely, "If you know what is good for you, you should hurry inside and not talk." He then stepped outside and went to find Abiodun. He found Abiodun with his chiefs in the middle of the biennial festival planning session and whispered into his ear. He stood up and excused himself, then followed Salim, swore some curse words, then hurried toward the palace where he had ordered his brother to be held captive.

Before they reached the palace, he made up his mind to get rid of Oyeade once and for all. He had not been able to gather the willpower to do this all these years; he had thought he was going to pass away by himself, and that way he would have rid himself of the blood guilt. However, now, with the threat of exposure, he had been left with no choice except to murder his own brother. He asked Salim, "Who else knows about this apart from that guard?"

He responded, "No one."

"Where is the guard?" Abiodun asked a follow-up question to which Salim replied, "I asked him to stay with Oyeade in the palace."

"When we get inside the palace, take the guard out and finish him off and come back inside to help me with the corpse of Oyeade."

When they got inside, they found Oyeade naked, in a kneeling position, with his hands outstretched as if he was asking for something from an invisible person in the room. He looked up when they came in and he said,

"I am prepared to breathe my last. It took me a few moments, but I eventually figured it out; you have taken my position as king and I am no longer useful to you. I have one question before you silence my lips forever; although I cannot recollect when I stopped being king, why did you keep me alive all these years and for what purpose? Why haven't you killed me?"

Abiodun was taken aback by the appearance of his brother and his questions and was first afraid of moving closer to him. He then summoned up courage, took a garrote in his hand and went behind him and put the garrote around his neck, then slowly tightened it. Oyeade did not resist at all and he slowly yielded his spirit.

As soon as Abiodun found out that life had been snuffed out of his brother, he pushed his body down on the hard floor and said, "I did not want your blood on my hands but now I have it anyway." Then he spat on his dead body before hollering out to Salim, asking him, "What about the other guard?"

He replied, "It's done, and I have instructed the other guards to instruct his family and give him a proper burial."

He then asked Salim to bring digging tools. "What do we need digging tools for inside the house?" Salim queried.

"We need to dig the place where we will bury my brother. His house will continue to be inside these palace walls, and no one should know about this forever and ever."

After they dug the grave and buried his brother, he left to join the meeting of the festival planning and acted as if nothing ever happened.

A few years later, a debilitated Keniola walked into Idumagbo after a year of travel and nineteen years in exile. Abdallab had succumbed to some strange diseases on the way back. She had tried everything she could to save him, but the claws of the disease seemed too strong and it snatched him away from this earth. Makuria had deserted her a few days later by saying he was coming, and he never came back; she could never say whether he was captured by the night marauders who torment travelers on this road.

She had managed to reach the large oasis, now called Lake Chad, on the northern tip of the Mamabilla plateau inhabited by several tribes speaking an eclectic connection of languages. Most were friendly, since they were predominantly defenseless and had to pay the Maradian king for protection.

After traveling south for many days, she came to the river that traveled down south and emptied itself in the Atlantic Ocean; the river is currently called river Niger. She knew this river very well as she had traveled up north several times on it so she became more confident that she would eventually get home to Idumagbo.

On getting to the outskirts of Idumagbo, she noticed that the neighboring hamlets and villages were deserted. She first thought that maybe they had all been captured and killed by marauders but after she looked around the huts, she discovered that everything was neatly tucked away and it did not look like there had been any form of looting. Then it hit her suddenly; the yearly festival of thanks and sacrifice to the thousand gods. The whole city and the surrounding villages went into a three-day festival by traveling to a location where sacrifices were made to the thousand gods, the protectors of the realm and the ancestors of the Yobas. It was a time of feasting and camaraderie, and no one was expected to bear ill will toward anyone; a time for confession and a time for forgiveness, and it was a must that everyone attends, including children and nursing mothers. It was also a time of rest for everyone as there was great entertainment, wrestling contests among the men, and dancing contests among the women.

There were about five women's groups and the choice of tie and dye patterns on the clothes to wear and the duty to prepare the festival foods fell on one of the groups each year and this year it fell on the women's group that Keniola belonged to, the Eso. She was very famished, and she really wanted to eat something but during this time, eating any food not prepared at the house of the gods was strictly prohibited and the penalty could be ostracization or death. Well, hopefully they would understand her predicament as she grabbed some smoked yam pieces off the shelf ate a little bit and put some in a bag to eat on the remaining part of the journey.

She hurried and hopped on the path leading to the house of the gods, a specially prepared place where the festival is held every year. It was another two days' walk for her and she was hoping she could meet some last-minute stragglers on the road to share their company. She tarried along and met Sango and his family along the way.

Sango was taken aback when he saw her coming toward him. He ran toward her and genuflected before her, and praised her by saying, "Welcome, queen of all queens, the one that goes into the lion's den and returns unscathed, the benevolent and the benefactor of all Yobas, the one that is equal only to the gods."

Keniola felt happy seeing someone praise her like this in such a long time so she smiled and collapsed into Sango's arms. Sango quickly ordered that a horse be brought so she could ride to the festival grounds. Keniola said she needed some rest and company first, so she was laid on a sleeping cloth by the side of the road while others surrounded and sang to her.

Before long, a young Adeolu and his Nubian mother, Elisabeth, came along. They saw the commotion and the crowd on the side of the road, so they decided to stop and see what was going on too. A year after Abiodun usurped Oyeade's throne, Adeolu was born in the palace of the king. When the mother could not say who the father was, King Abiodun sent her away and she went to live in a farm village far from the city, where they lived a life of a peasant. There was a distinguishing birthmark on Oyeade's shoulder which incidentally repeated itself on Adeolu's shoulder. No one knew about this but Abiodun, Aremu, and Elisabeth, his mother.

Adeolu wanted more but his mother cautioned him against it and said they should be contented with their lives. Adeolu went on to join the army in Karounwi, and his wisdom and heroism set him apart from the rest of the other soldiers.

A year before this, King Abiodun nearly lost his life during a battle with one of their enemies and Adeolu had come to his aid, only for him to sustain injuries and save the king's life. After the battle, Abiodun and Aremu were present when they took off Adeolu's clothes and they saw the mark on his shoulders, and both became transfixed for a long time as they continuously stared at the young man that saved the king's life.

After he became well, the king celebrated him as a hero of Idumagbo and asked him to invite his mother, and once both King Abiodun and Aremu saw the mother, they knew instantly that this was Oyeade's son and the mother had deceived them.

Aremu went on to befriend Adeolu and they became very close friends, shielding him away from the prying eyes of the king and his chiefs. Aremu would later tell Adeolu's mother that he knew that Oyeade was the father of Adeolu. Elisabeth denied it.

Adeolu and his mother lived far away from the prying eyes of the public and now that Adeolu had become a war hero of Idumagbo, he had pressured his mother to come to the festival with him. When they came closer to the road leading to the festival grounds, Elisabeth saw that this was the former queen of the land sleeping peacefully, Adeolu did not know who that was and he asked his mom, who had stepped back quickly after seeing who was resting by the roadside. He saw the look of consternation in her eyes and he drew her aside and asked, "Who is that?"

She responded, "Your grandmother, former queen of Idumagbo, Keniola."

Adeolu was instantly elated. Now he would have someone he could confide in, and someone of immense value and power in the polity who could help him reach his dreams. He studied the environment carefully and saw Sango in deep conversation with some people in his entourage, so he moved closer so as to eavesdrop on the conversation. His mother gently tugged at his shirt to discourage him from poking his nose in this business. Elisabeth was a scarred woman, a woman that had been captured and sold into slavery, raped several times until Oyeade saw her and admired her beauty and she bore him

a son. Adeolu listened carefully and he overheard Sango saying to Salim and

some of his entourage that the appearance of the queen portended danger for

King Abiodun and one of them asked, "Why is that? Shouldn't our king

rejoice at the reappearance of his mother? Should it not be a thing of joy? As

a matter of fact, I think the king might just declare a double celebration."

Sango replied sneeringly, "A kid does not know what a potent

concoction is but would rather call it a vegetable."

Sango gave the young man a terrible look, which signified that he'd

better shut his trap now. Sango said, "We had better send someone along to

go warn the king quickly of the arrival of his mother so as to prevent an

unpleasant surprise."

Sango replied, "Good idea." He chose someone and told him to

gallop ahead and inform the king of the arrival of Queen Keniola back to

Idumagbo.

Adeolu sensed that something was wrong immediately and that a

plan was in the making to accuse his grandmother of some crime and deny

her some privileges due to her, so he moved quickly and returned to his

mother and told her he was going to stand guard with her. His mother's tears

and cries could not prevail him of acting on his desires and so he crept beside

Queen Keniola, who was already awake and was also cautiously studying the people around her.

When Adeolu approached her, she smiled and Adeolu whispered his introduction into her ear saying, "I am Adeolu, son of Oyeade and Elisabeth. I was not yet born when you were captured, and it looks like your return is creating anxiety among the chiefs and the rulership of Idumagbo. Sango has just sent someone to warn the king of your arrival. King Oyeade passed away shortly after you were declared missing and his brother has ruled in his place ever since." Adeolu had listened to many stories and myths about Keniola when he was growing up, she was a champion Archer and bested many men who competed with her and now she is here in the flesh.

Keniola nodded gently and smiled, not giving anything away from her facial expressions. She said to him, "Stay beside me and we can travel down to the house of the gods together." She then called on Sango to issue an order and asked him to bring the horses; that she would like to start riding now. She also asked that a horse be provided for Adeolu too. Sango looked at Adeolu, remembered him as the war hero of Idumagbo, drew him aside and said, "Don't dabble into what you do not understand."

Adeolu gave no response.

Sango then said to Keniola, "We can only provide a horse for you and a guard who will ride with you."

Keniola replied, "When did you start countermanding my orders? I have chosen a guard and he is now responsible for my safety and protection until I get to the place where my son, King Abiodun, is."

Sango was taken aback as to how she got to know that Abiodun was the new king but being a warrior, he knew when he had been trounced and had no further cards to play and quickly acceded to the request by bellowing out to his subjects to bring two horses. Adeolu took one and asked his mother to come along and helped her on top of it. He climbed on it too. He was surprised at the agility of his grandmother when he saw her mount the horse without any help. Even Sango was surprised, and he said, "We will all ride beside you."

Keniola replied, "Then you will have to hurry because once night falls, we will be late for the opening ceremony of the festivities." As soon as she said this, she whipped the horse into line and charged forward into the early nightfall with Adeolu and his mother in close pursuit. Sango quickly called on his entourage to get on their horses as well and they charged forward quickly into the night. The remaining folks without horses also ran after them.

On getting to the festival grounds, the messenger quickly located Abiodun and told him of the arrival of his mother, Keniola, and also of the half-eaten food found in her sack of books. Abiodun was shocked and was very afraid and did not know what the next move would be. This was something unexpected and a few minutes later, Keniola galloped in followed

closely by Adeolu on a horse. He quickly descended the throne created for

him and genuflected before his mother as she alighted from the horse.

Keniola smiled, greeted him, and asked, "Where is Oyeade?"

Abiodun stood up and said, "He passed away. His disease caught up

with him after you left. It became worse, and I believe that was what led to

his untimely death."

Keniola nodded without any emotions and asked another question.

"I see that you were the one on throne currently; what happened to Oyeade's

sons? His wife was pregnant when I was brutally captured and sent to exile."

(She never wanted to say she way sold into slavery so as not to demean the

throne.)

Abiodun replied, "She had a stillbirth and died at childbirth, so

Oyeade has no surviving legitimate children." He stammered, then continued

and said, "However, we later found out that he had an illegitimate child, and

that is the young man that rode in with you just now."

Keniola heaved a sigh. "So according to the rules of our fathers, the

rulership of the kingdom of Idumagbo should ultimately rest with me as the

regent when the king passes away, before it becomes the turn of the children."

Abiodun had never heard of such rules before so he turned around

to see which of the elders around could corroborate it. This was the moment of truth for the whole kingdom, so no one dared lie. His chiefs, Arese and Abioye, looked down and pretended they did not hear what Keniola said for fear of not knowing who would win this battle of wits.

Babagun stood up and some other members of the Oro. Babagun said, "This is the way it has always been for the first set of people that first inhabited these lands; our kings have always put their queens before their children, particularly when they have not named any heir to the throne. They have done this to ensure that the queen does not get sidelined when the children take over. It is the prerogative of the queen to say she will relinquish the regency in favor of the first son. If there are no sons, the regent reigns supreme until such a time when a worthy king is found and crowned."

There was a hushed silence on the grounds such that if a pin dropped, everyone would hear.

Then Sango rode in, shattering the silence of the night. He alighted from the horse, surveyed the mood of the entire body of citizens, looked at his king and saw that his demeanor was very dull.

Abiodun spoke again, clutching at the last straws to save his rulership. "I will vacate the throne for my mother only if my mother has not committed any foul act that would be defiling our gods." Then Sango raised his hands and asked that he wanted to speak.

Keniola figured out quickly what was going to be said and she mentioned, "It is about time to start the festivities. Let's start with some wrestling matches and some feast. What special meal do we have for this celebration?"

She continued, "We will come to the part where we speak about offenses later on," effectively seizing control of the situation and power.

Abiodun looked at the throne he had constructed and could no longer ascend to it. Someone came back and said that the wrestlers were not ready yet. In the meantime, Sango had slipped into the gathering of the Oro cult members and had shared what he saw with Keniola. Then Oloro, second-in-command to Babagun, asked to speak. Abiodun quickly recognized him and said, "Speak, for you have listening ears."

Oloro, a very short and stout man, said a report had just reached him that a significant member of the ruling class had defiled the gods by performing an act which is sacrilegious to the gods. "We would invite the person to come out and confess before he is accused and charged."

Keniola knew this report was made to castigate her but she refused to cower. She would rather play her own card so as to be on the attack and to continue with her delay tactics, hoping it would yield fruitful results. She said, "It was confirmed that prominent members of the ruling class were responsible for the assassination of the king and the kidnap of the queen. Why was there no investigation done?"

As soon as she finished the sentence, she knew she played the wrong card because she did not take into consideration that there might be a lot of conspirators; she sensed this immediately because of the expressions on the faces of Abiodun and the chiefs. Since no one answered, Oloro continued, saying, "Our beloved former Queen Keniola was caught eating yams before the declaration, which we all know our gods frown upon."

Abiodun spoke up immediately, seizing control of the situation. "If such an allegation is proven, such person cannot be in a position of authority; one that does not respect our deities is not fit to govern us," he declared.

He then turned to Keniola and asked how she intended to plead with respect to the weighty allegation brought against her.

Keniola knew she was trapped at this time and she decided to weigh her words carefully; otherwise, she might be put to death at the hands of her own people, a scenario she had not considered previously. She had thought herself invincible after she survived a kidnap, multiple sexual abuses, and slavery. She said, "I have come a long way from queen to slavery and a very long and harrowing journey, survived many wild animals, many roaming marauders who were looking for prey, lost many friends, lost my husband, lost my son, and rose up again to become one of the most learned in

Timbuktu where I was held and would later escape and leave everything behind because of my love for my land."

She sobbed and then continued. "I trekked many days without food and did not even know that there was a festival about to start and that the no eating of yams was in place until I met other people on the road here, so I ask that this law should not be applicable to me because of my predicament."

Many of the women and children that sat and listened to her wept and Elisabeth led the pack by coming forward and hugging her before Abiodun put a stop to it by saying, "Everyone should go back to their seats. This is not meant to be an emotional affair but a religious and legalistic affair and should be dealt with in the same manner."

Adeolu raised his hands to speak on behalf of his just reunited grandmother. The king was flustered but had no choice but to call on him to speak, as was the custom at Idumagbo, especially when it came to such festivals in this part of town.

"I greet the king and salute the esteemed chiefs of this town. I saw my grandmother for the first time today and I am very glad that she is here, hale and hearty after a harrowing journey and I thoroughly understand that she has done something wrong in the eyes of our gods and must be punished." He paused and looked around and saw faces of anger, consternation, and fear in people's eyes.

Then he continued in a hoarse whisper, "Let's appeal to the sense of forgiveness from the gods," then added humorously, "I mean, the gods love Keniola too; they would not want her to die," oblivious of the ongoing power dynamics.

"We have a duty to serve our gods with our highest level of devotion and we as representatives of our gods have a responsibility to correct any wrongdoing on behalf of the gods and punish every crime committed against our gods," said Abiodun.

A few people chorused ayes while others gave a non-committal nod in response. Abiodun, glancing around, identified those that were in support and against it before continuing again. "Our former queen, my mother, Keniola, has been found guilty by the people for failing to abide by the fasting rules preceding our yearly festival, which we all know the gods clearly frown upon."

Then he paused for a brief moment, looked around, saw the uneasy calm around before pronouncing the sentence. "The queen will be spared of the ultimate punishment, which is death, because of her harrowing experience and her travails and because of that, we will send her to live outside of the city walls for the rest of her life. She will only come into the city if she seeks permission from the king."

After seeing the look on everyone's face changed to one of relief because they knew that this was very magnanimous of the king and usually a death sentence was passed of which there was no appeal. Then the king turned to Keniola and asked whether she had any words.

Keniola stood up with tears in her eyes and said she would gladly spend the rest of her life outside the city, but she would like Adeolu and his mother to come and stay with her. The king said, "Adeolu is a war hero and we will gladly oblige you." The king laughed at the scorn and said, "Is that all?" She nodded affirmatively in response, and thus she began another life of exile in her own city. She went on to live in exile for about ten years before the epidemic and during this time she trained and taught Adeolu medicine and surgery, astronomy, arithmetic, geometry, and the healing science. Adeolu later went on to learn other things from himself and remains the only person that defeated Keniola in archery. After they had increased the target distance many times, Adeolu had perfected the art of shooting the arrows in an upward trajectory and using the resulting potential energy to cover the rest of the distance, he also added some feathers to the tail of the arrow, a mechanism no one has done before.

Grandmother was very impressed and Adeolu had shown her how he arrived at the process through one of the geometric and parabolic equations she had taught to him earlier. Grandmother knew that his grandson is a maestro.

The Council of Rulers

Present-day Idumagbo, just before the break of dawn, Adeolu hurried quickly toward the palace for the first council of rulers in which Keniola would be presiding. He loved his grandmother but felt that she was overreaching and not doing what was right for the people of Idumagbo. This was the right time to let the people have a voice in the decisions that affect them. Although she had left her family out of the council, he had a nagging feeling that something might not be just right with Keniola. She used to be able to confide in him and suddenly she was putting some distance between them, which was making him feel kind of weird now. He never once thought that she could leave him out of the ruling council but when he thought about it again, he knew she was probably right and was doing it so as to remove all signs of corruption.

The previous day he had gone back to his former compound that the previous king confiscated, and he had seen that the compound had grown derelict due to his absence. This morning as he crossed the market square, a feeling of déjà vu came over him as he remembered the last time, he did this, which led to his charges and eventual exile.

Then from the corner of his eye, he saw Ibraheem the Arab going into an empty market stall. He did not pay much attention at first until he saw Itiade going into the same stall and a few minutes later Fero, his own daughter. Now his curiosity was aroused, and he knew he had to stay hidden to see who else was coming in for this meeting. Then a few minutes later, Aremu also entered the same stall. He could not remember seeing Aremu at the palace yesterday and he thought he may have come and then decided not to come to the palace. He waited a little and could not see anyone else go in and there was no way he could move closer without being seen. He decided to continue the walk down to the palace and he would have to ask Fero what was going on there.

Aremu arrived at the outskirts of the city with about a thousand of Araba's men and he had been met by an emissary from Araba who told him that the city was theirs and that it would be proper to leave the army in the camp and come with a few men into the city. He then sent a messenger to Ibraheem, one of his most trusted allies, to meet him at a secret market stall and was surprised to find Fero and Itiade at the meeting.

Ibraheem spoke first, since he was the only one who knew about everybody that was coming to this meeting. He then said, "You are all welcome to this august meeting. I have called this meeting because I believe we need to help the regency choose a good successor to the king."

Aremu said immediately, "Why is Fero here? She is not supposed to be here; she is not in line for the throne. If she does not leave immediately, I will have to leave," he said conclusively, looking indignantly at Ibraheem.

Ibraheem looked unperturbed and simply said, "Keniola specifically asked that Fero be brought to this meeting."

Then there came a cacophony of voices; everyone was trying to speak together at the same time. "What do you mean, Keniola said what? I was under the impression that this meeting was at your behest and was a secret from Keniola. If I had known she organized this meeting, I would not have been here at all," said Aremu.

"And neither would I; if I had known that a traitor was coming to this meeting," Itiade said.

Fero laughed aloud, which made all of them stop and look at her. She said, "Keniola is now the master puppeteer. She pulls the strings and we all dance to her whims and caprices. She formed a ruling council that she heads, then she forms a rebel council and puts a foreigner in charge. Let me tell you, I think I understand the game she is trying to play on us; she is trying to get us to kill each other!" she said.

Fero said this with her tongue in cheek, baiting Ibraheem to defend himself. Ibraheem, seeing that this was not going the way he had planned and having not anticipated any hostilities toward Keniola but expecting hostilities among these contenders for the throne, was really a source of trouble for the overall plan. He could not adjourn the meeting until the objective of the meeting itself was met. Keniola had set the meeting objective after he sought audience with her immediately after she announced the ruler's council. He had been invited to Keniola's inner chambers to discuss it. He had initially thought the discussion with Keniola had gone very well because he had gone to her with his credentials, hoping to convince her to give him a position so he can start whipping up support and sentiments in her favor, thereby retain the regency at least for the remaining part of her life on this earth. He was still telling her how he could be useful to her regency before she surprised him by saying that she was making him the topmost chief in the kingdom, the right-hand chief, and she had an assignment for him immediately.

The assignment would be to collapse the opposition and make them lame ducks or get them to finish themselves off so that she can reign for as long as she was alive. The main contenders for the throne would be Aremu and Itiade. She then told him that she could handle Araba and that he would be satisfied when he saw what was on the table for him and his men. She did not share the offer details with him and asked him to go figure out how he could achieve the objective she had placed in his lap.

So, he was here now, and all his plans seemed to be falling apart. Seeing the looks on their faces, Ibraheem started by refuting Fero's statement about Keniola's diabolical machinations and he said, "It is quite untrue that Keniola would want you to kill each other. You are all her grandchildren and one a great-grandchild, albeit all from different mothers, so she would not want any bad things to happen to you all. As a matter of fact, she told me how much she loves you all and would want someone amongst you to succeed her, but she does not want the succession to be a free-for-all fight that can result in blood feuds, so this meeting is actually a conciliatory meeting," he concluded.

Everyone seemed to be appeased, as the looks on their faces became ones of relief. Aremu then asked again, "Why is Fero here? What purpose does she serve in this meeting? She cannot be a king and she has no royal blood whatsoever. Is Keniola planning to pass the regency onto her?" He stared interrogatively at Ibraheem.

Ibraheem was unperturbed, as he already expected such comments, so he said, "Fero is here to ensure that peace reigns between both of you." He looked at Aremu and then at Itiade.

"She will be mediator because of the known angst between the both of you."

Itiade said, "I have no ill feelings toward Aremu; he is my uncle, and ordinarily he should have been in line to succeed my father, but he is illegitimate, and as such, disinherited from the throne of our forefathers. He has no claims toward the throne at all."

Aremu flew into a rage and said, "If you knew what you were talking about you would keep your mouth shut because if you knew who *your* father was, you would keep your mouth shut."

"I have heard the same rumor flying around about you being my father. It is very hard to believe that I can come from you; I have very good manners and moreover, no one is going to believe this."

"If I claim you as my son, it would invalidate my claim to the throne because I would have committed a sacrilege by cheating with the king's wife to make a son, so you see what dilemma I am in."

"What that tells me then is that you are not man enough to be my father."

"I have very limited options available to me in order for me to get the throne of my fathers—and one is killing you!" And with that he drew his sword and cut and thrust into the stomach of an unsuspecting Itiade, killing him instantly.

Fero and Ibraheem, both shocked, took to their heels in different directions as far as their legs could carry them. Aremu whipped out a whistle made from thin bamboo, blew it hard, and five of his trusted men materialized behind some bushes. He instructed them to give chase and catch her alive. They were able to catch Fero, so they bound her and took her far into the bush and kept her prisoner.

Meanwhile, Ibraheem had run as fast as he could into the bush while Aremu was hot on his trail. Aremu finally caught up with a spent Ibraheem. Ibraheem pleaded with him that he should not kill him and that he would keep his secret and be his support in the regent's court. Aremu was very confused and did not know what to do and kept on cursing that Itiade had provoked him, knowing what had transpired between them over the years and for him now to be talking like that to him. Ibraheem massaged his ego and said, "Don't worry; Itiade probably deserved what was coming to him."

He then continued and asked him, "Please do not kill Fero, because she is carrying Araba's child."

This made him curse more. After the curses subsided, he said, "What next? I cannot hope to take the city with Araba's men now. Who is going to support me for killing the city's beloved hero?"

Ibraheem placated him and said, "Don't worry, there is a lot that needs to be done and we still have a lot to achieve. We need to find a way to implicate someone in the death of Itiade."

He told Aremu of Tela, his former servant turned traitor, and said, "We should quickly go and capture him and frame him for the murder of

Itiade so as to put all the blame on the Maradians." He concluded by saying, "I will vouch for you and you will be exonerated, but please remember me."

Deep inside of him, he knew that Aremu had fallen into a well-laid trap and it would be extremely difficult to extricate himself. He had only said those placating words to safeguard his own life.

Aremu felt very relieved and asked two of his men who joined him to go back into the city and find Tela, deceive him and lure him to a lonely place and then kill him. Once the deed was done, they should come back and let him know and they would all go into the palace together with the bodies and shed crocodile tears.

Adeolu got to the palace right on time as Keniola was being ushered into the room where the court was going to be held that morning. The ruling council's inaugural meeting was held shortly before the beginning of this general one, which was supposedly for the planning of the festival. Adeolu quickly glanced around and observed the presence of Araba and Babagun right beside Keniola and Bankudi standing tall behind her. He learned Bankudi had been given the title of regent's chief protector. Ogunde was sitting down quietly on a stool in front of Keniola, carefully avoiding his eyes. They had not spoken to each other since after he was announced as the economic chief of the whole city.

Adeolu had taken a detour to his caves to get the medicine gourds he wanted to prepare for his daughter, Fero, later during the day. He'd discovered that she was pregnant yesterday as well, and he made a mental note to start taking good care of her; she was the only one he had now. So, when he did not see any Fero and Itiade on the seat an alarm bell went on in his head, but he refused to panic just yet.

Just before Keniola declared the meeting open, in came Ibraheem and Aremu. Keniola seemed pleased to see Aremu's arrival. She said, "This afternoon, we will begin preparations toward the commencement of the yearly festival of the thousand gods. We have selected some of our men that would proceed to the grounds and make it ready for us in three days' time. Our women have also promised us that our clothes will be ready by the time we get to the hallowed grounds. The foodstuffs to be prepared during the festivities will also be transported by of our women who will be accompanying the men on the trip.

"I am also pleased to have in our presence Aremu, who has just joined us this morning from his exile." She then laughed mirthlessly, a laughter that Aremu perceived was directed toward him and which seemed to taunt him as he rose to speak.

The words slowly formed and crawled out of his mouth as he spoke. "I am pleased to be here and believe that our Regent Keniola is steering us in the right direction and we are pleased to have her as our temporary head ruler. But we urge her to sooner or later hand over power to the rightful heir to the throne. I, Aremu, the first among the rest, the beloved of the gods, should be crowned king as soon as possible."

As soon as he finished his statement, Ogunde decided to speak and said, "We as a people have banded together over the years, lived in caves and learned from other cooperating bands of men sojourning across this vast space we call our home. We never had kings, we had councils in which everyone was allowed to speak freely—women, men, and children—everyone was heard. We had security councils, the occult where we freely traded our healing secrets among the initiates, but never kings. The title of king was brought to us by sojourners from the East who took over our lands and gave us new cultures. Our current regent is an offspring of one of these sojourners; her uncle Abdallab benefited immensely from the reigns of his family members in Idumagbo. They became rich and thus impoverished many of our people."

While he was speaking, everyone's head at the court kept bobbing up and down, signifying that he spoke the truth. He looked around, seeing that to every word he spoke there was not a dissenting voice, not even Ibraheem. So, he continued.

"We have had great things also come from the East; crops like corn, beans, and tomatoes, which we farmed in large numbers and are able to trade and bargain with. We have also had many animals brought to us, which we also reared and traded across many cities in our realm. We had currency introduced to us, which made trade and bargaining easier for us. We have had medicine and healing potions brought to us, which elongated a lot of our lives and most recently, we have had education brought to us through our most learned Regent Keniola, who has taught what she learned to Adeolu, who had used what he learned, like algebra and geometry, to develop machines like carts to improve our lives, improve our navigation at sea and on land. But the concept of kings has been the debilitating factor that has caused blood feuds and deaths among family members and friends and I say today we should let the regent lead us on the path and restore us unto glory."

All that were present stood up and applauded everything Ogunde said. Keniola stood up and said, "Aremu is not wrong to demand the throne but he should first learn to stop living in the past and start living in the present, where we have decided as a nation to move on. We are going to carry out a series of experiments in making leadership choices. I and the ruling council will be directing the affairs of the nation in the interim.

"One of such experiments is this ruling council, and the next will be to get our people to select who represents them in the ruling council and we will see how that one pans out. But in the meantime, we must ensure that all hands are on deck to forestall any disturbance and any rebellion during this transition period."

As she finished speaking, some of Aremu's men entered into the king's court. They conversed with Aremu while everyone looked on. Some of the palace guards also came in and they spoke with Babagun and Araba, who then quickly whispered something into Keniola's ear before following Aremu and his men into the palace grounds where the bodies of Itiade and Tela lay.

In the meantime, Keniola stepped into the inner courtyard and beckoned to Ibraheem to follow her. She then asked, "What happened? Give me a summary of who killed whom—and where is Fero?"

Ibraheem replied, "Aremu fell into the trap and killed Itiade and he is trying to use Tela as the fall guy."

"Good, very good. Now let's join the others in the palace grounds," said Keniola. On getting outside into the courtyard, they could see that Aremu seemed to be in control of the situation, praising his men for catching the culprit in good time.

As Keniola appeared on the palace grounds she looked around and said, "Who is going to tell me what is going on here?"

Babagun looked at Aremu and asked him to say what he just told everyone. Meanwhile, Adeolu had knelt beside Itiade and was checking out the circumstances surrounding Itiade's death. He was busy inspecting the cut-open body parts and the expression on Itiade's face as he departed this earth. Aremu spoke once more, saying, "My poor little nephew has met an untimely death at the hands of Tela, a known traitor who traded secrets with the Maradian and almost got all of us killed."

Keniola asked the first question. "Where was Itiade killed?"

Aremu replied, "Somewhere around the market, as reported by my men. My men saw Tela commit the act, gave chase, and then tried to arrest him but he resisted, and they had to kill him too."

Ibraheem spoke up, giving tacit support to Aremu by saying, "We only have the gods to thank that Aremu's men were around when the incident happened; otherwise, it would have gone unpunished. I suggest we begin preparations toward the burial of our prince and hero, Itiade."

Adeolu stood up from where he was, looked directly at Ibraheem and said, "Were you not with Aremu and Itiade and Fero this morning?"

Ibraheem replied quickly, saying, "No, I was at home with my family."

He knew that was a lie because he had seen them earlier nevertheless followed up with a different line of question that mattered to him most, "Where is my Fero? She is the only one I have left in this world. What did you do to her?" He looked at Aremu.

Aremu said, "I have not seen her since I arrived in this town, but we will start a search for her immediately."

Araba too then became suspicious and beckoned to Bankudi to not let Aremu leave the palace grounds. Bankudi walked up to Aremu and attempted to dispossess him of his sword and Aremu's men pushed back on Bankudi, which led to a free-for-all melee resulting in a flurry of fights. Bankudi and Araba engaged Aremu and quickly dispossessed him of his sword and when his men saw that he had been subdued, they gave up their swords as well.

Adeolu spoke again after the fights ended and said, "Ibraheem, I saw you this morning together with Fero and Itiade and if Itiade is dead, does that mean Fero is also dead?"

Everyone turned in the direction of Ibraheem and he said, "I was with them previously but left her and Itiade in the company of Aremu. I met them to intimate them of the plans of our regent for our kingdom and I wanted to use the opportunity to convince Aremu to be part of the future of Idumagbo. I left them together and came back to the palace for this meeting."

Babagun, who had never shown any affection for Ibraheem because of his foreign roots, spoke while looking at Keniola and said, "It seems Ibraheem knows more than he is willing to divulge. Do you want us to arrest him as well and apply the truth serum on him?"

Keniola responded, "We will let Aremu do the talking. If Aremu can confess to the crime and he implicates Ibraheem, then we know we have a criminal in our midst. In the meantime, we will suspend his announcement as the king's right hand."

She then rose, which signified the end of the court for that day. The guards dragged Aremu on to the king's prisons followed closely by Bankudi, Araba, and Adeolu. An ominous silence passed as they journeyed through the back-city roads that lead to the king's prisons.

Upon arriving at the prisons, they took him directly to a private room and Araba asked him again, "Where are you keeping Fero?"

Aremu refused to answer any of their questions, saying, "I do not know, I am not her keeper, and I was not with her during the incident."

His other men were then taken to a different room where Bankudi started dishing out blows to them in a bid to make them confess where they had hidden Fero or whether she had been killed. Adeolu was left alone outside the prison gates and was not able to gain entry and so could not partake in the investigations and interrogations.

Araba came back outside and told Adeolu that they would need truth serum for Aremu. "Could you help us prepare one?" Adeolu took his leave a few minutes later thinking a waste of time staying around when he could not do anything to help the situation. He decided to go to the caves and get the truth serum. He had to travel to certain places to get certain ingredients he would use in preparation and he knew that the journey would take him at least three days but he knew nothing else he could do in the meantime, so he set forth.

Ibraheem attempted to see Keniola, but Keniola had instructed Babagun not to let anyone come inside her court, particularly Ibraheem. Ibraheem thought instantly about what Keniola might be up to and he knew that he had better find a solution to absolve himself from this mess, otherwise he would also be having his head on a stake soon. So, he hurried in the direction of the city prisons and kept out of sight so that no one could see him. He hid and watched Adeolu in the distance for a while and as soon as Adeolu left, he went into the prison where he was allowed inside. Bankudi saw him and came over to him and there he told Bankudi, "I have some truth serums that we can use to extract the truth from Aremu's guards. They will confess in a few minutes and we will have evidence to nail Aremu."

Bankudi grinned and showed him his fist and said, "Only this is capable of breaking them."

"Take me to where they are," Ibraheem said.

Bankudi him took him to where the prisoners were and said to him, "You know you are no longer a chief and you are not supposed to be here, but the regent called me aside and asked me to help you with anything you want to do and if I cannot help you with any matter, I should let her know immediately what the matter is."

Ibraheem smiled and said, "That is why I am telling you, take the serum from me and administer it on the prisoners and let's get their confessions."

"The question is, I do not know whether this is something I should just escalate to her or just take the serum and administer it," said Bankudi.

"Take the damn serum and administer it."

Bankudi replied to him, "Don't worry, the boys are going to break soon, and we will find Fero." He showed Ibraheem his fist and then grinned sheepishly.

Ibraheem said, "This will make them confess quicker and we will know that it is the absolute truth and if you do so, I will not forget this favor for the rest of my life, and neither will the regent."

Bankudi looked into Ibraheem's eyes and seemed to think that this might actually be quicker, asked him to go bring it. A feeling of relief came over Ibraheem. He then said, "Where is Aremu being kept?"

Bankudi responded, "Araba is in charge and he will not even allow anyone near him."

"Then I'd better go quickly," said Ibraheem, hurrying out of the prison huts. Ibraheem knew that Aremu would not confess to anything, as he would believe that the best would happen to him anyways and he knew that once he confessed, then the opportunity to become a king would vanish. His only fears were the two guards who saw him with Aremu, and they were the ones that took Tela's life; they knew the whereabouts of the camp and probably the location where they were keeping Fero.

He went back home and retrieved the poison potion made from a rare kind of mushrooms that produces hallucinogenic effects before paralyzing the whole body and eventually snuffing life out of the body. On the road he noticed that people of the city were in a festive mood; they had just resisted an incursion into their territory and won a war against the dreaded people of Timbuktu. He thought, "Innocence can be very exhilarating; little do they know what kind of news they will hear soon."

The kingdom of Idumagbo had not done this festival in many years. The last king just could not afford it and he had other priorities, so he just kept postponing it. Now a new king, a woman, has made it possible; she was their darling.

Araba sat opposite Aremu for a while and asked, "Why did you do it? We had an agreement that every operation you would do had to have my imprimatur and you betrayed me. I brought you into my camp, I trusted you with the command of my soldiers and yet you still do this?"

Aremu stared at him and said nothing for a while, then spoke.

"Fero is not dead. I will tell you where she is, and you can go get her. I did not kill Itiade, I only wounded him; but Itiade and Fero attacked me first and I was able to overpower them, disabling Itiade by cutting some blood vessels in his legs."

Araba found that information very unpleasant; not because he distrusted Aremu, but because he also knew that Aremu might be trying to use his love for Fero to manipulate him. He continued to stare at Aremu without giving away any emotions; he nudged him on. "So, what happened after you killed Itiade?" he asked Aremu.

Aremu said, "I did not kill Itiade, He was alive the last time I saw him . Fero was with him as well, my boys took her prisoner."

"So why did your boys report to us that it was Tela that killed Itiade?" Araba queried.

"I did not know that the boys killed Tela until I saw them report it at the palace court just before I could get some time to inform the court of what went wrong. I ought to be sitting on that throne, it belongs to me. My father before me was King Adebayo, I am his direct descendant!" He raised his voice in a little fit of anger.

Araba said, "I believe you. Now tell me where Fero is so I can go and bring her back." Aremu described the location of the camp where she was kept and the soldiers that were on guard at the camp location. Araba stood up and exited the prison hut where Aremu was kept. He spoke to the guards at the door. "Do not let anyone inside." They murmured a yes response.

Araba then called some of his guard commanders and they brought a detachment of soldiers to him and they all got on their horses and galloped in the direction of the camp location. Araba kept on thinking as something at the back of his mind kept on telling him that he had made a mistake; he should have verified Aremu's stories with the captured guards. At the same time, he did not want Fero suffering a single minute after he had the information about her whereabouts, and he was in a position to do something about it.

He was also troubled about Aremu's revelations about Itiade and Fero fighting together. For what reason can they be fighting together? were they lovers again? He shook the thought away from his head and concentrated on the task at hand; rescuing Fero. He knew the next thing would be to get the captured guard's stories before he could come to a decision. He then increased the speed at which he was riding the horse and every one of the members did the same and they rode across the forests, darting through trees and fallen branches until they got to the first guards at the tip of the camp.

Araba issued orders for them to take him to the location where the guards were. The border guards then took Araba straight to the tents where

Fero was kept. As soon as she saw Araba, she whipped one of the guards a dirty slap. Araba asked one of the guards to arrest him and they should bring him along. Fero snatched the key to her chain from the belt of one of the other guards and as soon as she freed herself from the chains around her feet, she jumped into Araba's arms.

Araba felt relieved and quite comfortable with her in his arms and they just held each other for some time while all the soldiers looked on and some just looked away. She then said, "Let's find Aremu. He murdered Itiade in cold bold and without any provocation."

Araba said, "Don't worry, we have him under arrest. But he claimed that both of you attacked him first."

"That is an absurd statement. Why would we attack him? And would I join Itiade in attacking him? in any case, Ibraheem was there and he can corroborate this in case you do not believe me," she replied.

"Very well then, let's get back to Idumagbo as quickly as we can so we can get to the bottom of this." With that, he helped her on top of her horse while he mounted his own and they raced toward Idumagbo as quickly as they had come, cutting through the same thickset bushes.

In the past the horses used to be very sick as soon as they came in contact with the tropical forests, but Adeolu had come up with a prevention medication that you could mix with the meals and a special potion that you could get if the horses fell sick. He had shared this information among the Oro cult members, and they all possessed this knowledge and they profited from it.

"The nearest Oro cult member's compound from here will take at least a day's walk and riding," said one of the soldiers riding with them."

Araba knelt down beside the horse, gave the horse an embrace, and asked one of the soldiers to take the horse to the herbalist member. Fero sat behind Araba on the horse and they journeyed toward Idumagbo as fast as they could.

On getting back to the prison, they went straight into the hut where the other two Aremu boys were kept. Upon entering he saw Ibraheem and Bankudi siting glue-faced to the two chained prisoners on the floor who were foaming in their mouth. He knew instantly that they were not going to survive so he said, "Why are these boys dying? Who executed this killing? Between the two of you, I know it cannot be Bankudi. I have known him half of my life, so Ibraheem, start talking."

He looked at Ibraheem very hard trying to see if his ugly face could make him confess quickly but he smiled back at him. Araba being the son of a foreigner had worked against him and he had worked hard to win the support of many of the teeming youths scattered across the farmlands and cities by working hard and rallying others to them in terms of their needs. He had suspected that Ibraheem had worked to earn the support of the elites only and as such, he could also have lots of enemies, especially when his supporter was not on the throne. He wondered how he had survived for so long and he thought he must have an extremely manipulative personality to have stayed around and be successful in these lands.

Ibraheem said, "I was not there. I do not know what Fero is talking about."

Fero was astonished and her mouth was left open. She looked up at Araba and said, "He lies, he lies! He is a bare-faced liar. We do have the truth serum; you will get it and you shall die."

Then they noticed a commotion outside. Only the Oro cult and the king could order the truth serum to be administered on a suspected criminal. The criminal was given an option; confess to the crime and get a lifetime of servitude at the king's farms or not confess and let the truth serum bring it out of you and you were sacrificed to the gods immediately. If the truth serum did not bring the confessions out of you, you were exonerated, and you were left to go about your normal business.

In this particular case, Ibraheem had no power to order one and did not even have the means to procure one, as this serum was held in very high secrecy by the Oro cult.

Keniola and Babagun entered the hut and they saw the dead Aremu boys. She asked that they be taken away immediately. Babagun bellowed to some soldiers who came in and took the corpses away. Araba said, "Ibraheem killed the boys, probably in conspiracy with Bankudi, your new personal guard."

"You mean the personal guard you appointed for me," she replied sarcastically and then turned to Babagun and whispered, "We need to watch Bankudi very closely."

Babagun beckoned to one of his lieutenant soldiers and asked them to follow Araba everywhere immediately. She then turned back to Araba and said, "I ordered Ibraheem to do all he can to find out who the killers of Itiade and kidnappers of Fero were. I guess he must have been overzealous about it. I, however, trust him, because I believe everything he did, he did for the security and glory of our kingdom. Now we need to begin the journey to the hallowed grounds for our festival."

Babagun told her, "It was Aremu that actually gave Araba the location where Fero was kept, and we still do not know who killed Itiade because the guys that killed Tela died just now. It was Tela that killed Itiade. Fero has claimed that she was there when Aremu killed Itiade. Aremu says that is not true and that Fero lies because she does not want him to be king."

"We will hear his defense properly at the festival grounds and if we find him guilty, we will sacrifice him to the gods," said Keniola. With that said, the whole group filed out of the huts and went to their horses. The soldiers assembled in a formation and they began their journey toward the hallowed grounds for their festival.

The festival usually takes place over a three-day period. The first night is the opening ceremony with dances performed by several youth female groups and wrestling bouts among several male groups. There is also a special drama session by the city drama troupe. Everything ends with the final wrestling competition in the wee hours of the morning and essentially the next night is when they execute judgements and make sacrifices. The third night they have a thanksgiving feast and before daybreak the next day everyone is on the way back to the city.

Keniola asked that Khalil, the prisoner, be brought along the journey and during the journey Keniola sought him out. They had never had a mother-son talk before this, so Keniola sat with him in his prison tent and asked, "My son, what are his objectives for coming to Idumagbo?"

Khalil responded, "I am only here to do the will of my father."

Keniola placed her hands gently on Khalil and asked, "What is the will of your father?"

"King Bashir, my father, wanted me to reunite both of you together and bring you back, Mum, into the fold where you rightfully belong."

Keniola looked at him, and could not help but notice the handsome features, the taut muscles of his arms and legs, before finally asking, "If war breaks out here, will you fight alongside me?"

Khalil did not hesitate and said, "Yes, that is what my father would have wanted for me."

"When is your father planning to attack Idumagbo?" Keniola asked suddenly.

Khalil, prepared for the question by his father, said, "It is not the intention of my father to capture and enslave the people of Idumagbo, but his intention is for the safe return of his wife. He is fighting for his honor."

Keniola kind of believed what her son told her, and she promised herself and said

"As soon as you are allowed to go, you should arrange a meeting between me and King Bashir of Timbuktu" and as she was standing up she said, "Bashir is not your father."

He replied, "I have been told you would use that line for me. King Bashir is my father," and then added, "I delivered your message to Adeolu."

Keniola turned her back and left the tent.

Adeolu found the plant materials required to make the truth serum and started running back home to Idumagbo so he could be on time for the opening ceremonies. Along the way he met a few farmers from neighboring villages also walking down to the hallowed grounds and they informed him that the regent's granddaughter had been found, rescued by her fiancé, Araba. He was unable to get more details from them but that made him slow his pace and he walked with the farmers and together they reached the grounds where the opening ceremony was in progress. One of the city's most celebrated musicians was singing melodies and there was lots of dancing on the grounds.

Keniola, dressed in a grandiose manner, addressed the citizens with humility by telling them that this would be one of their greatest years as she would be reducing the amount of taxes on the goods each and every one grew in their farms. Within the last few months since she became regent, she had started up the harvest measurements and the equitable levy of taxes and not just the blanket tax that was levied by previous kings, which sometimes excluded the elites and put a higher burden on the peasants.

With Keniola's knowledge of how the kings of Timbuktu levy taxes on citizens, the ruling council, and as such Ogunde, had a lot of cash and resources. It was a period of unprecedented surplus.

Then came the wrestling matches. Ogunde and Adeolu belonged to the same wrestling camp in their youth days while Araba was younger than them but admired the duo. Araba later became an apprentice under Ogunde, and they developed a very close relationship.

After the dances ended, Ibraheem saw Adeolu but tried to avoid him. Adeolu ran after him and greeted him, as this was hallowed grounds; no form of argument, fighting, or malicious intent was tolerated with or without evidence. Then Fero saw Adeolu and she asked, "Father, why have you not shown your presence at the regent's court?"

"I want the regent to have a great chance of making decisions by herself and do not want to be a bore on her and the court."

Fero knew when something was hurting Adeolu, but she chose not to press it any further, as Keniola also appeared backstage. Adeolu looked at the many people fawning upon her, some because of what they stood to gain. Adeolu felt sick to his stomach so he turned off and became lost in the past when they lived together and remembered the things they shared, the kind of ideals that were noble, enduring, and enviable. To him she was the epitome of all wisdom, understanding, and moral authority. She had once told him, "Every individual on this earth can withstand a famine and giving power to an individual is the ultimate test of that individual's personality." She then narrated the stories of several kings who had failed to pass the character test and nearly bankrupted their kingdoms.

At the dawn of the next day, Babagun, Araba, and Bankudi arrived at Aremu's prison tent where he was held prisoner. Both his hands were tied together at the elbow behind him while he lay face down. Araba cut the cord that was used to tie him, and he sat up properly. Babagun then said, "In the next few hours, your trial for the murder of Itiade and Tela will start at the court of Regent Keniola and will have all our gods as witnesses. If you have someone that will speak on your behalf, now is the time to let us know."

Aremu responded, "This is not right; it is not the way to treat a prince, a most exalted king. I have not killed anyone and do not deserve this humiliation."

"You will be given three chances to confess to the crime, if you do confess to the crime, your life will be spared but you will spend the rest of your life as a laborer in the king's farmlands. And if you allow the truth serum to be administered on you and your confessions come out, you will be sacrificed to the gods. But if you do not confess to any crime in the truth serum-induced delirium, you shall be set free and compensated for whatever loss you incurred," Babagun said.

The Undoing

It was time for the festival to be kicked off properly and this saw the mass of people moving into the arena of the gods where each person of means sits on a stool on which a sculpted image figurine of a god is the headrest on the stool and an exact replica of the figurine is displayed on shelves behind the throne of the king of Idumagbo. The figurine on the headrest of the throne is made of gold and it represents the highest god of them all, Orunmila.

The titled chiefs and Ogboni also have figurines of bronze and brass on their seats; other individuals in the society have figurines of earthen clay dyed in various colors, or brass. A requirement is that these must be made in exact replicas and there are very few qualified craftsmen that can make figurines in exact replicas. These figurines were known as the twin figurines and it costs a fortune to get it made and even more to get deified. Very few people ever get deified over the course of the years and according to the stories passed down from generation to generation to generation, the number of gods had increased as people become notable men of valor, means, wisdom, and expertise in the community.

Keniola sat on the pyramid throne of Idumagbo with a figurine made from shining gold overlooking an amphitheater in which all members of the community, including men, women, and children of age, sat in silence. Keniola stood and addressed the worshippers, onlookers, constituency, and jury rolled into one.

A few days before arriving at the festival ground, Adeolu went to meet Khalil in his prison camp where Khalil told him that Keniola was going to ask him to stand for election to the throne of his father and that all the members of the household would support him to ensure that he was made the king. "She believes you would be a very wise king." Adeolu did not trust for a moment what Khalil was telling him. Why would his grandmother send Khalil to him? Why could she not tell him by himself? he asked himself.

Adeolu stared at Khalil with a bewildered look that changed to expressionless momentarily. The message was not lost on Khalil as he continued, "my father, Bashir, is coming with his army to conquer Idumagbo. He is coming with hundreds of flame-throwing catapult siege engines and he has vowed to either bring Keniola back alive or leave Idumagbo in smolders and ruins."

This piece of information was news to Adeolu but he quickly adjusted and asked Khalil, "when is the army going to be here?

"The army will be here any day now. The ones you defeated a few months ago were just part of the advanced cavalry and the surprise introduction of guns did the trick; but the king of Timbuktu is bringing bigger fiery weapons this time around so do not be under any illusion that you are going to win."

Adeolu then said, "What then is the purpose of my kingship when it is going to be taken away from me as soon as I get crowned? What then is the use of the crown?"

Both fell silent for a moment before Khalil said, "You know I am one of the most widely traveled and educated amongst the sons of King Bashir. I have heard stories of what religious intolerance does to a society during my travels, but I dare not speak against my father and the rulers that be.

"My father, King Bashir, is cloaking and selling this war as a war of religion to the chiefs and elites of Timbuktu and not one of his deflated ego charred by the scorned love of a woman, Keniola, my mother.

"My mother had me for Bashir's brother, Audu, who forcefully had carnal knowledge of her, was the story I grew up to hear. I have decided that I am going to stick with my mother during this war. My death or survival is of no consequence in this regard, so I would like to help you, Adeolu," he said, concluding his statement.

Adeolu thought quickly about what had been said and what had been left unsaid and he asked, "Is this a religious war whose intention is to snatch Keniola for the second time and impose an Islamic regime and culture on the populace?"

Khalil nodded his head in affirmation and said, "Even if Keniola gives up without a fight, he will still impose Islamic rule on the populace, and he will demand that everyone worship the Islamic way—and also secure all the trade routes as well."

Adeolu fell silent for a while and Khalil continued to stare directly at Adeolu and after a few more minutes, Adeolu said, "Is that all? Tell my grandmother I will consider it as soon as I can."

Khalil answered, "No, you will be required to become an Islamist if you are going to be the king of Idumagbo. The earlier you become an Islamist, the better for the citizens of Idumagbo."

Adeolu gave no response. He stood up and walked out of the enclave they provided to house Khalil. As soon as he was out of eyesight, he quickened his pace and then broke into a frenzied run and arrived at Ogunde's enclave as quickly as his legs carried him.

Ogunde was in some talks with two of Babagun's lieutenants; Isegun, leader of the army, and Akara, leader of the running messengers, an arm that can run hundreds of miles in a day. In some places they can use horses and chariots and when not possible, especially if they want to travel through the rain forest, they use runners.

Adeolu said, "Can we talk for a moment?" and immediately Ogunde stepped out with him into the corridor leading out of his current location.

As soon as they were out of earshot, he said, "We have to get someone to go to Karounwi and bring more of that gunpowder; the Maradians are coming with a full invasion."

"We decimated their whole army and those that ran away will tell the stories of what our guns did to their soldiers," Ogunde said mockingly.

Adeolu said, "Yes, we surprised them with the guns, but what do we know about these Maradians, their culture, and their politics?"

Ogunde, trying to piece together what Adeolu was trying to drive at, did not say anything. Adeolu, not getting any response, continued, and said, "We know nothing; the only person that knows the most about them is Keniola."

He continued. "Today I learned that they are a predominantly monotheistic nation of Islam and they are pretty advanced compared to us and that the king had not heard about Idumagbo before and decided to send an expeditionary force to fight, believing that this unknown country could be easily run over, demobilized, and the culture of the people seized. In summary, the king believes his people have a superior culture and religion over us."

Ogunde now was all ears and then responded, "And so, if he thinks so, he is mistaken. We bested him anyway. Let him send the next force, we will still defeat them. We have enough gunpowder and guns to keep them at bay."

"The king is coming with siege engines that will lob a payload one thousand times of what the gun will shoot."

Then Ogunde realized the enormity of the situation and why Adeolu seemed to be in a panicky situation.

He asked Adeolu if he could describe what the siege engines looked like. Adeolu took a stick and went over to the sand in front of the building and drew the engine; it showed its wheels and its huge catapult arm.

Adeolu, seeing the scared look in Ogunde's eyes, said, "Now you realize what I am talking about. Idumagbo is not even on the map anywhere and you wonder why anyone would want to come that far, bring horses and lots of men into the forest where they barely know what diseases and evil lurks there?"

Ogunde replied, "Since economics is out of it, kings and people will do this for religion and for the love of a woman. Those two things men hold dear to their hearts."

Adeolu nodded in affirmation. "Now you understand what I am talking about. In this case, this king has those two things dear to his heart, which makes him twice as dangerous; the love of Keniola and the religion of his people.

"His people are following him because he said he was coming to claim the land of Idumagbo for Islam, according to Khalil, his nephew, Keniola's son with Audu, the king's late brother.

"I suggest we move fast; we need runners to get to Karounwi and bring that gunpowder," said Adeolu.

"Yes, we will move fast but in a different way. We can turn Idumagbo into a war-making plant too. There are sulfur deposits and charcoal in plentiful supply. The only thing is we would need more saltpeter, which the Mongolian man knows where we can find it. He brought some the last time he came around," said Ogunde.

"We need Ekunogun to locate the Mongolian man. They are usually in the same location around the same time; while one sells medicine, the other sells weapons of war," Adeolu said, and Ogunde burst into laughter. None of them have ever seen the Mongolian man, they get their sales through Ekunogun.

"Let's get Akara and Isegun to organize the runners and let them know that we need the saltpeter as quickly as possible," said Adeolu.

On getting back to the enclave, Ogunde instructed Akara to begin running to Karounwi and search for Ekunogun and give him a message for the Mongolian man to supply them with drums of saltpeter. Akara, together with two of his runners, saddled their horses and began on the journey to Karounwi.

Karounwi was on a hill and not reachable by horses because of a huge rainforest that separated this town from its city, so after they galloped for a few hours they found a nearby farmland and left their horses with the farmers and began the rest of the journey on foot while asking around to see if anyone knew the whereabouts of Ekunogun and his family train.

By nightfall, they had found someone with information of where Ekunogun had camped his family. Akara and his fellow runners entered into the court of Ekunogun who, as usual, was painted in ash and clay. He granted them audience and after a few words of banter, Akara announced why they had come to see him. Ekunogun replied that the Mongolian man would be in touch and that they should proceed to make available his payment as well, which was usually in clothing, jewelry, and cowries.

Then Jade entered into the court. Akara recognized her immediately and pretended not to know her by looking away and as she was about to greet Ekunogun's visitor, she saw it was Akara. She remembered him. She greeted him, then went to Ekunogun and whispered into his ear and then left. Then Ekunogun said, "I am no longer inclined to pass your information to the

Mongolian man." He paused looked into Akara's eyes and said again, "No longer interested in doing business with you or members of your community."

Akara, obviously flabbergasted, asked, "What did Jade tell you?" He then continued. "Whatever she has told you cannot be the whole truth and you should not trust her."

Then stepped in two of Ekunogun's hefty guards. They stood in the doorway, apparently to keep an eye on any mischief that Akara might want to cause.

Akara, seeing that he had no other cards to play, said, "What do you want me to tell Adeolu and Ogunde?"

"Tell them once they release Aremu, the Mongolian man will deliver what they asked for," Ekunogun replied.

Akara went outside to meet the two runners. He told them what transpired, and they began the sprint back to Idumagbo. On getting to the edge of the forest, they saw a massive assembly of soldiers and equipment preparing to cross through the forest. They quickly hid themselves and watched as the commanders of the army gave orders and then some of the soldiers came out with machetes and they started to cut down the forest. They would need to cut down the forest in order to get the heavy equipment to Idumagbo. They were able to count about ten siege engines. They were made in the shape of a pyramid, and each was about fifteen feet tall.

Akara said to his counterpart runners, it would take them at least twenty days to cut through this forest and move all that heavy equipment across the forest.

One of the runners said, "We should go quickly and get back to the city, mobilize the army and go for a surprise attack. It would be a real coup. We would cripple all their war effort right there."

Akara said, "That is very wonderful advice, but if I were a general leading these armies, I would have sent people ahead to the edge of the forest on the side of Idumagbo to ensure that the kind of attack you mention would not happen. Let's be careful how we move through the forest. We need to wait until nightfall before we move."

They continued to watch the Maradian army do their work and the more they watched, the more afraid they became. As the first shadow of nightfall fell on the forest, the trio crept into the forest and started running. They had not even run for up to five minutes before spears and arrows started flying through the night in several directions at the same time and hit one of the runners in the back, protruding through his rib cage and pinning him to a tree. The remaining two increased their pace and continued to run in zigzag fashion so as to confuse their attackers, which they could not see but they could hear them behind them.

As they were about to get to the edge of the forest, an arrow hit the second runner on the leg, immobilizing him. Akara wanted to help him by pulling him along. He said to Akara, "Please go, leave me, take care of my family, and please do not let my sacrifice be in vain."

Akara left him and sprinted outside of the forest onto the flatlands. He decided not to go to the farm where they kept their horses because he thought that must have been compromised. He ran all the way to Idumagbo, where he met and told Adeolu and Ogunde what had transpired. Adeolu and Ogunde disagreed on the way to handle it. Adeolu wanted to keep it a secret from Keniola while Ogunde wanted to tell Keniola so she could be prepared. They agreed to report everything to Keniola except the fact that they saw Jade with Ekunogun.

Keniola was briefed about the episode with Akara and Ekunogun by Ogunde and she said to him, "It is about time that we try Aremu. Go and bring Aremu so we can let him have his trial and after the trial we will elect a new king who will defend Idumagbo from the bandits."

Ibraheem and Bankudi were very happy inside when they heard the news of Aremu's impending trial from Adeolu and Ogunde. The death of Aremu would free them from an impending doom over their lives. They had come into the festival grounds immediately after their early morning hunting expedition. "You seem happy after you heard the news about Aremu's trial," Bankudi teased him.

"You looked happy too. What if he was not convicted but set free? have you given that some thought?" said Ibraheem.

Bankudi said, "That is not going to happen," then he paused, seeing the disbelieving look in Ibraheem's face and then added, "Why would he be set free?"

"When it comes to elites and rulers dealing with themselves, they tend to be less ruthless, and there are many unseen hands at play, that I can tell you."

Keniola stood up a second time from the podium where she sat and asked, "Where is Bankudi?"

Babagun said, "He went hunting and should be back any moment."

Then Bankudi appeared and stood behind Keniola as Babagun carried in his hands a big, black calabash containing people's wishes to the gods. Babagun then went to join the leaders of the Oro cult in a procession and together they danced and sang songs to the praises of the thousand gods that had supported the kingdom and had provided wisdom and healing to men. Everyone also joined the procession of the Oro, the only time the uninitiated were allowed to join in the ceremonies. They sang praises and danced while Babagun passed the calabash around to each person in the procession in a relay and each person invoked the spirit of one or more gods onto the calabash. The calabash was passed around in a circle several times until all the names of the gods were invoked.

Then the sacrifices began with the members of the hunters' group. They brought with them to the gods an antelope and many types of living animals, as the gods would not accept dead animals. After the hunters, next came the farmers with their fruits and crops. They danced joyously and sang melodies to the delight of themselves and others. A majority of the people were farmers and after the farmers, next came the traders, the women involved in tie and dye, the blacksmiths, the professional soldiers, and all those involved in one professional trade or the other.

Keniola was very pleased with the display of love and affection shown by everyone and it was now her turn to dance. She stood up and walked down the aisle, the big conga drums preceding her every step, her legs and her body movements seemed to sync rhythmically with the drums and gongs. Everyone marveled at this seemingly old but young-looking woman and they joined her in dancing and thanking the deities that had spared her to this date.

After the euphoria of the sacrifice had worn off and everyone sat down for meals and drinks, they ate until their bellies were aching. None had eaten all day, which was the custom then. Then the big conga drum started sounding again for everyone to assemble at the amphitheater once again. This time around, Babagun and Ogunde stood at the podium and they announced that it was time for the trial of Aremu. Aremu was going to be on trial for killing Itiade and Tela.

Then Babagun signaled that Aremu should be brought forward he was brought forward and made to sit on the floor facing the people who would be his jury tonight. Araba stood up; he had been asked to prosecute the case against Aremu. Araba started by saying, "Murder is alien to our culture. We love our neighbors like we love ourselves; that is what has made us succeed as a nation, having tolerance of each other and respect for morals, and agreed authority in good standing with the people has always been our watchword and this has produced excellent leadership for us and has earned us admiration from friends and enemies alike. We frown upon murder, no matter what the other person did wrongly. We always discuss and find a compromise acceptable to both parties. He who does well that was considered of him, we label him a well-behaved Yoba."

He then went into a local tirade reeling of praises of the Yoba people, their ancestors and their gods, and everyone glowed and basked in the euphoria of being a Yoba. As he continued, everyone around paid rapt attention to his words. He further said, "Aremu is a son of the late Oba, who has been accused of killing his own nephew who was also contending for the throne; this is not the way of our people. It is not the way we do things around here. He did it in front of people who had given evidence against him. He claimed that he was protecting himself. People that were there said he struck first and his life was not in any danger and he did what he did because he is a wicked man and he deserves to die."

He looked around as silence engulfed the whole arena and he could swear that if a pin dropped, he would hear it. He was not sure at first what was causing the eerie silence; was it his words or the humiliation of Aremu sitting on the floor in front of his own empty seat with his own godly image? "I am moving a motion that we should kill Aremu in the same manner that he killed our brother, a crime borne out of rage and hot blood." He paused and then continued. "A traveling medicine man who helped me once told me of a faraway land in the East, where the seas flow with milk and honey, about a great man called Moses who gave them laws and it said one law among the laws, says he who kills must be killed too. If you kill by water, you die by water. If you kill by fire, you die by fire. If you kill by the sword, you die by the sword. And Aremu here has killed by the sword and he should die by the sword.

"If there is anyone here who has anything to say for or against what has been said, they should do so now," Araba said, concluding his message.

A few people in front of the theatre said, "Kill him! All those that have killed should be killed as well."

Then Akara stood up from where he sat and spoke. "Our culture forbids killing but does recommend that we kill whoever has killed in the same fashion. Our culture seeks to know what could be responsible for a human being to take the life of another, so in this regard I salute Moses of the East that Araba mentioned. But we shall refuse to mete out punishments based on prophets from the East." He paused and looked around to see people's reactions. There were a few people that reacted positively, so he felt encouraged and continued as follows by asking a rhetorical question. "Do our laws permit a father to kill his son if the son would bring him to disrepute?" There was a rise of murmur around, people were asking many questions at the same time, and it was turning rowdy. Keniola signaled to Babagun to speak to it. Babagun did not like the plan that Keniola, Ogunde, and Adeolu brought to set Aremu free using such trickery but he had no way of countermanding them and he signaled to Oloro, his second-in-command, to speak, as Babagun could not trust himself not to misspeak.

Oloro stood up and said, "Yes, we as people do not have the Moses law to kill someone that kills, as we try to ascertain for a fact reasons behind the killer's actions before judgement and our judgement could be that he should be killed or should be made to suffer before being killed or we can simply take away all his wealth, and yes, we do permit a father to kill his son if his son will bring shame onto him. This is what our ancestors and those that have come to this land before us have done. They have inhabited this land and have passed these traditions down to us. They prospered, and we have also prospered. However, in this case, Itiade is not Aremu's son and as such, what Akara said does not apply in this case."

There was an uproar as some people murmured, "Aremu *is* the father of Itiade!"

"Abiodun was a sterile king."

"Abiodun was not capable of fathering a child."

"Jade should be brought here to confess as well."

The people went on and on saying that Aremu is the father of Itiade and the truth is in the open.

Ogunde quickly stood up, trying to make corrections to what Oloro said. Their plan to get the Mongolian man to supply the needed saltpeter for their gunpowder was fast dissipating before his eyes because it seemed some of the leaders of the Oro did not even believe that late King Abiodun was sterile so he said, "If Aremu is truly the father of Itiade, he would have to tell us how Itiade was going to bring him to shame before killing him."

Then someone shouted from the back of the theatre: "He killed him because he was contesting the throne with him, which was bringing Aremu to shame!"

Then a hushed silence fell over the audience. Ogunde had no further words, as their plans just got back on track and he sat down beside Adeolu, who had not said a single word since the start of the ceremonies.

Keniola stood up and said, "It is our tradition to ensure that judgement is fair and that is the reason why we have all of as jurors in this shrine. Most recently we had some people against the judgement of death for Adeolu because of an existing tradition. Now Aremu is facing an imminent death sentence that some people are also opposing."

She continued. "I will also follow traditions and what has happened in the past. Especially in my case, Aremu did wrong. He slept with the wife of his brother the king, the wife of the king had a son for him, yet he continued to deceive all of us about the paternity of Itiade.

"Just because Itiade wants to contest for the throne, he cut him down in cold blood; this is not the reason why our forefathers made this law.

"Aremu is my stepson. He stayed with me in the palace when King Adebayo was on the throne and I am utterly disappointed in his behavior. Itiade, our hero, Idumagbo's beloved prince, we will forever remember him.

"As for you, Aremu, what you did is gruesome, and I will make sure no father kills any of their children under any of our laws, and by the powers conferred on me I declare that no father shall henceforth kill any of their children without recourse to the king and the ruling council. If any father does that, he will be put to death as well.

"Since it would be unfair to retroactively apply this law on Aremu, I hereby deliver this judgement according to our tradition and banish Aremu out of our lands and surrounding villages. If he ever comes in contact with any member of our tribe, they are at liberty to kill him. He is no longer welcome here and is now dead to us."

A majority of the people cheered for the judgement and they praised Keniola for her sagacity in coming up with this judgement that suited all parties just right. Babagun rose next and ask Bankudi and some soldiers to unchain Aremu and lead him outside of the towns and city of Idumagbo and its environs and they should bid him goodbye. Akara walked up and volunteered to help see him off, which was part of the plan. The plan was to lead him to where Ekunogun could claim him.

Keniola acceded and granted his wish as part of the plan to mask the real reasons why Aremu was being released.

Aremu raised his hands up and was very pretentious in his humility and gratuity to his people. He wanted to speak and address the people. Keniola and the rulership disagreed so he raised his hands in a triumphant gesture and his supporters within the shrine hailed and praised him, much to the annoyance of Araba, Fero, and their supporters.

After the exit of Aremu, Akara, and Bankudi, Keniola declared the wrestling championship open and everyone moved away from the theatre to a part of the festival ground specifically made for the wrestling bouts. Several teams competed in the wrestling matches and new champions were made and old champions defeated.

Adeolu was less concerned about the wrestling bouts and much concerned about what would come next after Bashir attacked. He had played out the scenario several times in his head and he had not found a single way of how they could defeat that mighty army that Akara and Khalil described.

Araba soon found him and was visibly very angry with respect to the recent judgement passed by Keniola and was about to start complaining to Adeolu. Adeolu raised his hand in a gesture of stop and said, "There is a lot more at stake than killing Aremu. The Maradians and their king are coming with a larger fighting force and they are hell-bent on decimating our lands and forcing a new way of life on the survivors,"

"How do you know about that?" Araba asked.

"I have been tracking their movement and from what I have heard, they are just about seven days' march from here. We will be overwhelmed with that kind of firepower," Adeolu responded. "We do have guns and gunpowder that would do the trick for us," Araba said slowly, seeing the look on Adeolu's face.

Adeolu responded slowly and with sadness in his voice, "They have siege engines and more gunpowder to incinerate the whole Idumagbo and surrounding towns."

They sat down on the ground, each lost in deep thought for a moment and were oblivious to the people passing them and celebrating one wrestler after the other. Araba asked suddenly, "How does this relate to Aremu's release? Please explain, as I seem not to get it."

Adeolu said, "I thought you were not going to ask." He then narrated the episode with Ekunogun and the gunpowder and how they decided not to let him into the secret initially so as not to give the people a sign that everything was slowly going downhill for the city.

Araba was bewildered and he said, "You mean that I only went through a charade of which yourself, Ogunde, and Keniola knew the outcome and you really made a fool out of me?"

Adeolu, not used to begging people, said, "I am sorry we had to do it that way to make it believable by the common folks that we lead; that is one example you will have to learn in leadership. Nothing is always what it seems to be, so do not believe anything unless you find out from the leaders that dangle the ropes behind the scenes," he concluded.

Then after a brief hiatus, Araba spoke again and he said, "I am no longer angry. I have learned a very good lesson here today, but I want you to keep me in your confidence going forward, not because of me, but because of the love I have for your daughter, Fero, and your unborn grandchild."

Adeolu's eyes lit up at the mention of Fero, his only surviving relation, who calls him Father. Adeolu asked, "How is Fero, by the way? I have not seen her around today."

Araba replied, "She is resting. She had some moments of morning sickness and she decided to take some rest. As soon as we get back to the city, I want to formally request the hand of your daughter in marriage and I want to hold a big feast in your honor."

Adeolu laughed and said, "There will be a lot to celebrate when we get back to Idumagbo. There is also a lot to prepare for in the next coming days and we have to plan our time very well. To everything there is a season and a time for every purpose under the heavens; a time to love and a time to hate, a time of peace and a time of war. It seems for us these times are going to be very fused together," he said, grinning.

The words spoken by Adeolu sank deeply into Araba and he knew the coming weeks were going to be a mix of joys and sadness and they fell into another round of silence before Araba asked again, "We have to have a king who will lead us into war. I do not think Keniola is capable, as she is the real reason why this king is attacking us, and her judgements would be very clouded."

Adeolu said nothing as the sounds of the big conga drums reached their ears for the next session at the temple.

The people of Idumagbo gathered once again at the large amphitheater of the thousand gods in which a graven image was built into the headrest of each seat. Keniola stood up as the people were filling their seats once again and announced, "Great people of Idumagbo, it is time for me to step aside for a new king. We have had a few selections from the people, and we would give the people the opportunity to speak and select their king."

Keniola then called on Oloro to call out the names of those whom the gods had preselected. Oloro stepped out and called as follows: "Araba, son of Hubertino and Eunice." Araba was not expecting his name to be announced but nevertheless he stepped out.

"Ogunde, son of Babagun and Idia; Adeolu, son of Oyeade and Fausat; these are the three people the gods have selected for us and from whom we will select our king. Anyone among the selected who is not interested in vying for the throne should say so now."

Araba stepped forward first and said, "I will gladly allow Adeolu to be my king and I will honor and serve him with my last breath." The people present erupted into a frenzy of applause and as the applause died down, everyone expected Ogunde to do the same thing because of his friendship with Adeolu. But he stood his ground and did not move an inch.

Then Oloro continued by saying, "We now have two contenders to the throne of Idumagbo. At this time, I would ask anyone that has anything to say about the candidacy of these men, they should say so now or forever hold their peace."

No hands were raised. Then he asked Adeolu to move over to the right of the theatre and Ogunde to the left of the theatre. Both men did as instructed and moved to the ends of the theatre. Oloro continued and looked directly at the people and said, "We have decided to do away with the things of the past and we are putting power directly in the hands of those to whom it belongs, the people.

"This is the time for you to make your choice. Your choice is the choice of the gods. It is in their presence you are making this choice and as such, you have received their blessings and I can tell you they are very pleased. And the spirits of our ancestors that have done this in the past before us are rejoicing now.

"If you are in support of Adeolu, move to the right and if you are in support of Ogunde, move to the left."

Everyone in the theatre that evening moved to the right apart from Babagun, Oloro, and Keniola, who refused to take sides. Then Oloro said, "The people have made their choice, the gods have spoken. Adeolu will be the new king of Idumagbo. All hail the new king of Idumagbo!"

Then everyone present genuflected before Adeolu, including Keniola, his grandmother, Ogunde, Araba, and Babagun, who once threatened to have him killed for defiling the culture of the land.

Adeolu's eyes became misty and he nearly ran to Keniola to prevent her from genuflecting, but he held himself back and thought a king should behave like a king and learn to accept respect and obeisance from his subjects and not shy away or prevent it.

Someone from the audience started the rendition of the king's song: "Oba to de ade owo, oba o oba alase oba, oba to wo ewu oye oba o oba alase oba, ki la n fi oba pe, oba o oba alase oba!" (The king that has a crown on his head is the king with the authority. The king that has the grand royal robes is the king with authority!) Everyone danced and the musicians beat the drums and there was a lot of dust in the temple arena.

After the dust settled down, Adeolu went up to the podium and everyone rose out of respect for the new king.

"Today marks the beginning of a new lease on life for our culture and our people. We have effectively put a death knell on sons of kings succeeding their fathers. We have given a peasant a chance to become the king of our land. We have made good behavior, good works, and effectiveness our watchwords and we have nipped in the bud the perennial fights that follow the death of every king. With this new approach, everyone that is capable can bid to become a king.

"In the times that I am going to be your king, there will be honey in the land."

The people chorused, "Ase!" (Amen!)

He continued. "There will be milk from the breast of nursing mothers!"

The people chorused: "Ase!"

"The pregnant women will deliver safely!"

The people chorused: "Ase!"

In wars we shall come out victorious,

The people chorused "Ase,"

Our coffers would be filled with gold and coins,

The people chorused "Ase."

He paused for a while and he looked at the people sitting and standing before him and he could see the happiness on their faces and the eagerness with which they were receiving his word and he thought, this is not the time to tell them about what is coming, about the second invasion. Then he said, "We should not give up on our culture and our beliefs. There are people that hate us, and our beliefs and they want to force their own ways of life on us. We should resist it with all the strength in our body and let them know that we will not be anybody's subjects. We would have to die first."

The last words drove the people into another round of dancing and singing and this time they sang: "Kaabo ooo, Kaabo, omo abile soro, omo abile soro, kile lanu kaabo o!" (Welcome the son of ours who speaks, and the ground opens up in obedience, welcome!)

Adeolu continued as soon as the song died down. "The new positions will be as follows: Keniola will be the queen mother and will be in council, as her advice will be very valuable. Ogunde will command the Karounwi king's army. Babagun will be the king's right hand and he will be in council too. Araba will command the king's security forces and those will be stationed within Idumagbo. Akara will be the king's left hand and he will also sit in council. Ibraheem will be in charge of the king's purse, and Oloro will continue to be the headhunter for all Idumagbo and neighboring towns and villages."

Those that he announced came forward, and Adeolu asked that they raise their right hands and repeat after him: "I will serve the people of Idumagbo land and protect its interests and culture and will not use my position to enrich myself and cheat others. This I solemnly swear to in the presence of the thousand gods and if I break this oath may the gods mete out any punishment, they deem fit to me."

They all repeated this, and the people shouted: "Ase!" followed by a round of applause. After the applause died down, Adeolu then looked at the people again and said, "Some of our children may not be farmhands, nor blacksmiths, nor hunters, but people that may be gifted in a different way to learn what constitutes discovery and advancement in modern medicine and as a result of this, we will be starting a school in which some of our children will be taught philosophy, writing, counting, algebra, geometry, astronomy, and medicine. Our able queen mother will lead this effort to build us a great nation. If we can effectively teach some of our children these subjects, over the next few years we will notice an explosion of innovation in the way we do things, which can effectively speed up some of our common processes, reduce the drudgeries associated with farming, hunting, and fighting wars. Our failure to do these may cage the curiosity of our people for many generations to come and we may become second-class citizens of this world."

The people did not know whether to clap or shout ase but nevertheless they broke into different groups discussing what the king just said and everyone gave their opinions on what the king had shared.

The king then concluded that he had good news. "I have accepted Araba's offer to marry Fero, and the marriage will come up as soon as we get back to Idumagbo." He then proceeded to declare the festival a success and asked that everyone prepare to depart for the city the next morning before dawn.

As everyone filed out of the amphitheater to their respective family tents, Ibraheem came up to Adeolu and thanked him for his graciousness and then said, "Idumagbo will be greater under your leadership," to which Adeolu replied, "Yes, certainly, I will be the greatest ruler that Idumagbo has ever seen."

They were then joined by Ogunde, Araba, and Akara. Adeolu said to Ogunde, "I need you to start going to the city tonight and prepare to attack the Maradian siege engines and cripple them before they get here." He also instructed Araba to go prepare to depart for Idumagbo and bring his troops into the city and bolster the city's defenses. Araba nodded and went to do as he was told.

Adeolu then asked Akara, do we have our saltpeter? to which he replied, "The Mongolian man sent his representatives and they brought two bags of saltpeter. We have to commence production immediately."

Adeolu asked Akara to follow him and they went to get their horses, together with Bankudi and a few soldiers, and they galloped into the night to the location where they had the sulfur mines and the gunpowder factory. They arrived there and they started making arrangements to make more gunpowder by mixing the saltpeter with the mined sulfur and charcoal and packaging it in small bags to be handed over to the specially trained

Karounwi soldiers who had been trained to shoot the guns.

Adeolu also began working on making the incendiary he had earlier

experimented upon that could be lobbed at enemy soldiers with a catapult

and sling that caused explosion and fire on anything it came in contact with.

By early morning the next day, he had made around a hundred of

such bags and he thought these would do. He then instructed Akara to deliver

fifty of these bags to Ogunde for the attack on the siege engines and fifty of

these bags to Araba for the defense of the city. They arrived back at midday,

and news of the impending invasion had reached every citizen when they saw

the arrival of Araba's army.

The citizens of Idumagbo had gathered in front of the palace and

wanted to know what the king had to say about the impending invasion.

Adeolu quickly dismounted from his horse and said to the people that they

should go home and that preparations were already in the making to defend

their fatherland. He said they should come back tomorrow for the coronation

ceremony and marriage rites of his daughter and Araba.

The citizens left, not wanting to disrespect the new king, and quietly

left for their homes. Adeolu asked for the whereabouts of Keniola and he was

told that Keniola had chosen to remain at the festival grounds and pray for

Idumagbo. In the evening, Adeolu sent for all the chiefs and instituted the war council consisting of Ogunde, Araba, Akara, Babagun, Oloro, and Ibraheem. He declared the meeting open by saying, "It is no longer news that we will be under attack soon. The Maradian army is close by and are about six days' march from us and this time they have engines that can catapult big stones of fire and gunpowder to break our walls and decimate our cities. Our discussion here today will be to make plans to thwart this attack and defeat the Maradians. When we defeat the Maradians, we will take the war to their lands to destroy their cities and farmlands and then make peace with a new king that will be favorable to us."

He then called on Ogunde and asked him his plans. Ogunde said, "We received the gunpowder and pellet stones, as well as the incendiary bags, and we will march on the siege engines tomorrow evening after the coronation."

Akara said, "Marching to meet the army will be suicidal, as they have spies all over the forest and I propose that we choose at least a hundred of the best soldiers who are also capable of running and subterfuge to do the attack. It will not be a direct attack but an attack similar to the attack of a mosquito on an elephant; we hit hard and run, disappear, appear again, attack, and run again. We do this over and over again until we obliterate all the siege engines and their plans and also delay their impending invasion."

Adeolu had discussed this plan of attack with Akara on their way back from the sulfur mines as he knew that Ogunde was not the best military tactician and he had gotten Akara to buy in, so he asked him to propose it during the council meeting.

Araba also spoke up and said that he agreed with Akara's plans and that as for him and his soldiers, they had started re-digging trenches around the walls and dabbing the surrounding plants and trees with the poison.

Adeolu then said, "As of the day after tomorrow, no one should go to the farms. Everyone should go and get whatever they need today and tomorrow. The people working on the farms should come home for their safety, and everyone capable of bearing arms should begin training immediately."

Oloro also chimed in and said, "Should the city walls be breached, we have begun preparations to provide citizens with resources, such as blinding powders and other poisonous substances that they can use in attacking the Maradians if they proceed to march from house to house."

Adeolu said he had heard everything that everyone said, and he said to Araba, "You have my permission to do what you have planned," and he also said, "I agree with Akara's plans and we should carry out the plans." Then he turned to Ogunde and said, "Do you have such manpower in your army? Those that can attack, run, and hide?"

Ogunde responded, "Yes, we do, and he will also be carrying out the plans as we have agreed upon here."

Adeolu said the soldiers would need some training in handling the incendiary bags and he instructed Akara to go with Ogunde so as to train the soldiers in the use of this new weapon.

Ogunde and Akara left the premises of the palace and hurried quickly to where their horses were tethered and before they mounted their horses, Ogunde asked Akara, "Where did you say you saw the Maradian army again?"

He replied, "It was about two days' march east of Karounwi; that was around the area where we found Ekunogun. They also have lots of spies occupying the forest around Karounwi and it will be very difficult to move the army from Karounwi without their knowledge."

"What do you suggest then?" Ogunde asked, seeking some more advice as he contemplated the onerous task in front of him.

Akara said, "I think we should split the army and move the hundred soldiers to the front of the Maradian army and target the siege engines while the rest of the army can fight from the rear, distracting them, which would be mostly suicidal because the Maradians have an army that is ten times larger than ours.

"Our people may have a fighting chance if we end up crippling all their siege engines, which can cripple their advance for many days and destabilize their battle plans."

Ogunde nodded his head and said nothing as he mounted his horse and they together with the other soldiers carrying their weapons galloped into the night through a narrow path that was less traveled and would take them into a pristine forest that no one dared to go to hunt; the forest was declared the forest of the gods. They galloped very fast and they got to a place where they could not ride again, and they tethered their horses and resorted to running the rest of the way.

On getting to Karounwi, they were sighted by the guards and they quickly opened the gates to the military fort and all the lieutenants called a parade and they were able to count about a thousand men. Ogunde called out the one hundred men and he asked Akara to give them some quick instructions on how to handle the new incendiary weapons while Ogunde went into a meeting with his commanders.

Akara joined them a little later and he could see that they had lots of map drawings on the ground and on the floor using charcoal showing different battle positions and how the attack would be carried out. Ogunde quickly briefed Akara and said, "Akara you will take the hundred men and their commanders and go through the same forest and there you will set up camp until tomorrow evening. We will go to the rear of the Maradian army and fire many shots and attack with four hundred of our best men to create a distraction. The army will concentrate on that and you can use that opportunity to come in and incinerate the siege engines. The next day, Isegun will also lead and mount another attack with the rest of the army and you can continue your hit-and-run guerrilla tactics of incinerating the motorized command of the Maradian army."

He looked up, not expecting any questions because this was now a military operation and he had just issued a command. He concluded by saying, "May the gods help us all," and with that he called for the four hundred soldiers under his command to fall into formation.

After giving the command and inspecting the soldiers' battle readiness, he gave orders to open the gate and they rode out on horses into the night to the rear of the Maradian army.

Akara, also in full battle regalia, also called into formation his one hundred men who were now trained and armed with incendiary and catapults into formation and as soon as they formed the lines, he informed them of the mission and then he led them quietly into the forest to the front of the Maradian army. They walked briskly for a while and then sprinted the rest of the way until they got near where they were attacked the previous night and he called for only hand signals and no more voice communication. It was pitch-dark, and he divided the soldiers into four teams as planned and they moved to surround the camp, which was about four square miles in area. Each team would attack from the four cardinal points and they were to wait for the signal from Akara.

Akara waited a few hours until he was sure that all the soldiers would be at their prescribed locations. He then lit a fire on his arrow and with his bow, he shot the arrow with fire up into the sky, which was the signal for the attacks to commence.

The last time they counted ten siege engines and the goal for each team was to destroy two siege engines each. The team from the east crept into the camp of the Maradians; some were sleeping, while some were busy keeping watch over their equipment. The leader of the team sighted a heavy equipment covered with large banana leaves and he saw that it was heavily guarded and surrounded by about fifty soldiers with bows and arrows and spears. From where they were within the camp, they could not move any closer without being detected so the leader took out his catapult and asked others to do the same and they fired the shots together at the same time. Some landed far away from the siege engines and exploded while some landed on the siege engine and exploded and quickly caught fire. Some of the soldiers around the engine were also on fire, some badly burnt, and the noise from the explosion threw the camp into pandemonium. The surviving Maradian guards around the first siege engine took up battle positions and advanced toward the Idumagbo saboteurs.

The leader of the Idumagbo east team called for retreat but it was too late, they were caught between the engine guards and the Maradian soldiers just waking up. The battle was quick, and all the twenty-five soldiers were killed within a few minutes.

The guys from the south had also advanced and this time the leader of this team had sighted two engines close to each other and he divided the team into two and he led the first team to attack the second siege engine. Their catapult shots were nearly perfect as all the soldiers guarding these engine were incinerated while the Idumagbo soldiers ran toward the third engine and fired more shots, but this time they were able to get off only a few shots and most of the shots went wide as the Maradian soldiers, now wiser, started shooting at them with arrows and their guns.

As soon as the first batch of the southern team were annihilated, there was silence for a brief moment before the second batch had crept behind the third siege and they also set it on fire with their incendiary catapult shots. As soon as they got that done, they started sprinting back into the surrounding forest, but the alarm was already sounded and the guns and arrows of the Maradian army found their escaping backs, killing all of them.

The northern teams and the western teams were the most successful, as Ogunde's army coming in from the northern flanks had arrived and were also shooting guns and arrows into the Maradian camp and the Maradian soldiers were now confused about what was happening. What they had thought was just an ordinary act of sabotage has blown into a full-scale battle.

As soon as both camps ran out of arrows and gunpowder, they threw away their guns and drew their swords. Ogunde ordered the four hundred soldiers into battle against the twenty-thousand-strong Maradian army. He knew they stood no chance, but this had to be done; a death today or tomorrow is still death. He mounted his horse and rode into battle with his men in tow, cutting down the Maradian soldiers.

The northern team also used the opportunity of the confusion to set fire to two of the siege engines with their incendiary catapult shots, but they could not get away as they were caught in between the melee and were all cut down and killed by the Maradian soldiers.

The western team were by far the luckiest, as they had arrived late to the planned location and the battle was already half gone as the Maradian soldiers concentrated all their efforts on fighting off Ogunde and his army. The western team started firing their incendiary shots at two of the siege engines and they immediately caught fire. By then, King Bashir of the Maradian army had taken control of the army and from his vantage position far away from the battleground he could see that Ogunde's army was diversionary. He asked some soldiers to pursue the western team of Idumagbo saboteurs who had run out of incendiary bags but were now confidently running toward the remaining engines with torches and setting fire to them. They were able to destroy three more and were on their way out of the battle zone while the Maradian army gave hot pursuit and many of them were killed in the process.

Akara and two of the remaining soldiers were able to make it into the forest and they hid in trees. Ogunde, whilst still fighting, counted eight engines on fire and saw that there were about two more still covered about a mile away from him. He had already been wounded and he saw that most of his men were already dead. He counted about twenty of them remaining and he saw that the Maradian army had them surrounded. He looked at the remnants of his army and he shouted, "Never give up!" and he mounted his horse and rode and broke through the ranks of the surrounding Maradian army, took out an incendiary bomb which he had kept for this particular occasion, and rode toward one of the remaining siege engines.

King Bashir quickly took a spear and threw it, piercing Ogunde's back, but he still continued. Then he threw himself off the horse onto the siege engine, causing a very large explosion, completely incinerating the engine.

The remaining soldiers from Idumagbo were not so lucky, as they were also killed bringing the battle to an end.

At the end of the battle, Idumagbo had lost about five hundred soldiers while the Maradian army lost nine out of his ten siege engines and about a thousand of his twenty thousand soldiers and about another thousand wounded and suffering multiple degrees of burns. Bashir was very unhappy about losing his siege engines and he quickly took account of what just went wrong and he knew this would create an incredible setback for his army. He really wanted to capture one of the saboteurs, so he asked more men to comb the surrounding forests for those that escaped and as dawn broke, his soldiers returned with a captured Akara and one of his soldiers.

they bound and tied him to a stake and started interrogating and torturing him about the next battle plans. Akara refused to talk, feigning ignorance, and claiming that he was just a low-level soldier in Idumagbo's army.

Then the king received a visit from Ekunogun in the afternoon; he had heard about the battle and wanted to sell weapons to the king. He also brought Aremu to King Bashir and Aremu told the king that he was robbed of his throne and that left to him, he would have willingly given Keniola back to the king as she was causing too much trouble in their kingdom.

King Bashir took him to the location where they had tied Akara and as soon as Akara saw Aremu, he knew it was game over. Aremu said, "You have caught a very important man in the army of Adeolu. This is a very resourceful man and he will be very much missed. And also, it is possible for you to do a bargain with the usurper in Idumagbo."

Bashir replied, "I am not interested in any form of negotiation, only their capitulation, surrender, and capture of Keniola alive."

Akara still feigned ignorance and was not talking and as the night sky descended onto the Maradian camp, Isegun and the remaining army came roaring full force into the Maradian camp again and they caught them unawares again as they were not expecting another attack and this time they killed about five thousand of their men, some of them still sleeping, and Isegun saw where Akara was held, freed him, and leapt onto a horse and took off into the forest, deserting his already decimated army. He knew Akara was very important and he could not be left with the army. Isegun's army also saw and killed Ekunogun and Jade, knowing that their presence in the military camp was treacherous and their death would be victory for Idumagbo.

Bashir was very baffled about the resourcefulness of these people and he thought that he had simply underestimated them. The morale of his soldiers was at the lowest, having lost close to half of his army by this ragtag army of hunter-gatherers, which is what he chose to call them. The most painful thing was that two of his fiercest warriors were killed in battle today and Khaleb, his nephew and adopted son, was wounded during his fight with Ogunde.

Khaleb was one of the most gifted commanders in his army. His injuries would heal but he would be out of battle for many weeks. He gave instructions that all the dead bodies be thrown into a pit and burned for the fear that diseases may start spreading in the camp. So, they quickly gathered all the dead soldiers and set fire to them and this time around he ordered round-the-clock surveillance of the surrounding forest. He ordered some of his men to make camp permanently in the forest.

He then called his most trusted commanders into a meeting and they discussed what their next plan of action should be. They agreed that they must have missed something and that it would have been impossible to move an army from Idumagbo without them knowing, with all the spies they have along the roads, and they concluded that there must be an army base nearby and they quickly chose a patrol of a hundred men and asked them to go in the direction the invading armies came from. The patrol had gone about twenty miles in the direction before they came upon a mountain and they climbed it and there they discovered a military fort but with no soldiers.

Isegun and Akara took a detour, as they could not ride their horses in the thick forest, and they continued to gallop nonstop all the way to

Idumagbo. It was as if the horse was also in the know as it refused to stop and continued to gallop until they sighted the mighty walls of Idumagbo in the distance. The lookout on the watchtower had seen them and they sent horses to get them quickly.

***

It was a solemn marriage ceremony between Fero and Araba in the midst of the ongoing war but nevertheless there were musicians playing all sorts of instruments, and lots of food and beverages were available to everyone. Adeolu was in a very good mood as he danced with his daughter before handing her over to Araba and he prayed for them.

In the midst of the celebrations there was an ominous foreboding at the back of every citizen's mind about the impending invasion, and in the midst of the celebration a messenger whispered into Adeolu's ear and he excused himself and left quickly for the infirmary.

They brought Akara and Isegun into the palace infirmary and Adeolu quickly went to check on him. He was the chief medical officer of the community and now he was king. Akara had been a very loyal soldier and Adeolu would not like to lose him. He quickly administered some medicine on his many wounds and after he had rested for a few hours, Akara woke up and they sent for Adeolu once again.

Isegun was not that lucky, as he gave up his spirit on getting to Idumagbo. He was badly wounded in the battle and his wounds had become gangrenous on the ride down to Idumagbo. Araba and Babagun also left the celebration after they noticed the absence of Adeolu, and they joined him at the infirmary. Akara looked up and said, "Ogunde is dead."

As Babagun heard that he burst into tears, and no one was able to console him. After a while he stopped and simply left the room altogether. Adeolu and Araba said nothing and just listened as Akara narrated what went on in the two-day battle near Karounwi. He told them about Aremu and Ekunogun selling weapons to Bashir. He also informed them about the estimated number of casualties on the Maradian side. He said, "Although we lost all of our men, we inflicted a severe blow on the Maradian army. Out of the twelve siege engines, we destroyed nine of them."

Adeolu was very glad on hearing the news and he said, "Do you think we might be able to negotiate with the king and offer him a truce?"

Akara was very glad the king asked that, and he replied, "It is an option we should explore, and it would be a very good option if we want to save lives."

Araba also joined in the conversation and asked, "You were there in their midst for close to a day; what do you think of the morale of the soldiers?"

Akara replied there was lots of infighting as everyone disagreed with each other and their morale was getting lower.

Adeolu said, "Thank you, Akara, you have done very well, and you are the hero of Idumagbo. We will leave you to take further rest and we may come back to you for further questions."

As they stepped out of the room into the corridors, Adeolu said, let's invite the king of Maradi to the final wedding event ceremony.

Araba said, "That is good diplomacy, and we will make sure we show him one of our best sides. Who do you plan to send to give that message to him?"

Adeolu said, "We will send Babagun."

"Do you think he will go" Araba replied. "Although he has been a soldier all his life, after losing two sons, yes, I think he would rather avoid further bloodshed."

They met Babagun sitting in the king's court surrounded by many women in silence just watching over him and consoling him with their presence and their somber look. Adeolu asked Bankudi, who was also present, to clear the court and as soon as the court was cleared, he said to Babagun, "We are sending you to Bashir, king of the Maradians, on a diplomatic mission to try and make peace with his army and ask or probe him for his price."

Babagun was silent for a very long time and he seemed to be very deep in thought as his face betrayed all his emotions and his thoughts as it danced from sad to angry back to sad and then finally it ended in a firm affirmation that could be interpreted as what can be better than trying to fix this? He replied and said, "I am highly honored and will gladly do as you wish."

Adeolu further said, "You should also invite him for the concluding part of the wedding ceremony coming up tomorrow between Fero and Araba. Tell him I am highly honored to host, and we will surely treat him well."

Adeolu signaled to Bankudi to go prepare and accompany Babagun on his trip to the Maradian camp.

Ibraheem came in afterwards and requested an audience with Adeolu. Adeolu granted this and everyone left the court. Ibraheem said, "Khalil visited me this morning and asked for my daughter Almitra's hand in marriage, but I refused because I do not trust him. I feel he is a spy in our midst, and he would do the bidding of his father."

Adeolu's face was expressionless as he carefully thought about the information that this man had brought. He himself had never trusted Ibraheem but he nevertheless brought him into the ruling council as a chief because he wanted him to be closer than away. Keniola had also done the same and he never asked her why, but he did it anyway. He made him keeper of the purse because he felt that might be the only way to get rid of him if he was ever caught in any form of corruption, but now it seemed he might actually be providing another avenue that could help us end this war. He responded, "Would you want anyone else to marry Almitra?"

"Almitra is very beautiful, and she has had a bevy of suitors, but she is very choosy. However, for some reason, she thinks she likes this Khalil."

Adeolu asked another rhetorical question. "Would you want your daughter unmarried? Do you think she will be happy if she marries Khalil?"

"Absolutely, I think she would be happy. But I do not know whether Khalil would be happy. It looks to me like he is scheming to get at something," Ibraheem responded.

Adeolu then said, "Your basis of suspecting Khalil is unfounded. You know he is my baby uncle and you should do what makes your daughter happy. But before you do that, let's put him to a test, have you seen Akara?"

He responded, "Yes, he was sleeping when I got here so I left him alone."

Adeolu continued, "Before you came, he gave us the battle report and he reported that nine out of the twelve siege engines were destroyed and thousands of their soldiers killed. We also lost all of the Karounwi king's army, including Ogunde and Isegun, Babagun's sons.

"We had a brief council meeting after that, and we decided to try and negotiate a truce and we asked Babagun to go to the Maradian camp and invite the king over here for Araba and Fero's marriage." He continued. "Now that you have brought this important information, we should include Khalil as part of the delegation to see if he will defect and if he does, that confirms your suspicion."

Ibraheem was very impressed and he responded, "You have spoken wisely, my king, and your wisdom is indeed very great. May the gods of our lands continue to protect you, and may they give you long life on this earth so that you can use your wisdom to the benefit of Idumagbo land."

Adeolu summoned one of the court's messengers and asked him to go get Khalil quickly, tell him it is urgent. He also asked that Babagun come back into court. Babagun came back into the court and Adeolu asked him when he would be ready to go, to which he replied that he had packed a few belongings and he was ready to go as soon as the king said so. Adeolu told him to prepare to leave first thing tomorrow morning and that he had another person that would follow him on this diplomatic trip. Babagun just nodded his head and never said anything. Adeolu then said, "It is Khalil. He wants to marry Ibraheem's daughter and we also want him to use that opportunity to invite his father or uncle, whatever he calls Bashir."

Babagun said simply, "That is a wise plan."

"You will still be the leader of this delegation and Khalil will listen to you," Adeolu concluded before Khalil stumbled in with Almitra in tow. Adeolu laughed when he saw Almitra holding Khalil and he said, "We only asked for Khalil, not you. Why have you come?" he further queried.

Almitra said, "After Khalil asked my father for my hand this morning and he refused, I saw that he was very agitated, and he was previously not making any plans to come to the palace before he suddenly changed his mind. I knew something was up and a few hours later, Khalil was sent for. I knew I just had to accompany him and show my king that I am really in love with him and would like to spend the rest of my life with him."

Adeolu then said, "That is so loving of you and it is very good of you, but we would ask you to excuse us for a moment while we speak with your future husband."

The words *your future husband* seemed to reassure Almitra that everything would be all right and she stepped out of the court.

Khalil sat down on the floor beside the throne on which Adeolu sat. Adeolu began by saying, "Khalil, you were my baby uncle and you know I would not do anything to hurt you or jeopardize your happiness in this city. You have served us very well and we respect your choice of not serving in our army but now that you have asked for our daughter's hand in marriage, we now have something to ask from you in return."

They all looked in his direction and he could feel their gaze burning through his skin so he responded, "What would you have me do, my king?"

His response was not very encouraging, and he quickly discovered this from the frowning expressions on the faces of those present. He knew not to toy with the emotions of these people; they were under severe pressure and he rephrased it by saying, "Whatever the king wants me to do, I will do as much as it is within my power."

Then they all responded, "Good boy."

Then the king asks Ibraheem to break it to him buy nodding in his direction. Ibraheem said, "Khalil, the reason I do not want to let you marry my daughter Almitra is because I do not trust you. You came here to fight us and we captured you and we forgave your sins and granted you clemency and allowed you to roam freely on our lands and now you want to marry our daughter, but deep inside you, have you thought about whether you deserve any of this?"

Khalil had never thought about this previously and he responded by saying, "I do not deserve the love your people have shown toward me."

Ibraheem smiled and then asked, "Would you be ready to prove that you are worthy of the love we have shown toward you?"

Khalil replied, "Yes, I am ready, and I will prove my love toward you and earn the love of your daughter and the people of this land inasmuch as it is within my power."

"We want you to go with Babagun to the Maradian camp and seek for truce and ask him to even come here for a feast."

Immediately his countenance changed, and he moved backwards a little bit and said, "I have not seen my father for quite some time now so I do not know whether he will come, but the man I know years back will not come."

"Then it is your duty to make him come," Adeolu interjected.

"You know what is on the table; you make him come and you marry Almitra and we have lasting peace."

Khalil said, "I will accompany Babagun and Bankudi on the diplomatic mission," and Ibraheem said, "Do not tell Almitra anything yet."

Adeolu added his voice to the instructions being passed to Khalil by saying, "Your horse is ready and as a matter of fact, you and Babagun and Bankudi will leave at first light tomorrow. You might encounter a lot of patrols on the roads so stay safe, and make sure you explain your mission clearly to anyone who accosts you."

At first light the next morning, the trio of Babagun, Khalil, and Bankudi began the journey on horses, galloping very fast on the plains outside the city walls. These plains could go for hundreds of miles before you reach the surrounding thick vegetation, which is almost impassable by horses. In order to get as much distance between them and the city walls, they galloped very fast and they were able to make the forest as quickly as possible. None of the three was a forest runner so they would have to make do with walking through the forest and at the current pace, they would get to the Maradian camp before dusk.

They had not gone more than 10 miles into the forest before they were accosted by some Maradian soldiers on patrol. Khalil spoke to them and explained their mission was to meet with King Bashir and fortunately one of the soldiers recognized him and they were spared a lot of torture.

The leading soldier asked some of the soldiers to accompany them quickly to their camp so as to deliver the message to the king.

On getting to the camp, the smell of burnt flesh permeated the air and they could see several burnt siege engines scattered around the camp. They could also see that some of the soldiers were working on trying to repair one of the siege engines.

The soldier led them straight to the palace tents which were in the middle of the camp and was surrounded by almost a hundred soldiers.

On their getting to the tent, the soldiers guarding the tent recognized Khalil and they broke into a euphoric shout, hailing his name, and the noise from the ensuing commotion alerted the king and he also came out to see what was going on.

On sighting his son, he was much elated, and he drew him closer to himself in a hug. He then asked, "Who are your companions? I don't think you escaped from your captors given the way you are dressed. Tell me what is going on. Why are you here and what is the catch?"

Khali replied, "Father, let's go inside and I can give you more details on the reason for my visit."

"Visit? I thought you had come here to stay and help us fight our enemies!" Bashir said.

"Wait until you hear what I have to say first."

The king led them into one of the tents with a very expensive rug on the floor and every one of them sat on the floor. With the king were five of his top commanders, and Khalil noticed that Khaleb was not present so he asked after him and the king replied, "He was wounded by your captors, and that is why you must join us to fight and avenge your brother."

Khalil quickly settled down. The fact that his companions, Babagun and Bankudi, had been completely ignored and snubbed was not lost on him. He continued to smile, and he knew that he had to manage these conversations very well because if anything went wrong with the conversation, his people, the Maradians, could be very wicked and they could simply execute Babagun and Bankudi.

So, he began by first introducing Babagun as the leader of the delegation and a former army commander of the Karounwi king's army. He introduced Bankudi as one of the king's most loyal and fiercest warriors. They murmured a greeting and grudgingly acknowledged their presence without a glance in their direction.

King Bashir's face was completely expressionless, and he asked Khalil to continue. "A famous astronomer once said you don't raise heroes, you raise sons. And if you treat them like sons, they'll turn out to be heroes. So, I have come here to inform you that I am getting married, and I want to invite you to Idumagbo for the wedding."

The king fell silent for a while then said, "Did their king agree to surrender or do we need to hasten our invasion then?"

He looked around at the soldiers and one of the commanders responded mirthlessly, "Then we will have a beautiful wedding afterwards," and then laughed.

The king reprimanded him immediately and asked that he leave the meeting. The soldier quickly apologized and then excused himself.

Babagun and Bankudi were not amused at all. After the exit of the soldier, Bashir said, "Is their king willing to surrender and convert from their graven ways?"

Babagun then said, "We are willing to negotiate and meet you at a middle point. We will never, never surrender."

"Then I will decimate your lands; no one will ever live there again. I will kill all living things in that area and will not leave any stones standing on another one. Don't you dare come here and tell me what you want," Bashir responded furiously.

Babagun said, "We almost destroyed all your engines; you can never get into our walls."

The king smiled and then excused himself. He went outside and then asked the soldiers present to detain Babagun and Bankudi and they should bring Khalil to him. They walked into a different tent, where they sat down. The first thing the king said after they were out of earshot was, "Where is Keniola?"

He was not surprised but he replied, "I do not know precisely, but it would be somewhere in the city." He then continued. "This is probably not going to end very well for any one of us if we continue along this path of war, but on the contrary, she might just change her mind toward you if you decide to be peaceful; imagine that for once." He paused for a while and looked into King Bashir's eyes.

King Bashir stared him down, then looked away.

"Consider yourself married to someone that you love and someone that loves you and you having the desires of your heart," he concluded.

"That is never going to happen. I would lose my position, trust, and authority with the people and I would surely be killed. I cannot even go into their city. What if they are planning to kill me?" Bashir said.

Both sat in silence for a while. Khalil could not guarantee that his father would not be killed if he went inside the city of Idumagbo and he could not guarantee that Keniola would be willing to accept his hand of love. Bashir finally said, "Tell him I am willing to meet him at a place of my choosing and we can discuss his terms of surrender, of which number one would be for him to vacate the throne and I will put a new replacement who will be of my religion."

Just then Aremu stepped into the tent with a turban on his head. Bashir wanted to introduce them, but Khalil interrupted him and said, "I know him very well; he is a prince of the kingdom of Idumagbo who slept with his brother's wife and murdered his son who was contending the throne with him, so I need no introduction," he said condescendingly.

"If Adeolu will vacate the throne and Keniola surrenders, we will spare Idumagbo, turn around, and vacate these lands. And I will take Keniola with me. With that in place, this will guarantee unity between our people and the people of Idumagbo, and we will have a wonderful marriage celebration afterwards," Bashir said.

Khalil looked at the king, briefly thinking how this plan would be to his favor. He excused himself and said that he was going to see his brother, Khaleb. He asked one of the soldiers to show him to the tent where his wounds were being tended.

Khaleb was happy to see Khalil.

Khalil said, "Such a horrible condition to be in;" referring to the bandages around his brother's arm.

"What happened? You really want to get yourself killed this time around."

Khaleb laughed and said, "Your man Ogunde did that to me in a one-on-one before I got rescued by other soldiers." He then beckoned to Khalil to come give him a hug. He walked over and they hugged each other. Khaleb asked, "How is mother, father's beloved? I heard you came to tell father to give up his ambition of incinerating Idumagbo and capturing Keniola."

"I don't think he will ever listen. As for me, I am not useful to his war efforts after my injury and I don't think I will be useful in the future as well. He is all alone, and the ruling council and kingmakers are on his neck to deliver something to delight the people."

"Well I am getting married, and I am inviting you and Father to come along and celebrate with me."

"I would love to come and meet the woman that has melted your heart," Khaleb responded.

"I do not think father will allow you to go," Khalil said.

"I can convince him to let me represent him, and I think he would like that idea. But one thing is that he would want you to come and stay beside him in Maradi, so you may have to promise him that. I know that is what is on his heart; he has discussed this with me previously," said Khaleb.

There was a slight commotion outside and both Khalil and Khaleb stepped outside of the tent and they saw that one of the soldiers was tied and being caned seriously. He was being accused of treason by speaking ill of the king's visitors in front of the king. Khalil moved closer and he saw that it was the same soldier that scorned him. He thought, he does not deserve what is coming to him. This is a well-respected senior soldier and is being humiliated in front of his soldiers. He thought the king had overreached but he dared not voice it.

Then one of the soldiers approached him and said the king was requesting him and Khaleb to come for a meeting. On getting there he saw Babagun and Bankudi being led into the same tent by some soldiers. On getting inside the tent, he saw two fierce-looking soldiers he had never seen before beside Bashir, and typical of him, he kept all of his cards close to his chest and never introduced them.

Khaleb said joyously, "Khalil said he is getting married and he is inviting us! And I know that you will not be able to go but I can go in your place and to guarantee my return, simply keep Babagun here with you until I return."

The king smiled and said, "Khaleb, seems like you read my mind; that is what we are going to do. We will keep Babagun here as our prisoner until Khaleb returns. We wish you happy celebrations."

Khalil knew this was not going to fly with his future in-laws, but he kept quiet and smiled too. Babagun, looking as if he had been stonewalled, finally found his tongue, and said, "Our king, Adeolu, will not deal with your adopted son," saying that to deflate his ego.

The king smiled and casually dismissed the comments from Babagun by not saying anything about it. He then said, "Khaleb, go prepare to go with your brother to Idumagbo for his wedding celebrations."

Then Khalil finally found his voice. "There is no need to come with me, as you heard what Babagun said. King Adeolu will not negotiate with Khaleb, and additionally, I will not be marrying Almitra with Babagun here in your prison," he said, still concealing the real reasons.

Then the king said, "You will find more beautiful women in Timbuktu; the most beautiful women are in Timbuktu."

This really annoyed Khalil, and he knew that he really did not care about his feelings but only cared for his own ambitions. He knew he had lost the battle. He then faced Babagun and said, "I am sorry. I know there will not be any marriage but let me take my brother back to Idumagbo and at least try to see if some semblance of truce can be negotiated."

Babagun nodded in approval, knowing that this Maradian king had the upper hand since they were in his territory. "You should leave first light tomorrow morning and if you are not back by the end of the third day I will assume that you have been killed and I will execute Babagun as well, and I will send you a message with his head on a pedestal."

He then stood up and dismissed the meeting. Khalil went to meet Babagun and said, "I will be back, and you shall be safe."

Babagun replied, "Who are you to make such guarantees? We both know that you hold no influence with this king." The words said by Babagun hurt him a lot. It seemed like a sharp metallic object pierced through his heart.

He bowed slightly and then left the tent as some soldiers came to take Babagun away.

At first light the next day, Khalil, Bankudi, and Khaleb rode out into the forest followed by a pack of soldiers who had been given command not to enter the plains and that they should come back on reaching the end of the forest. They walked for several miles, and Bankudi excused himself to ease himself only to come face-to-face with Adeolu and Araba carefully hidden, camouflaged. They asked him not to make any noise and they said, "Where is Babagun?" and he narrated a summary of what transpired with the king at the Maradian camp.

They then told him to continue the journey and that they would always be nearby. As soon as they reached the edge of the forest and waved goodbye to the trio, the Maradian soldiers, numbering about ten, were ambushed and killed by Adeolu and Araba and a couple of other soldiers and they quickly replaced the Maradian soldiers with their own soldiers, took off the dead soldiers' clothes and they put it on their bodies and also covered their faces and with mud from the forest and they asked the soldiers to infiltrate the Maradian kingdom and break Babagun loose.

Shortly after Babagun, Khalil, and Bankudi left Idumagbo, Araba had hatched this plan and brought it to Adeolu, saying that he did not trust the king and as such, they needed a way to know what was going on and the only way would be to surreptitiously follow the trio and as such, know the location of their patrols and be able to avoid it. To do this, they communicated using bird calls and re-echoes mimicking the canary bird also present in the forest, but only the trained and the discerning ears could distinguish. Adeolu had agreed on the plan and he agreed to follow them on the mission.

As soon as Araba donned one of the Maradian uniforms, it dawned on Adeolu that Araba may never come back if the mission failed. Araba said, "I will go, and I will come back and I will bring Babagun back safely with me and we will defeat this heartless king."

Adeolu placed his hands on his soldiers and mumbled some words about having the gods with him. He had never been a man of religion and as such, could not bring himself to say even the commonest prayers at times like this. Adeolu then bade Araba goodbye and he asked Bankudi to lead Khalil and Khaleb back to Idumagbo while he and the rest of the soldiers followed a different route back to Idumagbo.

Araba and his cohorts broke into a jog and they climbed in trees when he sensed a patrol in the distance. He hooted a canary warning to alert the others. Even though they were now dressed alike and some of them could speak the Maradian tongue, including Araba, they still tried to avoid them until it was necessary.

They finally got to the camp and they were accosted by one of the sentries who asked, "Where are you coming from? You were not part of any patrol earlier today."

Araba replied in fluent Maradian, "We left on a special mission. We escorted Khaleb and the other visitors back to the forest." He then pretended to be walking away, even though he did not know his way around in the camp. He could see many, many tents, but he did not know which one they kept Babagun in, so he asked the sentry, "Where did you move the remaining prisoner to?"

The sentry replied, "He was not moved." He then called on his fellow soldier, "Did anyone move the prisoner from his location?"

The fellow soldier said he was still over there, pointing in the direction of a tent.

Araba replied, "Yes, he is still in the same location." They quickly walked across, darting amongst tents until they got to the one to which the soldier pointed. Araba peeped inside and saw only one soldier with Babagun. Babagun's hands and feet were bound and he was lying on the floor, helpless.

Araba signaled to one of the soldiers to distract the guard and that he would come in after him. The other Idumagbo soldiers were to keep guard outside the tent.

The soldier entered the tent and thus infuriated the Maradian guard, who told him that this place was out of bounds to all soldiers and that he should leave now. Just then, Araba slipped in through the other opening and encircled his arm around the guard's neck in a sleeper hold. The other soldier went to Babagun and untied his arms and legs quickly. They took off the clothes of the soldier and gave them to Babagun to wear. Babagun dressed up feverishly, not saying anything.

As soon as he finished, they went outside the tent and signaled to the hidden soldiers on watch to let them go. They advanced in the direction where they had their latrines and all of them pretended to be going for a latrine, and each slipped into the forest behind them one by one with Araba in the lead. They could not go through anywhere else as they could not allow the sentries to see them again.

As soon as they had gotten far enough, they settled down, too the roll call, and found that no one was missing. They knew they could not go back into that forest because if Bashir discovered that Babagun escaped, he would throw a lot of soldiers into the forest to chase them and kill them all. So, they went the opposite way, looked for some farmers and purchased horses from them. Now they had to go around the forest through another forest called the forest of the gnomes, which would take at least three to seven days to get to Idumagbo.

Babagun looked at Araba and said, "I have known you to always have a brilliant mind; that was a brilliant plan that was well executed."

Araba replied humbly, it will be considered a success when all of us get into Idumagbo safely.

Meanwhile, as soon as Khalil and Khaleb and Bankudi got within the walls of Idumagbo, they proceeded to the king's palace, where they stayed. They waited a few hours. Khalil decided he would come back later and decided to take his brother to meet Almitra. Bankudi wanted to prevent them at first but decided to discreetly follow them so at least he would see all that they were up to.

At Almitra's place, Ibraheem was not home and after brief introductions, Almitra's mother came out and told them to leave quickly because Ibraheem would soon be back and he would not like them to be with Almitra. Both of them stepped out again and this time Khaleb said he wanted to see his mother, Keniola. He had not seen her in a long time and would not mind at least seeing her before anything else. They proceeded back to the palace where they were informed that Keniola was at the festival grounds. Khaleb asked, "What is that?"

Khalil replied, "Don't worry, I will let you know later."

Then they were told that Adeolu was around now. Adeolu came back, had a bath, and was all dressed sitting elegantly on the throne as if nothing happened. Then he asked, "Where is Babagun? Did you forget to bring him back? And who is this, by the way?"

Khalil introduced his brother, saying, "That is my twin brother, Khaleb. My father has agreed for you to keep him and he will keep Babagun until both of you meet at a neutral ground in two days' time."

Adeolu said, "That was not the instructions we gave you. What did he say about your marriage?" It was then that Khaleb knew that Khalil did not tell their father the whole truth. "Then your marriage will be postponed until we figure out how to get this invading army out of the way," he said, then added, "You can go now."

Khaleb was shocked that he was not arrested and bound as a prisoner, as he knew his soldiers would have done to Babagun. He asked his brother, "Is this the same people that came to burn down the siege engines? Because I don't think they are that strong. Look at him, he cannot even order my arrest."

Khalil responded, "Just because the lion tiptoes does not make him a coward. Beware of your assumptions."

***

As soon as the discovery of Babagun's escape was made known to Bashir, he flipped his lid and was very angry that he deployed a quarter of his army and ordered them to do a full-scale search of the surrounding forest immediately. After they were gone for a few hours, he ordered another section of his army to start cutting down the forest and that the rest of the army should follow behind and start moving their large machineries, wagons, siege engines, and large catapults. Bashir knew that this was a very deadly blow and if he was not careful, he might be drawn into a battle that he could not win.

Some of his army commanders came to meet him and asked him, "Where will the army camp once we clear the forest?"

He replied, "We will camp directly out on the lands in front of their wall and we will start a full blockade of their city. We will kill anything that attempts to enter or exit through their gates."

The most senior commander replied, "Don't you think we will be leaving our food sources behind and we will be open to any form of guerilla attack because we are way out in the open?"

Bashir replied, "In our present position, did they not make mincemeat of us? Did they not steal a prisoner under our very noses? Did they not come and destroy more than half of our equipment? I even think it is because we are close to food sources that was why we are not vigilant."

He then continued, visibly irritated, "I am the king here and I give the orders. Besides, once we capture Idumagbo, we will have all the sources of food within the walls of Idumagbo city. It will ensure our victory. Eternal vigilance will be our price for victory," he concluded.

The senior commander wanted to say something else; the look on the king's face indicated otherwise and he quickly joined the rest and bellowed orders for movement to commence.

After about three days of circumnavigation of the forest, Araba's team eventually arrived in front of the gates of Idumagbo and they could see that a substantial part of the forest had been cut down by the invading Maradian army. They carefully followed the paths where they had not placed traps and incendiaries. The guards on sentry ushered them in quickly and informed Araba that they had been monitoring the Maradian army since yesterday evening and they told him that they expect that the full army and their equipment will be out of the forest by noon tomorrow.

Araba proceeded straight to the palace where he was welcomed, and a musician came to serenade him. He first wanted to refuse, but changed his mind after Adeolu said, "You may never know if you still have your life after tonight." They danced and celebrated Araba and Babagun for their daring and victorious escape.

Adeolu ordered Araba, Babagun, and the rest of the soldiers that partook in the raid to go to bed and come to the palace at dawn, as he would be ready to reveal the battle plans and how Idumagbo would be defended.

"We will not surrender. They may have more men than us, but we shall overcome."

Then, Keniola entered the palace court and asked, "Where are my sons? I heard the lost one was looking for me."

Adeolu asked one of the messengers to go and fetch Khalil and Khaleb and let them know that their mother was looking for them. Adeolu said, "The Maradian king is at our doorstep and we shall be expecting an invasion any moment now. Hopefully we can hold them for as long as we have food."

"No, you will not be able to hold them that long. Even if we train all our citizens as soldiers, they would still outnumber us. The best move for us is to assassinate their king," Keniola said.

Adeolu was thoughtful for a while, then he said, "It will be very hard to get close to him unless we draw him out of his comfort zone."

"He is also a very decisive person and I am sure he knows that his death would put an end to all this assault and warfare, and he would not dare expose himself—"

"Unless we lure him into a trap using a bait," Adeolu completed Keniola's sentence.

Keniola said, "I will not be that bait, but you have his son Khaleb. He seems to be a gift from the gods, and he can turn the tides of this war."

Just then, Khalil and Khaleb were led inside the court by the messenger. Khalil prostrated the usual way the Yobas pay obeisance to their kings while Khaleb went to hug his mother. His mother hugged him back, stood, and said nothing to him.

Then Adeolu asked two soldiers to come in and restrain Khaleb. He told him, "You are now a prisoner and we will ask your father to move his army out of sight in exchange for your life. Otherwise, you will be executed. A message will be sent to him tomorrow morning."

Khaleb said, "You cannot do that! He has your Babagun and he will do the same to him as well."

"Babagun is back with us, hale and hearty," said Adeolu.

Keniola said, "I am going to take my leave. I refuse to be part of this."

"You are excused. I understand that these were some hard decisions. This a very hard one, but it is one we must make if Idumagbo is to survive," Adeolu said.

Keniola stepped out of the palace court with some of the soldiers she came with, Khalil wanted to follow, he was restrained and told that her mother would rather be alone now. The remaining soldiers followed Adeolu to the city walls where they inspected the sentry and the guards, they climbed up to the newly constructed watchtowers that now surrounded the city walls and they saw thousands of torches shining in the distance where the Maradian had made their camp.

The next morning at dawn, Adeolu, Araba, Akara and Babagun were dressed in full battle regalia. They had Khaleb bound and tied to a stake, which they now raised up so that the invading army could take note. Then they sent a single horse rider along to give a message to King Bashir. When King Bashir saw the stake on which Khaleb was tied come up in the distance, he asked his troops to stay action and some of them withdrew to a safe location. He decided to meet with Adeolu and his chiefs, who were already galloping on horses to the center of the fields dividing them.

Bashir had managed to send some spies into Idumagbo as well and they had managed to send him a message that they knew the whereabouts of Keniola. He had sent a message that they should take her immediately and ferry her through the end of the towns and that they should raise the green flag of Maradi so that if they come in contact with any Maradian soldier, their lives would be spared. He did not have any reason to settle any truce with these people from Idumagbo; he had a larger army, more equipment, and his army morale had improved over the last few days after they started their movement toward Idumagbo. However, he would make a counteroffer to Adeolu and his council to release Khaleb for their own lives; hopefully, they would take it.

He jumped on his horse and so did Aremu and eight other army commanders and they rode to the center of the battleground. Adeolu, Araba, Babagun, Akara, Bankudi, and six others also saddled and jumped on their horses to the center of the battleground. Representatives of both armies met in the middle without anyone bearing weapons.

King Bashir spoke for the Maradian army. "Your city is going to be in ruins in a matter of hours, so I implore you to give up right now, surrender Khaleb, Keniola, and install Aremu as your next king."

King Adeolu spoke for the people of Idumagbo. "Surrendering our principles and way of life would not be negotiable; surrendering Keniola would not be negotiable and surrendering Khaleb is negotiable and trying to cow us into submission is not going to work, so I suggest to you to let us give you back your son and some payment and you can turn your army around. Otherwise, you will suffer another massive defeat as with previous ones and lose your title and heritage."

Bashir spoke again. "I will not waste much of our time in a fruitless conversation that will not produce any results. Let's go back to our respective bases and fight this out."

Bankudi and another soldier were the farthest away from the location of the truce discussion and as Adeolu and Babagun turned their backs on Bashir, Bashir and his soldier mates also turned their backs. Adeolu and Araba galloped furiously away from the center of the battlefield, then Bankudi took out a hidden spear from a pouch sewn onto the side of the horse and threw it in the direction of King Bashir.

Only Aremu looked back; saw the projectile flying through the air. He rode his horse furiously toward it and dove in front of it. The projectile hit him in the shoulder, badly wounding him and missing Bashir. By then, Adeolu and his soldiers were only but specks of dust in the distance.

Bashir disembarked from his horse quickly and ran to help Aremu, and so did others. They carried him, put him on a horse, and rode back to their camp. Immediately he ordered the army to move and they began moving their soldiers and equipment across the battlefield. When then got to a specific location, Bashir asked them to halt. He was very furious about the attempt made on his life. He could not believe the treachery of it, and now all he wanted was to annihilate all of them and destroy their lands forever.

He gave orders and the first salvos from the remaining siege engines flew off, hitting the walls and some going above the walls into the city. He continuously and blindly gave orders until all that remained of the walls were smithereens and fire; even his son Khaleb that was tied and hoisted on a pole was nowhere to be seen anymore as several salvos from the siege engine got him and incinerated him.

Then Bashir ordered the salvos to stop. He ordered the first division of the army to advance forward and they moved quickly and advanced toward where a wall once stood and as they got closer, the majority of them fell into a pit where sharp arrows, stones, poisoned water, and mud were placed. Bashir, not wanting to lose the momentum, gave orders for the soldiers behind to step over their dead colleagues and use them as bridges into the city. He ordered them to torch every single building in the city, take whatever valuables they could take, get as many slaves as possible and above all, leave no stone upon another.

As soon as Adeolu and the rest of his truce delegation got into the city walls, Adeolu knew they were screwed, and he asked Araba to go fetch Fero and ask that they begin evacuating the city now. Araba said he was going to fight until death too but Adeolu looked at him and said, what is the use of having an unborn child if you do not wish to see him grow up? I want you to go now with the women and children that are not capable of bearing arms and this is an order. Go to Katunga; you will find help.

Araba bowed in obeisance and then went to fetch Fero, who was heavily pregnant, put her on a horse and with the rest of the women and children went to the footpath underpass leading outside of the city. As they departed their lands, he could hear the sounds from the flying projectiles from the siege engines and the cries of the people whose flesh was burning.

Adeolu and the rest of the fighting army stayed hidden in a rock-like bunker in the far eastern part of the city where they knew the siege engine salvos would not get to. After the salvos subsided, they heard shouts as the Maradian soldiers rushed forward trying to breach the perimeter. They heard their agonizing noises as they fell into the first of many traps laid for them. From their hideout, Adeolu and the rest of the army saw the first set of Maradian soldiers entering into Idumagbo and as they advanced toward the palace halls in the middle of the city, they were met with an explosion that consumed over a quarter of the advancing soldiers. After a few minutes they could hear agonizing noises from the soldiers, their anguish and pain, and the fresh orders from their commanders urging them to take the lands for their glory.

As the next set of Maradian soldiers appeared in the horizon, Adeolu had already divided the army into two. He asked Bankudi and Akara to lead the guerilla army; they hide, strike, and run, while he and Babagun led the rest of the soldiers in an onslaught against the rest of the Maradian soldiers. They ran toward them and cut them down as they advanced through the burning and smoldering remains of their colleagues, then more and more of them kept coming.

Adeolu and Babagun fought until they were tired, then an arrow hit Adeolu in the shoulder. He looked up and saw that it was Bashir that was shooting. He threw down his sword and reached for the arrow in his shoulder and he broke it, leaving the stub in his flesh. He had not been a fighting man all his life, but he'd changed in the last few years. He reached into his undergarment and reached for a gourd containing painkillers. He gulped it and dabbed the remaining over the wound.

Bashir fired another arrow; he dodged it. Then Bashir alighted from his horse. Adeolu reached for his sword again and with one useless hand he fought the Maradian king until he noticed he was the only one out of his army fighting. He saw Babagun captured and tied and he knew these soldiers were also trying to capture him and he was never going to let that happen.

He was feeling very tired and his legs were about to give way. Bankudi came on a horse and swept him off the ground. Bashir ordered his soldiers to give chase. He also got on his horse and gave chase as well.

Bankudi rode straight to the festival grounds, hoping to lose the Maradian soldiers on his tail along the way. The Maradian soldiers galloped fast too and were about to catch up when Bankudi made a quick decision by riding straight to the edge of the cliff where they usually make sacrifices and he pushed Adeolu off the horse and threw him into the river below. He was about to make his jump when a spear hit him in the back, and he fell into the river as well.

Bashir and the rest of his pursuing soldiers came to the edge of the cliff, watched, and saw that no one was swimming to the surface at first until Bankudi came up with a spear in his back. The king took another spear and threw it straight into Bankudi's back, piercing it, and he said he was dead. "He is not going to survive this, and neither is their king, Adeolu."

They turned and went back to the road and they met some of his soldiers that had been spying for him in Idumagbo. They told him that Keniola was in one of the rooms in the king's palace at the festival grounds not far from here.

Bashir asked them to hurry along. They got on their horses and once they got to the festival grounds, he could see that a lot of thought went into putting this place together; it was indeed a place of beauty. He had heard the spies tell him before and now he could confirm it himself.

He quickly went inside the room that the spies told him Keniola was in. He saw her perched on the bed with a sword, Khalil beside her with blood and soot and ashes. Bashir said, "Do not bring destruction onto your city. I once told you that this is what I was going to do if you forced my hand, and I did it."

Keniola said, "I am ready to fight for my freedom. If I kill you, I will walk, and if you kill me, you kill me, or you spare me and take me as a slave forever."

Bashir thought about that for a few minutes and said, "Let's go do this."

Keniola led the way into the amphitheater of the gods and the rest of the soldiers followed. They marveled when they got inside. They could not believe the human works that adorned the seats and shelves, and some of the soldiers balked and smirked that this was a pagan temple and they should not be going inside. Bashir ordered them to come inside with him.

He took out his sword and faced Keniola, who was already poised and ready to fight. Then they fought. Bashir first played with her and he quickly saw that she was all out to get him when she cut his forearm, then he changed his tactic and started fighting her like he fights a warrior. He could not believe how fit Keniola was; she could somersault and roll on the ground, giving her fight a colorful and stylish look.

Bashir managed to get the sword from her and then he went toward her, grabbed her by the throat and pointed the tip of the sword in her right eye. He then beckoned to the soldiers to bring a bamboo twine and with that they tied her feet and hands, then led her outside. Then Bashir looked around, saw all the figurine artifacts, and asked the soldiers to gather all the figurines on the shelves and remove the twin doubles on each seat and put them in a carriage. "We are taking them with us."

One of his commanders said, "That would be sacrilegious, taking unknown gods with us."

Bashir replied to him by thrusting his sword into his stomach, saying, "What do you know about gods, idiot? This is going to fetch us a fortune. Unfortunately, you will not be around to spend it with us."

He looked at the other commanders and soldiers and said, "Any more questions?" They shook their heads no. "Then get to it. Go and fetch the other soldiers and carriages from Idumagbo and bring them here. We will make camp and tomorrow morning at first light we will be on our way back to Maradi, our beautiful hometown. I understand that there is nothing of much value after we burned down the whole city, but I can assure you that this thousand set of twin figurines will make your families some fortunes."

Then the soldiers removed all the figurines and placed them in a horse-drawn carriage. The rest of the soldiers soon joined them. Some went in search of game back and made a barbecue and all the soldiers ate, drank, and sang joyously for their victory except for Keniola, who refused to eat and drink with them.

Epilogue

A week later, after their escape from the war-ravaged and now desolate Idumagbo, Fero gave birth to a baby girl. The remaining members of the clan, consisting mainly of women and children numbering about thirty, decided to stay and care for her. They stayed a while in a forest and allowed the child to be strong enough before they started moving again until they arrived at Katunga.

The people of Katunga welcomed them but wanted to know what drove them from their enterprising home that everyone envied. They told the people of Katunga that the people of Maradi laid a siege on their city and destroyed everything they owned and now they were refugees in search of assistance.

The king of Katunga, Alele, said he did not have any issues with them as long as they kept the culture of the land. He further mentioned that they worship the Osa Oko here and asked them what their gods looked like. They could not understand why he would ask that question but Fero, with her baby girl on her back, answered and said, "Our gods are in twos; two of a kind." he then asked them to follow him.

The rest of the people of Katunga also followed and they were led into the bush where they saw disused horse carriages, some dead bodies, and most of the twin figurines from the festival grounds of the thousand gods. Fero looked around and said, "where are all the other dead bodies?"

The king said, "Our major work in the last few days has been to bury these unknown people to prevent diseases and death."

Fero saw a white cloth stuck on one of the figurines and she knew it was Keniola's clothing and she knew instantly that Keniola must have been here. Araba held her back, seeing that she wanted to pick up the cloth. She adjusted and watched the emotions of the people of Katunga who had started looking at them funny. Then the king of Katunga said, "If you are going to live here in our city, you will worship our gods and you will not worship these other gods again."

They settled down in Katunga and never saw or heard from Keniola again; no one knows her whereabouts. Some other war refugees came into Katunga a few days later and they told them how Adeolu and Keniola killed all the Maradian soldiers. Adeolu, knowing that the spear throwing during the truce conversation might fail, had planned with Keniola, who poisoned all the water wells around the festival grounds and purposefully waited for the Maradians to arrive. The news we heard that she not only poisoned the water, she also poisoned the surrounding vegetation around the festival grounds and anyone that came in contact with this vegetation became sick, so one by one they died off on their journey back, the war refugee said.

He then added that all the twin figurines of the thousand gods from the amphi-shrine were carted away by the Maradians and no one knew where they were now. Araba and Fero kept quiet and did not say that the twin figurines were in a location close to Katunga. Until today no one knows where the figurines came from.

The people of Idumagbo have since disappeared into other Yoba cultures, their culture of curiosity and searching out the truth through experimentation forever caged as well.

Tayo Olajide, born in Ibadan, Nigeria, a Sojourner, Engineer, Inventor, and an oral Historian, trained and worked as a Software Engineer. He lives in Texas, USA with his wife and two children.

CPSIA information can be obtained
at www.ICGtesting.com
Printed in the USA
LVHW040842280720
661664LV00001B/31